PRAISE FOR THE HUNTRESS

Carrie's first foray into the medieval time period does not disappoint! This enemies-to-lovers, marriage-of-convenience romance captures the heart and vividly transports readers to the wilds of Scotland. Full of action, drama, suspense, and profound spiritual truths, *The Huntress* will leave you clamoring for book two and another chance to visit Carrie's excellent cast of characters!
~ Ashton E. Dorow, Author of The Royals of Acuniel Series

Cotten sweeps you into the lives of these unforgettable characters immediately, depositing you into a world so vividly crafted it is a sensory experience from cover to cover. I was captivated by the trials and triumphs along the way, and both challenged as well as encouraged by the themes throughout. A tale of loss and gain, joy and sorrow that points the reader to the only One who offers peace everlasting. Truly storytelling at its best.
~ Kelly Ferguson, Book Reviewer

Carrie Cotten pens yet another tension-filled tale of faith, love, and sacrifice. With immersive medieval settings, complicated characters, and a swoon-worthy marriage of convenience, *The Huntress* had me riveted from the first page to the last.
~ Jamie Ogle, author of *Of Love and Treason*

Masterfully told, The Huntress is immersive and delightful, cementing Carrie Cotten's reputation as a skilled storyteller who rightly divides the word of truth.
~ Heather Wood, Author of *Until We All Find Home, Until We All Run Free, Until the Light Breaks Through, and Until We All Share Joy*

A must read! Carrie Cotten delivers her most riveting story yet. She's managed to write the perfect blend of historical drama, battles, family ties, legend, and epic romance, all wrapped into a perfectly executed origin story for her lionheart women, centered on Christ.
~B.R. Goodwin, Author of *What Remains in the Wilderness, What Remains When Flowers Fade,* and The Sugartree Romance series

THE HUNTRESS

CARRIE COTTEN

CARRIE COTTEN
Gripping Christian Fiction

Edited by Heather Wood.
Formatted by Brianna Goodwin.

ISBN: 9798859412754
ASIN: BOCJQPB52G

ACKNOWLEDGMENTS

Every word of The Huntress belongs to the Lord, first and foremost, but he put so many essential people in my path on this epic journey without whom, none of those words would have been possible.

Thank you to my friends and family who listen to me endlessly ramble on and on about story ideas and characters who they don't know but live in my head.

Thank you to Ashton, who's expert eyes helped shape and make accurate the very first drafts and who's amazing design skills created an incredible graphics kit for this campaign. Thank you to my amazing developmental editor, Jennifer Q. Hunt, who spent endless hours answering endless questions, reading and rereading, and taking the deep plunge into the lives of these characters with me. You truly shaped this book into something incredible.

Thank you to Jamie and Kelly, my faithful friends, who are willing to read anything and everything and offer their support. Thank you to my beta team! Every single one of you have a huge hand in making The Huntress happen. Thank you to Joy who spent countless hours creating the most perfect digital art to make these characters really come to life.

Thank you to Heather and Brianna. My ride or dies. Your friendship, prayers, and advice bring me back to life when I feel like I'm dying. God knew I needed you both and he is so, so good to have brought you both to me.

Thank you to my prince charming. To my true love. The one who all the good parts of my heroes are based on. Every bit of romance I write is because of you.

Thank you most of all to my Lord and Savior, Jesus Christ. We have words of hope to share only because of his love. We have light to shine in dark places because he has gone into the deepest depths of that darkness and conquered it. We have happy endings because he has written the final chapter.

DEDICATION

To those who find themselves facing impossible choices. To those who are living a life they never planned.

Do not lose heart. The One who loves you has already gone ahead and knows the way. Keep your eyes on him.

Remember not the former things, nor consider the things of old. Behold, I am doing a new thing; now it springs forth, do you not perceive it? I will make a way in the wilderness and rivers in the desert.

Isaiah 43: 18-19

PRONUNCIATION GUIDE

Cyrene – /Sih-reen/
Beli – /Beh-lee/
Derelei – /Deh-rih-lee/
Bercilak – /Bur-sih-lak/
Traigh - /tʰɾaːj/
Cathala - /Kah-ha-lah/
Ailbhe - /al-vuh/
Dorcha - /do⟨r⟩-huh/
An t-aon - /ahnt-ay-on/
Eowin - /ay·uh·wn/
Rìoghachd - /ree-oh-gacht/
Nàbaidh - /nah-bee/
Taranau - /Ta⟨r⟩-nah/
Faidh - /Fee-ah/
Alasdair - /A-laz-dare/

PROLOGUE

Cyrene

821 AD

"We canna win."

Cyrene froze at his words, any semblance of a smile fading from her lips. Her racing heart would have leapt free from its place in her chest, had her throat not tightened so that it barely allowed a breath.

Duncan braced himself on strong arms, a map on yellowed parchment unrolled over the table before him. Thin inked lines represented the borders of their lands. A simple jagged edge between moors and woods, tower and trees. Borders she once thought unbreachable now seemed so fragile when stretched across the page. He lifted his eyes to meet hers, their deep blue now a dull gray. They'd been that colorless before, just days ago, when he'd laid bleeding and near death on the cot in her healer's tent.

1

She'd only come to the hut to bid him farewell. To offer a blessing for the battle he'd face and see him off, allowing her quiet sanctuary hidden deep in the woods to remain untouched by the world outside. That's what she'd rehearsed, anyway, on the short walk through neatly placed huts with their identically thatched roofs and walls of waddle and daub, built in a perfect spiral around a ceremonial clearing in the center. It was a place of order. A place where she knew each face, where she knew what to expect, where they were safe.

She'd been friendly when she stepped through the curtain; humorous, almost. Now the tense line of his bearded jaw and near-green shade of his skin made her regret letting him see a side of her that she kept hidden from nearly everyone, even those close to her.

"What's happened?" Her words sounded rough as she turned to call for her captain, who was engaged in a battle of wills and swords with Duncan's captain just outside.

"I . . . nay . . . nothing happened." Duncan waved his hand, calming her panic. Barely.

As she waited for the rest of his explanation, her mouth turned as dry as sand and eyes remained glued to the man who'd interrupted the dependable ebb and flow of her people's lives. The man she had allowed in. The son of her sworn enemy. What had she done?

Sliding a hand to his injured side, Duncan straightened, and Cyrene took an unnoticed step toward the doorway.

"I've just realized that I canna win." His other hand pressed against the lines of worry that carved deep tracks across his forehead before he swept it over the map still before him on the table. "No matter how I play it, wherever I position my men, I lose. The kingdom of Tràigh loses. My people . . ."

His voice broke, and his hand moved across his mouth. Cyrene lowered her eyes to the packed earth floor, keeping her own hands busy by brushing back a strand of flame-red hair that had escaped from her complex but loose braid. She knew that feeling all too well. Had walked the same path, only she had been a child with the desperate eyes of her people looking to her for life. She knew about impossible choices.

"They'll destroy what's left of my army, if they havna already. They'll take my kingdom, and when they've decimated my villages and stolen away our children"—he paused, watching her as the gravity of his words sank in—"they'll march for the woods. For yers."

Ice snaked up her spine, every muscle tense and ready. He moved as if to approach, and she took a warning step back, stilling him. A sharp sting against her palm as she tightened her fist reminded her of the gift she'd planned to offer, and she slipped it in the pockets sewn into the folds of her skirts, humiliated that all it took was a handsome face for her to nearly forget the suffering Tràigh had poured out on her people.

"Are ye threatening me?"

Every decision she'd made in the last five days played in her mind. All the motives and implications of his arrival. Every word they'd exchanged, every look, every touch. He'd been broken but had also broken down her defenses—but why? Had he been planning to give them over as . . . as what? A bribe, a bargain?

"Nay." He lowered his chin, eyes flaming with sincerity and holding hers hostage. A kingly authority driving them into her head. "M'lady, nay."

His answer was direct but incomplete.

She watched his throat move as he swallowed hard. A bead of sweat slowly made its way from his temple to his jaw, and Cyrene was on instant alert. Working hard to keep her expression impassive, she reached subtly behind her back to grip the hilt of the dagger she kept tucked in the leather of her belt. There was danger, but she couldn't determine the source.

Her chest grew tight with shallow breaths she struggled to control. Her ears pricked at the sounds of clashing swords from outside. They followed the usual rhythm of training battles. There were no shouts of alarm, no unusual silence. If this was a trap, there were no signs.

"What do ye want?" Cyrene glanced at the curtained opening of the hut. It only moved at the breath of a gentle breeze.

"Fight wi' me."

She swung her gaze back to Duncan, nearly laughing. "What?"

"Fight wi' me," he repeated, crossing his arms over his broad chest.

"We only fight to defend ourselves." Cyrene matched his pose. "We dunna seek war."

And they certainly didn't join their enemies in losing battles. *My people . . .* The way his voice had broken. Something in her heart ached. This was wrong; everything inside of her felt torn to shreds.

"War is already at yer borders."

She knew it wasn't a threat, but her eyes narrowed on him anyway, and she spoke with her own queenly authority.

"Then we will face it when it comes. I willna ask my people to run again. We spent too many years hiding, scraping by, dying alone and scared. This is our home. And this is where we will stay."

Even as she said it, she knew they'd face the same fate as Tràigh, but what else could she do? Cyrene turned, as if the answer to everything was hidden in the shadowy places that remained untouched by blocks of sunlight pouring through raised patches of the thatched roof.

She heard him sigh, releasing a sadness, as if he knew her answer already. "Ye canna win either."

She wanted to deny his allegations. To say that they would defeat any enemy, they would remain hidden and safe. To call him a liar and drive him out.

"But . . ." Her fingers moved to her lips as if to catch her words before they escaped. She drew in a deep breath and folded her hands together at her waist. She'd not ignored all that he'd revealed about his enemy. She'd counted and mapped and planned just as he had. He'd come to the point of honesty with himself; mayhap it was time for her to do the same. Even if the outcome remained the same. "Yer right."

She turned to find him staring, as if he'd expected her response and was surprised by it at the same time. She lifted a shoulder and looked toward the patches of light peeking in through the roof.

"Stories and legends will only hold the enemy's greed at bay for so long. If they take Tràigh, they'll come fer us—fer this land—and even if we defeat them, my people will suffer, and I . . . I canna find a way to stop it."

"Then fight wi' me." He presented empty open palms, urgency in his request. "Together, we stand a chance."

The torn-up shreds inside her became tangled and knotted, a painful tight mess that shot spears of near panic through her veins. She was no prophetess, but she could look into the future and see what it held for her people. Either decision opened their sanctuary to the pain and death they'd been sheltered from for so long.

Eyes squeezed shut, she clutched the folds of her skirts, her knuckles protesting the force of her grip. She chastised herself for ignoring her initial instinct to leave him where she'd found him in the first place. It had been an impossible choice. Just one of the many she'd made in her life.

A queen's first duty was to her people. Mercy and benevolence weren't risks she could allow to those outside her kingdom. Not when her people had suffered so much. He would have surely died, but they could have remained unseen, unknown—but now he knew about them. Now they were exposed and at risk. Saving him had been the right thing, but the cost was great. So very great.

"Cyrene." Her name was soft on his lips. As if they were friends. As if he knew her.

Dunna trust the tower king. Her mother's warning, issued with her final breath, released a torrent of emotions which stirred that tangled mess into a bubbling, rolling boil that threatened to spill over. If it wasn't enough that his father had driven her people to near extinction . . . If it wasn't enough he'd banished them, starved them, sold them . . . Now his son was asking her to send those very people into war alongside the kingdom that abandoned and betrayed them.

"'Tis the only way." He sounded as breathless as she felt.

How dare he have the nerve to share in her torment? No matter how right he was about the coming war, he was the intruder. He was the trespassing spy, come to infiltrate her village, calm their fears, and then . . . and then . . .

Bribes. Bargains. She whirled on him, her narrowed eyes targeting his.

"Thief," she hissed. When his eyes grew wide, she stormed toward him, aiming a finger at his face, teeth bared. "Ye came to steal what yer father left behind."

Despite his weakened state, he remained an immovable wall as she drove her finger into his chest, bone meeting bone.

"We fight, and then yer men will turn against us, taking the rest of our lives and land." She pushed harder, wishing her finger was a blade. "I'd rather yer enemies have it. Fool!"

Fool? He's not the fool—ye are. He took her prodding without response.

"Or maybe that 'tis yer plan. Turn us over as yer way out. Give my people to save yers."

She finally struck a nerve.

"I am *not* that king." The muscle in his jaw feathered as he snatched her hand away.

She raised her other hand, prepared to fight, but he captured it, too, his fingers wrapping fully around her slender wrist. He held her still, chest to chest, so close, they nearly shared a breath, but she refused to cower, to shrink away. She met his gaze, fire for fire, even as the truth of his defense sunk in.

"I give ye my word. Yer people willna be harmed by my men." His nostrils flared as the words sneaked out through his clenched teeth.

Dunna trust the tower king. It echoed in her mind, her ears, her heart.

She jerked against his hold, but his grip was firm. He stood nearly a head taller, and she tilted her chin, her face inches from his. Defiance fueled her courage. "What is yer word to me?"

He waited three long breaths before opening his fingers to release her. She remained rooted in place, forcing him to be the first to step away, both of them fuming.

There was no compromise, no middle ground on which they could meet. To ask her warriors to fight was to send them into battle on two fronts: the war before and the threat beside. Duncan paced, hands on his hips, except for when he reached up to rub the place on his side where a bandage still covered his wound.

Cyrene had her own scars that ached with memories of betrayal, and she laced her fingers together to keep from touching that tender place across her ribs.

Duncan finally shoved his hand through his mop of wild blond curls and turned to face her.

They were enemies.

There was no treaty that could be drawn that would ease the fear in the hearts of her people or calm the suspicion in his. There was no trust to be found between her, the queen of the woods, and him, the king of the tower.

"We have to fight our own battles." Cyrene felt the thickness of regret coating her throat, and her words nearly choked her. "There's no other way."

She wanted to ask him to keep what he knew of their village secret, but there could be no requests made between them. Not now. Duncan's chin dropped to his chest, hands at his hips. Her fingers found the small gift still hiding in her pockets and turned it over in her palm, wondering if he would receive it after how she'd accused him. Deciding against the offer, she turned to go, whispering under her breath, "I'm sorry."

"M'lady, wait."

Cyrene stopped, her hand on the curtain, ready to draw it back and let their paths be forever separated.

"There is one way." Duncan's voice was raspy. He waited until she looked over her shoulder.

He'd moved closer but was still a full step away. Another bead of sweat chased the same path down his face, and her eyes darted to the spot on his throat where she could see his pulse pounding.

Whatever he suggested would be only a desperate attempt to avoid the inevitable. There was no accord or agreement that could be struck to unite their kingdoms, none that she'd ever agree to. Nothing short of . . . Cyrene found his eyes searching hers, and as his lips parted to speak, her breath caught, and she turned away, suddenly acutely aware of what he was about to say.

Nay. Dunna ask it of me. 'Tis too sacred.

Time slowed, then stilled. It seemed an eternity as he drew in a breath and exhaled a request that sent a boiling tear streaking down her cheek.

"Marry me."

I

CYRENE

806 AD - 15 Years Earlier

Tiny embers from twin circles of fire lazily, happily drifted up until they joined the scattered stars winking across an onyx sky. Pipe and drum, verse and song, dancing and twirling, and joy above it all—Cyrene and Beli ran toward the celebration. Even though he was younger, Beli was faster and crested the hill far ahead of Cyrene. He'd always been quick.

Quick to run, quick to plan, quick to act.

Cyrene took a much slower pace. She let her arms swing out at her sides as she spun in her own private ceremony on their way to the clearing. There were two new lives born to the neighboring kingdom of Tràigh. They were princesses, just like her, and Queen Fiona of the Firth was Pictish, just like her. They were the first bairns sharing blood equally with both nations.

She dared not say it aloud for fear Beli would roll his bright blue eyes and call her silly, even if he was her younger brother, but she almost felt as though she'd gained sisters herself.

"Hurry, or we are sure to miss all the good food." Beli tugged on her arm, jerking her out of her twirl.

"Is that all ye can think of?" Cyrene stumbled behind him, laughing as he slapped his biceps where muscles would have been, had he any.

"I am the man of our house. A man needs meat and ale!"

"Aye, a man of seven winters." Cyrene nudged his shoulder with hers, but he ignored her chiding.

The clink of mugs and bursts of laughter kept rhythm for the musicians who played and played until the dancers collapsed from joyous exhaustion on woven blankets, only to rest a song, then rise again.

Cyrene and Beli clapped along with the songs, their throats raw from shouting the chants of celebration. Beli's stomach growled over the sound of the music, and he flashed a crooked smile before he moved toward the edge of the crowd, promising to return with food.

"Dunna get lost! I promised Mother I'd watch after ye!" Cyrene grabbed at the sleeve of his tunic, but he was too fast.

"Yer only older by one winter, Cyrene. Besides, as yer future king, I dunna need coddling."

Cyrene tossed a mocking look after her brother as he disappeared into the fray of villagers from both the Pictish lands and Tràigh. She was secretly glad he went to fetch food, as her stomach rumbled too. Her feet ached inside her small leather boots, but the music called to her, drew her from the shadowed edges of the clearing toward the spiraling circle of dancers. She bounced on her tiptoes, searching for Beli's thin frame and mop of bright red hair, the same color as hers. Surely, she had time for one dance before he returned.

She yelped when a lad with soft blond curls piled atop his bobbing head spotted her wiggling with anticipation and snatched her hand as he skipped past, flinging her into the spiral of laughter.

His woven brat flapped behind him like crimson wings as he threaded his fingers through hers, and they were enveloped in a sea of song. Its melody was a perfect blend of her people and his, the Picts and the villagers from Tràigh.

Strung between smoothed poles, the rich green silk flags of the Picts and the bold red flags of Tràigh were touched by the gentle breeze whisked inland from the gray waters of the Firth of Clut and moved in their own silent dance.

The deep emerald color always drew up a swelling pride in Cyrene's heart, though she was only a lass of eight. The Picts were a mix of peoples, come together under time of hardship to defend their lands against the invaders from a place called "Rome" hundreds of years before. Together they'd remained since. As one.

And because her mother, Derelei, queen of the Picts, had wed her true love, Bercilak, half Pict and captain of the king's army, the Picts were once again mixed and blended. Armies united. Lands expanded. Allies. Friends.

King William even took the lovely Fiona, daughter of the Pictish harbor master, as his wife. It was for her twin daughters, just a week old, that they now danced and sang and feasted. The celebration would last three days, until the princesses' naming ceremony.

Cyrene grinned until her cheeks hurt. She was surrounded by such joy after so long mourning their heavy losses from the attacks from the west, including that of her fearless father. Both kingdoms had suffered. King William and Fiona's wedding had ensured the friendship between the two nations would continue, and Cyrene prayed this happy event would ignite the healing they all needed.

She was young and didn't understand much of the talk in her mother's meetings that she and Beli were forced to join, but she recognized the strain across Derelei's brow was from more than a widow's grief. It had been a long year, but not so long that she'd forgotten her father's face, his emerald green eyes that matched hers, his smile, the feel of his arms as he gathered her up and peppered her cheeks with kisses. *Look,* he'd said, rubbing his calloused thumb over her freckles, *I've left my mark on ye, lass.*

The sudden memory gave Cyrene such a shock, her feet tangled together, and she tumbled from the ring of dancers, landing hard on her backside in the trampled grass.

"Are ye hurt?" The lad who'd pulled her into the dance stood above her, hands on his hips and chest heaving as he tried to catch his breath.

"Nay." Her voice was wobbly, eyes stinging from the tears that pooled behind her lids.

He offered his hand, which she was about to accept when another lad slammed into him from behind. He had similar features, except his hair was as red as Beli's.

"Where have ye been? We arna even supposed to be here. We must go, now!" The second lad, older and much taller, barely acknowledged Cyrene before hauling who she thought to be his brother through the crowd, giving him only enough time to mouth an apology before they disappeared.

Cyrene pushed herself up and slapped her palms against the dark green and gold fabric of her skirts before wiping the backs of her hands across her tear-moistened cheeks. She dragged in a fortifying breath, determined to be brave for her father despite the gaping hole in her heart carved by his absence.

Beli spotted her from across the clearing and waved, a roasted leg of pheasant in each hand. Cyrene smoothed her skirts again before weaving her way through the snaking line of dancers to join him.

Cyrene and Beli ate until their stomachs bulged, danced until they could no longer keep their eyes open, and finally collapsed in a heap by one of the fires.

Cyrene was awoken the next morning by the thundering of hooves on dirt and Beli's hands pushing her shoulder.

"Get up," he urged, his blue eyes wide and wild. "Mother's warriors are riding to the tower. She is wearing her green cloak."

"Her cloak?" Cyrene asked, still half asleep.

"She only wears that one when she carries her sword."

Cyrene was instantly awake, accepting Beli's hand as he dragged her to her feet. He beat her to the top of the hill overlooking the farmland that bordered Tràigh's, and when she arrived, he was standing as still and stiff as a hemlock. Cathala and Ailbhe, two of her mother's maiden warriors, stood behind him, Ailbhe's hands on his shoulders. Below, the queen and her guard were a shrinking black cloud as they rode on horseback along the winding dirt road that snaked through the village of Tràigh toward the tower.

Beli made to race down the hill, but Ailbhe's grip was strong. "Ye both are to remain wi' us until yer mother returns."

"Is she going to the tower?" Something turned in Cyrene's stomach, and it wasn't because of all the sweets she'd stuffed in her mouth the night before.

"Aye," Cathala said, her words clipped. "'Tis custom to bring gifts fer the bairns on the second day of celebration."

She caught Beli's wide blue eyes. He'd only been six, but she knew he remembered. Beli remembered everything. The last time their mother had gone to the tower, it was to learn of their father's death and the king's wedding to Fiona. Derelei had remained there until after the wedding, but when she returned, she began fortifying her army.

Cathala guided Cyrene and Beli down the hill toward the distant sounds of villagers waking to continue the celebration. "She'll return before nightfall. All is well."

But she didn't. And it wasn't.

At dawn the next morning, Cathala, stone-faced and silent, woke Cyrene. When Cyrene reached to wake Beli, she found the space on the mat where he'd been sleeping empty.

"He's already wi' yer mother," Cathala said.

Rubbing her eyes free of sleep, she followed Cathala, her eyes drifting across the great swath of Pictish land that separated Tràigh on one side from the dark woods at the foot of the mountains and from the firths leading out to the sea on the other. They followed the winding path from the hill toward the firth where the roundhouse Cyrene and Beli shared with their mother was perched on sturdy stilts near the shore. With each step, the joyful sounds of celebration were replaced with dreadful whispered rumors she didn't understand.

Prepare for battle.

So few of the guard have returned.

They say it 'twas the king's own blade.

Those poor bairns.

She stopped outside the roundhouse, and Cathala's hard expression softened slightly as she held back the curtain, nodding for Cyrene to enter.

"Mama is in there?" Cyrene asked.

Cathala nodded again.

"And Beli?"

Cathala shook her head. "He is with Ailbhe."

"Come, dear one." From inside, a voice beckoned her, familiar but weak and raspy.

Cyrene took only one step, timid at the shocking sight of her mother's condition. Queen Derelei's usually pearl skin resembled grayish lichen that grew on the seaward side of stones overlooking the Firth of Clut. Her hair, which had always reminded Cyrene of the dancing flames of evening fires, now lay matted around her face like the ash that remained in the mornings, doused and darkened by dew.

Brígid, the healer, hurried between her mother's bed and a table cluttered with pots and jars of fragrant herbs.

Cyrene's eyes darted from wall to wall, searching for some sense of familiarity. She was certain she'd been led into her mother's chamber, separated from the rest of the roundhouse by merely a thin curtain, but nothing looked as it had before.

Darkened rags spilling out of half-filled wooden bowls spotted the floor around her mother's bed. The metallic smell of blood overpowered even the herbs Brígid fervently mixed in a bowl. The Pictish queen's deep green cloak lay draped over a stool in the corner, not across her powerful, sure shoulders.

Now the great Derelei, the Battling Queen, lay still, covered by skins and strips of cloth. But it was the reddened eyes of the two warrior women who stood guard near the wooden posts of her mother's bed that frightened Cyrene and deepened a pit of dread in her stomach.

"'Tis not just the wound that grieves our queen."

Cyrene glanced back toward the roundhouse entrance, her ears pricking at the voices of two village ladies delivering fresh water. They deposited the buckets at the entrance but didn't dare enter. "'Tis the betrayal that has injured most. And our dear Fiona . . . the bairns . . . 'tis too much to bear."

All murmurs fell silent when a shadow darkened the opening of the roundhouse.

"Eden?" Derelei's eyes flashed something between relief and anger.

Her mother's warrior captain, whom Cyrene hadn't seen since her mother returned from Tràigh after Fiona's wedding, was silhouetted by the rising sun and filled the space of the doorway, sending the chattering ladies in search of some other place to be.

Cyrene was instantly in Brígid's arms, hauled into the shadows and shoved behind a small trunk while the warrior maidens moved to shield the queen.

"Stay," Brígid ordered before moving back to the queen's side in a motion so fluid, it was almost as if she'd never left.

"It canna be true." Derelei groaned as she tried to sit up, but grasped her side and fell back against her bedding. Brígid was in motion again, replacing dressings and fussing over the queen.

"What has he done?" Eden rushed forward, stopped by the maidens who hissed curses that sent waves of chills across Cyrene's skin. Eden wasn't dressed in fighting leathers as the others, but a tunic and long skirts like the village women.

"Let me be! I must speak wi' the queen." Eden whipped her arms free from the maiden's grasps, stumbling backwards and facing off against them with a murderous look in her eye. Her golden hair was wild, mussed and loose from her braids. Cyrene noticed her skirts were torn and ringed with dirt at the bottom, as if she'd been running along the shore.

"Let her come." Derelei breathed through the pain that drew her features tight.

When they reluctantly parted, Eden stepped through the wall of closely paired maidens, meeting their warning glares with defiance. She sank to her knees at Derelei's bedside, lowering her head in reverence.

"Where were ye, Eden?" Derelei gripped Eden's hand, her pleas so desperate, they drew the air from the room and left Cyrene's chest tight.

Eden glanced over her shoulder, eying the warriors at her back, an expression Cyrene had never seen on any maiden turning the captain's skin as white as snow. It looked a lot like fear.

"I had to . . . there's something I need to tell ye, but . . ." Her eyes slid even to Brígid, who braced herself on fisted hands on the bed opposite Eden. "I dunna ken who to trust, m'lady."

Derelei dragged in a broken breath, then motioned to her warriors to leave. Even in her weakened state, the sharp look she fired when they resisted was enough to urge them into obedience.

Brígid glanced at Cyrene as she, too, was dismissed. As she turned to leave, a pointed look warned Cyrene to stay hidden. And ready.

Once alone, Eden lowered her head again, her shoulders sagging from exhaustion. When she finally lifted her head, though, her eyes burned. Eden leaned so closely and whispered so softly, Cyrene couldn't hear the news she delivered. She nearly burst from her hiding spot when Derelei released a cry and covered her mouth with a shaking hand.

"It had to be done." Derelei's hand fell away from her mouth, then rested limp at her side as if she'd surrendered in a fight. "They canna be used now."

"Aye." Eden formed fists at her side, her jaw still tight and muscles twitching under her skin.

Cyrene's small fingers ached from her grip on the side of the trunk, but she remained crouched in the shadows. Waiting. Listening.

"I'm sorry to have asked it of ye. It will not go well now, Eden. There will be a reckoning." Derelei's eyes drifted closed as Eden nodded. When the queen opened them again, she found Cyrene's hiding spot and spoke as if directly to her instead of Eden. "I need ye to protect our people."

Eden nodded, drew herself upright, and bowed to her queen before darting out of the roundhouse as swiftly as she'd entered. The warrior maidens did not return. Only Brígid rushed back to Derelei's side after a whispered conversation just beyond the entrance. Cyrene crept from her hiding place, lingering at the corner of her mother's bed.

Though a fire burned in the hearth, Cyrene shivered beneath her wrap, and Derelei stretched thin fingers, beckoning her daughter closer. Furs fell back from her arms, marked with the symbols of her people and fresh wounds from battle.

"Go on. Dunna be afeared." Brígid's gentle hands fell upon Cyrene's small shoulders, ushering her across the smoothed wood of a planked floor. Lapping water against rocks beneath their round-house seemed to whisper a secret Cyrene didn't wish to know. A song of farewell.

"Hush now, shush now," it sang. "For not long now till she fly."

Forced forward by Brígid's urging, Cyrene dropped to her knees at the side of her mother's bed as Eden had done, her small hands working free from under the skins that did little to keep her warm. Her mother's body burned with fever, but her hands were as ice. Cyrene clung to them, winding her small fingers through her mother's. Derelei's once bright blue eyes were now barely the color of fog that hovered over the water in winter, and a sheen of sweat coated her skin.

"Who hurt ye, Mama?"

"Never mind, my love."

"I dunna understand. Why did this happen?"

If she could only find the reason, she could make it right, and her mother would be well.

"The king wanted something I couldna give." Derelei's words were soft, laden with sadness.

"But he was . . . wasna he our friend?"

"Nay, lass. Never our friend."

Shocked, Cyrene looked at Brígid. The healer was silently filling a bowl with steaming water. She seemed not to be listening, but her shoulders stiffened at the queen's reply, lifting and falling from a deep sigh.

"What does he want? I'll find it. I'll give it to him." Cyrene pressed the back of her mother's smooth hand against her own rounded cheek, praying for something called a miracle. She didn't yet fully understand what it was, but her mother had told her it meant something greater than any man could do, making possible the impossible.

"'Tis too late." Derelei's answer carried a pain much deeper than her injuries, but her free hand touched her side where cloths had soaked through with her blood. "We canna undo what has been done. We can only try to stop what is to come."

Cyrene shook her head, lost to the workings of a world she didn't understand and couldn't control.

"Listen closely, my child." Derelei's voice sounded like chains dragged over the edges of their fishing boats. "I am not long for this world. But dunna ye cry for me, for I have assurance of a kingdom far greater than any we ever ken, and I will go there soon to be with *An T-aon*."

"Can we go wi' ye, Mama, Beli and me?" Cyrene squeezed her mother's hand, her voice a mere trembling whisper. If she could just hold tight enough, no matter where her mother went, they could follow, even to the great *An T-aon*, whom her people worshiped.

"Nay, ye must remain. I need ye. Our people need ye. Both of ye." Derelei pressed her lips together, face pinched as she struggled to swallow. Derelei's next words shocked Cyrene, as if she'd been tossed into the frozen sea in the dead of winter. "Ye must rule as queen, Cyrene."

"Nay." Cyrene choked on her tears, sobs breaking her words into short bursts. "Beli . . . Beli will be king. It's always been such."

Derelei squeezed Cyrene's hand, fading strength darkening her blue eyes. "In yer father's world, Beli would have been king. But Bercilak is gone, and this is the land of the Picts. 'Tis ye, Cyrene. The crown falls to ye."

Cyrene couldn't find words to reply. She only shook her head, tears flowing freely down her chilled cheeks. She didn't want to be queen. Couldn't be queen.

"The warriors will fight, they'll protect ye, but ye must protect the people, teach them, care fer them as I have—even better than I. They need to ken the lionheart beats strong still, and it beats in ye."

The stories of ancient fierce warriors had chased Cyrene into dreams since her first memory. But those were tales of mighty women called by *An T-aon* for his purpose. They were blessed with gifts of strength, or bravery, or great faith. Cyrene was but a lass who trembled at the thought of a life without her mother.

"Ye must find yer courage. Ye are a lionheart, and one day ye will find yer gift. Our people are counting on ye, Cyrene." Derelei's image blurred, and Cyrene's eyes burned. "Brígid will help ye, but 'tis the way of our people, and blessed we are for such a people. 'Tis rare for a woman to lead and fer people to honor her rule."

Another sob broke past her small lips, dry and cracked from the cold winter winds. "Nay, Mama. I canna. I want to be wi' ye."

Derelei pulled Cyrene's hand to her own lips, just as dry as her daughter's. The act forced Cyrene's attention, and she blinked hard to clear her vision.

"Ye are the truth-keeper now. I ken ye will be a good and kind queen, Cyrene. Be strong. May yer aim be true." Derelei's eyes squeezed closed and face twisted in pain.

Cyrene buried her cries in the thick skins that covered the bed, her hands working their way around her mother. Her small head lay on the barely moving chest of the queen, and she clung to her, as if she could anchor her mother to earth, to herself. If she could just hold tight enough, Derelei would have to stay, or at least, they would go together to wherever her mother journeyed next.

Derelei's shallow breaths warmed Cyrene's head, and she whispered a warning that seeped deep into Cyrene's bones, hardening something in her young heart. "Dunna turn yer back, daughter. Dunna trust the tower king."

Brígid's hands pried Cyrene away, and though she protested, Cyrene was no match for the woman's strength as she passed her along to Cathala's waiting hands.

"Mama!"

As she was forced from the chamber, she caught one last glimpse of Derelei before the curtain fell closed. The queen's body was still, eyes fixed and empty. Cyrene had seen such a look before, and it was always followed by a sharply cut hole, then a mound of dark dirt. That empty stare meant her mother was gone from the earth, like her father, Bercilak—and Cyrene and Beli were truly alone.

Her mother said *An T-aon* would always be near, always listen when she prayed, but her voice made no sound as she screamed. There was no one to hear.

She'd been afraid before, of a shadow in the night or the sound of howling wolves at dusk, but never like this. Never grasped so tightly by terror that the breath was forced from her lungs. She wanted to run and run and run until she found the life she'd known before the fighting—a world without the clashing of metal swords and buzzing of arrows. A place where sun warmed the earth, where color bloomed across the fields, where she was safe and loved.

One day. Just one day had passed to carry her from life to death. A beloved princess to an orphaned queen.

She had to flee from this . . . this cold gray land where the only things that sprouted from the reeking black soil were death and sorrow. She had to find Beli.

Twisting free from Cathala's grasp, Cyrene sprinted across the dock, her slipper-covered feet slapping against the wood. She clawed her way up slick grass coating the hill, sliding to her knees at the crest.

Word of the queen's injuries had reached the villagers, and the clearing was a chaos of cries, of women snatching up their children and following the men to their homes.

Beli was nowhere among them. She screamed his name, but her voice was trampled beneath the pounding of hooves on earth.

Eden, atop a speckled gray mare, led a group of warriors toward the border of Tràigh. The rumors were true—there were so few of them.

The same rich red flags bearing the tower's crest that had been mixed with the Pictish green just the night before breached the horizon, moving to meet Eden. Somewhere a lonely horn bellowed as the skies darkened and gray clouds were drawn ashore by the rising tides.

Everything was changing. Even the air turned crisp, stinging Cyrene's pale skin. The sun was gone. Autumn had fled. Only the dreary, dull sky of winter remained.

Ignoring Cathala's calls, Cyrene tore through the fading day and plunged through the barrier of trees into the dark woods.

Mingled with her mother's heroic tales were warning stories of those woods. Hiding amongst the crags, dwelling beneath waterfalls, and feasting on the rich mossy growth of the gorges, fang-toothed fairies and goat-eyed sprites would carry away lasses who dared wander in, but Cyrene no longer feared those things as her heart was gripped by a horror much worse. She raced deeper into the trees, only stopping when her skirts caught the jagged, jutting claw of a fallen branch, and she fell face-first into the softened floor of the forest.

She moistened dry, dead leaves with her tears, pounded soft black soil with her clenched fists, and screamed into the emptiness that threatened to suffocate her.

A crunch from behind her sent her gasping and scurrying backwards until her back met with the rough bark of a birch tree.

"Beli?"

His face was swollen and tear-stained, his eyes as red as the dawn. He launched himself into her arms, and they clung to each other as if breath and life depended on their embrace. He worked his small hand up and presented Cyrene with a clenched fist.

"I dinna really want to be king." His whisper was a confession that shattered Cyrene's already fragile heart. "I swear, I dinna mean for this to happen."

"'Tis not yer fault, Beli." Cyrene kissed his sweat-soaked brow.

"Mama gave me this." Beli uncurled his fingers, and Cyrene gasped at what lay in his palm.

"The ring Father made fer her?" Cyrene dared not touch it, though she didn't know why.

"Aye." Beli sniffed, slid the back of his hand under his nose, then rubbed his thumb over the faded design etched into the silver. "She said I am to protect the queen. I am the fearless son of the warrior Bercilak. She said ye are a lionheart, and I am a lion sent to guard ye."

Cyrene tightened her arms around her brother. Beli held the ring between his thumb and forefinger, lifting it so Cyrene could see. Carved on its surface was a lion, reared and ready for battle.

"I dunna feel like a lion, Cyrene," he whispered.

"Nay. Neither do I."

Shouts from the edge of the woods brought them both to their feet. Beli positioned himself in front of Cyrene, his hands reaching behind to hold hers.

They rushed to the clearing and watched in horror as a nightmare in the daylight unfolded. Waves of red silk coated the fields, leaving a dark crimson stain across the ground as it moved.

Cyrene screamed as she was grabbed from behind. Cathala's arms were a vice around her middle, and Ailbhe had hold of Beli's arm as they were dragged back toward the hidden safety of the woods.

With a sword dropped at their feet and an order to "Keep them safe," Cathala and Ailbhe shoved them behind a tangled thicket, where a group of crying children were already huddled. Some were but toddlers, and others, the same age as Cyrene.

The maiden warriors disappeared through the trees in the direction of the battle. Cyrene and Beli watched, terrified, as two tower soldiers breached the tree line and started for their hiding spot. Cyrene drew two of the younger ones in her lap, clamping her hand over their mouths as they trembled in her arms.

Beli turned to Cyrene, something passing over his expression that sent her heart racing to a near stop. He began to inch to the edge of the thicket, and Cyrene grabbed for him, but as always, he was too quick, and she had to quickly regain control of a squirming child.

"Beli, nay." Her gasped plea was lost in the panic of breathlessness.

The soldiers crept closer. Another ten steps, and they were sure to hear the muffled whimpering of the children. Heartbeat thundering in her ears, Cyrene searched the ground around her for something . . . anything.

Her eyes fell upon the jagged end of a broken branch. She whispered a "Shh" to one of the children, and the second the soldiers looked away, she lobbed the branch as far as she could to distract them.

The relief she felt as they turned disappeared when she realized Beli had darted from the thicket to a wide hemlock nearby. Panic seized her again, and her eyes began to sting with tears.

"Beli!" she mouthed his name, not willing to risk the soldier's attention again.

He zipped from one tree to the next, putting more and more distance between himself and the thicket.

No, Beli . . . stay with me. Stay with me! Please.

Terrified, Cyrene's throat became too dry and tight to swallow. Beli was still moving, but so were the children, and she struggled to keep them from snapping a twig or rustling the bushes.

Beli pointed toward the clearing, just another few sprints away, and Cyrene nodded as she realized he was going for help. But just as he readied himself to slip from one hiding spot to another, a little lass tried to crawl toward Cyrene. Her knee snapped a dry twig hidden beneath a blanket of dried leaves, and she gasped in fear. The soldiers both turned, aiming straight for the thicket again.

Cyrene gathered the children closer, pushing up onto her heels. They'd have to run. She glanced back at Beli.

Go, Beli. Cyrene silently pleaded with her brother. *Run!* But he didn't. A small, brave smile lifted the corner of his lips as he raised the sword that was nearly as long as he was tall and burst from behind the tree, sword swinging in wide arcs around his small body.

Cyrene slapped a hand over her own mouth, which gaped with terror as Beli led the soldiers away. They closed in, towering over him, their laughter a disgusting taunt that made Cyrene tremble with the desire to help him. *Beli!*

If she stepped out of the thicket, she'd expose the children. If she didn't help him, he'd be captured . . . or worse. She was trapped.

What do I do? What do I do? Tears blurred her vision. Chest aching with shallow breaths, she tried to think through the panic. *What do I do?*

Then she heard the whisper of her mother's words as if she was there beside her. *Protect them. Find yer courage.*

Beli had found his courage. He was following their mother's instructions. He was protecting her, and she had to protect them. He kept luring the soldiers away, and Cyrene pushed herself to her feet, urging the children to do the same. A boy about her age that she'd seen a few times in the villages grabbed her hand, determination in his eyes. He nodded before releasing her and gathering one of the youngest in his arms.

As she ushered them further into the woods, a giant roar ripped from Beli's little lungs, and Cyrene sobbed at the sound of his blade meeting that of the soldiers.

2

DUNCAN

806 AD - A Week Later

A storm blew through the tower of Tràigh in the form of King William, and nothing in his path was spared his wrath. Including Duncan. It was he, the second son of the now twice-widowed king, who faced the raging monarch that morning.

"I told ye never to come in this room!" William nearly trembled as he roared, forcing Duncan to retreat to a corner when he surged forward. "What are ye doing in here?"

"I . . . I . . ."

"Answer!" William's shout was broken by a cough, but his thick fingers snaked around Duncan's arm, squeezing until he winced from the pressure.

"Nothing, Father." Duncan attempted to extract himself from his father's grasp, but only earned a tighter hold. "I just miss her."

William clicked his tongue in a disgusted response and threw rather than released Duncan's arm. Duncan tried not to rub the painful, pulsing spot. At ten, he was expected to be strong and unwavering, just like his father. Just like Brodric.

Duncan had long grown sick of hearing the praises sung for his older brother. Brodric was born without fear. Brodric could slay a hundred men with a stone in his sling. Brodric was so loved, he could make peace between the chicken and the fox. Brodric made the sky rain silver and the fish leap willingly from the sea into the fishermen's nets. Brodric would turn their father's silver crown to gold when he took the throne.

But Duncan could make a claim that Brodric never could. Brodric hadn't been the one to trade his life for his mother's at birth. No, that was Duncan's crown to wear. An invisible adornment worn by an invisible prince.

Duncan ran his fingers through his hair, his nails only snagging on tangled blond curls and not that unwanted crown. Fiona had been the one person who made him forget his shame. It was his stepmother's memory that had driven him to defy his father's orders and breach the threshold of her empty chambers for the fifth time in the week since she'd died. No. Not died. Since she'd been murdered.

Despite the disgust on his father's face, Duncan didn't grovel and swear to never enter again. It wasn't a promise he could keep. He would never stop longing for Fiona. He'd face whatever punishment, even if only for the chance of meeting the ghost of her memory or to capture the last lingering bit of her scent.

But she was gone, and with her, the tenderness and compassion Duncan hadn't known he needed until she'd graced him with it.

Head hung low, he waited for his father to empty the remainder of his outrage. But it never came.

The king coughed again, a deep, wet rumble that had plagued him since the winter months began. When Duncan looked up, his father stood, arms limp at his side, staring at the late queen's empty bed. The blood-drenched bedding had been removed, but Duncan could picture those haunting reddish-brown stains as if they were still there. He wondered if his father could see them too.

Did the king long for her as he did? Did he still hear her voice in the quiet moments? Surely, a husband grieved for his wife, even though Duncan had never seen a smile shared between them beyond the eve of their wedding. If not the queen, certainly the king ached for the children she bore him.

"Do ye think they live, Father?"

The king made no move to face Duncan nor even acknowledge his question until the shuffle of Duncan's feet against the stone floor broke the silence.

"What?" William's voice was raw, like stones rubbing together.

"My sisters. Do ye think that . . . that there's hope?"

William didn't turn to Duncan. He only ticked his face to the side a fraction, revealing the same hard expression he always wore. His eyes grazed the empty cradles that had been moved near the wall from their place next to Fiona's bed. His large hand rubbed a spot on his thigh before he charged toward the door with a growl, a slight limp hindering his steps.

"I can help." Duncan spoke quickly, his words having the desired effect and slowing his father.

William shot a harsh look over his shoulder.

"I ken the village well, and the woods. I've been there many times. I can help look for them."

The king turned fully at Duncan's offer and raked his eyes over his small form.

"Please, Father, I want to help." Duncan braved a step toward the king, but was stopped by William's raised hand.

Duncan watched his father's throat move as he swallowed to quiet another cough. He shrank under the burning glare of the king's dark eyes.

"Ye dunna go near The Dorcha." The king aimed a finger at Duncan when he opened his mouth to protest.

There wasn't a child in the kingdom that hadn't been warned of that endless expanse nestled between the Pictish lands and the mountains. A forest so dark, it was called just that—*The Dorcha*— The Dark.

Duncan didn't believe any of the stories, though, and if someone was going to capture his infant sisters, the blackness of that expanse would be a perfect place to hide them.

"I can be like ye. Imna afraid, Fath—"

Duncan's argument was cut off by his father's hand twisting the fabric of his tunic at his chest, nearly lifting him off the ground.

"No one defies me!" He shook Duncan, stealing any resistance and replacing it with fear. "No one!"

Duncan stumbled, barely able to keep himself upright when the king released him.

"That is where those . . . those savages who murdered the queen go to worship their pagan gods. Nothing good grows there; it only gives birth to evil." The king's jaw flexed, his teeth clenched in fury. "Ye shall not go near that place again."

The hardness in the king's tone frightened him, like black skies that promised a violent storm. Fiona had been one of those "savages," but even she had been wary of The Dorcha. Mayhap his father truly was stricken with grief, and in his rage, became confused. But even if that was so, Duncan's infant half-sisters were still missing. They still needed to be found.

"What will ye do?"

William snapped his eyes to Duncan's, meeting them directly for the first time in weeks. Duncan was paralyzed by the darkness he saw brewing there.

"I am the king. I will do what needs to be done."

"Yes, Father." Duncan prayed the king didn't hear the tremble in his voice.

"And stay out of here." William turned to the side, making room for Duncan to exit through the doorway.

Duncan felt his father's eyes as he forced himself to walk instead of run down the corridor. Before he turned the corner, he heard the king mutter under his breath, "Ye are nothing like me."

When he was free from his father's judging gaze, he sprinted to his own chambers and threw himself face down on his bed, where the softness of his feather-stuffed pillow absorbed his sadness.

"What is this?" Even at just fourteen, Brodric's voice was as deep as their father's. "A prince isna supposed to weep."

Duncan felt the weight of his brother's body as Brodric sank next to him on the bed. He pushed himself up to sit, running the back of his hand across his wet cheeks. Brodric's soft smile bore no judgment, and he rested a warm hand on Duncan's sunken shoulder.

"I hear her sometimes." Duncan couldn't meet his brother's eyes as he confessed, "She whispers my name."

"Aye." Brodric snatched the pillow from Duncan's lap and tossed it behind him as he flopped back, his arms stretched up behind his head. "'Tis natural, I suppose."

"She calls me to pray."

Brodric didn't move, but cut his eyes toward Duncan, auburn brows jerking together in question.

"Pray fer whom?"

Duncan shrugged, picking at a loose thread on his tunic. "Me. Ye. Father . . ." Duncan risked a glance at his brother. "The Picts."

Brodric shot up, instantly tense. "Dunna let Father hear you speak such treachery."

"Can all be guilty of the actions of one?"

"They are a ruthless people, Brother. 'Twas only our influence that kept their true nature hidden all these years." Brodric leaned in, forcing Duncan to meet his eyes.

"But why?" Duncan felt his hand cramp from the fist he'd clenched so tightly. "She was beloved by them, and she united our kingdoms through this union. Our ships, their access to the firth. A whole new trade industry. It was only to their benefit."

Brodric scowled and dropped back onto Duncan's pillow, arms folded across his broad chest. "Evil doesna need a reason."

Heat bloomed in Duncan's insides. Mayhap it was simply his desire for Fiona to still live that made him question what he knew to be true. Allies of the kingdom betrayed that trust, murdered his step-mother, and kidnapped his half-sisters.

"Fiona was lucky to escape them, but it dinna do any good for her in the end." Brodric sighed, his dark blue eyes narrowed at some memory. No doubt the same image that was permanently burned in Duncan's brain from the night Fiona was found. "They wouldna let her go."

"I hope Father hunts down the one who brought us such misery." Duncan didn't know when his thoughts had taken such a dark turn nor that he'd spoken his deadly wish aloud until his brother answered.

"Careful, Little Brother. Ye are starting to sound like His Majesty." Brodric's answer was teasing but cold. "Besides. Father and his men took care of the queen and her guard when they came under the pretense of offering congratulations."

Brodric chuffed a sharp breath. "She had the nerve to feign surprise. As if she hadn't ordered it done."

Duncan felt a cold wave of shame wash over him. Brodric didn't have to remind him. He'd been there. Summoned from his bed on the cold, misty morning when the Pictish queen's guard had arrived with a chest full of hack silver and gifts from the Pictish villagers.

He'd watched the servant disappear into the darkened tower door. Gasped with everyone else when he stumbled back out, red on his raised hands and a wordless mouth gaping with horror. The king roared, and that man lost his life simply for delivering the message. As had all the guards and servants who'd been in the tower that night.

"What's worse, she came simply to watch her sick plan unfold." There was hate in Brodric's voice.

He suddenly wanted to take back his threat, but Brodric was summoned by his tutor and left with a promise to come back after his lessons. Duncan scoffed at the suggestion that he needed keeping, but secretly counted the minutes until his brother's return.

It was when he was alone that the memories threatened to

consume him. In the quiet, Fiona's soft voice beckoned him to a place he wasn't ready to venture. A place where he would face himself and the truth of his heart. A place where he wrestled with his own hate and anguish.

Duncan, seeking reprieve from the stale air of his chambers, walked the halls until he found himself staring through a window at the steeple of the church Fiona had dragged him to every service. It was the beautiful dark-haired queen who had introduced him to a High King who sacrificed himself instead of his people. A Savior who loved enough to die for the ones who hurt him.

"Eternity and forgiveness," she'd softly answered when he rolled his eyes and asked what her king could offer him that his father couldn't. "And peace when you canna understand it."

How could such a light as Fiona come from such darkness? How could they have taken her from him so cruelly? How could he do what Fiona said God required of him and pray for his enemies?

When he heard servants whispering in the hallway, whatever softness or compassion he'd felt toward Fiona's former tribe turned to stone.

By the time Brodric returned, Duncan had cried his last tear, though his eyes still felt swollen and raw.

"What has happened?" Brodric stood in Duncan's doorway, frozen by the ruined state of his brother.

"Our sisters . . . their wraps." Duncan's throat constricted, his voice cracking as he shared the news he'd overheard. "They found them washed up on the shore, along with . . . remnants of an offering basket."

Duncan's throat was so tight, he couldn't speak to explain what that meant. But he didn't have to; Brodric knew of the ancient ceremonies. The ones the Picts claimed to no longer observe. The offerings of infants to the gods of seas.

The unmoving doorframe caught Brodric as his knees buckled. "No."

"Who would do such an evil?" Duncan screamed, pounding his

fists against his legs, repeating the question aloud he'd asked himself over and over since he learned of the discovery. "They were just bairns!"

Brodric slid to his knees, his forehead meeting the cold stone as he groaned in rejection of Duncan's announcement.

Duncan was without words. He could only watch as his brother, a pillar of strength, knelt and wept for the loss of their innocent half-sisters. Finally, Brodric lifted his head, eyes hard with conviction.

"Father *is* right." Brodric's words sent a chill through Duncan.

"What do ye mean?" He wasn't sure he wanted to know the answer.

Brodric stood to his full height, squaring his shoulders. "This evil must be eliminated."

"H-how?" Duncan's mouth went dry, something wormed its way through his stomach, and he wrapped his arms around himself.

"Does it matter?" Brodric turned, tossing a cold look of indifference over his shoulder. Then he nodded toward Duncan's window, where the sound of soldiers' pounding footsteps floated up from the courtyard. "'Tis already begun. It began the day that . . . that heathen dared show her treasonous face here."

"I canna understand." Duncan's words weren't meant to be heard. "Why?"

Brodric huffed again, as if Duncan was brainless. "Canna ye? The sea, Brother. 'Tis all about the sea."

Brodric disappeared that afternoon into his father's meeting hall, and the brother that emerged was not the same as the one Duncan knew before. The spirit of anguish and vengeance soon permeated the tower walls, soiling every surface with its rage. A terrible and violent revenge burrowed into the men of the tower, and Duncan was trapped there with it. The spirit of light Fiona had introduced him to was buried more with each passing day, and soon he mirrored his father's scowl of satisfaction at each glance of the black smoke that rose from the ground where Pictish homes used to stand.

3

CYRENE

808 AD - Two Years Later

Taut flax string dug into the crease of Cyrene's knuckles as she drew back, her thumb brushing against her cheek. Skimming her gaze down the line of her ash-carved arrow, she caught the buck in her sights, his great rack of mature antlers branching outward toward the sky.

Breathe in, still. Breathe out, release. Cyrene internally chanted the instructions as she followed those spear-sharp bone antlers through the foliage that blocked her shot.

A breeze cut through the trees, creeping up her back and lifting strands of her auburn hair. She fought back against a shiver that threatened to break her concentration. It was almost as distracting as the sharp pangs of hunger rolling through her stomach.

At least she was still alive to feel those pangs. The remembered echo of a child's cry as he was pulled from the lifeless arms of his mother cleaved through the wintery silence. She had to physically shake away the image of a dingy white cloth in Brígid's hands as the healer covered yet another of their people.

In one night, joy had turned to sorrow. The gentle Fiona and her infant daughters were slain, and the blame placed on Cyrene's people. Then her mother, most of the warriors, her friends . . . all gone. And Beli.

Derelei's ring, too large for her thin fingers, was strung around her neck by a leather cord and thumped against her breastbone. She'd gone back to look for his body. Even though Brígid warned of the dangers, she had to bury him. All that remained was the ring, though. She closed her eyes and could still see it, glinting in a single ray of sun like a beacon leading her to the spot where Beli had made his brave stand.

She eased back on the bow and shoved the dangling jewelry into her tunic. It had been precious to Beli, but now it was just another reminder of how the stories their mother used to tell were nothing more than empty words. If there had been such a thing as a lion-heart, it died with Derelei. Her ancestors might have found favor with *An T-aon*. The great Creator might have gifted them with courage or wisdom or strength or speed, but his gifts must have long run out.

Cyrene had none of those things. She only had her bow and the unwanted responsibility of a crown. That and the stubborn will to keep living.

The hope of being with her mother again was the only thing that kept Cyrene from losing all faith. *An T-aon keeps his promises.* Whether or not she believed her mother's words to be true depended on each day, sometimes each hour.

With every loss, every day without food, every heartbreak, Cyrene's already weak belief diminished even more. If nothing changed, it would soon be lost completely to despair.

A movement from the corner of her eye picked up the hairs on the back of her neck, and Cyrene drew back her bow again, refusing to lose the buck. All around delicate white flakes floated silently through the trees. Several landed on Cyrene's bare arms and soaked through the thin cloak covering her head and shoulders.

They'd hoped the last snowfall was the final one for the winter and spring was but days away. Her heart lurched at the feel of those flakes. Another big snow meant more sickness, less food. Death.

"Where are ye, *An T-aon*?" Her broken whisper sailed heavenward, dissipating into the cold air. "We need ye."

A sting of salt blurred her vision, but she allowed the tears to fall instead of lowering her bow to wipe them away. That buck meant another day. One more day.

The crack of a branch snapping somewhere in the distance jerked the buck's head up from where he was nibbling at the bark of an ash.

Cyrene pleaded for him to just take one more step. One more, and he would reveal that spot where her arrow could land.

Dunna run. Please dunna run.

He seemed to stand there for an eternity, staring into the woods, ears ticking back and forth, listening for danger. Finally, when the pish-pish-pish of snowflakes landing on dry, dead ground was the only sound, he lowered his head again. Cyrene's muscles burned. She should not have drawn back so early.

But to lower her bow now meant the possibility of missing the shot if he moved too quickly or got startled again. She'd just have to hold on until he gave her a few more inches.

He sniffed, nudged the ground, and took that final step. *Breathe in, still. Breathe out, release.*

Cyrene's arrow flew. She wanted to close her eyes. She didn't want to witness the impact. Despite their need for his sacrifice, death of any creature still gripped her tight in the gut.

This beautiful world wasn't created for death; it was created for life. But it was broken. Everything was broken. She thought mayhap beauty still remained, but it was so mingled with ashes, she could only ever see the gray.

At ten years of age, she should be sitting at her mother's feet, listening to stories of love and adventure. She should be running carefree with Beli through sun-drenched fields, not trying and failing to lead her people. To keep what was left of them alive.

The king had stolen everything. They no longer had safe access to the sea, no land for growing crops, no means by which to trade, so she did the only thing she knew to do. She hunted.

Cyrene secretly coveted the hunts. It was the only time when her world was quiet. It was the only place where no one was looking at her for answers to impossible questions. The movement kept her limbs from freezing, and the search for the camouflaged prey kept her mind sharp.

Cyrene allowed herself a long blink before training her eyes on the struggling animal. A whispered prayer of gratitude that her aim was true and his agony was only momentary lingered in the crisp air. She bounced her longbow in her palm.

Mayhap it was enchanted somehow; mayhap she had been gifted by *An T-aon* after all—for ever since she drew back the first time at eight years old, letting fly the arrow that would light the ceremonial fires at her mother's funeral, every release after that had met its mark. Without fail. Out of duty, she thanked *An T-aon*.

Waiting until the stag had stilled, Cyrene crept across the ground, holding up the loose trousers that swallowed her thinning frame. Delicate gowns belonging to a Pictish princess weren't fit for a hunting queen, and she'd grown out of them in less than a year anyway. Propriety had long given way to necessity.

She reached the stag, placing her near-frozen hand on his still-warm neck.

"Thank ye," she whispered. "For yer sacrifice. Ye will save many lives."

Once Cyrene had prepared him properly with her blade, she bound the hooves with bits of twine she carried in the pockets of her threadbare cloak. She released a lonesome whistle into the air, signaling for the others to come to her aid.

Pulling her cloak tight around her shoulders, she waited. And waited. None came. Night would fall soon. They wouldn't risk torches, not with being so close to the edge of the wood. And she wouldn't risk leaving the buck for other starving creatures to find.

Her shoulders trembled and ached as she attempted to drag his massive body without success. The felled animal wouldn't budge, and Cyrene slid to the ground at his side, exhaustion toppling the weak wall erected around her emotions.

Reining in the tears, she whistled again, hoping one of her friends was close enough to hear, that anyone would hear.

Do ye still hear, An T-aon? Did ye ever hear?

The stag was cooling but still retained a slight bit of warmth, enough to convince her to curl up next to him, at least for a few more minutes.

The crack of snapping branches jerked her awake, and she instinctively reached to her quiver for an arrow. She loaded her bow, scanning the forest, feathers brushing her frozen cheek. Shadows grew long in the darkening evening; they played tricks on Cyrene's tired mind.

She brushed her cheek against her shoulder and rose to her knees, a thin layer of snow fluttering to the ground from where it had piled in her lap. Where were the others? They should have come.

Bow drawn, Cyrene stumbled to her feet, scanning the woods. Something moved.

Shoulders hunched, knees bent, weapon at the ready, she inched forward. Her muscles burned as she scrambled over large stones dotting the uneven ground.

The sound of laughter sent her flat against the trunk of a hemlock. The voices were young, mayhap as young as she. Rolling along the trunk, she flung her gaze toward the sound.

Two lads marched along an unmarked path, punching each other's shoulders and smiling in the way of those who had no cares. Their cheeks were ruddy and warm. Brightly colored brats secured with ornate brooches covered their shoulders, the fabric thick and warm, not like her thin cloak. One walked backwards, facing her. He moved with more purpose than the other, as if he was the leader of the two.

He looked to be about her age, maybe a winter or two older. Not yet of the height of a young man, but there was a deepness to his voice indicating he was in his last days of boyhood. There was strength to his jaw, but his cheeks were still round, still a child's.

Like her. Like she should have been. Like Beli should have been.

His mop of blond curls bounced as he walked. He turned then, revealing the design decorating the back of his crimson brat. Cyrene gripped the curve of her bow so tightly it hurt.

The length of cloth he wore wrapped around his body bore the insignia of the tower. An elaborately decorated serpent coiled behind crossed swords. Cyrene hissed, the vision of her mother's unseeing eyes staring heavenward breaking something inside that had been broken and mended and rebroken hundreds of times in the last two years.

Tethered rage snapped free inside of her, loosening the memories she'd smothered. They uncurled inside her chest and ran through the length of her limbs until her fingers and toes tingled with the sensation.

She was there again. Drowning in a sea of chaos and terror. Glimpses of the past assaulted her mind. A soldier's hand brutally dragging a child away from his father as tears cut clear tracks down the lad's dirty cheeks. The glint of a blade, shiny and clean before it was plunged into the father's back. That same blade marred with blood, being wiped carelessly across a soldier's arm.

The shriek of a bird became the shouts of her mother's few remaining warriors. They were brave, Beli the bravest of them all, but bravery wasn't enough.

She shut her eyes to the memory of what had happened to her brother, what her last glimpse of him had been. She couldn't allow that image to materialize—not then. Not when there was danger in the woods.

It was all unleashed, all flowing through her as if it was still happening, and she looked at the lads with seething rage. She hated that blood-red cloak. That crest. That king.

Cyrene centered her aim on the blond one's chest. It would be so easy to release that arrow. To take from the king as he had taken from her. Whoever this lad was, if he wore the colors of the tower, surely his sudden absence would be mourned.

But it would also draw attention to the woods. That was the last thing she needed. A subtle tug in her mind sent Cyrene's gaze flecking over her shoulder to where the fallen stag lay. Shame weakened her limbs even more than the hunger.

She'd felt more compassion for that animal than this lad. How had she come to be so hardened that she'd even consider taking his life for no other reason than spite?

That was the evil king's fault too. He drove her to this place, this condition.

Cyrene turned her full attention back to the trespassers as they headed toward the edge of the woods, all the while running through all the reasons she shouldn't allow them to leave. The most tempting sprung from the fact that they were not afraid—at least, the blond one wasn't. Had their warnings of the woods finally worn off?

Were people no longer scared enough of the woodland fairies to stay away?

What if they'd seen her camp? What if the lads returned with soldiers to finish them off? Was that why they'd been laughing— were they making fun of the foolish Pictish people who thought they could outlast the king, escape his cruelty? Her cracked lips pulled back at the growl that slipped through her teeth.

She froze as the lad's gaze drifted past his friend directly to where she was watching. His blue eyes landed on her hiding spot, settling there. Even though she was barely visible behind the sturdy hemlock trunk, he'd seen her. She knew it.

He paused just a step, and Cyrene rolled herself back around the tree, lowered her bow, and drew her blade, holding it in both hands at her chest.

She could run. He wasn't so close that she couldn't get away. But her eyes darted to the stag again.

What if they tried to take it? What if they chased her until she lost it? Cold, hunger, anger, and hopelessness pounded in Cyrene's head, her knees practically a drum as they knocked together. She found herself once again trapped between the decision to fight or hide.

She risked a glance around the tree. The lads were moving away, the blond one's arm slung across his friend's back.

He dropped a look over his shoulder, finding her hiding place once again, but he didn't stop or alert his friend of her presence, if he recognized her as a person and not some human-shaped trick of the eye. He simply tightened his grip and urged his friend on toward the edge of the woods.

I'll let ye go this time. Cyrene willed him to hear her thoughts. *Just this once.*

Once they'd disappeared, she clambered back to her stag and whistled a final time, desperate and near panic. In minutes, Astrid appeared, wisps of her brilliant moon-white hair loosened from her braids, and thankfully astride a winded gray mare. Though she was but three years older than Cyrene, Astrid's hair was as colorless as the oldest women in their village.

Together, the two lasses lashed fallen branches into a makeshift sled and heaved the stag's body atop.

"Where were ye?" Cyrene groaned under the weight of the animal.

"Following a doe. Followed her deep too." Both Astrid's hair and accent were remnants of her Nordic descent.

"Did ye fell her?"

"Nay." Her friend's answer was breathless, Cyrene guessed both from disappointment and the labor of dragging the stag. "She got spooked and ran."

Astrid slapped the rump of her mare affectionately. "Cuddie and

I gave chase, but we got lost. Then I heard yer whistle. *An T-aon* led me to ye."

Cyrene stilled at Astrid's explanation. *"An T-aon?"*

"Aye." Astrid lashed the stag to their sled. "I was riding in circles. 'Twas getting dark, and I was lost. Then I heard yer whistle. If Cuddie hadn't turned at the sound, we'd have slipped off the edge of a gorge. I dinna even see it."

Cyrene worked in silence, unsure where to store the battling feelings of doubt and hope that wrestled inside her mind. Cuddie made light work of carting the stag once they'd secured the sled to her shoulders with ropes Astrid had used for traps.

Cyrene took Astrid's offered hand and climbed atop the horse's back. Navigating deep ravines and jutting boulders made for a lengthy ride. Cyrene was so weighted by exhaustion, she nearly fell off twice on the way to their camp. Unable to keep her eyes open, warmed by Astrid's fur wrap against her frozen cheeks, she sagged against her friend.

As they neared, women ran to help the lasses dismount, to start fires, to gather blades for skinning. They worked and moved in sync like the sun and moon and stars. Despite their circumstances, she saw hope alight on their faces.

Cyrene couldn't help but smile at the strength on display. She imagined dragging the ugly tower king by the collar and throwing him at their feet. She imagined the shock when he realized that though he'd slaughtered nearly all their men, the Pictish women and children survived. And they were strong.

They would not be so easily extinguished.

Soon the two other hunting groups arrived with their bounty. In addition to her stag, they added a doe, three rabbits, and a few pheasants to the evening's bounty. Seeing such an abundance nearly made her weep tears of joy. Everyone would eat that night. There would be enough to dry for jerky and to tan pelts for warm clothing. Her thoughts slipped back to Beli. How he would have danced at the feast they'd soon enjoy. How he would have made jokes about absorbing the strength of the buck through a savory stew.

Her heart ached with each beat. She missed him.

Though her bones groaned with weariness, Cyrene trudged to the largest hut in the camp, where the orphaned children lived with several of the older women.

"How fares the little one?" Her words grated against her raw throat.

"Much the same." A straw-haired woman pulled back the fur covering a small mound to allow Cyrene to gaze upon the sleeping toddler.

Because of her thick midnight hair, they'd called her Revna, though no one knew her true name. There was such chaos in the days after Derelei's death, Revna was not the only child to appear amongst them, nameless and orphaned.

A flicker of memory skipped through Cyrene's mind—Brígid handing the infant to the women, her only explanation that Revna had been found, and she was one of their own. Cyrene determined to ask Brígid about that memory, but . . . tomorrow, if she remembered. Her mind could barely form a thought through the thick exhaustion.

Like Astrid's exotic silver locks, the combination of Revna's black hair, olive skin, and striking blue eyes enchanted everyone in the tribe. But even their doting and affection weren't enough to give the babe the strength she needed.

She was frail, sickly, and Cyrene never failed to seek her out, hoping against hope Revna survived another day.

"There's nothing wrong with her, but she doesna thrive." The woman spoke over her shoulder as she gathered soiled clothing into a basket. "Brígid says 'tis as if the strong half of her is missing."

Cyrene placed her hand on the child's back, needing to feel the rise and fall of her body as she breathed.

"I wish I ken what to do fer ye, little Revna." Cyrene pulled the fur back into place and rose, nearly stumbling from hunger.

Grateful the women had busied themselves with the other children and hadn't witnessed her moment of weakness, she delivered the good news of their great haul before leaving.

Cyrene collapsed by a kindling fire as a lass with bright eyes dragged a fur from her hut and draped it over Cyrene's lap.

"Thank ye, Gertrud."

Gertrud was but six winters, and her broad smile looked strange on her thin face. Cyrene watched her skip through the crowd before finding her mother and tugging on her cloak. Her mother, Brígid, scooped up the lass, who whispered something in her ear before pointing a tiny finger in Cyrene's direction.

Brígid followed Gertrud's inclination, and when her eyes fell on Cyrene, she offered a knowing nod.

"I'm sorry," it seemed to say, and then with the soft smile that followed, "Ye've done well."

The mounds of fresh dirt covering the bodies of those they'd lost would say otherwise, and the undeserved approval of her mother's dearest friend released an ache in her heart so deep, she couldn't breathe. She buried her head in her arms that circled her drawn-up knees so no one would see the tears.

If only she'd been older and wiser, she could have stopped her mother from going to the tower that morning. If only her father hadn't died in battle just days before that horrible king married their own Fiona. If only she'd been quicker and grabbed Beli before he slipped away from that thicket. If only, if only.

Keeping her head lowered, Cyrene found the hard metal of her mother's ring beneath the fabric of her tunic and ran her calloused thumb across its smooth surface. Her mother's stories hadn't died. Not really.

Brígid had been there. And a few other elders who knew the traditions and knew her mother. They'd not only advised Cyrene in making decisions, but Brígid had taken up where Derelei left off and filled Cyrene's heart with those same fantastical tales of old. Unlike her mother, Brígid had a flair for the dramatic and wove in great love and romance to her stories.

It was those stories that had taken long, hopeless nights and made them bearable. Turned her nightmares into wondrous dreams.

But it had been nearly a year since she'd sat at Brígid's feet and listened to well-spun stories. The nights had turned dark and cold again. Mayhap a child's hope was all it had been.

Cyrene barely registered someone placing a carved wooden bowl of stew next to her, barely remembered gulping it down. Weariness dulled her senses as Astrid plopped down at her side, and Cyrene lifted the fur, allowing her best friend under.

"How's Revna?" Astrid asked between bites of stew.

Cyrene answered with a shrug.

"I was worse off when ye found me, and I recovered. She'll do the same."

"Aye." Cyrene leaned closer to Astrid.

She'd never forget the night they'd snuck to the sea with hopes of finding fish in their hidden nets and returned with a barely breathing lass instead.

Clinging like a stringy lump of seaweed to the shattered remains of her ship, the young stowaway was the only survivor of a failed attempt by the Vikings to blindly navigate the maze of the firth and breach the shores of Tràigh. The shores that used to belong to the Picts.

From that night on, Astrid was her sister. Never alone again.

Astrid finished her stew in silence, then wiggled down further under the fur she shared with Cyrene. Cyrene linked arms with her friend, their heads together as they fought sleep.

Astrid's story from earlier floated through Cyrene's thoughts. Beli had been the one to make plans. The one with all the ideas. The one who noticed every detail. But *An T-aon* had helped Astrid. Guided her. Mayhap he still cared for her people. Mayhap he would guide Cyrene too.

She breathed deeply. Praying. Listening. Waiting. Until suddenly, she knew the answer. Or . . . mayhap the beginning of an answer.

"We have to move." Cyrene flexed, squeezing Astrid's arm with her muscle as Astrid hummed a disgruntled response. "I saw lads today, from the tower."

Astrid turned a panicked gaze on her, instantly tense. "What happened? Did they harm ye, Majesty?"

"Dunna call me that." Cyrene frowned, staring at the fire with eyes so tired, they burned. "But no. They dinna do anything. They looked . . . happy."

"I dunna remember happy." Astrid's reply was dry. She became entranced by the flickering fire along with Cyrene.

Mayhap that's what little Revna needed. A place to be happy.

"We must move on. We canna survive like this." Cyrene rested one arm on her bent knee, waving her limp hand toward temporary tents that barely stayed upright and were patched beyond usefulness. "This is no life."

They never stayed in one place more than a few days, and the constant relocating was wearing everyone into exhaustion. They no longer needed escape; they needed a home.

"But where? The mountains are bare, the sea is at our side, and the king has taken our lands as his own. Even now, he builds a great wall of stone and wood around the village and tower. Shall we crawl to his gates and beg for mercy?"

"Nay. I'll na bring us back under that tyranny. I say we go into the wood. Deeper." Cyrene ticked her head toward the darkness ringing their firelit camp.

"Deeper there might be worse things than soldiers." Astrid shivered against Cyrene's side.

"I dunna believe that. Besides, I'd rather face a thousand real fairies than one of those brutes." Cyrene dropped her hand, pulling it back under the fur and into a fist. Lingering flecks of hope from Brígid's fantasy world where light always defeated darkness swirled in Cyrene's tired brain. A vision forming.

"We've managed to sneak into the villages a few times. We even have horses now. We can make one more trip, and then we will go so deep, no one will ever find us. We can forge our own army. Cathala and Ailbhe can train anyone able to fight. We will make our own world. Our own life. We will become the legends and stories they tell. He builds his walls, and we can build ours too."

Astrid didn't respond for so long, Cyrene thought she'd drifted off, and Cyrene remembered the day she stood over the empty grave commemorating her mother. Empty, because by the time she'd snuck back to the roundhouse, it was nothing more than a pile of wet ash. The king had taken too much. Lands and lives and even the respect for the dead. She'd made a promise that day, whispering it over the freshly turned black earth.

I'll never be subject to that crown again.

"The others might be scared." Astrid's voice was soft, sleepy. "But wherever ye go, I'll follow ye, Sister."

Cyrene didn't want to be followed. She didn't want to lead. It should have been her parents, strong, confident Bercilak, and wise, courageous Derelei, making decisions and barking orders. Or even young Beli. But not ten-year-old Cyrene.

Brígid promised to be at her side and continue to guide her, but no amount of advice or instruction could conjure an army to defend them or turn their meager camp into a home. It would be up to her.

"The lads?" Astrid muttered, her words dragging with sleep.

"Aye?" Cyrene laid her cheek on the top of Astrid's warm head.

"Were they verra braw?"

Cyrene couldn't help the giggle that shook her shoulders, growing as Astrid laughed too.

Somehow, her friend always knew when she was drowning in her own thoughts and needed to be rescued. Astrid continued to goad Cyrene until neither could fight sleep one more moment, and they slipped off, warmed by dreams of summer nights, full bellies, and soft beds.

4

DUNCAN

818 AD - 10 Years Later

The bells of the abbey rang clear across the courtyard, signaling the beginning of midday prayers. Duncan dropped the stone he was unloading from the cart and slapped his dusty hands against his robes.

There were few things he appreciated from his years spent learning the art of war, but when the head priest issued the proclamation that every student would assist with the building of the new sanctuary, Duncan was entirely grateful for the training his muscles had already received.

He'd arrived at the war camp as a scrawny prince and left with the moniker Duncan the Bold. Here at the abbey, he was just plain Duncan. He stared at his palms. They were raw and calloused from both wielding a sword and building a house of God. While his fellow classmates were straining, sweating, and sometimes falling out from exhaustion, Duncan found pleasure in the thoughtless, though strenuous, task.

He had not once regretted his decision to enter the ministry. Though the choice had earned him a scathing letter from his father, who had in no way hidden his disappointment that Duncan would not be leading his army. Quickly moving up in rank was the one achievement his father had not scoffed at, so turning down a further appointment had continued his mastery of disappointing the king.

As he made his way from the site of the new construction to the garden reserved for prayer, Duncan once again reminded himself he was not meant for the tower. *I am not my father.* That was Brodric's destiny.

Through five years of hard training in battle, Duncan rose to the level of captain, and with each swing of his sword, chipped away at the jealousy he carried for his brother until the space it had once filled was empty.

In the near six months of silence and self-reflection he'd spent since arriving at the abbey, he'd realized he'd never desired the crown, never lusted after the power that seemed to ignite rage in his father instead of pleasure. What sparked the jealousy was that Brodric was certain of his purpose. His brother knew exactly what he desired.

It was a burden he gladly relinquished, but even now, two and a half years later, at twenty and two years of age, he had not committed himself to a permanent ministry.

"Duncan." A young student dipped his head in greeting as he passed. Duncan returned the gesture but didn't miss the subtle judgment in his eye. He was practically an old man in their eyes, and they were little more than lads in his.

Most came for training upon entering adulthood. Duncan looked again at his hands, which had seen more of war than prayer. He'd seen much more of the world than these lads ever would. He'd experienced the sins they taught against, heard the Lord's name taken in vain more than in worship, and prayed he did the right thing by handing over his captain's charge to his best friend, Eowin.

Well over six feet, broad as an oak, Eowin's strength alone was enough to catapult him into leadership. But he was also as wise as he was strong, with a quick mind and affinity for planning that made the choice easy for Duncan when he decided to not renew his term in the service. If anyone could resist the temptations that came with power and violence, it was Eowin.

Father Malcolm spied Duncan from across the grounds and lifted his chin in greeting. While the other students and priests sought places of solitude throughout the garden, Malcolm clapped his bony hand on Duncan's shoulder, guiding him to a shaded corner.

"What will ye pray fer today, lad?" The old man's voice was gravelly with age, but his gray eyes held a spark that made Duncan think he already knew the answer to that question.

He also knew the priest wouldn't share his thoughts on the matter, even if he begged. Duncan felt like he knew nothing, only that there was a space inside that needed filling. For the second son of a king, his choices were limited. His father and brother encouraged him to wed the daughter of a wealthy laird in a nearby kingdom, but Duncan couldn't even entertain the idea. In his experience, marriages arranged to increase the kingdom hadn't been very successful.

His father had nearly torn Tràigh apart after Fiona's death, but Duncan had never witnessed even one second of that passion while she lived. There was only coldness and then chaos.

Peace.

That's what Fiona had promised her God could provide. It was that claim and the hope of finding the thing that would satisfy that emptiness that sent him to the doors of the abbey.

"I'll pray my purpose will be clear, Father." Duncan flexed his hands, his palms still burning from the roughness of the stones.

Father Malcolm nodded. "A good prayer."

"Is there another I should pray instead?" Duncan felt the hint of a smile on his lips.

"Oh, nay, nay." Father Malcolm pursed his lips, clearly holding back his own grin. "To find one's purpose is a fine thing."

He thought he'd known at fourteen, when he began his military training. Now at twenty and two, he was not much closer to that purpose than the lad he'd been when he left the tower on the back of a chestnut mare.

"I ken ye would say I should accept the offered priesthood." Duncan lowered himself onto the seat of a stone bench and looked up at the priest, who had clasped his hands together in front of his brown robes.

"I wouldna suggest it unless ye were certain that was the path the Lord lay before ye." Father Malcolm offered a slight bow before taking a few steps toward the cobblestone trail leading toward the center of the garden. "Ye canna walk in two worlds, Duncan. Ye must choose."

"There is only one path to righteousness and salvation."

"Aye. To follow Christ is the only way, but he doesna travel only within these walls." Father Malcolm lifted his hands and gazed across the well-kept grounds of the monastery. "If this is where ye can commit yerself and give yer heart, then accept the offer. But this is not a place to hide. The Lord doesna call us to be cowards."

Father Malcolm didn't wait for Duncan's reply, not that he had one to give. He wasn't hiding. Going against his father and entering study for the priesthood—wasn't that the brave thing?

Duncan did pray for purpose. He also prayed for courage if he was lacking it, but before he could finish, the jingling bells signaling a visitor at the gates drew the attention of everyone in the garden.

Tucked into the foothills of rocky mountains and miles from any port, guests were rare to the secluded monastery. Duncan lingered in the garden, attempting to continue in prayer, but eventually gave in to curiosity and followed the group to the gates.

The visitor was gone by the time he arrived, but he'd delivered a message that had the men murmuring and concerned. Something was wrong.

As he made his way through the crowd of hushed whispers, wide, tear-brimmed eyes, and hands shaking over mouths, Duncan was ten years old again, watching that servant stumble from the tower, fall to his knees, and with soundless sobs, raise his bloodied hands to the king. A knot twisted and tightened in his stomach.

He dared not ask, but the word came anyway, spoken from trembling, pale lips and carried mercilessly to Duncan's ears on a cruel wind.

Plague.

Immediately work on the new sanctuary ceased, and prayers began. Yet even still the bells of the gate rang again two days later. Then again the next day. And the next.

Each visit brought word of loss. Entire villages nearly destroyed by this disease. The abbey became a place of mourning, though it was shielded from the sickness.

Priests, students, and servants all abandoned study and service to fast and pray. Duncan remained in the garden, even when the others had chosen to move inside.

At dusk on the second day of unceasing prayers, heavy with the burden he carried for his homeland, Duncan's eyes finally closed. In a fitful sleep, he drifted through time and space to another night. A night he'd long forgotten and never wished to remember again, where events both real and imagined unfolded in his anxious mind.

He was a lad again. Woken not by a strange or loud noise, but complete silence.

Nights in the tower were quiet, but there was always some sound from behind his closed oak door. The scrape of boots on stone, the clink of metal mugs from the great hall, a burst of roaring laughter from his father's fighting men. Lately, it was the tiny newborn cries of his twin half-sisters. There was always something to break through the thick silence of night.

Duncan rubbed his ears, relieved at the soft shush his palms made against the side of his head. Once he realized he hadn't been buried underground, his second fear was that he'd lost his hearing like the servant lass who'd been struck with the fever.

He closed his eyes and listened. It was still too quiet.

Had something happened, and everyone fled the tower? Would they have forgotten him? Duncan dragged the back of his hand under his nose, wiping the sweat that prickled his skin.

Brodric might have forgotten him, even his father, but Fiona wouldn't have.

Duncan wrapped his crimson brat around his shoulders. It still smelled of smoke from the fires at the celebration he and Brodric had snuck off to earlier that evening. He slid his bare feet into the leather boots waiting at his bedside and stealthily eased out of his chambers toward the queen's room. Toward the light.

They'd nearly been caught when Brodric had finally dragged him back to the tower, and he hadn't gotten to tell Fiona of the great joy the joined peoples shared. In a world that was hard and cold, she was the one thing that was soft and warm. He imagined how her face would brighten as he described the laughter and dancing. Then she would bless him with smiles, conversation, tender touches, and whispered words of encouragement. He often thought Fiona was the only seeing person in a country full of blindness. She was the only one to see him—that was certain.

Duncan mashed his lips together, smothering the smile that pushed out from inside, and he peeked around the corner, earning himself a view of the queen's chamber door.

Just days before, Fiona had pressed a kiss to the dark head of one whimpering infant as she sighed a lament for lost sleep.

Father had grumbled about there being servants and wet nurses for such things, but Fiona was insistent.

"Pictish women care for their own." Her defiance had sent him into a rage, and Duncan hadn't seen them speak since.

She'd taken to walking the halls all night with her lady in waiting in an attempt to lull the babies to sleep. He secretly hoped he'd find her doing the same that night, but Duncan felt his brows furrow when he noticed her corridor was empty and chamber door unguarded. Duncan glanced over his shoulder, from where he'd come. It was strange. All the corridors were empty.

Then he remembered. At supper, he'd sat as close to Fiona as he could, missing her nearness in the days she'd been confined to her room after his sisters were born. One of Fiona's ladies had whispered to her, begging her to let her take the infants to her chamber for the night. To allow the queen to rest. She must have agreed.

He pushed off the wall, prepared to peek in her room, just to see her face, when the creak of a door from further down the hall sent him crouching in the shadows.

He couldn't tell from which door the sound had come. Both the king's and Fiona's ladies' chambers were in that direction. His hope sprang to life. Mayhap it was Fiona, returning with her bairns to her own chamber. He moved to greet her when the heaviness of the footfalls registered in his ears.

Fiona would have hushed her guards and welcomed Duncan's presence had she been awake, but he was sure to receive a harsh scolding for roaming the halls if he were caught by anyone else. He'd rather suffer through the silent night than face the wrath of his father or the teasing of his brother.

He melted into the darkness that painted the stone walls black and waited for his chance to dart back to his own chamber. Someone was approaching. It must have been her guard returning to his post.

A flare of heat raced up Duncan's back. He should tell his father to replace that guard. It wasn't right for the queen to be left unprotected, even for a moment.

But the king would demand to know how he came to know that information. Making himself one with the rough stone walls, Duncan eased further down the hall.

The sound of the footsteps stopped at the queen's chamber. There would be no visiting her tonight. He swallowed the giant lump of disappointment that had formed in his throat and made a move to race back to his own chambers when the person outside Fiona's room coughed. Duncan froze. He recognized that sound, and panic soared through his nerves. His feet were soundless as he stole back through the dark night to his chambers and buried himself under his blankets.

He laid awake, waiting for someone to burst into his room and drag him out of bed, doling out a harsh punishment for sneaking through the village and roaming the halls. Just before sleep finally captured his consciousness, he thought he heard footsteps again, but outside his door. One step slightly heavier than the other, as if the person favored one leg. And once again, he heard the familiar gruff cough he would recognize anywhere.

In a dream within a dream, Duncan rode dark ships on stormy waters that tossed him about his bed, nearly sending him overboard. He awoke to his father's hands on his shoulders, shaking him into wakefulness.

Somewhere inside, Duncan remembered it should have been Brodric waking him to get dressed and gather in the courtyard for the Pictish queen's arrival, but in the reality of this nightmare, King William loomed over his shrinking form.

"What have ye done?" the king roared, his voice like thunder.

"N-nothing." Duncan squirmed to free himself from the king's pinching grasp, but his father's hands became shackles that fixed him in place.

"Ye killed her." William's features twisted into something dark and unnatural. "Ye murdered her."

"Nay." His protests were growing weaker, diminished by the guilt pressing on his chest.

"Ye saw someone, and ye did nothing, said nothing." William's face was no longer human. The thing accusing him was gnarled and grotesque. "Ye let her die."

"I was scared."

"Coward!" the monster hissed sharply. "Liar."

It leaned in, pushing on Duncan's chest until no air could pass to his lungs.

"They asked ye if ye heard anything, and ye lied. Ye were too scared to speak."

Duncan couldn't respond or defend himself, both because of the merciless pressure on his chest, and the truth of the accusations.

From behind the hideous creature dripping its venom onto his face, another vision appeared.

Fiona.

Beautiful, innocent Fiona. Sadness bathed her in a soft blue light, her gentle hand outstretched toward him.

"Dunna let it happen again, Duncan, my love." Tears flowed down her soft cheeks. "Not again."

"Duncan." Someone shook him.

Fiona became a wisp of smoke. The creature shifted back into his father and cast a long, disapproving look. Just before he vanished, Duncan saw something that turned his insides to ice. His father's hands were stained red with blood.

"Duncan." Father Malcolm's voice was tight, strained.

Duncan opened his eyes, nausea overtaking him as he shot upright. The priest sat on the bench next to where Duncan must have rolled off onto the ground in his exhaustion. Behind Father Malcolm, the sky was blossoming into dawn with delicate shades of pink and orange. It should have been beautiful, but it seemed like an unwelcome messenger.

He rubbed his eyes and shook himself awake as he crawled off the ground to sit next to Father Malcolm. The priest didn't speak for a long time. Duncan felt his heart begin to pound inside of his chest, and not only from the disturbing dream.

"Word has come from Tràigh." Father Malcolm's words were dry.

Duncan clasped his hands together over his mouth, waiting for the news Father Malcolm would deliver next.

"The king is dead."

Blackness edged in on Duncan's vision, bringing with it the

sharp sting of saltwater against the back of his eyes. He clenched his teeth, willing himself to stay calm.

"My brother?"

He felt Father Malcolm's hand on his shoulder. "I'm sorry."

The two didn't speak again until the sun had fully breached the horizon, heating the air enough that sweat formed on Duncan's brow. The priest simply stayed at Duncan's side as his mind rolled through every emotion and implication of this news.

When the abbey bells rang for morning mass, Duncan finally cleared his throat and stood.

"I canna take the throne."

Father Malcolm rose, though significantly slower and not without the popping of his joints.

"Is there another in yer family line?"

"I have a cousin. He bears the same name as my father." Duncan scrubbed his hands over his face, forcing his mind into clarity. "But he has left the country, and when last I heard from my brother, he was not any sort of man fit to lead Tràigh."

Those words stuck in Duncan's mouth, held there as if he should spit them back out in reference to himself.

"Duncan." Father Malcolm's usually soft voice was firm.

Duncan met the old man's eyes, his brows arching at the certainty he saw there.

"Though there is much sadness and ye shall surely mourn, I believe yer prayers for purpose have been answered."

Duncan shook his head. "Nay. I wasna meant to rule."

"What will ye do then?"

"I dunna ken. Mayhap the neighboring kingdom will take Tràigh as its own."

"Is that what yer father would have wanted ye to do?"

Heat flashed up Duncan's spine, warming his face so that sweat formed across his brow.

"Does it matter anymore?" He knew his voice was too loud, his tone too harsh against his mentor and friend. "I amna like my father."

Duncan was breathless when Father Malcolm placed his hand on his shoulder.

"Mayhap my mother had a relative who can make the claim, but . . ." Duncan's words felt jumbled in his mind. "But it canna be me."

"Then I pray the Lord will lead the right man to Tràigh."

"Aye." Duncan rubbed his hand hard across his forehead, attempting to force his jumbled thoughts into clarity. "I will leave at dusk. I will settle the matter and return as soon as possible."

He aimed for the abbey.

"Duncan." Father Malcolm's call stopped him, but he didn't turn around. "Ministry isn't only conducted inside the walls of a church."

Duncan didn't reply. He only swallowed hard and continued on his path to his chambers.

As the sun sank to its resting place, Father Malcolm accompanied Duncan, who had traded his robes for a léine and brat, to the gates. Duncan placed his few belongings on the ground as the old man drew him in for a shaky embrace.

"May the Lord bless ye and keep ye, lad." Father Malcolm's hands held Duncan's shoulders. "May his face shine upon ye and be gracious to ye, the Lord turn his face toward ye . . ."

Father Malcolm paused, forcing Duncan's eyes to his. "And give ye peace."

5

CYRENE

818 - A Week Later

"'T is finished, m'lady."

Cyrene looked up from the drawn map she'd been staring at but not really seeing.

Liam stood in the opening of her hut, his long arms holding back the thick fabric covering the entrance. When she met his eyes, he ducked inside and offered a presumptuous half-smile before folding his arms across his chest. Any excitement she'd felt over the news melted into annoyance at the casual confidence of the lad-turned-man she'd grown up with.

"I thought ye might need an escort." Liam chucked his chin upwards, one brow arching, as if she should be honored by his offer.

Cyrene fought the urge to crumple the parchment beneath her hands and lob it at his head. It enraged her that he thought he could take such liberties just because she'd let him hold her hand once, when they were a pair of terrified children hiding from the tower king's soldiers. She was no longer a child. She was the queen, and he ought to act accordingly. She only tolerated him because he'd been brave that day, and she couldn't spare any brave souls.

"I willna be going anywhere." She smothered a smile at his shocked expression.

"Ye arna going to see it?"

"Nay." Cyrene turned her back on the warrior. "I willna risk losing its secrecy to satisfy my own curiosity. And neither should ye."

"But . . ."

"That will be all." Cyrene waved her hand, dismissing Liam before he could further protest.

She heard him draw in a long breath, and rubbed her hand over her mouth to hide the taunting grin that spread across her lips.

"As ye wish, m'lady."

There was a sharpness to his tone, and Cyrene was tempted to reprimand him for it, but she held her tongue and allowed him to leave.

"'Tis finished." She repeated Liam's words as she sank into the large wooden chair at the head of her table.

This time, she allowed the smile tugging at her cheeks. She traced her finger along the route of their completed project.

"Finally."

"Talking to yerself again?" Astrid glided through the folds of fabric and plopped into a chair neighboring Cyrene's.

"Does no one in this village respect their queen?" Cyrene's harsh glare didn't affect Astrid in the least.

"Liam dinna seem verra happy." Astrid tossed a handful of hazelnuts into her mouth from the bowl on Cyrene's table.

"He expected to escort me to the tunnel." Cyrene nearly growled the explanation.

Astrid released a throaty laugh, slapping her hand on the table. "I wish I coulda witnessed that request."

Cyrene rolled the map and secured it with a thin leather strap before placing it in a basket with other spirals of parchment.

"I want to be happy." Cyrene's soft remark landed at her feet as if she'd dropped a stone. "Do ye think we can finally be happy?"

Astrid didn't have a reply. Cyrene turned to face her friend, feeling exposed and vulnerable. Her fingers twitched, tempted to stroke the fabric of her dress where it covered an ugly scar across her ribs. She laced her fingers together instead, stilling their movement.

"I want to take a breath that isna burdened with all the ways we can be hurt again, and sleep through the night without hearing the sound of soldier's boots and swords in my dreams. Where Beli's roar doesn't chase me awake every morn."

Astrid lowered her eyes, turning a shelled hazelnut between her fingers. She'd not met Beli, but knew him well enough from Cyrene's stories.

"I want to forget the pain that brought us to this place."

"We canna forget." Astrid didn't lift her eyes, but her fidgeting stilled. "I ken I wasna there for the worst of yer heartache, as ye werna there fer mine, but we can never forget."

Cyrene took her seat at the head of the table again, propping her chin against her palm as her fiery red hair fell in waves across her shoulder.

"This tunnel is a great victory, m'lady." Astrid finally raised her chin, searching Cyrene's eyes for understanding. "After nigh ten winters, ye finally have safe access to the village again. There are those who will help us. Those who ken what kind of man that king is and will stand against him, even in secret."

Astrid drew a dagger tucked in the leather belting her waist and flipped it by the blade with expert hands.

"But even though we have built a home here in the wood, even though we have found a way to trade with the village of Tràigh without our scouts risking their lives crossing the open fields, we can never forget what it cost to get to this place. That's what makes it so valuable."

Cyrene's throat went dry. Faces of those they'd lost were permanently etched in her brain and drifted to the surface of her memory as if summoned by Astrid's words. Cathala. Ailbhe. Eden. Brígid. Mother. Beli. So many others.

"Yer right." Cyrene touched Astrid's arm and stood, making her way to the hut's opening. "I suppose I am just tired."

Cyrene drew back the fabric and gazed across the rows of fortified huts that spiraled out from hers. Laughter drifted over their roofs from somewhere on the outskirts, and the smell of cooking meat permeated the air. She could even make out a faint melody from some happy soul playing a flute.

For so long, she'd only ever focused on the next step forward. Survival. Each minute of each day had been crucial and dire. But now, now that she had space to breathe, where she should have found that happiness, she only found all the thoughts she'd silenced over the years waiting for her.

"Our people havna always been faithful to *An T-aon*." Cyrene didn't turn, but heard Astrid move from the table to join her in the doorway. "Sometimes I wonder if all the suffering came because of some fault, some doubt?"

"I dunna think so." Astrid moved to lean against the doorway, holding back the curtain with her shoulder. "If we were punished for every wrong, then we'd have to earn every joy, and dunna the teachings say our works canna earn us anything?"

"Aye." Cyrene fingered the delicate embroidery sewn into the sleeve of her tunic. There was a time when she'd thought she'd never again experience such a simple pleasure as a clean garment that didn't fall off her shoulders.

"I have seen more of the world than ye." Astrid's pale eyes squinted against the brightness of the sun. "Suffering is not limited to worshippers of *An T-aon*."

A decade of work brought them to this place. A place they called home. They were even expecting to soon hear the sweet cry of bairns.

"I ken ye would seek answers. A reason fer all the hurt." Astrid nodded toward the village. "I think our people suffered because that king is evil, and now our people can risk joy again because *An T-aon* is good."

Cyrene gazed at her friend. A look of certainty relaxed Astrid's features, reminding her that Astrid was only a few winters older. She envied the peace Astrid found in *An T-aon*. As if he wasa friend.

"It was a good choice to name ye as captain of my warriors."

Astrid jerked her head toward Cyrene at the sudden compliment. Cyrene couldn't help the smile as Astrid twisted her mouth to keep her own expression neutral.

"Someone had to keep Liam's confidence from swelling his head till it burst."

Cyrene's laugh drew the attention of a group of passing ladies, their eyes wide at the unusual sound. They looked at each other and smiled as they walked but quickly stopped at the sight of something just out of Cyrene's view.

She straightened, instantly alert, and noticed from the corner of her eye that Astrid did the same. Her captain's fingers already curled around the hilt of her blade.

A shock of black hair announced the arrival of Cyrene's young scout, who stormed toward the hut with purpose.

"Revna?" Cyrene barely spoke her name before Revna drew close and offered a brief bow in greeting.

"I have news." Revna's light eyes were blazing, brilliantly contrasting her dark hair and honey skin, her jaw clenched around the words she forced through her teeth.

Revna usually kept her quiet rage as close as the daggers she hid in her waistband, but this day, it was on full display, and Cyrene jerked her head to urge her and Astrid inside. It had been a risk to name Revna as scout. She was but twelve winters, but there were none more stealthy or sharp. And none more in need of purpose, as she'd taken to stealing to the villages on her own anyway.

Once the folds of the hut's fabric door fell together, Revna spun on her heels and captured Cyrene's gaze with a pointed stare.

"The king is dead."

Cyrene nearly laughed, certain she hadn't heard correctly. She looked at Astrid to see if her captain had understood the same.

"What? When?" It was Astrid who spoke, stepping toward Revna as if to hear her better.

"A week past. I hadna been to the village because of finishing the tunnel, and just got word."

Neither Cyrene nor Astrid spoke for a full minute.

"Should I summon the elders?" Revna tilted her chin, urging a response.

"How?" Astrid asked. "Er . . . how did he die?"

Revna's eyes danced between Cyrene's and Astrid's waiting gazes. Her nostrils flared, and she shook her head as if forcing the answer through unwilling lips.

"Plague," she said flatly.

Astrid retreated, eying Revna as if she carried the disease herself, but Cyrene noticed the veins bulging against the skin of Revna's forearms from the force of her clenched fists. This news enraged her, and Cyrene couldn't imagine why. He was their most hated enemy.

Cyrene swallowed hard, her dry throat resisting the action, and she stared at the rug-covered floor of her hut. The king was dead.

The tower-dwelling tyrant who murdered her mother, who stole Fiona, and who slaughtered her people was gone. She'd always imagined receiving her vengeance against the man. Mayhap when she'd trained enough warriors to face him, or when she'd slowly worked her way through his kingdom, turning his people against him enough to start an uprising. Every imagined outcome ended with her confronting him and spewing all of his terrors back in his face until he crumbled to dust under his own sins.

It didn't seem fair that he escaped her wrath so quickly. "What of the elder son—will he rule in his stead?" Astrid had taken to pacing the small space between the table and doorway.

"Nay." Revna's soft answer stilled Astrid's route. "Brodric is also gone."

Astrid and Cyrene met stares.

"The kingdom is without a ruler?"

"Nay." Revna's answer froze them both in place. "A new king has come."

6

DUNCAN

821 AD - Three Years Later

The clash of metal against metal jerked Duncan upright from his bed. The hearth's fire long extinguished, only blue light from a full moon seeping through cracks in the shutters illuminated his chambers. His room was empty. He stilled. Listening. Hearing nothing but the hiss of his own breath, he pushed relief down his dry throat.

He dashed to the window and shoved open rough wooden shutters. Except for the rhythmic rush of the sea against the shore, the night was as quiet as his chamber. From his bedroom on the highest floor of the monstrous stone tower his grandfather had constructed, Duncan could survey the seas and almost the entire kingdom. His kingdom.

His eyes shot to the shores that had once belonged to a conquered kingdom of Picts, finding them empty.

Duncan sucked in lungfuls of the cool night air and allowed the chilled breeze to coat his sweat-soaked skin.

The same dream had plagued him night after night for weeks. Striped Viking sails, armed Norsemen, and kidnapped villagers.

Even with the soldier's warnings, he'd arrived too late less than a month before when their enemy breached the shores just before dawn. Now phantom sails were all he could see, and cries of loss were the melody that rocked him to sleep at night.

Duncan scrubbed his hands across his bearded chin, then shoved both hands through his wild blonde hair before he braced himself on the window sill, still unsettled by the nightmare. He set his gaze upon the sea and worked his way across the kingdom, searching for anything out of place.

Large grass-covered mounds snaked the perimeter as an outer defense. Deep black gashes sliced the earth along the interior, trenches cut to delay an enemy's advance.

If the trenches were breached, a thick wooden fence with poles sharpened to a point surrounded the village, and a ten-foot stone wall encircled the tower, courtyard, and keep.

Beyond the tower, the village, and the farmlands grew an impenetrable labyrinth of trees, gorges, and waterfalls—The Dorcha. Even bathed in moonlight, that forest beyond his borders seemed to gobble up the light, leaving only an endless space of utter blackness.

Duncan didn't allow his gaze to linger on that shadowed expanse, instead skipping his eyes over the sleeping town and grounds below his walled tower. Pale stones gleamed in the light of a half-moon. If it weren't for the relentless dreams and preceding attack, he would have thought his father insane or paranoid for draining Tràigh's coffers of hacksilver to build such defenses in the years Duncan was away. Despite the hardship it placed on the villagers and his reluctant successor, King William had been quite ingenious in his design. Duncan wondered why his father never thought to wall off the sea. Maybe he did, but he never had the chance. There would be no opportunity to ask him, not anymore.

Duncan closed his eyes to the world, dragging in one deep breath before allowing his gaze to rest on the small cemetery just beyond the tower's stone boundary.

Six graves dotted the well-kept garden. Two mothers, a father, a brother, and though their bodies belonged to the sea—two infant sisters, taken before they'd even been named.

"It's a tragedy too great to bear. Best the people forget." It was the gruff explanation his father had given when Duncan asked why he'd not spoken the names they would have been given.

Mayhap they had forgotten, but the merciless sea wouldn't allow such grace for Duncan. Each brush of the tide whispered hints of the names they might have received, and each stone on the shore became a marker for their short lives.

Memories from that terrible night and what followed crashed against the walls he'd built in his heart as the waves crashed against the rocks below. In a dream, a monster with his father's eyes accused him of playing a part in Fiona's death. Accused him of hiding instead of acting.

Not like the former king. He acted swiftly. Duncan's eyes flicked to the place on the shore where a colony of roundhouses used to be, to the empty spaces in the village, and noticeably vacant spots amongst the fields.

The sea had washed away the charred remains of the round-houses, but long-standing superstitions kept the villagers from building over the destroyed Pictish homes.

What else could his father have done, though? A people who would murder the wife of their ally and sacrifice her children to pagan gods? There was no choice but to drive them out. Still, an unease crept along Duncan's skin, raising the hair on his arms and tying his insides in knots. *Ye are nothing like me.* His father's insult added to the chill seeping into his bones.

His entire family forever rested just beyond the home he now kept, forced upon him by cruel chance or divine providence—he could never decide which.

He leveled a finger at the largest of the shadowy markers in the cemetery bearing his father's name.

"I never wanted this from ye."

Three years, he'd dwelt in the tower and was still trying to understand how his path had ended there. He'd certainly not found the peace Father Malcolm prayed for or Fiona had promised.

Lanterns burned in the windows of the little church tucked quaintly between the tower and village, spilling rounded arcs of light across lush green grass. His eyes traveled up stone walls to an iron cross atop the thatched roof, moonlight illuminating its speared top. A deep longing pulled at his chest, threatening to crush the heart beating within.

It had also been three years since he'd passed through the doors of a church. Duncan sent his gaze heavenward, searching the starless sky for hints of the Creator.

"They say that because of Christ, I can talk directly to ye. Do ye ever speak in return?" Duncan waited in silence. He blew out a long breath, shaking his head against his own dashed hopes.

He still believed in God. As strong as he believed himself a living, breathing man. There was no doubt in his heart of the Almighty's existence and authority. Because of Fiona's instruction, he'd confessed as a young man his many errs and trusted God to forgive him.

Yet. His heart still felt as far from God as the stars were from his fingers. He looked again to the cross.

"Would I ken yer voice if ye did?"

A cloud passed over the moon, blanketing the land in a cover of pitch black. Duncan's eyes skittered across the kingdom once more before he shifted his shoulders, prepared to return to his bed when a dot of light bobbled up from the village. Duncan stiffened, his palms scratching against the rough stone as he leaned forward.

The orb wove rhythmically between homes toward the outer wall, bouncing as if carried in the hand of a runner. A momentary break in the clouds bathed the land in moonlight once more, and

Duncan's eyes focused on the light bearer. A hunched figure, nothing but a shadow, snuffed out the light and wrenched open the gates that kept the village secure.

To Duncan's horror, dark shapes rose up from blackened sands of the shore as spirits rising from their graves. They morphed from nothing to a small army that crept toward the village and the now vulnerable, slumbering villagers. Unprotected. Where were the sentries commissioned to guard that gate and walk the length of the boundaries at night? Who were these intruders?

Then as he looked out to sea, sharp lines of Viking sails rose as deadly spears behind the towering mountains that dotted their shores. He jerked his head to the warning towers. They remained dark. But the signal tower, the light directing ships safely through dangerous fjords—that beacon was lit!

Not again! The memory of wailing mothers, lifeless bodies of fathers, and empty beds of children sent flares of rage through his blood. He would not fail to act again.

"Eowin!" Duncan's roar filled the courtyard below. "Call the guard!"

Before Duncan could dress and reach his armory, Eowin had assembled what remained of the war band in the great hall and tossed armor toward his king. The captain knew better than to suggest his king remain behind.

Duncan counted soldiers as he strapped on his leather breastplate. Too few. Far too few. And some not yet fully recovered from the last attack.

Breathless, Duncan sheathed his sword and waved the men away from the stables. Horses would only announce their presence; this defense depended on stealth.

As the men huffed toward the village, his mind was tumultuous with questions. How could the ships have arrived undetected? How could they have known the signal fires would be lit to lead them through the dark and dangerous curves of the firth?

"Where are the watchers?" Duncan's growl was met with a stern glare from his captain, whose ghost-white face was drawn, showing as much fury as Duncan felt in his own chest.

"I dunna ken yet, m'lord. I've sent scouts."

How could this have happened? So many things had to go terribly wrong for another invasion to be possible. He couldn't tarry any longer, though. Until he knew for certain there was disloyalty, he would trust his men. Duncan allowed one long breath before he straightened and turned to his waiting soldiers.

"Be bold. The Norsemen have returned. Dunna let even one of our people be taken this night!"

7

CYRENE

821 AD - The Same Night

Clicks and whispered whistles summoned warriors crouched in the wood. Lithe figures rolled across the plain like a purposeful fog. The Viking ships spotted by Cyrene's scouts from the cliffs meant slavery. Torture. Death.

"There, m'lady." Astrid's breath met the cold air and snaked a wisp of smoke toward the darkened sky.

From their place high in the branches of a redwood, Cyrene narrowed her eyes at the target of Astrid's gaze. Over the high walls of the city, she spotted a squirming bundle hefted over the broad shoulders of a hulking Norseman.

Astrid released a hiss. Cyrene clutched the warrior's arm, stilling her with a stern glare. Astrid had never revealed the reason she'd secretly boarded the Norse ship that brought her to their shores, but Cyrene had seen the hand-shaped bruises purpling her too-thin body and drew her own conclusions. There was no love lost between the leader of Cyrene's warriors and Astrid's former countrymen.

Another bulky figure stalked between homes. There could be dozens more slithering through the village like venomous snakes, striking their prey before devouring innocent lives.

"We must go." Cyrene lowered herself from branch to branch, her feet near silent as she landed.

Her resolve was settled until she reached the edge of the wood, where roots met grass.

She'd not entered the open plain that stretched between The Dorcha and the village since she was sixteen. A tightness grasped her chest, forcing her breaths to shallow. The people of that village needed their help, but Cyrene hesitated.

She'd not forgotten. Her memories from well before that last trip into the meadow were as fresh as if they'd just been formed the day before. She could still smell the smoke as soldiers from the tower tore through Pictish homes and burned them to the ground. She could still see the indifference on the villagers' faces as they watched and did nothing. Even though the plague had claimed most of the ones old enough to have been present, Cyrene still felt a measure of wariness.

"Have ye given any more thought to Liam's proposal?"

Cyrene jerked her head toward Astrid, whose wide grin made her teeth glow in the moonlight.

"I hardly think this is the time," she grumbled, taking the first step into waist-high grass.

Her stomach rolled at the thought of lanky Liam. For some reason, he still felt he was a worthy candidate to rule at her side, though she'd bested him more than once in the training ring and made every effort to directly ignore his advances.

"'Tis the only time ye canna start shouting." Astrid nudged Cyrene as she loaded her bow with an ash arrow and crept on bent knees through the meadow. "Yer three and twenty already. Sooner or later, ye must choose a mate."

"Later then." Cyrene drew from her own quiver, sliding an arrow through her fingers, coating the slick feathers with oils from her skin. *Mate.* The word twisted her stomach in knots. They might live in the wildness of the forest, but they weren't animals. "And I never shout."

Astrid's distraction had brought her thoughts back into focus, and before panic could find her again, she pressed her back against the rough bark of the thin poles that formed the fence around the village. The night was yet quiet, but as the sun broke the horizon, the morning would be filled with the cries of loss and grief.

It wasn't only the colors and crest of the tower that had changed in the three winters since the old king died. So much of their lives had become intertwined with the people inside those walls. Her scouts traded their meat and berries for grain and vegetables they could not grow in the woodlands. Their blades were forged by the village blacksmiths, and the rich cobalt of her arrows, made so by dyes from the fabric makers.

Though her people had no direct contact with the villagers save for the few scouts who did the trading, they were essential to their survival. She felt obligated to protect them. It was tyranny that drove her people into the woods, and tyranny she would fight against until her last breath. Besides, if the new king of this land wouldn't defend them, to whom could they look?

She only hoped he did not capture her own people in the process and turn out to be even more ruthless than his predecessor.

"To the gate." Cyrene's subtle nod toward a hidden opening in the wall drew a sneering grin from her captain, who was ready for a fight.

Thanks to their tunnel, half her warriors were already inside, stealing through the night to strategic vantage points.

Since the first raid, her archers in the wood had been watching. Waiting. Cyrene scowled at the thought of that looming tower on the other side of the village. Though she'd been told the soldiers attempted to drive back the savage men from the North, they'd only come once the Vikings made for the inner walls. The king's army clearly didn't care for the lowly villagers, only peasants to them—easily replaced.

"Why are there no guards protecting these people?" Cyrene didn't intend her question to be answered, but Astrid leaned in close, her breath coming in short bursts.

"There were." When Cyrene shot her a demanding glare, Astrid dragged her finger across her throat, indicating the cause for the absence of patrolling soldiers.

"Seems this king has more problems than he realizes." Cyrene drew in a deep breath, schooling her ire and reminding herself that the Vikings were the only enemy she needed to focus on that night.

She looked upon her warriors, both pride and protectiveness swelling in her chest. Even for Liam, whose arrogant, lopsided grin made her want to bare her teeth. She'd make many sacrifices as queen, but marriage was one she would put off for as long as possible.

Revna appeared behind her, materializing out of the darkness like a ghost. It was Revna who had come, breathless, hours before dawn, with news of sails on the horizon.

"What word, Revna?"

"One ship, m'lady. Some villagers already taken on board." Revna's blue eyes blazed, consumed by fury as she delivered the news.

Cyrene placed her hand on Revna's shoulder, lowering her head until Revna held her gaze. "We will get them back."

"Aye." The assurance in Revna's answer unleashed a squirming dread in Cyrene's stomach. Revna clenched her fists at her side. "I'll get them all back."

Cyrene lifted her hand cautiously, as if Revna were a wolf with hackles raised, poised to bite. Her scout stalked back into the night, flipping a blade between her fingers. Cyrene's childhood hope for the orphaned lass to find her strength had come to pass, but not in the way she'd imagined. Revna was still young, though, and Cyrene formed a new hope. Someday, she prayed, Revna would find peace.

Tonight, though . . . tonight, Revna's rage might very well save lives.

The queen turned back to face her waiting warriors.

"May yer aim be true." The hissed challenge of their queen fortified their will, proven by the heightened stance of each maiden and man.

As Cyrene passed, she touched the tip of her curved bow to meet the same of each of her warriors. To each, she spoke a prayer before slipping through the blackened entry of a city under silent siege.

"May *An T-aon* be yer eyes when ye canna see. May he let your arrow fly straight and true. May he return yer heart to mine at battle's end."

8

DUNCAN

821 AD - That Same Night

Duncan melted into the shadows of the rough daubed wall of a village home, searching the dark for Eowin's signal as one hand found the tightest grip on his spear and the other confirmed the position of daggers strapped to his belt. The faint thud of a sword rapping against a wooden shield made him wince and shoot a warning glare at the soldier to his right.

Someone lit the flame that guided an enemy ship to their shores. Duncan prayed the culprit wasn't hidden amongst his warband, waiting to plunge a blade into his back.

There was no time to wait or investigate. The invaders would be gone by morning, taking all the young village women and children with them. A rich bounty they would then sell for an incalculable profit.

Fury washed over him, a rage of righteousness drowning any

semblance of fear. They'd not succeed in capturing even one of his people. Not this night!

Tossing his spear from hand to hand, he sucked a silent breath through clenched teeth and begged a blessing from the heavens.

Lord, be near. Send yer angels to watch over us and guide our steps to save yer people.

His prayer was a thought that seemed to dissolve into the blanket of clouds, never to reach the ears for whom it was intended. Father Malcolm had reminded him that though he may wander far from God, God would never wander far from him. He clung to that promise as tightly as his weapon.

Though flanked by soldiers, Duncan's loneliness consumed him, and he physically shook his head, hoping to dislodge its hold. The war between king and man raged within him, but he could only fight one battle at a time. This was not the moment to lose heart, to have courage fail.

Dunna let it happen again. The ghostly voice of Fiona escaped from some hidden place in his memory. No. He would die before he allowed any more of his people to be taken, and he beat back the weakened man within, drawing forth the strength of the crown.

A flash of movement from above diverted Duncan's attention. But as he squinted to focus in the dark, he saw nothing.

"Watch the rooftops," Duncan whispered to the men who waited shoulder to shoulder beside him. "There might be danger from above."

Only soft grunts indicated their understanding, and Duncan tightened his grip on his shield as Eowin signaled with a wave.

Duncan and his men flowed through the streets, a river of vengeance, clasping hands over the mouths of Norsemen, driving spears deep and wielding swords with deadly accuracy in a silent flood of defense.

The metallic bite of blood and death filled Duncan's nose, quickening his heart as he searched for his next target. From the shadows, the scrape of a blade rang much too close in his ears, and Duncan was forced to the ground by a booted foot to the back.

His shield skidded across the dirt, inches too far from his fingers as he flipped to his back only in time to see the glint of metal slicing through the air, aimed at his neck.

He had less than a second to work a blade free from his belt when his attacker was driven suddenly back, dropping to the ground by the force of an arrow to his chest.

The tip of Duncan's spear ended any remaining fight before he whirled around, searching the thick woven thatching of the roof behind him for his savior. None was there. He dared not tarry; the Norseman was surely not alone.

After lugging the fallen Viking into the shadows, he became as the night, listening for breath, for the muffled cry of a villager in need of saving, for the scrape of footsteps.

Again, Duncan's eyes were drawn to the sky as overhead flew the straight, steady shaft of another arrow. Between passing clouds, a second of moonlight caught the flash of blue feathers, its archer as invisible as the wind. Mayhap his prayer had reached heaven after all. Mayhap there were angels among them that night.

The leather-wrapped handle of his shield creaked under his grip, and he bounced his spear in his palm to regain the hold. With each buzz of an arrow cutting through the black night, doubt dissolved, assured victory in its place. Shoulders lifted in confidence, he tore free from the shadows. Cutting through the air with power and purpose, his spear found its target. Neither hesitation nor fear slowed Duncan's pursuit, as he knew azure arrows would keep him safe until the last Norseman fled from the village.

9

DUNCAN

821 AD - The Next Morning

"'Tis true then." Duncan's fingers dove furiously through his wet hair, curls darkened from the water he'd used to scrub away the last remaining clumps of dirt and blood from the previous night's battle.

They'd fought until dawn was summoned by the orange flames of a burning ship. Duncan's army dragged weary yet victorious to the keep. Though not all had returned, including the sentries they'd found murdered at their posts. Not enough. Not nearly enough.

Not one Viking surrendered and survived to reveal how they'd come to know of this kingdom, or how they'd known the signal fires of Tràigh's watch towers would be lit.

"Aye. We have a traitor in our midst." Eowin gripped the hilt of the dagger he'd presented to the king so tightly that his knuckles turned white.

A dagger found buried in the chest of their final watchman, who would have stopped those signal fires from being lit had he lived. A dagger that bore the crest of Duncan's kingdom.

One of their own had driven that blade through the watchman's heart. Not only his, but the bodies of the other sentries found at their posts, faces frozen in a grim cry only heard by the night.

All measures of protection had failed, his men slain. Fathers would not return to waiting children, nor husbands to worried wives.

Duncan's fist collided with the wooden surface of his table, the trencher and cup from a barely touched meal nearly toppling over the edge.

"Could this have been the work of one man?" The swirling patterns around knots in the wood teased him. Leading his eyes on a hunt for answers that didn't exist. "Or are we looking at a revolt?"

Eowin's fingers combed through his shoulder-length dark hair. He tied it back at his neck using a strip of softened leather. "Could be one, sire. If he were quick . . . or trusted."

This had happened before. In this very tower. A traitor, a murder, a kingdom betrayed. The dread of his father's accusations, even if only in a dream, resurfaced. He searched his memory, cataloging every decision to see if he was somehow responsible for this attack. He'd not been wise enough to intercept the traitor that night. He would not let it happen again.

Duncan's eyes fell to the dagger Eowin placed back on the table. The tip of that small blade pointed him in a direction he didn't want to travel. And the road was paved with nothing but suspicion and distrust. Questioned loyalty amongst his guard, every soldier in his ranks, and every member of his household.

When his father faced such a dilemma, nearly every tower guard and household servant met the sharp end of his vengeful blade.

"What will ye do?" Eowin, braced by clenched fists on the wooden table, eyed Duncan, certainly wondering if the son would follow in the footsteps of the father. He had been there too. He knew.

Duncan released a sigh, his conflicted emotions quelling any clear thoughts that tried to form. "We must act, but keep this between us fer now."

Eowin nodded, folding a crimson cloth over the dagger to conceal it. The metallic bite of disgust seeped into Duncan's mouth, and he resisted the urge to spit. How could one betray his countrymen? How could one sell his own people, innocent women and children at that, to a merciless, godless enemy? The reward must be great or the hate deep.

Brodric hinted that greed was the reason behind the attack on Fiona. That the Picts had wanted to keep control of the firth—but Duncan assumed a long-held hate had also played a part, finally bubbling over until it was too hot to contain. In the end, his father had cleared the kingdom of the scourge of godless Picts. At least, that was what the kingdom was led to believe. Duncan couldn't help but rake his gaze over the tops of the black-green treetops in the distance.

Could some have escaped? Had they returned, seeking revenge for the harsh punishment his father dealt? Mayhap it wasn't harsh enough.

"Sire." Eowin's gravelly tenor broke through Duncan's crimson veil of rage. "We shall find the traitor."

"Aye, we shall, Eowin." Duncan examined his man's visage. His expression revealed nothing but determination, and Duncan prayed for discernment. *Please, dunna let it be Eowin. Not my friend.* "In the meantime, we must fortify the kingdom. Next time they come, they will come in force."

"Agreed, sire. If word of our trouble reaches yer cousin—"

"I ken." Duncan's raised hand silenced Eowin. "If William should think the crown weak, he'll waste no time in coming fer it. But be it my cousin or the Norsemen, someone is after Tràigh."

A soft knock on the great doors of his meeting room echoed off the stone walls. With Duncan's permission, a weary scout trudged through the hall.

"What word, Ronan?" Eowin offered the lad a mug of ale, which he greedily drank in one gulp.

"An army assembles, m'lord."

Eowin sent a glance to Duncan, warning him to remain calm before he demanded the details of Ronan's report.

"I couldna see a crest of flags of any kingdom I recognized. They must be keeping them hidden. But there were at least a hundred men gathered, and more arriving."

"How close to Tràigh is this army?"

"At least four days' ride, sire."

A weight nearly more than he could bear pressed on Duncan's chest. Attacks from the north, a mystery army gathered in the south, and who knew what kind of evil lurked in the depths of The Dorcha. He had no shortages of enemies.

When Duncan fell silent, Eowin released young Ronan with a hand on his shoulder.

"In the days it took Ronan to return with this news, how much larger did this army grow?" Duncan finally spoke. "We dunna have but seventy men ourselves now, after the attacks."

"Shall we call for aid from Rìoghachd?" Eowin tilted his long face, catching Duncan's eye and returning his mind from a wayward journey of possibilities.

Duncan splayed his fingers wide across the map unrolled before him. Rìoghachd was their closest neighbor, only a range of hills between their lands. King Theobold was as wealthy in the currency of soldiers as he was silver. Long had they kept peace by weak trade agreements.

"I dunna put much faith in our alliance. 'Tis frail at best. We havna much to offer but access to the sea."

Eowin folded thick arms across his broad chest and examined the map Duncan still hovered over.

"Theobold would just as likely help defeat the Norsemen, only to turn around and attempt to conquer Tràigh himself." Duncan squeezed his eyes closed, a thrumming pain brewing inside his skull.

His advisors would have been better suited to make these suggestions. It was their purpose to know of the business of neighboring kingdoms. But with an unknown traitor in their midst, there was too much at risk. Once again, it was left to him.

"Here." Duncan pressed a calloused finger to the yellowed paper. "Nàbaidh. 'Tis where we should seek aid. The mountains between us are too broad for King Laorn to attempt an invasion, and they are in need of our access to the sea. We will have sway."

"I shall send riders."

"Nay." Duncan's quick reply caused Eowin to tip his chin in curiosity. "I shall ride myself."

"But, sire. If that waiting army is yer kinsman, and yer cousin should hear of an empty throne . . ."

Duncan turned his back to Eowin. The captain was right. Even if the one who'd slain their watchman wasn't one of his own, there was still a spy in their midst, mayhap hiding in his very household.

"Word could reach Laird William in days." Eowin moved to better view the map, large fingers testing different routes to Nàbaidh. "I'd say we have four days . . . at the most."

Duncan chewed his bottom lip as he scanned the map over Eowin's shoulder. There was only one route to take them there and back that quickly.

As if reading his mind, Eowin drew close, voice lowered as if sharing a secret. "'Twill take too long, unless . . ." Eowin moved to drag his wide eyes over Duncan's expression. "Unless we pass through The Dorcha."

"Aye."

"There's got to be another way. We canna go there. They say the woods are guarded by a ghost queen. She'd sooner drive a dagger through yer heart than look at ye."

"Dunna ye remember our trips to the woods? Are ye still afraid of a few shadows and fairies, Eowin?" Duncan's brows clicked up in sync with the side of his mouth. "Besides, if there be a queen in that wood, I should quite like to meet her. Mayhap she's just the bride I need."

Eowin's head jerked up, ruddy cheeks growing redder as he took in the taunting smirk of his king. Wouldn't he like to see the looks on his advisors' faces with that news. They'd been pressuring him to wed. A fairy queen would certainly seal their sour mouths for good.

"I suppose yer right." Eowin's smile was stiff, clearly unconvinced by Duncan's teasing. "Still, ye canna go, sire. We canna be certain that no men from the North were left behind. They could be hiding there and spring upon ye."

Duncan folded his arms across his broad chest, muscles still sore and bruised from the fight. Though he didn't know whom to trust, Eowin was right again. His own gut told him not to leave his throne unprotected. Every nerve warned that the second he did, it would be overtaken.

Duncan's thoughts drew up an image of a single light bobbing along the village streets the night before. Someone had been on the inside. Someone opened the gates to allow the intruders in. Was it the same someone who'd slain their watchman and lit the signal fires?

His heart clenched within his chest. The woods could very well be full of more than just myths and legends. The stories had never frightened him, but when he'd explored the woods in secret as a child, he'd always felt an unnerving presence. Still, he'd rather face a legion of goblins and trolls than one ship of ruthless Vikings. The king finally raised his blue eyes, freezing Eowin in place.

"Will ye go in my stead, Eowin?" Duncan's resolve wavered despite his attempts at confidence. "Can I trust ye?"

A flash of pain darkened Eowin's eyes, and muscles rolled along his strong jaw as he straightened and bowed before his king.

"Ye are my oldest friend, and I have pledged my life, sire. I shall go wherever ye ask." As Eowin raised his chest, Duncan registered a reddening in his complexion, hinting of uncertainty. "Though . . . I dunna ken the way."

Duncan dropped a hand on Eowin's shoulder, which reached a few inches higher than his own.

"Thank ye." Duncan's voice deepened with gratitude. "I shall take ye through the woods. Then I shall meet ye four days hence to lead ye home."

"Aye."

"I canna send ye alone though."

Eowin eased closer as Duncan dipped a quill in a pot of ink and scratched a list of names on a parchment.

"Wi' these alone shall ye travel. None others are to ken of our journey, not even their wives. I shall send ye wi' what's left of the silver. It's enough that King Laorn will lend ye his ear. But we must ride this night, under cover of dark."

"Aye." Eowin accepted the parchment and, following a quick bow, made haste for the door.

Duncan sank like a rock into the hard seat of his chair. A shape hiding in the shadows caught his eye. It was a trunk full of his father's belongings that he'd had moved from the former king's chambers. He'd intended to sort through the contents weeks ago. Before the first Viking ship arrived, before chaos shattered his orderly life.

Duncan pressed his fingers against his drawn brow, failing to smooth the tightness that encouraged the terrible ache in his head. He finally drew his hands to his lips, fingertips pushed together as he poured an aching heart into a broken prayer.

He beseeched God on behalf of his people. He prayed that the angels from the night before would remain in his absence, and hoped, mayhap, there were enough to accompany his men on their journey. He begged that God's favor would continue for just a few more days until they returned with promise of aid from Nàbaidh. It would cost him, but if it meant a trusted ally in this coming war, it was worth it.

Drawing in a deep breath, Duncan covered the dagger once more.

When he shoved through the meeting room doors, he nearly plowed over a maid carrying a tray of food.

"Are ye hurt?" Duncan stepped away as the lass gathered her spilled tray.

He didn't immediately recognize her from his staff and paused at her unusually tanned skin. For half a breath, he was a lad, meeting his olive-skinned stepmother in almost that exact same spot.

"Nay." Mayhap it was the looming threat of that unknown traitor toying with his mind or the fact that he'd crashed into her, but he thought he saw a flash of rage in her dark eyes before she curtseyed and lowered her head, eyes to the floor.

He opened his mouth to ask her name when she curtseyed a second time and took slow, retreating steps.

"Pardon, Majesty." Her voice was quiet and accent strange. "I am new and dunna ken my way yet."

"Hilda brought ye in?"

"Aye."

That would make sense. The plump head of his kitchen was as kind as she was skilled at cooking, earning Duncan twice as many servants as were needed for his small household. No orphan or widow would go without work or food as long as Hilda had a say.

"I shall bring ye a fresh tray." She bowed again and hurried away after he kindly bid her to return with his advisors instead of food.

He doubted his ability to secure a confession, if the traitor was one of his own council, but he hoped for enough vision to sense a guilt-ridden reaction when he revealed the discovered blade.

IO

CYRENE

821 AD - Later That Night

From her perch in the wide-reaching branches of an alder tree, Cyrene narrowed her bright green eyes at the small troop moving slowly through the wood.

One, two, three . . . she counted six in all. Their shapes were barely visible under the light of the dimmed torch they carried. They clearly meant to travel unnoticed.

"They've come from the tower." Astrid's whisper came from behind Cyrene, where she hovered. "Though they dunna bear the new king's crest."

The new king. She knew little of him, but the image he'd chosen for his crest never settled well with her. The former monarch was represented by the serpent across a blood-red flag—fitting, she thought, for such a vile human. But the new king . . . he chose blue, and the animal of his reign was a great beast reared on hind legs, its mane coiffed and proud. A lion.

It seemed to hint at secrets that should not be known. It seemed too close to the worn engraving on the ring that now encircled her thumb instead of a strap around her neck. A ring she'd almost grown into.

Heat engulfed Cyrene's ears as violent thoughts forced themselves into her mind. Her grip on the branch tightened, and legs ached to leap, desiring to glide like a silent assassin to the ground.

Her huntress eyes narrowed, fire from her heart lighting her vision as she considered the small band of men. Her prey. Heads covered in hoods and swords wrapped tightly in cloth so as not to make a sound, they walked, leading horses under blindfolds through tightly spaced trees. With each brush of leaves and snap of twigs, the horses' ears piqued to attention, but the coverings over their eyes and the assuring hands of their masters kept them calm.

After the attack on the village the night before, Cyrene's instinct was to rid her wood of any who breached the treeline uninvited, especially tower-dwelling scum. Though his men were unaware of their presence, her warriors had worked in tandem with his to send the Vikings fleeing. And that was the way she intended to keep it.

Although, despite their victory, she knew it wouldn't be long before the enemy returned.

She tapped a rhythm on the deep green cloth of her cloak, weighing choices. There were but two elders left to counsel her, but this was a decision that needed to be made quickly. Cyrene recognized the brush of arrow against quiver as Astrid loaded her bow, as if Astrid had read her mind.

The men walked with purpose, as if on a well-trodden path. But there were no trails through these woods. A black stallion in the lead shook his head, releasing a nervous snort against unfamiliar surroundings. His master turned, a dark hood falling to his shoulders. Cyrene pushed forward, bracing herself on the strong branches to see his face. He was the one leading them, the one who seemed to know the way through *her* wood.

A shifted torch bathed his face in a halo of light. Her eyes grew wide, silently searching. His features, the curve of his jaw and bow shape of his lips . . . he looked familiar. Yet she could not place the memory. The man lifted a gentle hand and spoke words to the animal that she couldn't hear. Once the horse was soothed, the man raised his hood and continued on his way.

"Shall we call the warriors, my queen?" The string of Astrid's bow creaked as she drew it back, arrow at the ready. "They might be spies returning to their own land. Maybe they're planning an attack on the tower."

Cyrene put aside her vengeful wrath and ran through the possibilities, exacting an outcome for each move.

"Nay," Cyrene breathed finally, her ire settling into disdain. "I care not for the business of the tower king. Their problems are their own. But follow close. If they veer from this course, sound the alarm."

Astrid's response was a graceful leap from her perch and a soundless landing below. She slipped off through the trees as Cyrene kept her gaze centered on the soft yellow glow of the men's torch.

A shrill call from the east drew her attention, and she snapped her eyes back to the travelers. Only the golden-haired leader lifted his head, and Cyrene felt the corner of her lips lift in interest.

To most, it would sound like the simple *chirr-up chirr-up* of a song thrush, but to those who inhaled the same breath as the forest, it was a warning—especially in the black of night when the birds were silent.

The men hadn't altered their course, so it couldn't have come from Astrid. Something else was wrong.

Cyrene lowered herself to the forest floor, darting soundlessly over soft, rich soil until she reached her meeting hut.

"What is it?" Cyrene's chest instantly grew tight at the sight of Revna. Her appearance could only mean one thing: danger.

Revna stood in the center of the hut, staff in both hands, feet planted as if ready for battle, tanned skin nearly buzzing with anticipation.

"A man. From the sea." Revna's deep blue eyes were wild and wide, her breaths short. "Captured."

Cyrene straightened to her full height, nostrils flared with venomous outrage. The slick, smooth wood of her bow groaned under her grip, and she sensed the same reaction from her gathered warriors. Twice in a night, her sanctuary was invaded; it was almost enough for rage to give way to fear. Almost.

"Take me to him." Her words were clipped, spoken through clenched teeth.

Revna nodded, her own lips pursed and jaw tight. The thick fabric of the hut opening snapped against the silent night as Revna threw it back to lead the way.

Cyrene felt her blood nearly boiling as she followed the scout, Revna's normally quick pace even quicker, her dark cloak whipping against her legs as she moved.

As she followed Revna's nearly invisible form, Cyrene fingered the silver band on her left hand. The memory of Beli uncurling his small fingers to show it to her carved a fresh stinging wound across Cyrene's heart. She'd searched for him, for years she searched. Hoping against hope he'd survived somehow and escaped, though she knew it was a fool's hope.

She did find the ring, though. In the spot where Beli had made his brave stand. It waited there for her, like a marker to commemorate such a courageous battle.

She couldn't decide who she hated more: the invaders from the North, or the neighboring enemy that lived just beyond the trees.

At least tower-dwellers came head on, in the light of day. They didn't slither around in the night like snakes. In that, she could find a semblance of tolerance for the men of the flat land. But not these new intruders, men without honor. Cowards.

Cyrene's ire grew as Revna led them to the edge of the village and beyond. Deep into the dark woods, nearly to the cliffs overlooking the sea, two maidens stood arm to arm, staves at the ready in front of a large redwood. Two torches plunged into the soft earth burned at either side of them, creating an orange circle of light.

"Your queen has come," Revna announced, signaling to the maidens to part.

Slumped against the trunk of the redwood and bound with ropes, a broad figure sat bloodied and motionless.

"Does he live?" Cyrene lowered only her gaze, chin kept high.

Revna kicked the man's leather-shoed foot. A weak groan escaped his lips as his head rolled to the side. Revna sat on her heels and took the man's filthy chin between her fingers, lifting his face before she stepped back and wiped her hands on the fabric of her cloak. "Not fer long, my queen."

"Send scouts to find Astrid." Cyrene didn't take her eyes off the captive. Revna, sensing the queen's hesitation, paused as Cyrene added, "And fetch Gertrud."

"My queen?" Revna's response sent a flame across Cyrene's cheeks, and Revna lowered her head in remorse.

"Gertrud, the healer." Cyrene raised a brow at her scout. "If he doesna live, he canna speak."

Revna bowed and sprinted into the black, Cyrene's hard tone clearly enough of a warning for her not to dare question a command again. Hands clasped behind her back, Cyrene kept her eyes on the prisoner as she directed the other maidens to search for any more men daring to hide in their wood.

The two who'd been standing guard remained, but backed away at Cyrene's nod, dissolving into darkness. She lowered herself to her knees, tilting her head until the man's barely opened eyes found her face.

She examined what little she could of his condition. His torn tunic bore a large red stain on the chest. His face was covered in deep gashes, one eye swollen completely shut, and the other that gazed at her, not much better. What had been the same near-white hair as his countrymen was now blackened by dirt and caked with dried blood.

His breaths came in pained, shallow bursts, and Cyrene knew his injuries were severe.

"Do ye wish to die this night?" Cyrene's voice was steady, certain, and regal.

The man's head lolled side to side, a groan his only reply. He couldn't understand her language. Cyrene scanned the darkness beyond the glow of the torches. If Astrid didn't arrive soon, they'd know nothing.

Almost as if summoned by her thoughts, Cyrene spotted the glow of Astrid's snow-white hair in the blackness.

"Can ye speak fer me?"

Astrid nodded, a mixture of curiosity and suspicion narrowing her gaze as she took in the man with features much the same as hers.

"I shall bring my healer, and if ye desire to live, then ye shall tell me of the plans of yer people." Cyrene spoke, and Astrid translated the words into the smooth guttural language she knew from a life before.

"N-n-n-" He tried to protest, but Cyrene only stood, silencing him with a hard stare.

"Then I pray ye ken *An T-aon*, for ye shall meet him before the dawn." She turned to leave while Astrid was still speaking.

"Wait." Astrid's whisper latched onto Cyrene's heels, stopping her retreat.

His strangled cry was nearly a gasp, but enough to bring Cyrene back. He coughed, wincing at the pain it caused, and spoke to Astrid.

"He says he will do as ye say." Astrid pushed herself to stand. "He did not die in battle. According to his beliefs, he will not go to Valhalla if he dies now."

Cyrene studied Astrid, wondering if she'd shared those same beliefs before she landed on their shores. Astrid's stone expression revealed nothing.

A tilt of Cyrene's head seemed to calm the man's ragged breathing, and she stood watching over him, her stance warning. He was weakened beyond threat of violence, but still Cyrene found her pulse speeding at each twitch of his hands and sputtering gasp.

She searched her heart for the compassion she felt burdened to show, but found only shame at its absence. Just before the silent forest released the shushing sounds of approaching maidens, the man's head fell forward, unconscious.

"My queen," Revna said, eyes still lowered in respect. "Word from the scouts."

"What word, Revna?"

"The travelers passed through. All but one."

"One remained?" A chill pricked at Cyrene's spine as she watched Gertrud direct several of the warriors to cut loose and lift the injured man upon a skin stretched between two sturdy cut saplings. Mayhap she was too quick to dismiss their presence.

"Nay, m'lady. They said he followed the same path back toward the tower."

"He led them through." Cyrene's observation was meant only for herself, but Revna exchanged a dark glance with Astrid before offering a slight bow and hurrying to assist Gertrud.

Ancient stories had always been warning enough to keep villagers and soldiers from breaching their borders. This was her land, her kingdom. Who was this man who seemed to know it so well?

"What shall we do wi' him?" Astrid jogged back to where Cyrene stood staring into the darkness. When Cyrene's expression didn't register her question, Astrid spoke softly. "The captive? Where shall we take him?"

Cyrene's insides churned with indecision. Perhaps in Gertrud's hut, the man might live, but then what? He was the enemy. She couldn't allow him to know where her people lived.

"Not wi'in our borders." Cyrene directed her maidens to fetch whatever Gertrud needed from her hut and to construct a shelter there in the outlying wood.

Cyrene remained, pacing outside the makeshift hospital. Waiting and watching, every sound pricking at her ears and causing her fingers to itch for the string of her bow. Astrid offered frequent updates but no news of his purpose nor the plans of his people. The man lived through the night and the length of one morning, never conscious long enough to be questioned.

Despite Gertrud's best efforts, the Viking's injuries were too severe. As evening approached, he drew in a ragged breath and exhaled a gargled whisper into Gertrud's ear as he gripped her tender hand.

Gertrud's golden hair fell, covering her face as she lowered her head, a shudder drawing her shoulders inward.

"My queen." Gertrud dabbed at her eyes with the back of her hand after several moments of silence. "I am sorry."

"Nay." Cyrene lightly touched the healer's shoulder. "'Tis not yer doing. I wish he had yet lived, and we ken of the plans of his countrymen, but ye arna at fault."

Gertrud nodded, running a gentle hand over the man's face, closing his staring blue eyes for the final time. His expression, which had been twisted in pain, was now soft, given peace in his last moments by Gertrud's compassion. The tenderness with which Gertrud placed the man's hands over his chest set a sting of conviction through Cyrene's own heart. Though he be her enemy, Gertrud was as kind in her care of him as of her own people.

"What did he say?" Cyrene asked.

Gertrud flashed her blue eyes toward her queen, then to Astrid.

"He whispered a thank ye, m'lady." Astrid bowed, her tone solemn as Gertrud's shaking fingers danced about her lips.

A tightness swept through Cyrene's throat, making words difficult to form. Gertrud had eased his pain when Cyrene had battled dark thoughts of allowing him to suffer.

"As deserved, Healer. Ye are the most gentle of us all."

Cyrene may have been queen, but she knew well there was much to learn from those in her care.

Gertrud stood and smoothed her skirts, head lowered and eyes ringed with red. As she gathered wet cloths and pots of herbs, she stopped, turning quickly to face Cyrene.

"In the night, we thought him to be mad from the fever, but . . ."

"Go on," Cyrene urged, her hand light on Gertrud's elbow as she led her to a stool in the corner of the shelter.

"Astrid said he spoke of ships wi' dark sails. A ghost fleet on black waters." Gertrud flicked her eyes toward Astrid, who nodded in confirmation.

"Which waters?" Cyrene searched Astrid's face for clarification.

"I ken not," Astrid said. "He dinna make sense. He said something about a stolen crown and keeping the kingdom. He spoke of a new moon and a storm that raged from both the north and the south."

Cyrene moved to the lifeless man, wishing against nature that he would come back to life and explain his secret riddles.

Both Cyrene and Gertrud spun as the shelter opening was torn back, golden evening light pouring around a silhouetted shape.

"M'lady." Revna's stone greeting turned Cyrene's skin to ice. "There's trouble in the wood."

II

DUNCAN

821 AD – The Same Night

uncan's thighs screamed as they clenched tightly to the leather saddle. The thunder of hooves across the meadow pounded ever closer, and he risked a glance backward in time to see another of his men fall under the swords of Norsemen who'd seemed to come from everywhere and nowhere.

Duncan pulled the reins to the side, silently pleading with the attackers to follow him away from his men.

Sire, Norsemen in the village! The warning had come through the panicked cry of the same young maid he'd sent to summon his council. She tucked thick strands of black hair back under her veil as she trembled in the open doorway of his throne room. Only two of his advisors, Toran and Ligulf, had been present, about to reveal some news they believed could lead to the traitor. When they questioned the girl, she was unable to name the guard who'd summoned her, unable to give any answers to his barked questions as he, once again, raced to the already gathered troops.

Now surrounded by Vikings, Duncan chastised himself for such foolish impulsivity between each dodge of a swinging sword. With Eowin and his most trusted men still away on their aid mission, he led the warband himself.

Straight into an expertly laid trap. A small fleet of Norsemen drew him and his front men further from the tower, only for them to be cut off from the following troops by another enemy group that laid in wait outside the walls.

He was surrounded. His larger army battling the throng that had divided them, more hidden Norsemen materialized to form an enclosing circle. They didn't seem interested in sacking the tower, only chasing down his small warband. Where were they coming from? There were no ships on the shore.

The slice of blades and screams of his men turned Duncan's will to ice. Somehow, they had to have known he would lead the army. That he was alone. This was planned—a plot to kill the king.

His stallion, Taranau, reared and spun, his sword cutting through the chill of the late evening air as he defended against neverending attackers. *Retreat. Retreat. Retreat!* The order was pulsing from his brain, but there was no opening in the line of Norsemen, no way out.

Woods at their backs, the enemy line thinned enough that what was left of his men could break through.

"To the trees!" Duncan drove his men forward, knowing their only hope was to get lost in the thickness of the forest and pray the coming darkness would hide them as they wound their way back around to the troops left defending the tower. He knew the way; he could still salvage this.

Duncan leaned in, his breaths matching rhythm with the pounding of his horse's hooves. He guided the animal, weaving and dodging, urging him on ever faster, away from the men who sought to end him. The sun had not yet set, but a waning moon was painted in the purpling sky, whitening their already pale skin and casting ghostly shadows that blackened their eyes. It was as if they were an army of dead, raised from the grave. Even their battle cries were swept up by the howling wind and turned to otherworldly moans. Duncan swore he heard some shout in his native tongue, but pressed back the fear that conjured that imagining.

One gained on him, the breath of his pursuer's steed hot on his calves. He glanced behind, catching a glimpse of the man at his heels. Beneath a Norse helmet, he spied fiery red tendrils of a Scottish mane, and the blade he bore . . . 'twas not a Norseman's weapon.

It canna be. Scots have joined wi' Vikings against their own?

There was no time to look again. He tightened his grip on the leather reins. He could not fall; he could not leave his people unprotected against this invasion. If accepted, his bargain with King Laorn of Nàbaidh would not stand unless he lived. But he would not sacrifice his men for his own life either.

Please, Lord. Hear me! Grant us favor!

Duncan jerked the reins to the right just as a sword made a wide arc through the space where he'd been. He dug his heels into the horse's side, urging him on, straight into the darkening woods.

"Steady now, Taranau." Each breath sent daggers down his throat.

Duncan became one with Taranau, hugging the dark steed's neck as they wove through the dense wood. The trees grew closer together, and Duncan was in just as much danger of getting his head knocked off by a low-hanging branch or leg broken by the trunk of a silver birch as being run through by the sword of his enemy.

Duncan guided Taranau stealthily through the maze, deeper into the wood, slowing only when the hoofbeats behind him grew quiet. Mayhap he had outrun them. Mayhap they all had. He pulled up on the reins, Taranau obeying the silent command and trotting to a walk. With what little daylight remained, Duncan scanned his surroundings, his sharp, skilled eyes seeking any break in the endless pattern of bark and brush. He saw none. He let out a long breath and drew in the same, his lungs welcoming the air he'd been withholding during his escape. A torrent of both relief and panic swept through the king's veins. Where were the rest of his men?

He pulled Taranau to a stop and listened. Nothing. His blood ran cold. Had they all fallen?

Please dunna let it be so, Lord. Even with the shame of his absence in the church services, he prayed that the words he'd learned in his studies of the scripture were true. That though he wandered, God remained near. A good shepherd, seeking after his lost sheep.

He knew better than to make bargains with the Almighty, but simply asked God to forgive his confusion and distance, if not for his own sake, for the innocents in his charge.

Duncan drew up the reins once more, turning his horse back toward the tower. At least, he thought it was that direction.

As he took in the fullness of his surroundings, Duncan found no familiarity. When they'd passed through the first time, he'd kept to the eastern side. It was closer to the village and the area he'd explored as a child. But this—the ground rose and fell in waves as if made of water and not soil. Great stones the color of wet ashes broke through earth painted with the remains of once-green moss, and in the distance, he heard the rushing sound of a stream or waterfall. The trees were so close, they were near impassable. Even the air was thicker there. A place he'd never been.

There was something almost enchanted about it, though, and he felt a pull in his stomach, as if something called to him. It drew him deeper and deeper into the thickening wood. The settling darkness shaped shadows into otherworldly, almost person-like forms. He wouldn't have found himself surprised if fairies were to rise up from the bushes, twinkling like floating stars just as whispered stories described.

He let his head fall back, eyes cast upward in search of any open patches in the canopy where he might gain direction from the sky. The only indication being a single bright star in the purple sky. He was headed north. His tower was westward.

As much as his still-pounding heart desired to remain in this secret pocket of safety, he knew his men would be searching for him, and if the Norsemen had circled back around, possibly in need of assistance themselves.

Duncan gently nudged Taranau with the heel of his boot, and the horse turned obediently, when a flicker of movement startled the animal.

Duncan shook his head, certain he hadn't seen what his mind imagined. A woman—or lass, rather—stood in front of him, a basket of berries spilled at her feet. Her yellow hair was unbound, tumbling in waves over her shoulders. She wore a simple gray dress, a leather belt cinching at the waist. A circlet of delicate green vines ringed her golden head, and Duncan was certain he was hallucinating.

He opened his mouth to speak when more figures emerged from the wood, sudden and swift.

From all directions, Vikings descended, leaving Taranau, Duncan, and the lass trapped against the barrier of stones protruding from the earth at their back. The horse reared, and Duncan tumbled backwards, reaching for but failing to grasp the leather straps of his bridle.

His back met the forest floor, a flash of light, then blackness veiling his vision as his skull connected with the rough side of a lichen-covered rock. The air in his lungs was forced out, leaving him gasping and dizzy as he scrambled to stand and draw his sword, white and black spots still disrupting his sight. He shoved the lass behind him, separating her from their attackers. Taranau stomped and prodded the ground in an arc around Duncan, protective and loyal.

The shallow wheeze of the girl's panicked breaths sounded even above the noise of Viking boots, and Duncan retreated, forcing her toward the stones behind them.

His assailants were just steps away. Duncan searched for some defense, spotting a dark cracked opening in one of the hut-sized stones. He shoved the lass into the opening and hissed orders to stay hidden before darting in the opposite direction.

A chaotic dance of clashing metal began as he battled the assailants. Taranau had regained his senses and assisted his master with kicks and rearing, sending men flying backwards at the impact of his strong hooves. Taranau's battle training was as effective as any soldier's. The sound of breaking bones matched the sounds of breaking branches as the battle moved around in the forest.

Duncan used the benefits of the densely populated forest to his advantage, dodging between trees and under low branches, the swords of his attackers missing his head and chest, becoming lodged into trunks instead. He kept the battle moving further and further from where he'd stashed the mysterious lass. But the fight was unequal, and Duncan saw he would be overtaken.

"Taranau! Come!" he called at the panicked shrieks from his faithful companion. "Taranau!"

Then Duncan did something unnatural, something he had never done, nor even considered—he fled. Taranau followed. Further away from the lass, deeper and deeper into the unfamiliar and darkening forest, he ran, the footsteps of his pursuers on his heels. Duncan didn't look back, knowing any delay in his escape would mean death; his only option was escape. To capture a king—it would mean the destruction of his kingdom. The Norsemen didn't merely over-take kingdoms. They desecrated them. They burned every home to the ground and slaughtered without discrimination. Women and children were taken and sold into slavery. They held no honor for life.

And if anyone remained alive, the second his cousin heard of his death, he would sweep in and destroy what was left. No. He had to live.

Duncan's ears pricked. The steps behind were closing in, forming a barrier between him and his horse. But it wasn't the Norsemen at his back that would be his greatest threat. It was the one from the side, who had crept ahead. The one who had waited patiently for him to come near. The one who now pounced from his hidden place and tackled Duncan, bringing the king to the ground.

As blows landed hard against his face and torso, Duncan caught flashes of plaid from beneath Viking armor. He was not set upon by a single enemy. This was a carefully coordinated attack, and even though his head swam with pain, he knew exactly who was behind it.

"William!" Duncan's growl fortified his resolve as he wielded his sword from where he lay on the ground.

Unable to challenge the throne on his merit, his cousin William's only chance to claim the crown would have been Duncan's death. But Duncan would not relinquish it so easily, especially not to one so reckless as to make deals with the Vikings.

The glint of his iron blade moved like the dance of the flame from the village pyre at a funeral—wild and without bounds.

Lord, spare my people if I fall. Dunna allow them to be slaughtered!

Duncan fought, though he felt the fire of steel as a blade pierced his side. His cry cut short, and his vision edged in darkness from the blow of a club. He could not—would not—succumb without giving all of himself for his people. Anger rose within him. Anger at his attackers and at God, whom he'd always trusted to lead him on the right path. But this road was dark, marred with death and ruin. How could he have gotten so lost?

As his life poured out through the wound in his side and he defended himself against blow after blow, he felt betrayed, misled, abandoned. Why had God called him to the clergy for all those years only to then force him to be king? Why, when his time would have been better spent learning to rule, to be prepared for situations like this? Now he was dying, and everything was for nothing.

Still. Deep inside there was a tiny spark, the hope that God would hear him, even in his rage. That he would still grant some kind of miracle. Praying without reservation nor dignity for help, Duncan's heart was laid bare.

The burning pressure of another sword pressed hard into his ribs. The thick leather of his breast plate held—a final defense against the iron blade—for beneath its tip lay the king's pounding heart.

Taranau's frantic whinnies faded as even he was driven back, refusing to leave his master.

"Run, Taranau!" He tried to set the animal free from his oath, but Duncan's cries were reduced to strangled groans by yet another blow to the chest.

As the last of Duncan's strength was spent and blackness surged inward, he felt the great pressure of bodies upon his chest suddenly relieved. Through half-closed eyes, he saw blurred images of his attackers arching back in agony, streaks of bright blue flashing across the dark sky.

The angels—they'd returned.

The *thwap* of arrows and soft squish of flesh as they met their target registered in Duncan's mind. Something quick and small collided with the shoulder of a nearby Norseman, and he twisted in pain before being struck again. The second blow drew an agonized howl from his lips and an unnatural bend to his arm.

As light as fairies, hooded figures emerged from the trees, moving as if carried with wings. Arms drew back, arrows flew, men fell. Drew, flew, fell . . . over and over.

Mayhap he'd died and this was his mind's way of easing him into the afterlife. Dreams of angels come to whisk him away.

Pain from another blow to his face squelched any illusions of a swift exit to heaven. Duncan rolled to his stomach, pushing up on arms that felt heavy with the weight of a thousand boulders. A white-blonde Norseman barreled toward him as Duncan struggled to get to his feet. The Viking raised both arms, preparing to bring a massive iron ax straight through Duncan's skull.

Duncan felt a wisp of something buzz past his cheek, and instantly, the hulking man disappeared from his vision. The smooth, rounded stone that brought the giant to the ground bounced into Duncan's view. Its surface was completely covered with strange black symbols, the dust of ash paint sloughing to the ground as it rolled to a stop. His vision blurred; he couldn't distinguish what was real and imagined.

His feet slipped from under him, and he reached for the stone that saved him. He could feel its cool, solid form against his palm. It was real.

He held onto the rock as if it could keep his heart beating. Such hope in such a small object.

Icy fingers crept up Duncan's limbs, freezing him in place and racking his body with shivers. He could no longer defend his men. He could no longer protect his people.

"Please . . . save . . . them." He prayed the angels or fairies or whatever they were could hear him.

Cold crept further into his chest, and the smell of earth filled his nose. He only floated, neither on earth nor in heaven. His limbs were numb, unable to find connection to the world, and the sharp, metallic taste of blood filled his mouth, suffocating him.

Thwap, thwap, thwap. The sound of arrows meeting their targets faded into silence, and darkness overtook the light.

One of the figures stalked toward him, and as she turned to release an arrow from her bow, her hood fell back. Midnight hair spilled from underneath.

"Fiona." The word only reached as far as the bed of leaves pasted to his cheek.

Fiona's face peered down at him. In the next instant, she was gone. He knew he would soon follow. Though his heart beat in an attempt to keep him alive, every pump sent more of his blood pouring from the wound in his side.

Just as his eyes closed for the last time, Duncan felt the warmth of hands on his shoulders and back, turning him over. A figure hovered, bending low, its face shielded in shadow but framed in a crown of wildly brilliant auburn hair.

12

CYRENE

821 AD - A Day Later

"Hhis injuries are grave, m'lady." Gertrud's dread siphoned the color from her skin as she gripped the queen's hands. Her eyes slipped over Cyrene's shoulders to the warriors standing guard before she lowered her head, speaking in a whisper only Cyrene could hear. "I canna watch another man die."

Ignoring less threatening wounds, Gertrud had tried to address the most severe injuries but turned to the queen, her tear-filled eyes revealing what she could not say. Cyrene felt the same desperation and squeezed Gertrud's fingers, her eyes raking over the trembling form of the man they'd rescued. A man who'd brought strangers through her wood more than once. Aye, she recognized him from four nights prior. The mysterious horseman who knew the way through her kingdom. There was no mistaking the bow-like curve of his lips and unruly tangle of dark blonde curls, though they were currently soaked with blood and matted with dirt.

As much as her ire was sparked by the nearness of this battle to her village, when a terrified young Brianna led them back to the place where the "tower man saved her," they'd tracked him, and she'd seen a blaze of courage in his fight. As if he were fighting for more than his life. Like Beli.

The pleading gasps for the lass and for his fellow soldiers, even at the risk of his own safety, echoed in her mind. And something else, something that, despite the fact that he was an enemy soldier from the tower, made her desire for him to live, if only to know who he was.

"Leave me." His voice was as the sea brushing the shore, barely a breath and fading. "Save her. Save them."

Even then, as life slipped from his body, in his delirium, he pleaded.

After so many years of vitality, suddenly death seemed an unwanted visitor that was overstaying his welcome. First the captured Viking, and now this unknown intruder. However dangerous he might have been, guilt at her satisfaction over the Viking's death, agony at seeing Gertrud's pain, or mayhap the same wound in his side that had her swatting away memories of her mother had driven Cyrene to do the unthinkable. She'd brought the injured soldier into the very heart of her village. Her sanctuary. Still, as she watched him labor to breathe and tremble under pain of his injuries, even that great risk didn't seem enough.

"Astrid!" Cyrene called.

When the captain appeared at her side, she turned sharply, hands clasped behind her back. A decision was made. "Call Revna to fetch the healer from Tràigh."

Astrid's lips parted in surprise, her eyes drifting toward the injured man before meeting Cyrene's. "He brings war, my queen." Astrid was tentative, her voice low and eyes flicking to Gertrud, as if she didn't want her to hear.

"It matters not. The man has entered our realm. He is in need of help, and that is what we will offer; now quickly, Astrid, call for Revna."

Astrid bowed and fled the hut with haste. She returned seconds later with news that Revna would fly on the back of her pure white mare, hopefully reaching the village by dawn. Revna's speed and severe beauty were not her only intimidating aspects. She would bring the healer, with or without his consent.

Cyrene stayed by the man's side, assisting Gertrud in his care. They moved silently about the hut, dancing in perfect balance around each other as they changed dressings and mixed poultices. A deep gash in his side was the most concerning wound. As Gertrud worked to control his bleeding, Cyrene tended to the multitude of less threatening injuries painting his arms and face.

"This one could use a sewing." Cyrene dabbed a wet cloth over a nasty opening above his right brow, the eye underneath nearly swollen shut.

"He wears the colors of the new king. But he doesna seem much older than ye, Majesty." Taking a mortar and pestle, Gertrud rambled as she ground herbs and oil into a paste, her words rushed and panicked. "He must be a hired soldier in the king's army, for his hands are calloused, but his skin too smooth to be a fieldsman."

"Aye," Cyrene said, allowing her eyes to trace the length of his muscled arm to the hands Gertrud referenced before moving to the hearth.

When she first spied him struggling with his assailants, she only saw a soldier of the tower, and she was eight years old again. His leather boots were the ones that had crept toward a thicket where she sheltered a terrified group of children. His sword was the one that caused a blossoming stain of red on the right shoulder of her little brother's tunic. The vambraces on his arms were the ones that, in her last glance over her shoulder, she had seen pressed against Beli's throat until his face turned from white to blue to gray. She'd frozen in place, a quieted child in her arms, not even acknowledging when Liam pulled at her, begging her to keep running. Beli didn't move either. Not even when they picked up his small body and carried it out of her sight.

She nearly held her warriors back and let this stranger suffer the fate those men deserved. But he wasn't one of them. Gertrud was right. He was young. He would have been a child like her when those terrible things happened. So she saved him. Her warriors were so swift and sure, she hadn't even had to notch an arrow before he was rescued.

As long as it was possible, she would escape taking a life. Even when they'd stormed the village against the Vikings, she shot to wound, not to kill. Mayhap it was selfish to allow her warriors to bear that burden alone, but there were enough impossible choices she was left to make, choices like the one that had cost Beli his life. Flee or fight. She had enough death on her hands.

"Were it not for the bruising, I suspect he would be quite braw."

Cyrene felt a flash of heat across her cheeks and forced her attention back to the rags she was soaking in a cauldron of boiling water. Gertrud had only been muttering to herself, as was her habit when she was upset or nervous, and didn't expect a response. Cyrene was grateful, as she was embarrassed to admit she'd had the same thought. At least, he was more handsome than lanky Liam.

Gertrud bent to spread her mixture over his wounds. When her fingers touched his skin, she froze, slowly looking toward Cyrene with wide eyes.

"My queen, he burns." Gertrud's normally full cheeks had transformed into shallow graves where her hope was buried.

Cyrene's boots made no sound as she darted across the straw-covered floor. Her long, thin fingers brushed aside the man's dirt-dusted locks, her fingers registering the heat from his skin, though she didn't touch him.

"We need the healer. He will have medicines; he will know what to do. I dunna ken . . ." Gertrud's wild gaze swept toward her meager supply of herbs, Cyrene almost able to hear her listing each one and its use as her lips moved soundlessly.

Filled with resolve, Cyrene straightened, grasping Gertrud's thin arms. She looked forcefully into her healer's eyes. "Think, Gertrud. What can we do? What do you have?"

Gertrud pulled her quivering lip between her teeth as her eyes darted around the hut as if searching for the answer hidden somewhere within. Her breaths came in short bursts, and Cyrene could tell the young woman was near panic.

"What would yer mother do?" At Cyrene's hushed mention of Brígid, Gertrud stilled, bright eyes settling on Cyrene's. There had been no better healer than Brígid, and the lass had trained under her since she was a bairn.

"Ye ken everything she ken. Even more." Cyrene encouraged her with a nod, and Gertrud drew in a deep, calming breath.

"He must be cooled," she said, certainty weighing heavily in her tone. "Wi' water from the lower falls—'tis even colder than the sea."

Cyrene risked a smile of hope and squeezed Gertrud's arms in assurance. "Go. Take Astrid and Fiadh. I shall tend to him."

Gertrud's steps were just as silent as Cyrene's as she dashed through the doorway and into the night.

Cyrene turned back to their patient, lowering herself to kneel at his side. She folded back the linen cloth covering his bare chest, surprised to find a thin silver chain around his neck. She lifted it, a small ornate cross pendant dangling at the end. She lowered it back into place and proceeded to inspect the dressings Gertrud had just fastened. They were already soaked through with his blood.

White lines and pink patches of puckered skin dotted his chest. This man was no stranger to battle. But none of his scars were like this wound. It was angry and red. Still allowing his lifeblood to escape, even after the full night and day he'd been in their care.

She pursed her lips, determined to stave off the redness and fever blooming at the site of his injury, but she lacked knowledge of the healing herbs. Remaining on her knees, she hoped for help to arrive quickly, for his presence not to bring hurt or fear to her people, and for her own heart to turn toward compassion instead of vengeance, as was its nature. Her whispered words were quick, unintelligible to anyone listening—of which there was none, for the man had taken a shuddered breath and grown still. Too still.

Cyrene leapt up from her prayer, hands moving across his face, his neck, his chest, searching for life. Hatred for the tower king and his soldiers had taken root in her heart for so long, yet she knew followers of *An T-aon* were called to forgive. To love their enemies. She could not, not yet. The best she could do was desperately wish for him to live.

"Breathe!" She pressed on his chest, and at her hissed order, his thick chest began to move, and Cyrene raised her hands in praise, then hurried to the roughly planed table, where Gertrud's herbs were laid in neat piles.

Cyrene gazed over the few choices, her eyes continually drawn to the pungent aroma of fresh clove leaves and juniper petals. Clove would stay the pain, and juniper . . .

She remembered a simple lesson from Brígid when they were younger. "If yer ever injured on yer hunts, find these plants." Brígid had lifted a sprig of juniper and leaves of clove, allowing her pupils to memorize their shape and color. "Chew the leaves, then place them on yer wounds."

There was something else she mentioned . . . what was it? Cyrene touched each herb and flower. Elder! That was it.

She drew a measure of thin cloth from Gertrud's basket, placed it over the opening of a wooden bowl, and with a pestle, blended oil with some of the juniper, clove, and elder until she'd created a thick paste. She crushed the remaining herbs into another bit of cloth and drew the kettle from where it warmed on an iron hook in her hearth. The boiling water sent the earthy aroma souring throughout the hut as Cyrene poured it over the crushed herbs, producing a small cup of fragrant liquid. She carried the tea and paste to the cot. The man had begun to tremble once more.

His shivering grew violent and state agitated as fever and pain coursed through his body. Cyrene hummed a low lullaby while she removed his bindings and spread the paste over his darkening wound with her fingers. His body jerked at the sting of the herbs, but quickly stilled as the powerful sedative of clove took effect.

She then slid her arm beneath his head, lifting it and coaxing his dry, cracked lips open with the edge of her cup.

"Drink. 'Tis but a bit of tea."

He didn't resist, and Cyrene whispered encouraging praises as the liquid slid easily into his mouth and down his throat.

When he'd taken in all the herbs, she gently laid his head back onto the stretched deerskin cot. Soon he stilled, head rolling to the side and breaths deepening with sleep. Cyrene lingered, examining his face in the soft yellow light of the torches, looking for the spark that resonated in her mind. She felt as though she'd seen him before. Not just the night in the woods as he led the band of men, but even before that.

She lifted her hand, the tips of her fingers moving to brush back a damp curl that fell across his forehead. Just as her hand touched his skin, he jerked. His eyes flew open, and he grabbed her wrist. Her hand, captured by his, hovered over his face.

"The crown," he groaned, the strain of forming words twisting his expression. "Is it . . ."

His loyalty, though to a monarchy she despised, impressed Cyrene.

"Be still now." When his hand relaxed and his fingers slipped from her wrist, she rested her hand atop his, which had fallen to his chest. "The healer is coming."

Through fluttering lids, she could tell he was trying to focus on her face, and she leaned a bit closer. As much as she desired to pelt him with questions, including who he was and what he was doing in her wood, a stronger urge to comfort this stranger took hold of her heart.

"The lass . . ." Another wave of chills took hold of his body, cutting off his words. "Is she . . ."

"She's safe. Yer safe," she whispered, lifting her hand to once again comb curls away from his face. "Rest."

His eyes fell closed, and Cyrene stood, planning to return the bowl of herb mixture to the table. A brush of warmth against her hand stilled her. His weak fingers gently took hers, filling her with a strange flood of heat.

Eyes still closed, his lips moved, throat rising as he swallowed. Cyrene remained frozen, wanting to both move away and draw closer at the same time.

"Thank ye."

His hand slipped away and mouth fell slack just as Gertrud and fellow maidens returned laden with vessels of ice cold water from the falls.

Cyrene felt the eyes of her warriors as they registered her nearness to the man, and she hissed in a sharp breath to command their attention.

"Help me move him to the basin."

The women obeyed immediately, each placing hands beneath and lifting him from the cot. Once he'd been placed in the large carved wooden basin, they began pouring the water over his burning body.

"What shall we do now?" Gertrud asked, her hands seeking comfort in each other.

"Pray fer mercy. And fer Revna's swift ride."

The warriors nodded and joined her in placing their hands on the trembling man. Cyrene counted the hours as he burned in the tub, her warriors bringing fresh pails of cold water. As the shadows grew long in the evening sun, a commotion from outside sent them all hurrying to the hut opening.

Revna appeared in the entrance, the dark undertones of her skin golden with sweat, and thin wisps of her hair loose from her braids hanging limp along the sides of her reddened face. She stepped aside, allowing a cloaked gentleman to enter.

The warriors, unbidden by their queen, took a protective stance, shoulders hunched forward and feet planted firmly. The sky-blue eyes of the village healer widened when met with the fierce wall of women, and he instinctively retreated into the unmoving barrier of Revna.

"Thank ye for coming." Cyrene's voice wafted above her warriors, who returned to a more demure posture at her comforting tone. "Please, he has been pierced by a blade and burns wi' fever."

The man hesitated one moment longer, clutching a brown leather satchel to his chest as a shield.

"I am Cyrene, queen of the dark woods. The berries and meat your village enjoys come from these woods and are felled at the tips of our arrows. Our trees build your homes. No harm will come to ye here, for we are the keepers of the peace. What are ye called?"

"I-I am called Thaedry."

"Yer the healer from Tràigh?"

"Nay." At the biting grip of Revna's hand on his arm, Thaedry lifted his hand in defense. "I am a healer, but I amna from Tràigh. My kinsman ken the old healer and bid me come when his eyes grew dim. I have just come a month hence."

Cyrene lowered her eyes and head in acknowledgment.

"Please, this man needs yer help, Thaedry. I would be most thankful for yer knowledge."

Thaedry surveyed the impressive band of warriors, each maiden bowing as had their queen, before he moved toward the basin.

"How long since he was injured?"

"One day prior."

After a short examination, Thaedry turned to Cyrene. "Ye were wise to use the waters. The fever has broken. May we move him? I need to treat his wound."

Cyrene nodded and raised her hands, motioning for her maidens to lift him once again. His drenched riding trousers clung to his skin and hung low on his hips. Cyrene directed the women to turn away as she placed a clean woven blanket over him to preserve his modesty.

"I shall take my leave, Thaedry. Gertrud and young Fiadh shall assist ye." Cyrene nodded to Gertrud and her assistant as the healer began to pull small jars and leather pouches from his bag. "We do not wish to hinder yer work."

"Aye, Yer Majesty." Thaedry's demeanor had relaxed, and he spoke gently to Gertrud. "Will ye boil some water?"

As Gertrud hastened to the kettle, Cyrene followed her warriors through the curtain, leaving Thaedry to attempt a miracle.

13

CYRENE

821 AD - Two Days Later

All her usual methods of capturing sleep when thoughts refused to fall silent had failed. Even under Thaedry's endless care, still the man's condition remained dire. Each passing hour increased the chances someone would come looking for him, be it ally or enemy.

Abandoning her cot, Cyrene dressed and slid one arm through the string of her bow, securing it across her back. She slung the strap of her quiver over one shoulder and tucked thin iron blades in her waist belt, hiding them beneath the fabric of her cloak.

In lieu of sleep, she prepared to join the next watch of warriors, their number double what had been assigned before. The threat of otherworldly dangers was no longer enough to protect them.

She glanced toward the hut where the man lay, and once again questioned her decision to bring him into the very heart of her kingdom. Had it been foolish? Even if not doing so would have meant his death?

"I humbly offer my services to protect Her Majesty on watch tonight."

Cyrene scowled at the husky sound of Liam's voice as he whispered over her shoulder. She'd been too engrossed in her thoughts to hear him jog up behind her.

Out of nowhere, Astrid also appeared. The hard rock of her shoulder against his ribs sent Liam stumbling aside, and Cyrene hid a laugh with her hand.

"Ye can take two shifts, Liam. And be at the training fields at dawn. Ye clearly need practice to be more aware of yer surroundings. What if I'd been a Norseman?"

Liam's reply was unintelligible until he murmured a furious, "Aye, Captain," before storming off.

"What a thorough leader ye are." Cyrene linked her arm through Astrid's, accompanying her friend to the edge of their village.

"There are no bounds to my loyalty, Majesty." Astrid rolled her hand in a flourish of dramatics and bowed between steps.

"Have the scouts any news?" Suddenly serious, Cyrene released Astrid's arm and gripped the strings of her bow instead.

"Not in our wood, but there is unrest in the tower king's land, just as the soldier reported." Astrid's fingers danced across the hilts of blades tucked into her waist belt. Unlike the village ladies, the warrior maidens had always preferred softened leather trousers under tunics and vests instead of skirts or gowns. "Shall we prepare to intervene again?"

Cyrene thought for a long moment. "Nay."

At Astrid's questioning glance, Cyrene straightened her shoulders. "'Twas probably a mistake to have done so before. I dunna want to risk exposing our kingdom again. We have remained safe wi'in The Dorcha this many years. Safe we will stay. But we remain diligent."

Astrid nodded in acceptance. "I'll keep our scouts stationed close to the border. If trouble comes near, we will be ready."

Once Astrid confirmed routes with each pair of warriors, she and Cyrene continued their patrol of the innermost perimeter.

"Have ye considered the elder's proposal?" Astrid's sharp eyes never stopped scanning as they walked.

"Ahh . . . I dunna ken." Cyrene sighed and brushed back a strand of red hair that had escaped from her braid.

"No hurry then. 'Tis only the future of our people."

Cyrene ignored the amusement in Astrid's tone and drew in a long breath, rolling her head to alleviate the stiffness in her neck.

"I ken ye would say 'tis time to find a way for our younger maidens to marry, but I am leery of making unions with the village lads, even if we are able to bring them here in secret. Thirty missing lads willna go unnoticed."

"Aye. 'Tis true."

"We dunna ken this new king. Just because his father dinna breech the deep woods doesna mean the son willna either."

"Aye. 'Tis true."

"And I havna forgotten how quickly those same village people abandoned our former alliance. We dunna ken if they'll do it again."

"Aye. 'Tis true."

"Aye. 'Tis true," Cyrene mocked Astrid, nudging her with her shoulder. "Have ye no helpful advice, oh wise captain?"

Astrid walked in silence for a full minute before answering.

"All that were just lads have now grown and married. Already many are expecting a bairn. But what about ye?" Astrid stopped, causing Cyrene to halt her steps as well. "Yer several winters past the age to marry. Will ye not give yer people an heir to love and care for them as ye do? Will ye leave them to fade into true legends of the wood or disperse into foreign lands? Yer the last of the royal Picts. Will we end with ye?" Astrid's reply was soft. She didn't chastise, but simply stated the truth.

If Cyrene was meant to wed, she'd have to consider a union from the outside. "Where is this from? Ye never showed interest in marriage. Why the sudden concern fer mine?"

"We arna talking about me." Astrid raised an eyebrow. "I amna the queen."

"Aye, 'tis true." Cyrene couldn't help but laugh.

"Mayhap Liam's strategy will work after all?" Astrid's casual comment sparked Cyrene's curiosity.

"What strategy?"

"To be the last man standing."

Again, Cyrene couldn't stifle the amused breath that burst from her lips. "I'd rather wed that injured soldier in Gertrud's hut."

"Mayhap ye'll get yer wish."

Cyrene hissed at Astrid's teasing and adjusted her bow, refusing to think of the action she'd have to take if her act of kindness toward that stranger backfired. More impossible choices.

She'd prepared a witty retort when a distant scream of pain sent Cyrene's skin prickling with alarm. "What is that?"

"I dunna ken." Astrid was already loading her bow.

Together they raced toward the source, landing at the entrance of the healer's hut. Throwing back the folds of fabric, Cyrene stormed inside, blades from her waist drawn and spun until they were secure in her palms.

She was immediately overwhelmed by a sickening smell of burning flesh that twisted her stomach into a painful knot.

At the sight of her sudden appearance, Thaedry threw his hands in the air, one wrapped around the end of a short iron staff. The other end was hammered into the shape of a small orb and was glowing bright orange.

Cyrene lunged forward, the sharp tip of her blade nearly piercing his chest at the heart. Astrid was a step behind, sweeping her loaded bow as she scanned the room for danger.

Once she was assured Gertrud and Fiadh were unharmed, Cyrene hissed through her teeth, an unnatural rage boiling through her veins at the memory of the stranger's scream. She hadn't heard such a sound since the same cry escaped her own mouth after the death of her mother. To hear it again filled her with unquenchable fury.

"What have ye done to him?" This stranger was no one to her, and yet . . . Cyrene inched further, Thaedry crying out at the sting of her pressing blade.

"M'lady!" Gertrud launched herself between Cyrene's advance and Thaedry's trembling form, attempting to push them apart. "'Tis well."

Gertrud's arm shot out, a hand raised to stop the captain's advance. "'Tis well, Astrid."

Cyrene's eyes darted from Gertrud to the quivering Fiadh before lowering to the soldier, who lay limp on the cot, his bare chest soaked with sweat and an angry blackened wound where Thaedry's brand had been.

"Please, Yer Majesty." Thaedry's voice quaked, but he moved toward his patient despite his evident fear. "I must tend to the burn."

"We had to seal the wound, m'lady." Gertrud placed her hand on Cyrene's blade, gently urging her to lower the weapon. "He was dying."

Thaedry, assured by Gertrud he was not in danger of being run through, hurried about the hut. He cleaned the swollen shape on the man's side until it was no longer black but red, and coated it with a thick white paste.

Though unconscious, Thaedry's patient jerked at the application.

"What is that yer doing?" Cyrene's nervous suspicion turned her tone hard and sharp.

"Mandrake poultice." Thaedry continued working without looking up. "For his pain."

Gertrud returned to the table, took a bowl and cloth, and knelt beside the man, dabbing at his moistened forehead.

"His fever has not returned, but we had to stop the bleeding. If he lives through the night, Thaedry says he has a fair chance." Gertrud glanced at the healer, who returned the look with affection before she turned her blue eyes again to Cyrene. "'Twas wise to call fer him."

"Aye?" Cyrene lifted a brow at Gertrud's familiar reference to the healer, and the maiden's fair cheeks flamed a bright crimson.

Cyrene returned her blades to her waist belt and leaned her bow against the hut's large support beam. Her heart finally slowed from its panicked pace, and her skin prickled, still on edge, uncertain as to why she suddenly seemed to care so much about the fate of this stranger.

"Has he spoken?" Cyrene reached for the bowl, taking Gertrud's place on a stool at the man's bedside.

"Not but moans and mutters." Gertrud wiped her brow with another cloth and attempted to tame wild curls that had escaped her braids over long days and sleepless nights.

Cyrene took in the circles darkening Gertrud's normally bright skin and the level to which her shoulders sagged. Thaedry still stood at her back, tending to the man's burn; when Cyrene stood, he took a defensive step in retreat, his hand rubbing the spot on his chest where her blade had pressed.

"I am sorry if I hurt ye."

Thaedry's hand froze, as if he realized what he'd done, and dropped it to his side, visibly relaxed. "Nay, m'lady. I understand; I should have warned ye."

Cyrene tipped her head in acceptance of their truce and touched his elbow, turning him away from Gertrud. "I thank ye for yer help. I have yet another favor to ask."

Thaedry must have understood her want for discretion, for he only lifted his chin to indicate he was listening.

"I fear exhaustion has taken hold of Gertrud and Fiadh. Can ye convince them to rest? I shall stay in their stead."

Thaedry bobbed his head, his simple smile not unnoticed. After completing his procedure, he straightened and approached Gertrud and Fiadh at the hearth where they were tending the fire and placing another kettle to boil.

Fiadh graciously accepted Thaedry's encouragement and skirted from the hut with a passing bow to Cyrene. Gertrud remained, though.

Cyrene kept her back to the healers, sparing Gertrud the embarrassment of watchful eyes as Thaedry insisted on preparing a tea to renew her strength.

"Yer no good to me if yer mind is not clear." Thaedry's tone was gentle in response to Gertrud's arguing. "He's resting. Take yer leave for now." Gertrud made a noise as if to protest, but Thaedry silenced her with a husky whisper. "Please. Ye have been by my side for nearly two days. I'll need ye when he wakes, but . . . but I canna bear to see ye suffering."

Cyrene risked a glance over her shoulder, spotting Thaedry's hand tender on Gertrud's elbow and her reaching to grasp his arm in return. Cyrene resisted the chuckle that rose in her chest. Gertrud had always worn her heart out in the open for anyone to see, giving it freely, and Cyrene was pleased it was a man such as Thaedry whom Gertrud had chosen to care for it. He shared her passion for healing, and Cyrene could tell by his demeanor, he was just as kind.

Mayhap the elder's suggestion of unions with the village men would not be the disaster she feared. Gertrud excused herself from the hut, clutching Thaedry's tea in both hands.

Cyrene joined Thaedry at the hearth, where he dipped his instruments in hot water before placing them on a cloth to dry.

"That wasna a love potion ye brewed for young Gertrud now?"

"Nay." Thaedry's surprise turned soft, and he breathed a laugh. "I admit I havna met a lass wi' a sweeter spirit."

"She is verra precious to me, and just now breaching the age to marry. I dunna have to warn ye to be careful wi' her heart, do I?" Cyrene squeezed his shoulder and gave him a pointed look with the sharp lift of one brow. She bobbed her head toward the bow that still rested against the post. "I never miss."

"I promise to keep it safe." Thaedry's tone was light, but his expression sincere, and as Cyrene looked deep into his eyes, she knew he was telling the truth.

He smiled, but weariness drew dark lines across his forehead, and Cyrene lifted her hand. "If ye think it safe, ye should go find rest yerself."

His eyes explored Cyrene's own tired features, but she raised her brows, warning him not to share those observations. He glanced at his patient before settling his gaze once again on her.

"I'll have my maidens take ye to a hut of yer own." Cyrene motioned toward the exit. "Dunna worry; I'll not leave him, and promise to fetch ye if he wakes."

"Thank ye, m'lady."

Once Thaedry had been handed over to Astrid with instructions to provide him a comfortable bed and full meal, Cyrene found herself back at the bedside of the intriguing stranger.

Thanks to Brianna, talk of his presence had permeated the village. She'd spent most of the day affirming shocked rumors that the stranger did save the lass and quieting fearful ones that he was a Viking come to lead them all to ruin. She shared many of their concerns, but what choice had she been given? Should she have left him to die?

No. Of that, she was certain. He'd been a lion. Like Beli. Besides, it was never the wrong decision to offer aid when it was needed, but where she should go from there was her true dilemma.

He clearly knew his way around her wood. What would stop him from leading the tower-dwellers into the heart of her kingdom and taking all that was precious? How could she convince him not to bring news of their presence to the new king?

She lowered her head, heavy with worry. Even as a child, even when her people were wandering, she had not forsaken the traditions of worship. She'd been faithful to honor *An T-aon*, and encouraged her people to do the same. But her heart had grown distant, her worship habitual.

Somehow, the arrival of this stranger and his dire situation had given air to the suffocated coals of her faith, and something suddenly began to burn within her chest where before there had only been ice.

Still battling the hollowness which her prayers had taken on over the years, she lowered her head and pleaded with *An T-aon* for wisdom. For favor and protection for her people, for an end to the invasion of the Norsemen. She begged forgiveness for the vengeance her heart simply could not release, however justified it was. Finally, she prayed for the healing of this stranger, though she didn't know his intentions nor even his name.

"Duncan."

Cyrene's head jerked up with a start, her mind suddenly alert. In the quiet of the hut, with the deep breaths of the patient as a soothing lullaby, she must have fallen asleep while praying and muttered her last thoughts aloud.

"My name. Duncan."

The patient gazed at her as she attempted to conceal her alarm. "The same as the tower king?"

"Aye." His eyes were half closed, the swelling still allowing his right eye to open but a fraction, but she noticed they were shockingly blue as they reflected the torch light. "'Tis a common name."

His gaze rolled about the hut, alarm shortening his breaths.

"Where am I?" He raised his hand, fingers tapping the stitched cut above his eye.

Cyrene took his hand, gently lowering it from the wound as she considered his question, hesitant to reveal secrets that had long kept them alive.

"Yer safe." Her simple reply seemed to satisfy him.

"How . . . how long have I been here?" His voice was raspy, words strained.

"Three cycles of the sun."

"Three . . . I must go." He attempted to sit up but sucked in a pained breath as his hand flew to his injured side. He looked at the injury as if seeing it for the first time, and then pushed against the cot. Away from her.

He thought she'd hurt him?

"The healer sealed yer wound. It was grave. I . . . we dinna ken what else to do."

Something flashed across his face, a wildness that spoke of strength and passion. Just as soon as it appeared, it was gone, replaced by a grimace of pain.

"I remember," he groaned.

Realizing her nearness, Cyrene shifted, putting distance between herself and the stranger. Mayhap she should be the one afraid of him.

"I canna hurt ye." He spoke through heavy breaths. "I wouldna even if I could."

Cyrene lifted her chin, asserting her royalty through her crisp tone. "I dunna fear ye."

The man called Duncan gave up his struggle and collapsed back onto the cot, breaths heavy, looking over the length of her. "Aye. I believe ye."

Cyrene felt uncomfortable under the scrutiny of his gaze and returned the inspection with fervor. She drew in a breath, prepared to begin her interrogation, when he offered an observation she didn't expect.

"Ye were there," he said. "Ye rescued me."

She only blinked in response.

"Are ye hurt?"

"Nay." She relaxed, but kept her eyes sharp. Something about the way he asked that question seemed familiar.

He offered the hint of a smile on what looked like a painfully swollen set of lips.

"Please." His breaths were labored. "Do ye ken what happened in Tràigh? What of the other soldiers?"

For the first time, Cyrene fully took him in. He was tall, evidenced by his feet dangling off the end of the cot. His arms and chest were toned from what she assumed was military training, but his beard was smartly trimmed, as if he were a nobleman. He'd only spoken a few words, but she guessed he was educated, as his speech was precise and confident.

Unruly curls of yellow-blonde hair were plastered in waves to his sweat-soaked forehead, and Cyrene was surprised by her desire to dab at his face with the cloth she still clutched in her hand.

This was the first time she'd seen a soldier from the tower up close since she was a child. Under the armor, he was just a man. As she was looking him over, she noticed he, too, was examining her. She retreated a step.

"What is this?" The man's brows perked in question, but Cyrene continued her inquisition. "Who are ye, and what were ye doing in my . . . in the wood?"

Though ravaged by suspicion and frustration, she chose her words carefully, still cautious. Mayhap he was too injured to inquire as to why she was also in the wood. Although if he remembered anything about his journey to her village, he already knew too much. She glanced toward the table, where her daggers were in plain view.

"Ye dunna waste time, do ye?" He attempted a smile, though it pained him.

"Nay. And I expect an answer when I ask a question." Cyrene tipped a brow, challenging him to defy her again. Then she asked the question she really wanted an answer to. "Why were ye not afraid to enter?"

He took a few long, ragged breaths through open lips and didn't seem to mind his place of disadvantage as she stood over him. He blinked at his surroundings and pulled his dry lips between his teeth before speaking again.

"When I was a lad, I dinna believe all the stories." Every few words, he stopped and gathered his breath. "Whenever I could, I snuck away and explored, looking fer the truth."

"By yerself?"

Duncan lifted a shoulder. The simple gesture provoked a grimace of discomfort. "Mostly. I wanted to see fer myself."

"What did ye find?"

"Trees." Duncan's eyes drifted closed, a smile tugging at his mouth.

Cyrene waited, wondering if he'd fallen back asleep. But he sucked in a slow breath, and his blue eyes found hers again.

"I dinna ken how I found myself so deep in the wood. My me- I mean, word came there were Vikings in the village, and we went to fight them back, but it was a trap. I only entered the wood to escape." He coughed out the last few words, and Cyrene had drawn a cup of water before he regained his breath.

"Thank ye." When he'd drunk his fill, he let his head fall back onto the cot and captured her gaze. "And for saving my life, I thank ye all."

"Unlike the men from the North, we are not beasts."

"What are ye, then?" Duncan's eyes sparked with curiosity and something else, a teasing humor that made Cyrene's insides squirm in its presumed familiarity.

"We are human. Just as ye are." She retreated another step, hands coming together in front, fingers lacing.

Mayhap she should have let him believe they *were* the wild Picts of old, the ones rumored to paint themselves blue and fight naked. The ones said to sacrifice bairns to the sea.

No one truly knew who had claimed the lives of Fiona's children, but like her death, the responsibility for theirs was lain on the Picts.

"I dinna mean to offend, m'lady." Duncan winced as he once again attempted to find relief by shifting on the cot. "It's just that I dunna recognize ye from the village or estates. May I ask yer name?"

Cyrene narrowed her gaze as she considered his request. Did he know every face in his kingdom? She couldn't imagine a nobleman, even one that served in the king's warband, lowering himself enough to mix with the commoners. If he were a man of ill-intent, capturing the queen would be his ultimate goal in overtaking her kingdom— not that tower-dwellers recognized Pictish royalty anymore. But he was hardly at the advantage in his current state, and her warriors were but a call away. Still, she opted for caution.

"I am called Cyrene."

"Cyrene." He repeated her name with reverence, his eyes dropping closed and throat moving as he swallowed hard. "Deer-chasing second Artemis, the huntress with lion-slaying hands."

Cyrene straightened, hands fisting the fabric of her skirts as she lowered herself to the stool by his cot. "Ye ken of the ancient stories?"

Eyes still closed, Duncan nodded. "Aye. I have studied many things, daughter of Hypseus. Though I dunna ken why."

"Ye dunna ken why ye studied?" Cyrene wondered if he spoke from dreams or pain-induced delusions. Maybe that was why he wasn't afraid.

"Seems . . . wasted."

His words came slowly, breaths deepening as if he were drifting to sleep again, and Cyrene bent closer to this intriguing stranger. A skilled fighter, a learned man. Who was he?

"'Tis said she be nymph, not mortal." His lips fell into a soft smile, words slurred. "Are ye nymph, Huntress?"

"Some say so." Cyrene muttered her answer, thinking him to be asleep.

"I ken I am in The Dorcha." His eyes remained closed.

Cyrene didn't respond. The less he knew, the better. Mayhap she could convince him it was all a dream. His next words stole her breath, though.

"I can feel it," he said. "The air . . . 'tis thick wi' memories and legend. Wi' sorrow and secrets."

With effort, he opened his eyes, meeting Cyrene's. "How long have ye lived here?"

She held his gaze until a whisper of cold caressed her skin, and she looked to the glowing embers of the fire instead. "Seems like forever."

"Please, Cyrene—bonnie huntress of the wood." The desperation in his voice drew her attention again. As he opened his mouth to speak, his body jerked, gripped by a sudden wave of pain, and he was alert again, mind sharpened by distress. He reached for her, his hands gripping her wrists and his blue irises blazing. "Please, tell me of the other soldiers. Do they live? Has the crown fallen?"

Cyrene, frozen under his touch, considered his questions. For a soldier, even in his injured state, he seemed to carry himself with authority. Mayhap he was captain of the army, or a laird in the king's command.

"We fended off yer attackers. I ken not of the other soldiers nor state of the crown. But we dinna find any others like ye fallen."

He breathed a sigh of relief and released her, seemingly unaware of his forward behavior.

"Were there others? Like me?" There was a measure of hope in his question. "They'd have come over the mountain wi' . . . wi' an army?"

"Yer king would bring an army through The Dorcha?" Cyrene jerked her hands free, her worst fears realized. She pushed off her stool, aiming for her longbow.

"Nay." Duncan's reply was soft but firm. "They'd come to the tower's aid. That is all."

She glared at him for a moment before diving to his side again, her fingers firmly grasping his chin until his eyes flew open.

"Tell me the truth."

Caught in her gaze, he sucked in a wet breath, his eyes barely staying open.

"Tell me." She roughly jerked his chin again, forcing him to consciousness.

"I swear it. Only to aid the tower." His words were tight, breath trapped in his lungs.

Satisfied, she released him. He raised a shaking hand to rub the place her hand had been.

"None others have passed through." Cyrene eyed him carefully as she answered his question, gauging his reaction and fighting the sadness of a forming reality. He knew too much.

Duncan's hands curled into tight fists before he again tried to push himself up. Cyrene sighed at his stubbornness and pressed against his shoulders, forcing him back down. He offered little resistance.

"Yer not well, Duncan." He stilled at his name on her lips, and she withdrew her hands at the anxiousness that rose in his eyes.

"Please." He grasped her hand again. "I must return wi' haste. The crown depends on it."

"Why?"

"Because I . . . I just must." Duncan's blue eyes darted back and forth between hers.

"I canna allow it." Her response was gentle, almost an apology. He couldn't be allowed to leave now, though she had no plan for how to make him stay should he recover. Choice after impossible choice.

He released her hand, his eyes closing and head falling to the side in defeat. Cyrene stared at the hand he'd grasped, her skin buzzing with some unknown sensation.

"Not until ye answer my questions." What was she doing? Why give him hope?

"Aye." He didn't open his eyes, and Cyrene felt a pang of regret.

She found herself making a promise she wasn't sure she intended to keep. "And yer strength has returned enough for the journey."

"I . . . there was a lass." His eyes remained closed, but he dragged in a deep breath. "Was she real?"

"Aye." Cyrene spoke softly, intrigued as his expression turned to concern. He must have forgotten how many times he'd already asked about Brianna. "She is well. Thanks to ye."

He looked at her once again, relief bringing color to his cheeks just before his mouth twisted, a groan escaping between his teeth. He tensed under some unseen attack, and Cyrene darted to the folds of the hut's entrance, sending word through a maiden to fetch Thaedry.

14

DUNCAN

821 AD - The Next Night

N ight had come again. A cool wisp of wind crept across Duncan's skin, teasing him with icy fingers. The healer's tea, laden with poppy and mandrake, had stolen all of his concentration and energy, leaving him to sleep the remainder of the day—or mayhap many days. He couldn't be sure.

Even now, he wasn't certain he was truly awake. It was too quiet, and his mind swam with the thickness of dreams—strange dreams that plagued his rest. He swatted away buzzing memories of the one called Gertrud soothing him with song.

Of all the blurred visions dancing in his mind, one image was as clear as the day. Cyrene. Faint freckles dotting her ivory skin made her emerald eyes all the more alluring. The defiant set of her jaw and rise of her cheekbones reminded Duncan of the Roman goddesses from the illustrated manuscripts he'd studied. Her hair, like flames of auburn braided in rows along her face, fell into thick waves down her back. And the way she moved—it was regal, important.

Mayhap her teasing wasn't such. Mayhap she truly was a nymph or wood fairy, as the stories told. Such beauty must have surely been a fever-induced dream. He groaned into his hands, praying the vague memory of his dopey grin and promise to make her his bride was a hallucination and not reality.

There was one thing he did know for certain. The Dorcha was not an uninhabited wilderness. There were people living in the wood, and he was their prisoner.

Duncan released a groan and rubbed his eyes, attempting to force his vision into clarity. He might have been confused, but the thrumming of urgency to return to the tower beat an undeniable pulse in his chest.

He pushed himself up, and the wound at his side screamed in rebellion when his muscles contracted. Ribs that must have been at least bruised, if not broken, protested as well, and it took him a full minute to catch a breath fulfilling enough to keep him conscious.

Once steadied, he let his eyes wander, blinking hard to force his vision clear. As he surveyed his surroundings, he shook his head, once again unsure if what he was seeing was real.

It wasn't a hut like those of his village. It was more a mix between a roundhouse and a tent. Large support beams stood as anchors for a cone-shaped roof that appeared to be covered with thick thatching. The walls were wattle and daub, but the entrance was covered with a fabric curtain.

A breeze caught the doorway fabric and snapped against it, capturing Duncan's attention and sparking the realization that he was alone.

Surely they wouldn't have left him unattended. He didn't know who these people were or how far from home he'd ended up, but he was certain Cyrene didn't trust him.

Had something happened? He rubbed his eyes again, still groggy from the tea and medicines he'd been given. He'd slipped in and out of consciousness since his conversation with Cyrene, but he was sure he'd heard a flurry of activity outside the walls of the hut.

Laughter and singing, voices carrying on in the ease of conversation, even the ting of blades in the rhythm he recognized as practice sparring. They were sounds of a vibrant village.

But as he listened then, he heard nothing. His heart sped up and ears perked at the absence of those sounds. Even in the abbey, evening bustled with activity. Only once before had he experienced such silence, and the next morning, Fiona was dead. His eyes darted about the hut in search of some explanation.

His panicked gaze finally settled on a slumped form at the table, and he blinked hard, rubbing his eyes a final time. Her arms stretched up and folded as a pillow for her head. Long golden braids masked her face, but he knew it was the lass they'd called Gertrud. At first, Duncan's pounding heart nearly stopped in fear she was dead, but as his eyes combed over her, he noticed the rise and fall of her back as she breathed the deep breaths of sleep.

Relief flooded like warm water over his skin. If Gertrud slept so peacefully, there was no danger. It was simply a quiet night.

Too quiet. He held his breath, silencing even the noise from his body and listened, finally hearing a soft noise in the distance. What was that?

A drumming? The trill of a pipe? He glanced back at Gertrud, still soundly sleeping. The hope of an idea surfaced among his still churning thoughts. Cyrene had all but promised to keep him captive until she was satisfied he was no threat, but he didn't have time to attempt to convince her of that.

Pausing at each creak of his cot, Duncan pushed himself to sit, giving his swimming head a moment to still. Gertrud didn't stir, and he doubted she would, from the empty cup turned aside, resting just beyond the reach of her fingers.

If she'd taken even a small taste of the man he'd heard them call Thaedry's mandrake tea, she'd be unwakeable—at least for a while.

He didn't see any sign of Thaedry, but surely he'd not leave

Gertrud alone long—if he were any kind of man—especially if she was sound asleep.

Though his legs felt as unsteady as young saplings, Duncan seized his opportunity. He was grateful they'd healed him but still didn't know to what end.

Lip clenched between his teeth to stifle his groans, he rose on shaky legs. His tunic was nowhere to be seen and had probably been too mangled to save, but his trousers, though torn, were slung over the back of a chair. He managed to get both legs into the softened leather pants before having to grip the hut's thick center beam for support. Sharp bolts of pain darkened his vision at first but slowly subsided. Near the hearth, he found his boots, thankfully in well enough condition to lace, and hanging over thin sapling racks, he found a brat nearly dry from being cleaned.

He labored to drape the heavy cloth over his shoulders and around his middle before he lurched toward the hut's opening. A staff waited, leaning against a pole near the doorway, as if placed there just for Duncan to use. He let it bear most of his weight as he hobbled through the fabric flaps into the crisp night.

He let his head fall back, sucking in lungfuls of fresh, cool, outside air for the first time in days. He'd been warm inside, but the oppressing suffocation of indoors had started to settle on his chest.

Those life-giving breaths hitched as his eyes fell upon an endless spread of huts erected between redwoods and firs so tall, they seemed to brush the sky. The black needles of the massive firs gobbled up the light.

He hadn't truly believed it, though he'd suggested it in a pain-induced stupor, but he suddenly realized he'd been right. He was in the woods. Deep within The Dorcha.

Visions from childhood stories meant to frighten him into obedience danced in his mind. Dead-eyed warriors that would materialize from the trees, silent as the grave. Beautiful pixies bewitching weak-minded men until they speared them through with talons that grew at the end of their hands instead of fingers.

He'd never believed them to be real, but there was also never supposed to be an entire kingdom hidden within either. Mayhap this kingdom had eliminated what Picts had escaped his father's reach. Mayhap they were worse than the Picts, and he was in real danger. He nearly crept back into Gertrud's hut, but couldn't reconcile those grim thoughts with the orderly rows of huts and the kindness of the sleeping healer. These weren't monsters; they were a people, just like his.

How had he never known of this place? Even so, his heart thundered with determination. If this was indeed The Dorcha, then he could find his way home.

What sky he could see was clear black and glittered with stars, just a sliver of moon to disrupt their glow. He immediately located the three blinking lights leading to the brightest in the sky. The North Star, a beacon for the sojourner, placed in the heavens by its Creator to always guide them home.

Duncan scanned the rows between huts. The entire village seemed empty. A rustle from beyond one of the huts captured Duncan's attention, and he hobbled in the opposite direction, ducking behind the corner of one of the small homes. Thaedry materialized from the darkness, juggling his torch and a large pail of water. Duncan folded himself into the shadows and listened, interpreting the thump, growl, and sloshing as poor Thaedry's misfortune with the heavy bucket. The sound of the healer retreating again into the night left Duncan pressing his forehead against the hut's rough wall in relief.

Heart pounding a thundering rhythm in his ears, Duncan tried to shake his head clear. He had to get to the tower. No matter what.

As long as he could see the sky, he'd be able to find his way. It was foolish to attempt such a journey in his condition, but concern for his people won over reason. Gertrud and Cyrene might be kind, but that didn't mean the leader of this group would be. He prayed God would give him the strength to at least make it to his own village, where he could acquire a horse.

Taranau! Another request shot heavenward that his trusted companion had escaped. Just days before, Duncan's prayers felt weighted to earth by doubt, his connection with God a faint shadow of what it should have been. But there, in the dark, in his desperation, he had no choice but to cling to the hope that God would guide him home, and if it was his will, would save his kingdom. He desperately wished for a word from the heavens, encouragement or direction or even chastisement—anything to know his prayers were heard. Mayhap it was only in the deepest valleys that a man's heart was humbled enough to hear from the Savior.

Forgive my doubt and pride, Lord. I was looking to myself for answers when I should have always been looking to ye.

He edged along the outskirts of the village, a wobbly staff his new companion. A growing concern at the nearing of a drumming beat lifted the hairs on the back of his neck. Checking his direction again by the stars, he continued.

Just beyond the rows of huts, a perfect circle of trees made way for a large clearing, bare inside save for a man-sized stack of wood in the center. On the other side of the clearing, Duncan could make out the faint color and shape of more homes. To the left and right of the clearing, he saw the same.

What he'd thought to be a whole village was only one section, and this man-made clearing was dead center of it all. There had to be nigh thirty homes in this secret place.

As he hobbled closer to the clearing, another light appeared, and another. They bobbed up and down in waves, making a circle inside the circle. The drumming rhythm matched the quick beats of his heart and seemed to beckon him even closer. A clear, pure tone whistled through the winter air, releasing a solemn tune.

He could possibly skirt around the outer edge of the homes, but it would take him off course, and he would risk getting lost or having to take a much longer journey, which his burning side warned against. Worse yet, he might be caught and lose any chance of getting back to the tower. He would have to simply attempt to sneak past them.

As he hobbled closer, floating lights became lanterns, and whistles became music. Bodies illuminated by the lanterns' fire became clear as they formed a swaying circle around a group of dancers dressed in white flowing dresses, who floated through an opening in the crowd.

Each dancer carried her own lantern as she jumped and twirled to the tune, and Duncan couldn't help but inch closer.

Suddenly, the dancers stilled, lanterns raised and bodies parting to form a path to the center of the circle.

From the darkness, a parade of warriors approached two at a time, side by side. Each carried a bow, outstretched as if presenting them to the people. They were mostly women with a handful of men; none looked older than he. As they reached the center, each pair split, marching in opposite directions until they met back on the other side. They formed a tight ring, then all was silent.

Duncan's eyes widened as he counted the growing circle of warriors. At least twenty.

He knew he should keep moving, but it was as if his feet had grown roots to plant him in that spot forever. He could only lean against the sturdy trunk of the redwood in front of him.

A clear voice rose from the silence, singing words in a language that Duncan didn't understand. The warriors parted again on the side from which they'd entered, and a single figure glided forward from the dark. A cloak of rich green shielded a thin, graceful shape, delicate trails of gold vines woven into the fabric from the hem to the hood that covered her head. Everyone, including Duncan, stood completely still in reverence.

The singer vocalized again, a beautifully haunting melody that ushered in the solitary dancer and wrapped around Duncan like winter wind.

Once the green-cloaked dancer reached the center of the circle, she extended her hands, accepted an offered torch, and approached the unlit stack of wood. In a smooth arc of her arm, she tossed the torch onto the wood, and flames devoured the cut branches, bathing each face with an eerie orange glow.

She stepped away from the blaze, standing perfectly still in front of the waiting crowd. In her hands, she held a long staff. She raised it to the heavens and spoke in the same language as the singer. Each person mimicked her movements and repeated the words. Then from the group, pipers and drummers stepped forward. The woman in the center reached up to lower her hood, a fountain of fiery auburn hair spilling from beneath, and Duncan felt his breath catch in his throat.

She swayed to the side, then back the other way, her hands moving in a dance that seemed ancient and sacred. She twirled the staff, as if a practiced tradition. Her back to him, she made a quarter turn, her position still concealing her face, and repeated the dance. When she made another turn, Duncan felt heat shoot up from his neck until it burned in his ears.

Even in his delirium, he'd memorized those features. The square tip of her nose, the fullness of her bottom lip. Defined cheekbones dusted with freckles.

"Cyrene." Only the smooth trunk of the redwood heard his declaration, but Duncan felt a jolt sweep through his limbs as if he'd been struck by lightning.

He pushed back into the shadows, scanning the faces of the crowd to see if he'd been heard. No. He was far too removed. Even if he'd been standing front and center, Duncan felt he would have been invisible.

All eyes were on Cyrene. She moved as though she had wings. Delicate and elegant, she lifted her arms, making sweeping motions through the air. When she'd made a complete turn, the warriors raised their bows to the heavens as if presenting an offering, then bowed to place them at their feet and joined in the dance.

The rest of the people followed, hands raised, then bowing, then dancing.

A warning slid up Duncan's spine, urging him to flee. To take what could be his only chance to run. But he was anchored to that spot, captivated. Villagers and warriors filled the clearing, singing and dancing in all directions, but Duncan could only watch one. The fascinating woman who wore a thin golden circlet over her vibrant, wild hair.

Then he knew, and his blood turned to ice in his veins.

He understood exactly who these people were.

They hadn't eliminated the Picts. They were Picts. They were what was left of the savage, pagan tribe which had betrayed their alliance with the tower and murdered the one person in all the world who'd loved him and his innocent sisters.

And Cyrene.

Cyrene was their queen.

His knees wobbled. He was forced to drop his staff and grip the redwood's trunk to keep from collapsing. He couldn't breathe, couldn't think. He could only stare at her angelic face.

How could something so beautiful be so godless and vile? His teeth ground together so hard, his jaw protested, and his fingers dug into the crumbling bark of the fir that supported him.

Cyrene suddenly stilled, her gaze scanning the crowd—and beyond. Just as her green irises settled on his hiding spot, he pushed himself back into the darkness again in time to hear a scream over the trill of a pipe.

It was a cry of panic, of fear. He jerked a furious glare back to the clearing. To Cyrene, who still focused directly on his hiding spot.

"What sacrifice will ye make now, Queen?" Duncan's seething accusation dripped from his mouth, and he ran the back of his hand along his chin.

He'd tarried far too long. He should go, get ahead of the warriors Cyrene was sure to send after him when his absence was discovered.

But again, he heard the cry. It came from the direction he'd just fled. He searched the woods, seeing nothing. None of the celebrating villagers seemed to have heard, not even Cyrene.

He took a labored step toward home but stopped. If this was some kind of pagan ritual, that scream could belong to an innocent victim. Mayhap even one from his own kingdom. Duncan slammed his fist into the unforgiving bark and hobbled back toward the healer's hut. Streaks of pain seared his side, and his strength was all but gone by the time he reached the first of the empty homes.

He fell against its sturdy corner, scanning the rows between huts, his throat lined with sand and breaths coming in short bursts. A commotion drew him further in, his fragile cane doing more than its share of holding him up.

A man held Gertrud from behind, her feet lifted off the ground as she kicked and fought and screamed. Thaedry lay motionless in a heap halfway inside the healer's hut.

"Where is he?" the man growled, struggling more than he ought against Gertrud's small frame. She was a wild animal in his arms.

Duncan took a step, his head swimming. The blurred shape of the man sparked a moment of recognition, but it faded as Duncan's pulse pounded in his ears.

Gertrud was a Pict. One of them. But she'd helped him. Saved him.

He had to move quickly before he joined Thaedry in unconsciousness and Gertrud was left alone. He might not be able to bring the man down, but he could break his hold, allowing Gertrud time to run for help. Lurching from his hiding place, Duncan stumbled forward, the cane raised above his head.

With one swing, the wood made contact with the skull of the healer's attacker, bringing both the man and his captive to the ground. Duncan followed them down, his chest so tight, and pain from his wound turning his breaths to wheezes. As his vision darkened, he saw the blurred shape of Gertrud scrambling toward him from beneath the heap of the man he'd felled.

15

CYRENE

821 AD - At the Same Time

The uplifted voices of her people filled Cyrene's heart with joy, and she found herself nearly dropping to her knees in reverence. The ceremony was one she'd witnessed and participated in dozens of times over the years. Though it had become an empty performance for her, she never once failed to attend and lead. She was and always would be faithful to *An T-aon*, but looking over the near-glowing faces of her people, she never expected to feel so . . . fulfilled.

She blinked back welling tears at the vision of her mother's face, which looked much the same. It was a memory she'd placed in the farthest corner of her mind, not willing to risk the heartache of revisiting it.

With the unrest they'd experienced and what was unfolding just beyond the borders of their world, she'd nearly postponed their ritual, but some unending ache in her chest wouldn't allow it. It was as if *An T-aon* was drawing them to himself. Especially with the unrest. Especially with the conflict stirring in her spirit. As if in rest, they might find their strength.

Something about the gathering together, as each individual gave of his or her heart—it strengthened them all. Cyrene felt a tightening in her chest, a conviction against the disdain she'd held onto for so many years. As if *An T-aon* himself was pleading with her to release it.

She'd thought all tower-dwellers selfish and immoral, thus justifying her feelings. Yet she'd seen with her own eyes at least one who'd sacrificed himself for his brethren. Even for one of her own.

Her thoughts were drawn to the man called Duncan. Thaedry seemed convinced he would recover, and he'd all but begged to return to the tower.

She gazed at the faces of her people. Their eyes upturned, hands woven together, they were free and protected. How could she allow him to leave? How could she betray her duty to them and risk their safety—all that they'd built?

Even if he didn't of his own accord, he could be persuaded by the Vikings. She'd heard of the horrors they would inflict to get the information they wanted. Not even the noblest man could be expected to resist that torture.

There was nowhere else for her people to go; she had to protect them here, in their hidden village. She'd promised them a home, and she kept her promises.

Her mother's last words rose up like the smoke from their fire offering: "Dunna turn yer back, daughter. Dunna trust the tower king."

All these thoughts of Duncan had her imagining his face in the shadows surrounding their gathering, and heat rushed up her spine. When she looked back to the spot where she'd pictured him watching, he was not there.

"My queen!" Astrid's bell-like tone rang above the celebration.

Something tight in her voice released yet another wave of fire across Cyrene's skin. "'Tis Gertrud! She's been attacked."

Cyrene's eyes darted to the space in the woods again, wondering if it had truly been her imagination.

"Was it—"

"Nay, m'lady. He is . . . I dunna know exactly what happened. 'Twasn't he, though. He saved her."

He saved her. Twice now, he'd helped her people. That news couldn't find a place to land inside her head. Tower-dwellers didn't save any but their own; they only destroyed. Her people were the kind ones, the ones who helped. An unexpected shame at her arrogance snaked around her wrists like binds and chilled her to the bone. She shook her hands as if she could free them from the invisible straps.

"Search the woods, Astrid. Take the warriors. And tell Revna to bring the soldier to my hut."

"Aye."

"Be vigilant; the night is black and shadows thick."

Astrid made haste to the warriors, and Cyrene gathered the skirts of her gown, tearing through laughing groups of people toward the healer's hut.

16

DUNCAN

821 AD - The Next Morning

The smell of pine and mint drifted through the air. Duncan's eyes were so heavy, he sought to use his fingers to lift leaden lids but found his limbs nearly as weighted. The wound in his side burned as he drew in a deep breath and exhaled a groan.

"Easy now."

That voice. He knew it, and his weary eyes crept open with great effort.

Cyrene appeared as a ghost, blurred by exhaustion and seeming to float toward him. Would he ever be fully conscious again?

"Do ye mean to kill me now, Huntress?" His attempt to flee would be known, and there was no need for tricks or games.

"Not today."

He thought the whisper of a grin played at the edges of her lips, but he could still barely get his eyes to focus. Murderous queens didn't smile, did they?

"How . . . what is the day?"

"'Tis the None."

The None . . . that meant he'd been gone a full four days. Again, he tried to sit up, but was nailed in place by the searing pain in his side.

"Here, some broth."

Placing the bowl beside the cot, she lifted Duncan by the shoulders. He stiffened under her touch, and she eyed him cautiously as she stuffed a fur behind his back until he was sitting up. He took the broth she offered but didn't drink, though its aroma was tempting.

Cyrene watched him for a moment, her eyes dipping to his untouched food. She moved to the hearth and drew her own serving, taking a purposeful sip.

He felt small under her stare, but partook of the broth until his vision had fully cleared.

This was not the healer's hut.

Rich colored stretches of fabric lined the walls. Furs covered a wooden plank floor beneath a table and chairs in the middle. One chair was larger than the others, with scrollwork decorating the arms and back—a royal masterpiece.

"Thank ye." Duncan lifted the bowl to his lips and gazed at Cyrene over the top, visions of her graceful dancing, however godless it may have been, drifting through his memory. "Yer Majesty."

Her brow jumped at his address, a flash of emotion reddening her cheeks before she brought it back under control.

"I suppose I should say the same to ye."

Specks of a memory dotted his mind. Gertrud's screams, a hulking figure, the crack of wood on bone. He'd thought it a dream, but mayhap not. Was she thanking him for helping Gertrud, or saying she knew who he was? An arrow of heat flew up Duncan's spine, the flames instantly frozen by Cyrene's characteristic wall of ice stacked between them. Cold. Impassable.

"So . . . thank ye as well, Duncan." The heat cooled as Cyrene lifted her hands, palms together as if in prayer, and gave him a slight bow of gratitude.

Duncan disguised his sigh of relief as a pained breath and attempted to keep his disdain for the beautiful, deadly leader hidden as well. At least his identity was still hidden.

"Is Gertrud well?" He chose an easy question to begin negotiations. Though she didn't know it, this was a meeting between two royals. Playing political games was his least favorite part of being king, and in his current state, Duncan's confidence in his ability to win was shaken.

"Aye." There was that brow again, arching over her grass green eyes. "Though she is quite furious with ye."

Under the heavy waves of fatigue and pain, Duncan had almost forgotten the question she'd just answered.

"Why is that?" Duncan forced his attention back to the savory liquid. Was it simply the knowledge that this woman led such brutal people that made his insides squirm?

"Ye nearly cost her a patient." Cyrene placed her empty bowl on the table.

"Please extend my apologies to the lass." When he finished, he lay the bowl in his lap, feeling energized by the pottage and whatever herbs had been added.

He didn't know what she would do if she discovered his identity, he didn't know the state of his army, he didn't know if Eowin had been successful in the mission to secure aid—he only knew one thing. He had to find a way back home. Mayhap his rescue of Gertrud would be enough for Cyrene to release him without a fight. A life for a life. Surely even pagans honored that understanding.

He allowed his gaze to sweep over her, a slight sadness worming its way into his heart. A fleeting hope that, like Fiona, surviving Picts had abandoned their godless ways in the years since her death faded at the memory of their ceremony. It was clear they still held to the ancient traditions.

146

His hand drifted to his side, finding fresh bandages, then to the empty bowl in his lap. He felt his mouth bend into a frown, and he placed the bowl on the stool next to the bed.

"Does it hurt verra badly?" Cyrene lifted her hand, motioning to his wound, when Duncan cocked his head to the side.

"Oh. Nay. 'Tis well."

Her question hadn't made sense to him. Her kindness didn't either. Nothing about this place or this woman made sense. They were nothing like the devils his father had described. If it weren't for that ritual he'd witnessed, he'd have thought his father mistaken at best and an evil liar at worst. Mayhap that was part of their curse—they were talented deceivers.

Fueled by frustration and desperation, Duncan lifted his feet, turning to sit on the edge of the cot with a stifled groan. He ran his hands through his curls and scrubbed calloused palms over his face before pushing himself up to stand.

"Ye shouldna—"

"I am well." Duncan's outstretched hand stopped Cyrene's approach, as did the clip in his tone. Just as quickly, he dropped his arm, chastising himself for such a blunder. That wasn't how a layman would speak to a queen. "I beg yer pardon, m'lady. I just meant . . . I canna lay down any longer."

Cyrene dipped her head, acquiescing to his request. She only watched as he stretched his arms across his body, working out the stiffness in his joints. They both knew he wasn't well enough to try to run, and her easy yet dignified pose showed no hints of worry or fear. His breath was still shortened by the pain in his side, and he'd be lost this deep in the wood without stars to guide him.

If he'd only kept going the night before. Shame at such a thought brought his eyes low, as did the imagined outcome of Gertrud's fate had he not intervened.

His gaze shot back up to the cool queen. Cyrene hadn't mentioned the stranger. Who was he? What had they done to him? So many secrets. Duncan held his tongue. Demanding answers was the response of a king, not a common man. He would have to play a game of a different manner.

Something familiar caught his eye over her shoulder. Held between two x-shaped limbs strapped together was the staff she'd used in her dance.

"May I?" He nodded toward the object, and Cyrene stepped aside, allowing him near.

Without touching it, Duncan examined the smoothed staff. It lay in a cradle of thin branches that had been cut, stripped of bark, and smoothed almost to perfection. Now up close, he could see intricate designs carved into the wood. Mayhap symbols of that language they'd spoken. Leather straps seemed to pour from each end, both decorated with the same designs.

"Will you tell me what this means?" His gaze traveled along the line of the staff and up toward Cyrene, who was eying him curiously, her chin tipped upward in that queenly way that made so much sense to him now. There had been something *other* about her—he'd recognized it even in his delirium.

In a step, she drew up beside him, close enough that the fabric of her skirts brushed his arm, and he could detect the scent of her hair. Fresh mint and wild elderflower.

He cursed his foolish senses for noting every scent and manner-ism, his idiotic brain for its acute awareness of her every move, and his defiant heart for finding pleasure in those minute details. No matter how delicate her beauty, she was the leader of the people responsible for ripping his kingdom apart and destroying him with grief.

Duncan schooled his emotions, keeping his expression placid.

Tenderly, she lifted the leather straps, allowing them to drag across her slender fingers before falling back into place. "The symbols say, Hear, O Israel. The Lord is our God—"

"The Lord is One." A tightness seized Duncan's chest as their eyes met.

"You know the scriptures?" A new expression replaced the usual suspicion on Cyrene's face, her eyebrows no longer turned disapprovingly down toward the other but now lifted in intrigue. Duncan shared her surprise.

She was Christian. How could she be Christian?

"I do." With her silent permission, he ran his hand across the carved surface of the wood, fingers exploring each intricately carved symbol. "He is the God of my people."

At this, he heard Cyrene's gasp, and her lips parted in a way that almost revealed an emotion, but much to Duncan's disappointment, they closed together again in nearly the same instant. Despite his confusion, he felt immense satisfaction that in the matter of a minute, he'd succeeded in breaking through a tiny bit of Queen Cyrene's cool exterior.

"I ken of a church in Tràigh, but dinna ken the building to be in use."

The truth of her statement stung. Though the priest kept the lanterns lit and doors unlocked, Duncan couldn't say for certain if any of the villagers attended his services.

This new knowledge was a paddle that swirled everything he thought to be true about the Picts into a muddled mess. "How long have your people been worshippers of the one true God?"

"It was before my mother's time. And even far beyond my grandmother. 'Twas the *peregrini* that came from across the sea to share, and they believed."

He knew that term, and not only from his studies at the abbey. A bit of Latin still infiltrated their language from centuries ago, when the Romans invaded. A remnant, apparently even among the Picts.

"The Wanderers." Duncan's hands found his chin, palms scrubbing across the coarse hair of his beard. "Because the Irish missionaries wandered after Christ."

Cyrene nodded. "The stories speak of a man called Columba who brought Christ to the land here. They say the fire of his temper caused a great destruction, yet *An T-aon* turned that into a passion for the gospel. Though he was the cause of much loss, he also became the voice that carried the message through which many were saved."

"*An T-aon?*" Duncan repeated the unfamiliar phrase.

"It means 'The Only One.'"

He knew that term too. It was what Fiona had called God. He stared at Cyrene, whirling thoughts unable to land. They shared more than a complicated and confusing past; they shared the origin of their faith as well.

That couldn't be right. "Then how could ye . . ."

Cyrene watched him as he felt the walls built from all he'd always known to be true suddenly start to crumble.

"How could we what?"

Duncan cleared his throat, searching for a way around the end of that question. "I meant to say, what made yer people turn from the old ways?"

"My mother told me once that when a person has only ever known darkness, their first exposure to light sometimes burns, but once ye be touched by that light—once ye can see when ye had been blind—'tis all ye crave."

Duncan could only stare at the staff. A simple carved stick had taken his world and turned it on its end, much as a simple hewn tree, built in the shape of a cross, had been the tool through which Jesus turned the world on its end.

The words of another missionary named Patrick floated through his mind and out of his mouth. "He watched over me before I knew him and before I learned sense or even distinguished between good and evil."

When Cyrene didn't respond, Duncan looked up to see a strange look on her face, as if maybe some walls inside of her were crumbling too.

"A beautiful sentiment," she said, her voice catching.

"'Tis something a wise person said long ago."

"Ye said before that ye have studied." Cyrene's statement was more of a question that drew a blank stare from Duncan. He blinked until her words made sense.

"Aye. Three years, I studied the ancient scriptures."

"Only that?" Cyrene shifted to face him.

"Nay; the priests felt it beneficial for us to learn history and sciences as well."

She would have been just a child when Fiona died. But when he realized the true identity of her people, his heart had branded her as a killer. Looking at her now, knowing her people had been subject to the same divine law as he, her image began to change.

He'd seen her eyes before, knew they were a lovely jade green, but as she stood close, he also detected flecks of gold dancing about her irises. Knowing of her faith only served to amplify her beauty, but something in that discovery also disturbed him greatly. If they were not responsible for Fiona's death, who was? And why had his father blamed them?

"Are ye true, Duncan?" His name on her lips nearly stole his breath, and the nearby torches must have caught the light in her eyes, because they blazed as if lit from within.

Who was he trying to fool? He was no match for her.

"Are ye an honest man?" The simplicity of her question broke him, for there in those five words, she revealed such vulnerability, and he wanted nothing more than to throw himself on the ground at her feet and offer her his undying allegiance.

"I . . . I try to be, m'lady." How could he be true though, when his whole life could have been one massive lie?

Nay. It couldn't be true. She might be Christian, but Christians had the capability to sin still. And just because she was a believer, mayhap some of her people were not. One of the former queen's guard could still have taken Fiona and the bairns' lives. He was not out of danger yet.

He looked up to find her staring at him, his gaze captured as if she'd thrown a net around him. She looked deeper, and he felt a tug in his gut, like she had reached inside and tried to pull something out. It drew him to her without his permission and kicked his heart into a sprint. The minute she looked away, the feeling was gone and his head swam, leaving him unstable on his feet.

"I believe ye." Her curt whisper added to his wobbliness.

It should have been the beginning of a treaty between them, but somehow his honesty seemed to bother her, almost anger her. As the questions now raised about his own history deeply disturbed him.

"May I sit?" Duncan's hand hovered over his aching side as he edged toward the table, slowly lowering himself into one of the chairs when she nodded.

Despite the lingering discomfort of that moment with her, a wave of assurance swept warmly over him. Now that he knew she believed as he did, he felt quite certain her plan was not to serve him up as human sacrifice to some unknown and powerless god. If he could get her to talk, mayhap Cyrene would understand why he needed to return to his throne. Duncan decided to extend the first offering.

"The staff you use," Duncan said, tipping his head toward the wooden totem. "'Tis like the mezuzah of the Jewish people."

Cyrene moved a chair but didn't lower herself into it. He tried not to shrink under her penetrating gaze, instead examining his fingers as he continued his explanation.

"In my studies, I learned they would fix their mezuzah to the doorposts of their homes. Even now, they carve the words into the wood or etch them into the stone. I see that ye and yer people do something similar. Ye bind them to yerselves."

Duncan nodded toward the bands that adorned her wrists and waist. The symbols pressed into the leather were the same as on the staff. Cyrene did smile then—at least, he thought it might have been a smile as she traced the markings with her finger. She stepped away from the table, and it was all Duncan could do to keep his jaw from dropping open in awe as she lifted the decorated staff in a move so devastatingly graceful, it hurt.

"To our hands, our head, our feet, and our waist."

Any sounds drifting in from outside fell silent as she spoke. The clear ringing of her voice took its place, and as she sang, her long fingers moved, dancing across each area of her body. The air in the hut became thick, pressing in on Duncan as if embracing him, and a chill prickled across his skin as he recognized the melody. It was the same song she'd performed at the ceremony, now repeated in his language.

"I bind the truth to my body that I might not forget." She lifted her arm, the staff rotating above her head between her fingers. With a perfect spin, the straps swirled around her.

"I fix the words of *An T-aon* to my hands, that everything I touch may feel his love through them." A flick of her wrist sent the staff sliding along her shoulders, leather straps snaking their way up her arms.

"I adorn my head wi' the Word, that all my thoughts be ever turned to him." She turned again, the staff gripped on both ends by her ivory-skinned hands.

Duncan's eyes widened as she pulled her hands apart and the staff became two separate pieces, the leather straps not attached at the end as he'd thought, but pulled through the middle by some hollowed-out tunnel. How had he not noticed during her fireside dance?

The revealed leather of the middle became a crown as she twisted the two ends of the staff behind her head but for a second before untwisting once more. The two separated ends of the staff joined together by the length of leather moved from one of her hands to the other as she twirled and tossed them in a perfectly crafted dance.

"I affix them to my feet, that they be ever moved forward in service to him." She flung one end of the staff downward, her foot catching and stopping its flight while the leather straps wrapped around her slender ankle like the ties of a sandal.

"And I fill my form wi' the bread of life, that I might feast on his righteousness for eternity." A tip of her toe sent the half-staff twirling back up toward her hands, where she caught it mid-flight and snapped the two ends back together as if one solid piece at her waist. Her final movements were strong, quick, and short—as if in battle.

Duncan was struck silent by the sacredness of her stilled pose. The stance of a warrior, humble yet fierce, elegance capturing Duncan's breath in his lungs. Only when she lowered her arms softly to her side was he allowed to exhale.

She extended the staff, presenting it to Duncan. He let it rest in his open palms, feeling unworthy to do anything more. "I dinna understand . . ."

"'Twas you I saw then." When Duncan flicked a questioning glance her way, she reached for the staff, which he returned. "Last night in the woods, when we were worshiping *An T-aon*."

"I thought ye were . . ."

"Pagan?"

"Bonnie." The word slipped out before Duncan could stop himself, but he recovered with a half-smile and bow of his head. "A bonnie ceremony."

When she didn't answer, Duncan gazed up at her through his lashes. Cyrene's lips twitched in a way that suggested she was in a battle for the correct response.

"Aye," she finally said with a wave of her hand. "'Tis a lovely offering."

Duncan lowered his eyes again, fully aware that wasn't what he meant. He heard the rustle of her skirt as she moved, and took the opportunity to assess her again.

Despite the way she allowed her fiery waist-length hair to remain unbraided except for delicate rows at the sides of her fair face, she was every bit as regal as any queen who ruled from a tower. Mayhap more. He wanted to come right out and demand to know if her people had done the atrocious things his father claimed. As king, it was his right, but he wasn't in his kingdom—he was in hers.

"M'lady. Will ye tell me what happened? How Gertrud came to be in such a state?"

Cyrene turned to replace the staff on its stand, her back to him as she spoke.

"'Twas my fault." Her words were so soft, he barely heard them but dared not ask her to repeat them.

Duncan rested his elbows on the table, fingers interlaced over his mouth as he waited.

"I left too few to guard, and pulled my scouts." Her shoulders rose and fell with a deep inhale. "'Twas just fer the night. We've not once missed a ceremony, but it was foolish to think ourselves invincible. Especially after . . ."

Her voice trailed off, and she took a step back, staring at the staff for a long second before she turned to face him, jaw tight and eyes blazing.

"A man from yer kingdom found us, found my home." Her words came through clenched teeth, and Duncan made himself a statue, frozen. "He slipped past my guard and found Gertrud in the clearing —looking for ye, I imagine."

If he came from Duncan's kingdom, was he a Viking or one of his own countrymen?

"He was looking for me?"

She nodded, that arched brow both suspicious and knowing.

"Toward what end?" Duncan's throat was instantly dry.

"I canna say if his words can be trusted."

"M'lady, I am sor—"

"Nay." Cyrene waved her hand, then approached, taking the chair across from him and folding her hands in the same manner as he. "Had ye not returned, I canna imagine what would have happened to her."

"The man? Does he live?"

"Aye."

"Does he speak?"

"Aye."

155

"What does he say?"

"Ye were leaving." Cyrene leaned forward, her movement trapping Duncan's gaze. "First tell me why ye came back."

"I heard her screams. I thought . . ." He could no longer say what he'd actually thought. "I couldna just leave her. Wouldna been right."

"Why?"

Duncan sat back against the chair, her question insulting. "Why? Because she needed help."

"Who is she to ye?"

"No one." Duncan's fingers raked through his curls again, her interrogation not making any sense. Did Cyrene think him to be smitten by Gertrud? That his actions were anything untoward? "She's a living, breathing person. Created in God's image. She needed help. How could I not . . . and ye . . . all ye did."

Cyrene's eyes narrowed as she considered his answer.

"Please, m'lady. What does he say?"

Her mouth moved to the side, lips pursed as she considered his request. Then she leaned forward again, eyes narrowed and voice no more than the whisper of the wind.

"He says naught but that ye are his friend."

17

CYRENE

821 AD - Half an Hour Later

"Eowin!" Duncan flew toward the captive and would have reached him, had not her warriors linked their arms under his and held him back. "What news of the tower? What news, Eowin?"

Cyrene observed the rage that befell Duncan's expression as he examined the captive he called Eowin, who had been bound and forced to his knees by her warriors. What of his dark hair not bound at his neck hung tangled and loose, nearly reaching his shoulders. A deep purple bruise encircled one of his stormy gray eyes, nearly swollen shut from the injury. A gash along his other cheek had stopped bleeding but remained red and angry.

Duncan flashed an accusatory sneer at Cyrene. It was the first violent sign she'd seen since he arrived, and while she'd made preconceived judgments, it still startled her after how civilized he'd been. Mayhap her initial instincts were correct, and he could only hide his true nature for so long. He might have studied the scriptures, but that didn't mean he lived by them.

"We dinna harm him," she bit back at his unspoken accusations. "He was such when we found him. Aside from the wound on his head from yer blow."

Duncan's expression twisted into a blend of fury and pain before he wrapped his arms around himself and doubled over. His wound was still grave enough that the walk from her hut to this one had him panting, and her warriors needn't work to restrain him, despite his size.

This captive clearly meant a lot to Duncan. Cyrene had hidden her surprise at the relief in his tone when they entered the hut on the farthest outskirts of the village. Astrid ordered the scouts to double their watch, but Cyrene requested no guards on the outside of the prisoner's hut. She wanted to avoid an unnecessary outbreak of fear.

Astrid obliged but packed the dwelling nearly full with guards on the inside and led an extra patrol of the village herself. Despite his size, mayhap six armed warriors, including Liam, was overkill for one man, but Astrid said she wasn't about to underestimate her enemies again.

"Si—" The man snapped his lips closed and struggled against his bonds, eyes wide with a mix of anger and concern. Cyrene wondered what he'd stopped himself from saying.

When Duncan groaned, breaths escaping through his teeth, the prisoner's zeal to be free was renewed. Liam was thrown to the ground by the shove of his shoulder, and Cyrene reconsidered her opinion of the number of warriors needed to subdue him.

"What have ye done to him?" The growl in Eowin's voice was enough for the two maiden warriors holding Duncan to release him and draw their spears, aiming sharpened stone tips at the captive.

Without their support, Duncan's knees gave way, and Cyrene moved to catch him as he headed to the ground. Unable to bear his full weight, she guided him gently down, Eowin's demands growing more frantic as Duncan descended.

"What have ye done? Release me!"

"Eowin, calm." Reaching past her, Cyrene felt the heat of Duncan's breathed plea on her neck as he pushed toward the captive. "Let me go to him."

She straightened, her muscles tense at his nearness, at the warmth of his hand on her waist as he gripped her to support himself. She ground her teeth, resisting the initial temptation to dart across the room.

She was Cyrene, Queen of the Woodlands. The mysterious enchantress that fed wild—albeit untrue—tales from the villagers. How could a single unintentional encounter draw up such strong emotions?

Pulling in a measured breath, she relaxed her hold, allowing him movement in the small space between them. Duncan didn't try to free the man, but simply placed his hand on the back of Eowin's head and drew it to his own until their foreheads touched in a simple and familiar greeting.

"I am well, my friend, and have these people to thank."

Eowin released a rebellious hiss as the maidens pulled him away from Duncan. Cyrene assisted as Duncan stood, stepping silently away from him once he was steady.

"They said ye were dead!" Eowin twisted and jerked, his muscles bulging beneath his tunic, bonds groaning against the force. Cyrene flicked her eyes to the maidens guarding him, signaling them to close in. Their spear tips at his shoulders stilled his fight, and he lowered his voice to a husky whisper as if sharing a message only Duncan would understand. "The villagers have assembled in the keep."

Cyrene narrowed her gaze upon Duncan. She'd decided her earlier prediction about his station was correct. He must be the son of a nobleman, mayhap enduring a term in the king's warband—he was too educated to be a common villager, too well-trained in battle to be a farmer, and lacked the inescapable sea salt smell of a fisherman.

But this news, word of his welfare important enough to cause a stir amongst the village, had her heart beating faster, and she heightened her stature in hopes Duncan couldn't read the interest in her expression.

"Nay, Eowin. Calm." Duncan moved toward Cyrene, hands extended in invisible offering. "Please, m'lady, release him. He'll do ye no harm."

His size alone was enough to fuel her suspicions, if not the memories of Gertrud's tear-stained face, which vividly reminded her of the harm most certainly intended for the young healer.

"This man attacked one of our own. We are merciful, but we have laws. There is only one fate for one such as he." Cyrene's hard stare did nothing to diminish Duncan's persistence.

His eyes widened as two warriors dragged Eowin to his feet until he towered over even Liam. Though it clearly pained him, Duncan straightened, his arms outstretched toward both Cyrene and Eowin.

"I've ken this man my entire life. He wouldna have hurt Gertrud; only meant to silence her screams, as he was in search of his . . . friend."

Eowin's vigorous nodding added proof to Duncan's claim.

"Ye were the one to strike him down."

"Had I ken the man I saw was Eowin, I wouldna struck him—I wasna in my right mind, m'lady."

The rough rope binding Eowin's hands popped and cracked against the strain of his resistance, his skin red and raw from the struggle. His eyes flicked in turn from each of her guards, then to Duncan. She could see the desperation as clear as the beads of sweat across his brow. It was killing this captive to be at a disadvantage while his friend was injured and vulnerable.

No. Not his friend.

For she had seen that same protective desire in the eyes of her own warriors. Duncan was no mere friend.

Cyrene stepped suddenly back, heat rising above the rounded collar of her tunic. Sensing her alarm, her warriors inched closer, Eowin stilling under the tips of spears that now pressed into the flesh of his neck and shoulders. Not piercing, but painful with the threat.

Duncan's eyes darkened but never left hers, and in a single blink, she witnessed understanding pass across his face, his countenance shifting almost instantly.

Not a friend. Not a soldier; not even a young laird.

Despite his injury, Duncan drew to his full height, chin lifting ever so slightly. The ease at which they had conversed finally made sense.

The man standing before her, the man they'd been caring for and allowing into their perfectly hidden world—was not at all what she thought.

He was the king of Tràigh.

The enemy.

Bloodkin to the one who'd killed her mother. Who nearly succeeded in annihilating her people. And Beli.

A different heat filled Cyrene's veins, the rage of an injustice done, and she reached for the longbow that was not in its place across her chest.

Instantly, a wall of warriors appeared between her and Duncan, two still struggling to restrain Eowin.

He was no longer the unfortunate injured soldier who mistakenly wandered into her territory. He was the evil tower king. She couldn't see Duncan's face; she could only see his father's.

The pulse pounding in her ears turned into the drum of marching boots. The hiss of her breath became the wheezing final gasps of every one of her murdered countrymen. And Beli's roar, quieted by the peace of many winters, awoke from where it slumbered, echoing so loudly in her mind, she covered her ears.

How could this be? How could he have found her, tricked her into welcoming him in, deceived her into nearly trusting him?

Whatever kindness she'd been considering vanished, replaced by the phantom sting of frost from so many endless winters. She'd been a fool! A weak, silly fool.

Duncan's eyes widened when she withdrew two short blades from her waist belt, and his hands flew out to his sides, shielding his companion. Not from her warriors.

From her.

Without an order, the warriors turned from guarding Cyrene to subduing Eowin. One pushed against the back of his knees as two others forced his shoulders down. He was on his knees again, more spears at his throat and chest. They pressed in close, causing him to suck in a sharp breath through bared teeth at the nick of a spear that sent a line of blood racing down his neck toward his collarbone. She advanced on him, lifting her hand with plans to push Duncan away with a hand to his chest and carry out Eowin's sentence herself. In an act that shocked every person in the hut, including Eowin, Duncan paled and dropped to his knees.

Cyrene's hand on the tower king's chest stilled, for as he'd knelt, he'd also clasped both his large hands around hers, his fingers covering the sharp blades still gripped in her fists.

If she moved even an inch, they would slice through his skin.

All manner of royal pride disappeared as he lowered his head, his forehead pressing against the back of her fingers. His grasp was firm, but didn't hurt her.

"Release the queen." Liam charged on Duncan, pressing the tip of his spear to Duncan's neck, dangerously close to the place where the king's pulse danced under his skin.

He didn't resist, but lifted his fingers and simply let his hands fall limply in his lap.

"Please, Yer Majesty." Duncan looked up at her.

How many nights had she dreamt of this moment? Of bringing the despicable king to his knees and condemning him to his face? But it wasn't William who knelt before her, and those weren't his empty, lifeless eyes. They were Duncan's. Clear and pleading and as blue as the sky. This man was an impossible choice in himself.

His raspy voice, humble and broken, tore something loose inside her chest. "We . . . I beg yer mercy."

"Mercy?" She nearly laughed. Calculated words gave way to an explosion of emotion. "The king, your father, slaughtered the Picts without cause. He offered no mercy."

Duncan's red-ringed eyes grew wide, his expression a mix of sadness and shock. That feigned surprise only stirred her ire. How dare he pretend not to know?

"And Fiona."

His mouth dropped open at her name.

"And her bairns."

He winced at the mention of his infant sisters.

"She was one of them. She was . . ." Cyrene's voice broke under the emotion, and she shook her head, unable to continue. Her eyes burned with the salt of tears she refused to release. She couldn't even speak as if she were one of the Picts herself. She had to step outside her lineage to keep herself together. "What he did to them, to—"

Grief choked off the rest. *Beli, Beli, Beli.* A shuttered breath chased the excruciating agony of that memory. Of leaving him behind, the courage of a lion his only defense. Of the impossible choices she was forced to make. Again and again.

"What did he do?" Duncan reached for her, but she curled her lip and jerked back. He lost his balance, but caught himself before he landed face-first on the packed dirt floor.

"As if ye dunna ken."

Duncan dragged himself to his feet, his face nearly as white as the moon, and sweat darkening his blond hair. One of the warriors grabbed his arm, but he jerked free, facing off with Cyrene, his determination equal to hers.

"Tell me, Huntress," he demanded, a rage of his own brewing behind cobalt eyes. "What do ye think I ken?"

Cyrene let her gaze bore into him, praying that even an ounce of her fury would somehow reach the late King William where he lay awaiting eternal judgment.

"She was murdered."

"By whom?" He was near shaking at those two tight words, his hands in fists at his sides.

Cyrene stepped forward, lifting her chin. His only movement was the heaving of his chest as he stared down at her, her face mere inches from his.

She spoke her next words as a curse through her teeth. "Her dear, loving husband."

"You lie!" Eowin roared from behind Duncan, and the warriors forced him back to his knees, their ready spears daring him to speak again.

Cyrene ignored Eowin's outburst. Instead, she followed the king, who stumbled backwards as if she'd struck him. Eowin made some noise, and Cyrene jerked her head toward the hut's door.

His shouts of protest fell silent under the warrior's threats as he was hauled outside.

"Leave us," Cyrene barked at the ones who remained to guard her. Most obeyed without blinking, but Liam hesitated, his eyes dancing between Cyrene and Duncan. "Out, Liam."

His jaw muscles feathered under his skin at the clenching of his teeth, but with one final warning glare aimed at the tower king, Liam whipped the curtain aside and stormed out.

Duncan seemed too stunned to register he'd been left alone with Cyrene.

"Explain." Duncan's order pulled her features into a sneer.

She didn't owe him any explanation. He could suffer in his ignorance, for all she cared.

"Huntress." He ran his fingers through his mussed curls, his tone suddenly soft and pleading. "I'm sorry."

He took a step toward her but stopped when she tensed. "Please, will ye tell me?"

She crossed her arms over her chest.

"Please," he said again.

She released a long breath and searched her memory for a way to speak aloud the truth she'd kept locked away in her mind. A truth pieced together from what she'd witnessed herself and from what she'd learned from Brígid and the elders.

"Derelei never fully trusted the king of Tràigh. When he chose Fiona, Derelei sent the captain of her warriors to play lady in waiting. To protect her. And she did. Eden never left her side, not for one minute."

Brígid had entertained them with many stories as children. Tales of their history, of lovers, of heroes, and even monsters. She would tell them over and over. But this story—this one she only whispered once through shaking, tear-quaked breaths—Cyrene had never forgotten—and never repeated, until now.

The hut was silent, the king frozen under the terrible spell of her tale. Cyrene kept her emerald eyes aimed at Duncan, examining him for any signs of recognition, any clue that he already knew this particular yarn.

"Until one night, Eden fell ill after a meal. She said it was as if weights were strapped to her limbs. She could barely move and soon fell into a deep sleep. When she woke, it was before dawn. She clawed her way to Fiona, certain she'd been poisoned on purpose. She thought she was dreaming the whole time, because there were no guards anywhere. When she reached the queen's chambers, she saw him." Cyrene's jaw clenched so tight it hurt as she glared at the fair king, who rocked on his unsteady feet, barely standing.

"Who?" Duncan didn't move, didn't even breathe.

Her next words were like the lashes of a whip, and he winced at each one. "The king. Though he dinna see her. He was slipping out of her door like a fox, bathed in blood."

Duncan choked on some weak denial as his head fell and Cyrene coolly delivered the tragic conclusion. "Fiona's body was still warm when Eden dragged herself to the queen's side and heard the horns sound to announce the opening of the gates at the keep."

Cyrene's ribs ached, her lungs burning as if she'd run miles and miles.

"But Fiona was a Pict, and Picts dunna give in easily." Her lips pulled back in a victorious sneer as she added the final detail to her tragic story. "Eden discovered a dagger still clenched in Fiona's hand. Her murderer dinna escape unscathed."

She saw Duncan's face drain of any remaining color, his eyes refusing to meet hers. He knew something. Something he didn't want to know.

"'Twas yer mother." Duncan's voice was raspy, strained. "At the gate?"

Cyrene tipped her head.

"Why?"

"Why else? 'Twas custom to bring gifts for the bairns." Cyrene watched him carefully, unsure of what lies he'd been told. "The king sent a servant to bring Fiona, but he returned, announcing Fiona had been found, and the king ordered his men to hold my mother and her guard as he raced inside the tower."

Duncan searched the ground, as if proof of her claims were scattered across the dirt.

"When he returned, making a show of his grief, he called my mother to a private meeting. I dunna ken what they discussed, but when they emerged, the news had come that the bairns were missing, and the king flew into a rage. My mother escaped the tower with a wound from his sword and only two of her guards."

There was more to the story, but he would have known the rest. It was no secret.

"Dunna ye ken, werna ye there?"

"Aye . . . but I was just a lad, and my brother took me from the keep as soon as the servant came with news of Fiona." Duncan's voice was that of a dead man, empty and lifeless.

"We learned later that Eden was accused of killing Fiona and her bairns." Cyrene watched as each of her words seemed to break something inside of Duncan. "He claimed the servant caught her in the act."

Cyrene cocked her head to the side. Did he know any of this? "Did ye not hear from the servant yerself?"

166

"My fa . . ." Duncan cleared his throat. "The king had him executed. All the guards and servants in the tower that night were executed before the sun set that day."

He turned away, and Cyrene sniffed a knowing breath. *Coward.*

"Does she still live? Eden?" Duncan didn't face her, but only turned his head to look slightly over his shoulder.

"She came to my mother and spoke of what she had seen. She rode in the queen's stead to face the king's troops at the border." Cyrene could still see the brave captain of her mother's army disappearing with her warriors over the foggy moor. "She dinna return."

He stood very still for the length of three deep breaths, her story drawing his broad shoulders down. Suddenly, he turned to face her.

"What of the bairns? Their wraps were found by the sea. It was said—"

"I ken what they said. We dunna sacrifice innocent bairns." Cyrene shook her head, disgust sharpening her tone.

"But the captain . . . Eden? The bairns were not in Fiona's chambers that night. The ladies attending Fiona were fiercely loyal to my father. They'd have brought his bairns straight to him if they thought there was danger. Eden dinna say if she saw them or heard them that night?"

"Eden hoped the same. She left Fiona and found the wet-nurse." Cyrene softened her tone. Those bairns were his sisters, and she could read the desperation, the hope, in his expression. He must have known what she would say, though. "The bairns were gone, and the nurse . . . ye must ken what happened to her."

Duncan's hands flew to his mouth, his eyes squeezed shut, and he shook his head as if trying to rid his mind of some terrible knowledge.

"Nay," he breathed, then shoved his hands through his hair, clenching handfuls of curls in his fists. "Nay, nay, nay. He wouldn't."

Was this display some kind of show? Some façade to gain her sympathy? It was her turn to demand answers. "What do ye ken?"

Duncan scrubbed at his face before he lifted his empty hands as if offering her something.

"I . . . I heard something that night. Someone coming from the direction of the ladies' chambers—I thought it was a guard. I dinna see who, but he stopped outside Fiona's chambers, then he made a noise . . . a cough . . . and I ken."

When she didn't respond, Duncan folded his arms, his shoulders curling in as if he were hunched against a raging wind.

"'Twas the king." He didn't seem to be saying this for Cyrene's benefit as much as his own. "'Twas before he met with yer mother."

It was true. She'd believed it from the beginning, but there had been no evidence to verify the innocence of her people. Duncan's face was as pale as hers felt. She almost felt sorry for him. Could it all be just another deception?

He didn't move as she approached and grabbed his chin, lifting his face so she could see his eyes. They were bloodshot and lined with silver. There was sadness there, but also a spark of anger. If it were some manner of play, it was convincing. *Truth Keeper.* That's what her mother had called her. Cyrene turned her gaze loose on his, winding through the halls of his mind, searching for that truth.

Duncan's chest stilled as she dug into his very essence, hunting down the lie. His lips moved, words held back by her capturing stare. There was no deceit in him.

"I'm sorry." The croaked apology was nothing more than a gasp, but powerful enough to break her gaze.

"Sorry?" She nearly spat the word.

Cyrene slammed the door shut against the memories that threatened to send her to her knees.

"Yer sorry isna enough." Did not her people deserve vengeance? There was no mercy shown them. Why should she extend it now?

"I . . . there are so many things that dunna make sense." Duncan's whisper froze her in place. He swung his blue eyes to hers, desperation etched on every line of his face. "I dunna ken the truth—the whole of it, I mean, but I am sorry for what he did to yer people. To ye."

Teeth clenched together so hard, she thought they might shatter, Cyrene's mind battled the rising whisper from her heart. The small breeze of irritation that carried with it a conviction against her anger and desire for revenge. Duncan's own words gave power to the wind, like a voice in answer to her own question.

I should show mercy because he was a living, breathing person. Created in God's image. He needed help.

Cyrene acknowledged the pain in her forearms and released the fists she'd been clenching. It had been so long since she'd felt the weight of *An T-aon's* presence so fervently; mayhap not since she was a lass and worshiping at her mother's side. Though it went against what was truly her desire, what *felt* right, she breathed in the soft correction from what she knew to be the Spirit of *An T-aon.*

The compassion she battled ached in her chest, and she marched to the doorway, gulping down lungfuls of fresh air.

"Release him." Cyrene waved her hand, signaling two maidens who had stationed themselves on either side of the entrance. Liam was noticeably absent. Cyrene was secretly glad he'd not been waiting with judgment in his eyes.

She stepped through the doorway, eyeing Eowin, who now stood free of restraint. "Release them both."

She witnessed a drop in Eowin's shoulders at her command, and a wary disbelief in his stare when Duncan was hauled out of the hut. He didn't trust her. She could respect that. She didn't trust him either.

Their silent battle of wills only ended once Eowin's bonds had been cut and he dove for his king.

"Sire," Eowin breathed, his arms folded around Duncan's chest, aiding him, but Eowin's eyes measured the threat still circling him.

Duncan knew swordplay, was obviously skilled in fighting, but Eowin was a true soldier—even captain, mayhap. She could see the plans he was making, the way his sharp eyes registered every threat.

169

In a matter of seconds, he assessed his surroundings, taking care to not let his gaze linger too long on any one place.

Even the way his muscles flexed as he seemed to give a small bounce in his hold of the man in his arms, as if estimating how far he could carry Duncan should the need arise. King Duncan.

Sire. That was the word he'd clipped before. Cyrene wasn't schooled in the hierarchy of a tower king's court, but the way Duncan had gone to his knees for one of his own made her think mayhap he wasn't either.

Mayhap he had become as she, a ruler of a different sort. Something . . . other. Mayhap together . . . no, the word tasted sour in her mouth. She still didn't know what to do with the two men.

"The Picts were blamed for someone else's crime. They were hunted, taken, abused. That is truth." Cyrene's voice grew in strength as she delivered her response.

Tapping the hand Eowin still used to support him, Duncan stood, sweating and near green, but on his own.

"Yer father massacred them. That is truth." Cyrene stopped to swallow the grief that nearly exploded into the volatile silence of the hut. "He used Fiona. Wed her, killed her, and then used her again as an excuse to steal the Pictish lands. He was a tyrant who cared only for his wealth and wishes. Why should I believe ye to be any different?"

Duncan moved like a lion, closing the gap between himself and the queen in one long stride. She stood her ground, and he didn't seem to notice the maidens who shifted to surround him with an arc of sharpened metal spears.

He towered above her, fierce, masculine power emanating from his form. A warning. But Cyrene refused to tremble before him. She would never crawl at the feet of the tower king. She bowed to *An T-aon* alone. She refused to break his gaze, even as she registered the feathering of his jaw, the flare of his nostrils, the rumbling of a smothered rage he was fighting to contain.

"I loved Fiona." When he spoke, the deep timbre of his voice was broken with a fierceness that tightened the muscles in Cyrene's stomach. "I am not the same, Huntress."

Chin lifted, she met his piercing gaze stare for stare. They were so close, they shared a breath as she challenged him without fear. "Doesna his blood run in yer veins?"

Though his breathing hitched and skin continued to drain of color, Duncan did not stumble, he did not falter. There was a calm strength behind his eyes, a gentle power he'd kept hidden from her until then.

"Doesna each man choose how he shall live? Whom he shall serve? And each king, how he shall rule?"

His words were so impassioned, a chill swept across Cyrene's skin. Something akin to admiration blossomed in her chest, and she considered how long it had been since someone had surprised her as much as this tower-dwelling king that was causing more than just an upheaval in their peaceful village. His arrival had unearthed something long buried inside of her heart as well. Something that grated against the comfortable existence Cyrene had grown accustomed to. Something that had shaken a finger at her meager faith and labeled it as entirely inadequate.

"Aye." Her simple response did little to quench the fire in his eyes, and she decided to do a little surprising of her own.

She turned to her warrior maidens still armed and ready with their spears.

"Help His Majesty to my quarters." She didn't bother to hide her sarcasm. When Duncan opened his mouth, presumably to ask after Eowin, she nodded in his direction. "The captive as well. I wish to speak in private."

The maidens moved in formation to flank her and the men as they traveled. Two maidens made to reach for him when he stumbled, but the king waved them off. They looked to their queen, whose subtle nod had them lowering their arms but keeping within a half-step. Eowin stayed even closer, Cyrene acutely aware of his keen eyes surveying their village as they walked.

"I was ten."

Surprised to find him at her side, Cyrene shot a narrowed glare to the rasping king. She didn't ask for clarification at his strange statement. She only flicked her eyes in his direction as they walked.

"When I lost Fiona. I was ten. How old were ye?"

She sucked in a sharp breath through her nose, committed not to share any more of her heartbreak with this stranger. At the sound of Duncan's labored breaths at her side, Cyrene quickened her steps, but he kept pace, though she could tell it was difficult.

He wasn't slowing, and kept his expectant eyes centered on her. She clicked her tongue, annoyed with his persistence, and turned determined eyes to his.

"Eight." She snapped the answer as would a starving dog at a bit of meat.

"And when ye took yer oaths?"

This time, she refused to look at him, her mouth drawn into a hard line. "The same."

At Duncan's wheezing, Eowin offered his shoulder for support. Duncan finally accepted, and she stormed out of the humiliating range of his pitiful stare.

18

DUNCAN

821 AD - Minutes Later

He barely made it to the wooden chair around Cyrene's table. Throat dry and the wound in his side sending streaks of sharp pain across his middle, he let his head rest on his fist. It was not proper for a king to appear so weak, but after all that had transpired in the last few days, especially in the last hour, he was beyond propriety with Cyrene and her people.

Her version of what happened to Fiona couldn't find a place to settle in his mind. It didn't fit with the facts long set in place, and her words were stomping through his brain, kicking up memories and tearing them to pieces.

She'd uncovered bits that he'd buried and strung them up like lanterns in the darkness.

"Sire." Eowin sat in the chair beside him, his hand warming

Duncan's shoulder. "Who are these people? Why do they care so much about the Picts?"

Cyrene had her maidens lead them to her hut, where the male warrior she'd called Liam waited. His disapproval was as evident as Cyrene's annoyance when he asked for a word with the queen. She'd nodded for Duncan and Eowin to enter while she remained outside. He could hear the murmur of a soft argument from beyond the fabric covering of her door and leaned close to Eowin to engage in his own quiet conversation.

"They *are* the Picts."

Eowin shot up, a growl tearing free from his lips. Duncan didn't raise his head, but jerked the captain back into his chair with a firm grasp on his arm.

"Sit. There is much ye dunna ken." By the time Duncan finished explaining all that he'd learned, Cyrene still hadn't returned, but Eowin had calmed and sank back into his chair with his head in his hands.

"It doesna make sense." Eowin sat forward again, glancing at the doorway. "Picts have been pagans for hundreds of years."

"I dunna think we were told the truth, Eowin." For the first time, Duncan spoke aloud the grating suspicion he'd felt even as a child. "I think my father lied."

"But . . . why?"

"Evil doesna need a reason to be evil." Brodric's claim floated to the surface of the sea of memories churning up waves in Duncan's mind.

"Duncan." Eowin rarely used his name, never taking advantage of their long-standing friendship. "Ye arna speaking against yer father, are ye?"

"I remembered something . . . something from that night."

Eowin leaned even closer.

"I heard someone outside Fiona's room that I heard cough." Duncan explained the significance of this memory while Eowin's brows inched closer together. "But there was something else too."

"Aye?"

Duncan scrubbed his hands over his growing beard, forcing his mouth to keep moving. "I heard it again outside my door. The same cough."

Eowin didn't speak. He simply stared at Duncan, waiting.

"It was my father."

"That doesna prove anything. He had the right to walk the halls of his own home."

"There's something else, Eowin. Something I canna explain." Duncan slammed his fist against the table, then tensed, glancing at the hut's entrance. He could still hear voices outside. Perhaps no one had heard his outburst. "Cyrene said Eden found a blade in Fiona's hand. That she'd injured her attacker. When I heard his steps approaching Fiona's chambers, they were as one would expect. But after, when he was at my door . . . my father was limping. He was wounded."

"There was a fight at the gates, we all ken as much. It could have been—"

"This was before anyone discovered Fiona. Before the Pictish queen arrived," Duncan hissed, raising his fist but flexing his fingers to keep from pounding the table again.

Eowin gathered his mussed hair and tied it back neatly at his neck, then rubbed his hands across his forehead. This information clearly disturbed him as much as it did Duncan. He swallowed hard and cocked his head to the side. He was about to speak when Cyrene entered.

Her cheeks were flushed, he assumed from whatever conflict had transpired with the warrior outside. When she noticed him watching, she narrowed her eyes and walked with purpose to the hearth, pouring water from a kettle into a metal mug. No doubt their argument was regarding his presence and what to do with him. From the possessive watch the warrior had kept on Cyrene, Duncan assumed the young man had some hope of a future ruling by her side. Now that they knew he was the king of Tràigh, he doubted

Gertrud's rescue was enough to secure his release. He needed something more.

Duncan exchanged a glance with Eowin, who raised his brows and tipped his head a fraction toward the queen.

"Tell me of the tower, Eowin." He turned his attention to his captain, pretending not to notice when she stilled and her shoulders stiffened. "What state did ye find it?"

Eowin glanced at Cyrene, then back to Duncan.

"'Tis well." Duncan lifted weary eyes to Cyrene, who had turned to face him and was regarding him more warily than she had ever before. Time was short; he had to take some risks. "I trust the queen."

Cyrene's eyes widened slightly, then, as he was learning was her way, she brought her expression under control, revealing nothing. He made himself a note to ask her to teach him how to do that.

"'Tis under siege, m'lord." Eowin seemed to understand Duncan's game and folded his hands together, his tone grave. "And two of yer advisors were killed the night ye disappeared."

Duncan felt the little food he'd eaten threaten to evacuate and pressed a palm flat against his stomach to school his muscles into submission. Cyrene poured another mug of tea and placed it on the table next to Duncan.

"Who?"

"Toran and Ligulf."

A flex of his hand was the only means to still the trembling. "They came to me that evening with something related to the traitor."

"What was it?"

"I dinna get to hear. A maid brought news of the Norsemen, and I left right away. What of the others? The rest of my household?"

"I dunna ken." With sea-gray eyes cut suspiciously to Cyrene, Eowin stood, pacing across the small space of her hut. "When ye werna there to meet us, we had to travel round the wood, and entered a battle already waging."

"Does the inner wall yet hold?"

"Aye." Eowin stopped pacing. "At least, it did. But now . . . I dunna ken." Eowin opened his mouth and closed it again.

"Speak, Captain." Duncan's eyes blazed, demanding the full report from his man.

Eowin swallowed hard before aiming his gaze at the statuesque queen. "They were gathered at the weakest points, m'lord. As if they ken just where to strike."

A shiver ran through Duncan's frame, and he felt himself sway, even as he sat in the chair. Two hands, one on each shoulder, steadied him. Eowin on one side, and Cyrene on the other.

Heat flashed across his skin, causing his pulse to race. There was no time. Someone knew their defense strategies. Someone wanted them all to die.

Duncan refused to allow his eyes to close, not even to blink. For each time, his mind flooded with visions of ant-like soldiers pouring across the land, devouring his kingdom in a sea of blood and ash.

"Wha . . . who?" Though he already knew, he needed to be sure.

"'Twas the colors of your kin, sire. Laird William."

Cyrene tensed, jerking her hand from his arm, and Duncan took his turn to reach for her. She retreated from his touch as if he were an asp. *William.* That name stirred something so deep and dark in her, he could practically smell the smoke of her burning rage.

"William is dead." Her words were a hiss, spoken through clenched teeth.

He'd witnessed the outcome of his father's rage against her people. He flinched at the echoing sound of the soldier's footsteps. He could feel Brodric's hands pulling him away from the window as he glimpsed an endless line of Picts, chained together, being marched through the courtyard. No wonder she hated him.

"William, my father, is dead." Duncan spoke, his voice soft as he worked hard to control his rage at both the past and the present. "William, my cousin, is very much alive. I suspected the gathering army was his."

"They attacked from the south." Eowin's expression morphed into something else, something angry and violent, and Cyrene's posture took a defensive shape.

"From the south?" Duncan heard Cyrene whisper, but kept his attention on Eowin.

"They dinna attempt to surround from the seaside, just pushed us back and waited, almost as if . . ."

"As if what?" Duncan clenched his fists, pounding one hard on the wooden table. "Speak, Eowin!"

"As if they're waiting for something."

The suggestion drained the color from Duncan's face, and a breath flew from his lungs as if he'd been struck.

"The men will hold the tower to the last, but the storehouses are still sparse from the last Viking raid. The villagers willna last long."

"What of aid from Nàbaidh? Will Laorn come?"

Eowin's expression fell further, and Duncan's hope with it. He felt the weight of a thousand bricks upon his shoulders, pushing him down and down and down until he would be buried under defeat.

"He dinna say nay, but he couldna promise aye either. His own kingdom was still rebuilding from a recent battle."

Duncan sighed in frustration. "What is left of the warband?"

"I was told no more than sixty."

"Only sixty?" As he spoke it, the number cut across his throat, choking him. Sixty of what was once nearly one hundred before the Vikings came.

"And what of William's forces—how do they fare?"

"Nigh three hundred attacked, sire. Many lost of that, 'tis certain, but their will is strong."

What was left to be done? Eowin began his pacing again.

"We were told ye'd been killed. I dunna ken how he got to them, but William even presented yer robe and crown—both covered in blood, but I ken it wasna true. The men . . . they created a distraction, and I went fer ye."

"How did ye find me?"

Eowin glanced again at Cyrene, the threat seeming to dissipate a bit from his glare, and he turned a smile on Duncan. "Taranau."

Duncan sat a bit taller at the mention of his horse. "He lives?"

"Aye." Some small twitch of a smile tugged at the corner of Eowin's mouth. "We returned from Nàbaidh and rode right into battle. I only ken what I told ye because some of yer army still remained defending what was left of the outer wall. We were pushed back toward the village, and I saw him. This was tucked under the saddle."

Eowin reached beneath his torn tunic, producing a bright blue feather. "I assume this belongs to ye, m'lady?" He bowed his head slightly as he presented the feather to the queen and grinned once more at Duncan. "'Twas Taranau that led me here."

"Where is he now?" Duncan's gaze darted between Eowin and Cyrene.

She drew in a slow breath as she unfolded her arms and extended her delicate fingers, accepting the feather. "He is wi' my maidens. We have a stable. Dunna worry; he is being quite spoiled."

"William has to ken ye arna dead. I ken he'd come looking for ye. I dinna want to leave the men to fight without their captain, but I had to find ye. I had to ken if ye were . . ." Eowin shook his head, emotion cutting off his words. Then he turned to Cyrene. "I am sorry for scaring the lass. I wouldna have hurt her. I was only trying to find His Majesty. I thought ye were part of William's people. I thought ye'd taken him."

Duncan clapped a hand on Eowin's shoulder, allowing both of them a moment of subdued celebration at their reunion. "Thank ye, my friend."

The moment passed too quickly, and a thick blanket of dread settled over Duncan's shoulders.

"If the keep is breached, he willna keep our men alive. He'll torture them and anyone they love to find me, and once he realizes they dunna ken where I am, he'll have no more use for them."

"What do ye want to do, sire?" Eowin leaned toward Duncan, his folded arms bearing his weight.

"What of the north? Are there any ships?" Duncan noticed Cyrene's chin ticked in interest at his question.

"Nay." Eowin pushed back a thick strand of hair that refused to stay captured with the rest. "But if the Norsemen return and attack from the sea, the tower will fall."

"I dunna think we vanquished them all at their last attack."

Eowin's brows jumped in curiosity at Duncan's suggestion.

"They came from nowhere, Eowin. When I took the men to defend the village, they surrounded us, but there were no ships. They must have come with the others and remained hidden in the sea caves."

"They'd have seen what happened to their countrymen." Eowin sat back in his chair. "They would have watched them all die."

Both men fell silent. Eowin spoke first.

"Do ye think yer cousin has made a bargain wi' the Norsemen?"

"Only a fool would strike such an accord, but of those that pursued my men into the woods—not all were Vikings." Duncan's eyes refused to focus as he pictured the state of his lands, fury stirring heat up his neck. "In the end, he'll get a blade in the heart. One way or the other."

"We need to return. Let the men see their king is alive. Rally what forces we have left and pray for aid from Nàbaidh." Eowin passed an obvious look across Cyrene as he bent closer to Duncan. "Before the battle spreads beyond our borders."

Duncan watched the queen. Her expression remained stoic, not revealing any sign she'd registered the implication of Eowin's warning. He lowered his head, attention focused on his folded hands.

"M'lady?" He cut his gaze up to Cyrene, unfolding his hands to present her with empty palms. "I thank ye for yer kindness, for saving my life. I ken the hate ye must feel toward my father. But I amna he. His battles arna my battles. I willna harm ye nor yer people. Eowin nor I willna even speak of this land, but please allow me to try to save my people. They are innocent in all this."

She remained quiet. He knew she'd been listening closely, weighing their situation and analyzing every word. She was smart, that much was clear—set on protecting her people. He just wasn't sure how far she would go to do so. Would she prevent him from leaving? Would she keep him prisoner or worse?

"I shall have my warriors take ye to the edge of the wood." Cyrene spoke finally, taking the chair opposite Eowin and next to Duncan. "I will let ye go."

She straightened, shoulders strong and regal. Then her emerald eyes turned dark, threatening. "But I willna wi'hold my wrath from anyone who crosses our borders again. It doesna matter which kingdom they are from. It doesna matter if they are soldier or farmer. There will be no mercy. Do what ye have to do to keep yer people out of The Dorcha."

Her words were so filled with conviction, Duncan's blood ran cold. She meant every word. It seemed like she had something else to say, so Duncan waited, flicking a look to Eowin, hinting for him to do the same.

Her shoulders relaxed so slightly, he wasn't sure he'd truly seen it. But when she spoke again, her voice was softer. "But what can ye do against such odds?"

What could he do? Sixty battle-weary soldiers against his cousin's hundreds and possible alignment with the Vikings. He looked at Cyrene, her expression expectant but removed. As if this had nothing at all to do with her. She had to know; she had to at least be preparing for the possibility of the battle reaching her woods.

"Would ye not again go for aid?" Cyrene left the table to retrieve a rolled parchment from a basket and returned, uncurling the paper to reveal an inked map of the lands.

Duncan examined the drawing, feeling certain his initial plan was still the best.

"I can send riders again to Nàbaidh, but we canna wait. Supplies and strength will run out." Duncan leaned forward on his elbows, catching Cyrene's attention. "Ye should ready yer warriors."

Despite the wariness leadening his bones, Duncan's tone exuded authority. A king back on his throne, even if an enemy threatened to occupy the actual dais.

"'Tis not our battle." Cyrene's brows arched together, her fingers threaded in front of her as if she'd just done something as simple as turn down a strawberry tarte.

"'Tis everyone's battle, dunna ye see?" Heat flooded up Duncan's neck.

"We are safe here. We have been for more than a decade, and here we will stay."

"Ye canna be this blind."

Cyrene's lowered brows piqued at his insult, but he continued. "I found ye. Eowin found ye. Ye arna as hidden as ye think."

"Are ye threatening me?" She was angry. He could see that, but behind her ire, flicked a spark of fear. He had to proceed cautiously lest she revoke her promise to allow him to leave.

"Nay. Of course nay. But the battle will come. If my kingdom falls to William, he will certainly claim this land for his own. And these woods arna so large they willna find ye eventually, even if by accident." Her gaze flicked to the side, and Duncan sat up taller. "They already have, haven't they? Someone else found ye?"

Cyrene didn't answer.

"Can ye take yer people over the mountain? Find safer lands?"

"We willna run." Her hands curled into fists, her determination matching his own.

"Then get ready to fight." He pushed back from the table, wincing at the pain that seared from his side.

"Ye brought this to us." Cyrene stood abruptly, her words biting as she leaned toward him, her weight braced on her hands.

Eowin slammed his fist on the table. "Dunna speak to the king in such—"

"Eowin." Duncan's sharp reproach silenced the captain, and Duncan turned back to the seething queen. Mayhap she was right. Mayhap he did bring this terror to her door.

"It doesna matter how or why; the enemy has come. We have to act. To decide how to move forward, how to protect our people now. It is up to us. Ready yer warriors, Yer Majesty." Duncan's tone softened. "I beg ye."

He felt the tension from Eowin at his side, his friend staring between the two leaders, waiting.

"My people have seen enough of war." Cyrene met him toe to toe, never wavering. "I shall do whatever it takes to make sure they dunna see it again."

Duncan wasn't sure what she meant by that, but she seemed to have ended the conversation, because she moved to the entrance of her hut and opened the fabric for a maiden warrior who stepped in and immediately set almond-shaped eyes on Eowin. She was dressed in fighting leathers, generously armed with blades at her side and a longbow across her back.

More than her distinctive brow, strong, straight nose, and high cheekbones, it was her thick white-blond hair that caused Duncan and Eowin both to freeze in place. She was a Viking. And she was loyal to the queen.

A spark of challenge filled the hut with renewed tension, and Duncan realized he was witnessing the captains of two armies squaring off.

Cyrene set her sharp green eyes on Duncan, their force pinning him in place. "If ye bring yer battle here, or try to return, ye will only find death."

Eowin tensed, but Duncan lifted his fingers in a silent order for the captain to remain still.

"Astrid." Cyrene's authority drew the warrior's attention. "See the king and his captain to a hut. Before dawn, have Revna and her scouts take them to the border."

Cyrene passed her gaze over Duncan and Eowin, stripping them bare with the ice in her eyes. "See they are well protected."

Duncan deciphered her order to mean she wanted them heavily guarded. There was to be no trust between them.

"Aye, m'lady." Astrid bowed but didn't lower her sky-blue eyes from Eowin's, defiance wafting from her as strong as the scent of pine in the forest.

The twitch of Eowin's lips into a subtle grin didn't go unnoticed, and Astrid released an unnerving growl in response. Duncan shoved Eowin toward the door before the two of them tore the hut apart.

"Thank ye." Duncan slowed as he neared Cyrene, who still waited by the exit. "Truly."

She only offered a formal nod. He paused, wanting to say . . . something, anything. His kingdom had plenty of enemies, and her people had been the greatest of them for most of his life. But for some reason, he couldn't stand the thought of her hating him. Mayhap it was because Fiona was as beloved to her as she was to him. Mayhap it was the slow realization that his father might not have been a monster only in his dreams. *Ye are nothing like me.* For the first time, he didn't consider those words an insult.

He searched his vocabulary, but there were no magic words to thaw the ice she wore as armor, so he exhaled a ragged breath of disappointment instead.

As Duncan took the final step toward the exit, Cyrene's hand grazed his arm, and she dropped the curtain, leaving them alone in the hut. She didn't look at him, but where her fingers touched his skin, he felt fire, not ice, and he stilled, his heart picking up its pace. He stopped close enough that if she looked up, he'd feel her breath on his face.

"Ye were right." Her whisper was so painfully quiet, Duncan remained frozen, waiting. "A Norseman did find us."

He was surprised at the fire that threat against her ignited in his chest, and his eyes roamed her face, searching for hints of injury. He saw none, but his jaw ached from the force with which he clenched his teeth. Neither of them moved, as if they were under a spell of truce and one flinch would break it. Cyrene sent one glance toward the curtain that cut them off from the rest of her village before she turned fire-lit eyes on him and delivered Gertrud's report.

"A stolen crown? A wind from both the north and the south?" Duncan scanned the floor, trying to put together the full meaning. "The Norsemen do ken of my cousin's plan. The fool!"

Cyrene nodded. "I think yer wise to keep close watch along the sea."

A warning. An offering he hadn't expected.

"Aye." Duncan's gaze danced back and forth between hers. He'd seen the moment she realized his status. She'd been so angry, as if she wished him to drop dead right in front of her so she could spit on his corpse. Yet as they stood almost breathing each other's breaths, she seemed . . . afraid.

She didn't wish for his kingdom to be destroyed. Of course she wouldn't. She might hate him and all he stood for, but since his father died, the tower was no threat to her or her people. Despite her stone exterior, inside was a human with a heart of flesh who had to feel the same sense of dread as he at what was coming.

He risked a soft grip of her elbow and didn't know how to feel when she didn't pull away. "I promise to keep them from the woods as long as I can. But, m'lady, if the keep is breached and my crown falls . . . I'llna be able to protect ye." He tipped his head, forcing her to meet his eyes. "Ready yer warriors."

"I will take care of my people." Her words were short but her tone soft. "There is safe passage for ye to the mountains . . . if ye need to flee."

He searched her eyes, not understanding what she meant. Then it sank in. She knew his army couldn't defeat such a strong enemy. She was offering him a way to live.

It was more of a gift than he'd expected to ever receive from her after what her people had suffered under his father's rule.

He pushed back the curtains, and as they stepped out of her hut, he followed Cyrene's gaze to the sky.

"He spoke of a new moon," she said.

Through the canopy of the forest, only a sliver of white appeared in a cloudless star-speckled sky. The new moon was only two nights away.

Long seconds passed before the walls she'd temporarily let down were constructed again, and Duncan knew his time was up. He bowed another thanks before meeting Eowin where he was engaged in a staring war with Astrid.

Once he and Eowin were shown to an empty hut, he shared what he'd learned from Cyrene, including a suspected timeline, and didn't bother suppressing a groan as he lowered himself onto one of the cots.

"What is it between ye and the wild queen?" Eowin collapsed on the second cot, a muscled arm stretched, propping his head up.

"I dunna ken what ye mean." Duncan let his lids fall closed, knowing sleep was near, whether he wished it or not.

Eowin snorted and grumbled something about Duncan being in denial. They lay in silence. He assumed Eowin was as suspicious as he that Astrid or possibly the scout Cyrene mentioned was lurking just outside to eavesdrop. Or mayhap neither wanted to state the obvious. With a coordinated attack from both land and sea, Cyrene was right—there was no hope of victory.

"Her warriors," Eowin finally said, his whisper husky. "Are they well trained?"

"They bested those attacking me. They bested ye." Duncan blinked, flashes of their quick end to the men who'd set upon him like bits of some long-ago dream in his mind. He was so tired, his eyes burned when he closed them, so he forced them to stay open, tracing the lines of the thatching roof above him. "They're as skilled as any of our men. Mayhap better with the bow than some, at least."

"How many?" Eowin either ignored or didn't catch Duncan's dig at his poor skills with the longbow.

Duncan turned on his side and propped his head up on his palm, eyes narrowed in curiosity.

"Twenty, maybe," he whispered, even quieter. "What are ye thinking?"

Eowin scrubbed a calloused palm across his bruised face. "If Nàbaidh willna send aid . . ."

"Ye think to ask the queen?"

"Ye said it yerself—the battle is upon us all. If we face them alone, we will fall. If she faces them alone, she will fall. But mayhap if we had a secret alliance of our own . . ." Eowin's voice trailed off into the silence.

"An alliance," Duncan breathed, rolling onto his back again.

"Or a union?"

Duncan twisted his head to see Eowin looking at him, a devious expression twisting his friend's lips into a half-smile.

"Ye canna be serious? The great Eowin . . . suggesting marriage?" Duncan scoffed at the cone-shaped roof. "Is this not the same man that said he'd rather be drowned in the sea?"

"We arna talking about me."

Duncan looked at his friend, catching the tail end of a full grin before Eowin's expression grew serious. "A true queen of Tràigh. The sacred uniting of her kingdom and yers? It's the only way our people —and hers—will believe a peace has been struck. The only way her warriors and ours willna turn on each other in the battle—or after."

"A wife, though?" Duncan hissed, flashes of Fiona's tear-stained face and his father's uncaring scowl filling his mind. Duncan's stomach churned at the thought. "Is that why ye dinna argue against staying the night?"

Eowin huffed a half-hearted laugh. "Somewhat. I also believe we should time yer return carefully. Use yer sudden appearance to our advantage."

Duncan hummed in agreement, then fell silent to his thoughts. A marriage. To Cyrene. Of all the men in the world, he would be the very last she'd agree to, and he wasn't sure he'd even want her to.

"Yer advisors will choose a bride for ye soon enough. Better ye choose fer yerself."

He suspected that's why Cyrene had given him the warning. She needed him to win. His crown was a safer enemy than his cousin and the Vikings. As preposterous as the suggestion was, Eowin had a point. At least this way, he'd have some say in the matter. Cyrene was certainly beautiful; he could do a lot worse. But it was folly to consider.

"She'll never agree. She hates us. Hates me."

"Canna hurt to ask."

"She might say aye just to kill me in my sleep."

Eowin's deep chuckle filled the hut with a lightness Duncan appreciated. "She's smart enough to at least bear an heir first."

At the mention of a bairn, Duncan nearly choked on his next breath and sent Eowin into a laughing fit as he coughed his way back to breathing normally.

"She may be wild, but there's enough civility here, she must ken the way of things. She wouldna risk the next king being worse. And she hasna killed ye yet," Eowin said, his laughter finally subsiding. "Besides, I see a lot of ye in her."

"What do ye mean?"

"Yer both unbearably stubborn, and both will do anything to protect yer people."

"I should have ye flogged for such insults to the crown." Despite his taunting, Duncan let Eowin's proposal settle over his bones, filling his thoughts with possibilities, both heavenly and nightmarish. But even considering asking her felt like the execution of his one selfish secret wish. "Even if she agrees, it would be eighty against three hundred . . ."

"'Tis the only way." Eowin turned his back to Duncan, soft snoring drifting through the hut a few minutes later.

19

DUNCAN

821 AD - The Next Morning

Duncan stood over the map of Tràigh he'd requested at dawn, comparing it with the numbers Eowin had scratched on parchment.

Too few. No matter how he positioned them, with the intel Eowin provided, there was only enough for a thin line—much too easily overcome. He'd be sending his men to die. And die they would, with honor, for their king and country. But their sacrifice would be in vain. It soured Duncan's stomach to even consider asking it of them.

He slammed a fist onto the rickety table, and a plate heaped with bread and dried meat jumped from the impact. An ache in his side reminded him he was still not completely healed, though Thaedry's poultice and herb teas must have been nothing less than magical potions, as quickly as he'd recovered.

If only King Laorn had agreed to bring aid. But betting on that frail possibility wasn't a risk he could take. There were no good moves, no turn of play that could result in their victory. Not without . . .

"I went to the stables." Cyrene appeared in the hut's opening. "They said ye hadna arrived."

Duncan straightened, clearing his throat. "Aye. Eowin felt it best to make a solid plan, get plenty of rest, and eat before the journey."

"I would agree." She glided into the hut, keeping something behind her back. From outside, a ting of blades colliding piqued Duncan's interest, as well as the half-smile Cyrene wore. "I thought yer journey delayed, as yer friend canna seem to leave without a challenge of skill wi' Astrid."

"Oh." The word fell flat. Duncan felt completely inept, given the other challenge Eowin had issued the night before. His men were waiting, the battle was waiting, and yet there he stood like a bumbling fool, wasting time.

"Revna has fallen for Taranau. I practically had to order her to ready him for yer travels." Cyrene's tone was pleasant, questioning, almost as if she, too, were stalling.

"Revna?"

"My scout. She will take ye to the edge of the wood." Aside from the brief moments she'd shared the faith of her people, this was the friendliest she'd been with him. It was a farewell, a Godspeed, and an unspoken understanding that he was about to face an unwinnable battle.

Duncan offered a weak grin and hummed in amusement before he let his gaze drift back to the parchment, every ounce of hope soaked into the ink that sketched crooked lines around his lands. It seemed so small drawn out there on the yellowed paper, but enclosed in that jagged shape were living people. Men, women, and children who depended on him to keep them safe. Doubt filled his bones, and he sank into a chair, hands plunging into his wild curls.

He would fail them. They would be slaughtered, sold, and enslaved, and as much as he would try, it wouldn't be enough. He wasn't enough. It was suddenly as clear as the map rolled before him.

"We canna win."

Cyrene stilled when he asked her to do what he knew she could not: "Fight wi' me."

As Duncan tried and failed to persuade her, to see the dangers that were coming, to lead her away from the conclusion he'd already reached in his mind, he could see the battle raging in the depths of her eyes, green as the forest she called home.

He captured her small wrists as she turned her wrath on him, and accepted her accusations. His patience wore thin and tone bordered on threatening as he made promises he fully intended to keep but knew she wouldn't believe.

She was right. His people would never accept her promise of peace either.

Unless.

He shoved his fingers through his hair and dropped his hands to his hips. Was he really about to do this? He had to. Eowin was right. There was no other way. He heard the shuffle of her boots as she moved toward the doorway.

She was leaving. It was over.

"I'm sorry," she whispered so softly, he was certain she didn't mean for him to hear.

"M'lady, wait." Duncan took a step, voice so low, she stilled, frozen. "There is one way."

She looked over her shoulder, her eyes scanning his face, his neck, his chest, measuring the panic he was trying to hide.

Then as his lips parted, she jerked her head away, as if she knew what he was about to ask. Of her. Of her heart.

God forgive me. He drew in a delaying breath before he spoke again.

"Marry me." The words came out quicker than he'd planned. Her only response was the tightening of her fist on the fabric of the curtain at the door. "Become the queen of Tràigh.

"Yer right. There is no accord or agreement we could strike in this short time that would satisfy the fears of yer people and mine. None except this."

He had to keep talking, keep her from darting through the doorway and sending Astrid in to drive him away with the tip of her sword in his back, or mayhap through his heart.

"As leaders, we are called to give all of ourselves. Our wants and needs, our very lives, surrendered for the good of our people. I can see ye have given yer heart to yer people. I see how ye care for them and would do anything to save them. I hope ye see the same in me."

He waited. Allowed her to absorb his words. She didn't face him but turned her head to the side, only the slightest nod giving him a hint that she would allow him to continue.

"I willna ask ye to love me. But . . ."

Duncan paused as she finally turned, her hands exchanging the curtain for the folds of her skirts, fists so tight, her knuckles were white. She looked . . . furious.

"Is this why ye came to the woods?" Her tone was harsh, words clipped.

"What?" That was not the response he'd expected.

She took one step toward him. "How did ye ken about us? About me?"

He threw his hands up in defense. "Ye were there—ye saw the attack. Ye ken how I came to be here."

He couldn't fathom what made her think he'd purposefully sought her out with the intention of marriage. He hadn't even known she existed. "I swear to ye. What ye saw, what I said, is the truth."

She didn't move. She only leaned forward, centering her gaze on his eyes. Something flipped in his stomach before she looked away, searching the ground for some answer she seemed not to find. When she squeezed her eyes closed and shook her head, he hated himself for the tension that coated her features.

He hated asking this of her, of himself. A king was afforded many pleasures, any he desired, but there was one wish he'd always kept in a secret place in his heart. A simple joy reserved for those not born of royal blood. A wife who truly loved him and that he loved in return. The tang of blades from outside was a sharp reminder that his wishes must yield to the duty beset him by the crown, and he squared his shoulders.

"But at the moment of our union, all that I have would belong to my queen. She could command my armies just as I, and their loyalty would be as unfaltering. Whatever she brought under my crown would become as one wi' the kingdom." Breaths trembling in his chest, Duncan held Cyrene's stare until she released a long-held breath. "Wi'out question."

"Do ye ken what yer asking, Duncan?"

They were laid bare before each other, not rulers of kingdoms, not heads of armies, only Duncan and Cyrene. The thundering of his heart pounded in his ears. Sounds from outside faded under that thrumming, and he flexed his hands before he spoke, his voice deep and clear.

"Aye. Be my queen. Marry me. Unite our kingdoms, and together, we fight. To save our people? To save us all."

The sound of her delicate gasp slipped between his heartbeats, and a lovely shade of a rose colored her cheeks, but her eyes . . . he saw the fear in them. The reservations. If she said yes, she'd bind herself to him for life. He knew what she wondered, what terrible questions swirled in her mind.

What if all he'd shown her of himself was a façade, and underneath it all, he was as cruel as his father? What if like Duncan now suspected King William had done to Fiona, Duncan broke her body and her spirit?

"'Tis just you and I, Huntress."

Her eyes shot back up at the softness with which he spoke the name he'd given her. He measured her every move, her every breath.

"Ye can say nay, and none will ever ken of this conversation. I willna blame ye, nor think poorly of ye. I ken 'tis too much to ask, but . . ." His voice faltered, and he took the length of a breath to draw up the remainder of his courage. "If we canna be allies, I canna see another way."

She didn't speak, but she didn't run or shout or drive the blades he knew were hidden in her belt into his heart. Her breaths had quickened though, and Duncan resisted the urge to rescind his proposal—to take away the burden of this terrible choice he was forcing her to make. This was a king's duty. To make the hardest decisions. Impossible decisions. To send men to war and make brides of enemies. Love was not a luxury afforded to one such as they. But he wouldn't force her. He would wait and let her answer decide their fate. That somehow didn't feel fair either—mayhap it was even worse. But she, too, was a ruler. A queen. One who must also put her heart aside.

It struck him then that if there was a woman in the world who could possibly understand him, the pressure he felt, the decisions he was forced to make, it would be the bonnie, fire-haired woodland queen that held him hostage in her emerald stare. A small corner of his heart warmed at the idea of her at his side, but as her lips parted, he knew she was going to turn him down.

Instead, she closed her mouth, eyes lowered to the bands of decorated leather she wore on her wrists, as if they called her name. Duncan waited in silence for a full minute while she stared at her arms. He watched, too, wondering if somehow, they were speaking to her.

There was something otherworldly about this place—he'd felt it the moment he lost his way in the wood and again during their ceremony. He understood why they guarded it so carefully, and he wanted to do so as well. But he held to his convictions not to force her. He would give her a choice, which was a greater gift than he'd been given in his life. A greater gift than most queens received.

"Are ye certain?"

Her question jerked him back to earth from where he'd been adrift in his thoughts.

"I canna love ye. Not like . . ." Her voice trailed off as she kept her eyes locked on the leather bracelets that hugged her wrists. She dragged in a long breath before she spoke again. "Are ye certain ye want to trade a chance to find that . . ." She finally looked up, the full force of her blazing green eyes heating his insides. "For a lifetime wi' only me?"

His tongue seemed glued to the roof of his mouth, and he had to work hard to swallow. He had asked himself the same question the entire sleepless night before, but with her heart in mind instead of his.

I canna love ye. Her honest admission was mayhap the saddest words he'd ever heard. But something in the way she'd asked her question—it was vulnerable. She'd allowed him further in than ever before. She, too, secretly desired a union of love instead of duty.

I see a lot of ye in her.

She'd also revealed another truth. *Only me,* she'd said, as if she weren't enough. As if she, too, had made costly choices in her past. Impossible choices.

"What choice do we have, Cyrene?" The air was thick, his words taking a second too long to reach her.

He watched her slender throat as she swallowed hard.

"I would fight wi' ye." Her response was hoarse, as if her throat was as dry as his. "But I canna ask them to."

Her answer snuffed out the breath Duncan had drawn, as if someone had punched him. A queen who would fight for the enemy but not force her people to do the same. She would not manipulate their loyalty.

The way they looked at her, honored her, protected her—surely every one of her warriors would follow their queen, but mayhap some with fear in their hearts and eyes cast both ways. He didn't have to speak it; he could see in the sadness of her downturned lips that it meant more of them would die.

He didn't reply right away, but stepped around the table. Tentatively, asking her permission with the tilt of his head. A dip of her chin brought him another step and another, until he was close enough to touch her.

"I wish there were more time, that the world would wait. I ken ye are afraid. I willna lie and say I am not. The past we share . . . I ken there are things . . ." He didn't know what he was trying to say.

"We dunna ken each other at all," she whispered, her eyes glistening with tears she refused to shed. The set of her jaw and quickness of her breaths told him she was as conflicted as he. She was working just as hard to rein in her panic.

This was too much. He was stealing her future and risking her kingdom. All for barely a chance that they'd even survive, much less emerge victorious. If she refused to flee . . .

The only way. 'Tis the only way.

Eowin's words echoed over and over. Sooner or later, to the Vikings or his cousin, all would be lost. They both knew what happened to the people of villages and kingdoms conquered by the savage men from the North. Better a loveless life than no life at all. Still, it felt so wrong. So very wrong.

She was waiting for him, though. For a king's strength and assurance.

"We are strangers, 'tis true. But there are things I ken about ye." He tilted his head, taking the liberty of examining the soft lines of her face, her defined jaw. "I ken ye are kind. And ye are wise. I ken ye have undying passion for yer people. I see how much they love ye." He started off softly, then, though his voice remained quiet, his tone grew in intensity. "And I ken that although ye dunna wear the fighting leathers, ye are a warrior."

He stepped closer, and she didn't back away as he gazed down at her, fisting his hands so as not to reach out and cup her cheek.

"I ken we serve the same God. Yer faith and mine—'tis the same. I ken ye will fight fer that faith, fer yer people, until yer last breath." He wanted to clasp her hands in his, begging her forgiveness for this request. Not just for her, for both of them.

"I swear to ye, wi' all that I am, Cyrene, bonnie huntress of the woods, that I will do the same for my people. And if we wed, if ye were my queen . . . my wife"—heat raced across his skin, blazing outward from his heart as her breath hitched in her throat—"I will die for yer people, too, for ye will be mine, and I will be yers. My heart, my body, and my soul."

He lowered his head. He had nothing left to swear and no way to prove to her that his words were true, that he would keep his oaths, only a prayer that she would believe him. At the warmth of her hand on his face, he met her eyes. They bounced back and forth between his, searching so deeply, he nearly lost himself. Then her gaze dug so far, he felt a pull inside, like she was reaching into his chest and holding his heart in her hand.

He could not move, could not breathe, could not look away until she lifted her hand, letting it hover near his face before lowering it back to her side. He exhaled a shuddered breath, feeling exposed and gutted.

"I believe ye." Cyrene was staring at the hand she'd touched him with, rubbing her palm with the thumb from her other, as if he'd left a mark on her.

He started to allow a smile, but realized she still hadn't given him an answer. And truly, he still wasn't sure which he hoped she'd give.

"What say ye?" His throat was tight again, making his words strained, husky.

Cyrene only stared at her hand, fingers moving from her palm to trace the designs pressed into the leather of her bracelets. When she spoke, her voice was so soft, Duncan thought mayhap he'd imagined it. But when she finally lifted her head, he saw something else he knew about her. Even though her eyes were begging him to be the man he said he would, he knew she was fiercely brave. And he knew he'd heard correctly when he'd heard her say, "Aye."

20

CYRENE

821 AD – Mid-Morning, The Same Day

Fingers of fire had uncurled in her stomach at the twitch of Duncan's lips when he registered her answer. A promise she'd made to herself as a child echoed in her mind. She swore never to be subject to the crown, and now . . . had she really agreed to marry that very king?

The son of the man who was responsible for her mother's death, the murder and banishment of her people?

Even though he'd called her beautiful, even though they'd plotted and planned out an elaborate and unbelievable scheme to secure victory, could kindness and honor truly come from such evil blood?

"Are ye certain?"

Cyrene could tell from the storm that raged in Astrid's crystal blue eyes, her captain thought she'd finally succumbed to the pressure of leadership and lost her mind. For once, Astrid had no distracting remark, no jokes to break the tension.

Mayhap Astrid was right to doubt. But she'd looked into his eyes, into his heart, and had seen only truth. She'd accepted long ago she might never find the heart-pounding, soul-crushing love that Brígid had woven into her stories, but this . . . this was not at all in her plans. A rushed wedding to her sworn enemy, no matter how handsome she thought he was at first.

Dunna trust the tower king. Her mother's warning cooled the heat in her chest, and Cyrene scolded herself for entertaining such thoughts. She might marry him, but she would keep her promise. Marriage hadn't saved Fiona, after all. She would never let herself become vulnerable to that crown and risk her people being hurt again.

It wouldn't come to that. He'd made it clear he wasn't after her heart. And she made it clear he would never win it.

She found herself unusually calm, though her insides trembled with uncertainty. She was not afraid he would be cruel, but terrified she'd just agreed to something much worse—that simply because of who they were, they'd exist forever as strangers. A shared life, shared bed, shared children, all loveless, lonely, and suspicious. A sinking feeling blossomed into nausea.

Her fingers found the softened leather of her bracelets, tracing the indentions of etchings that reminded her of Whom she served.

I ken ye are good, An T-aon. I have been so far from ye all these years, though ye remained close to me. Please let this be the right choice.

He was good. *An T-aon* was good. She would repeat this truth until her treasonous heart accepted it. Mayhap in that goodness, *An T-aon* would allow her and Duncan to find something good together. Mayhap the king could become her friend. And that would be enough, more than enough, if it meant that her people would be spared the horror of what followed an invasion.

Mayhap, like Astrid, Cyrene could grow to find friendship with *An T-aon* as well.

"I am certain." Her answer to Astrid's challenge was as final as the grave. "'Tis their only hope. And ours."

Though the muscles in her jaw rolled under her skin, Astrid bowed in submission.

"When, m'lady?"

"This afternoon."

Astrid's posture went rigid again, as Cyrene suspected her friend hoped there would be time for the queen to change her mind.

"There is much to be done." Chills swept along Cyrene's skin as she suddenly pictured herself standing before Duncan with the eyes of her whole village watching them.

"Shall I tell the warriors, m'lady?"

"Nay. I wish to do that myself. I ken it will be a shock, as I'm sure it was for ye."

"Aye." Astrid's hard expression softened into something akin to pity. "But we trust ye."

Cyrene placed her hand on Astrid's shoulder, a soft squeeze declaring her appreciation for her loyalty.

"Gather them, bring in the scouts, and . . . and . . ." Cyrene stumbled over her words.

The weight and finality of what she was about to do singed solid thought into mere vapor. She turned her back to Astrid, unwilling to show the tears that had disobediently pooled. Just as quickly as they'd formed, Cyrene willed them dry and cleared her throat, keeping her back to Astrid.

"And send for Revna and Gertrud." Cyrene didn't turn, but busied herself rolling the parchments Duncan had returned to her after their meeting.

She'd never forget that expression on his face when he'd confessed his fears. He'd looked more near death than when they'd found him bleeding and unconscious in the woods. The sorrow and desperation in his eyes had broken something loose in her.

Tower-dwellers had been the enemy, cold and cruel. They didn't care for common folk. But Duncan—he tore apart every notion she'd held as truth. He'd saved more than one of her own people and grieved for even the lowest of those in his kingdom.

His fingers had traced the lines of his lands, lips moving as if beseeching *An T-aon* to turn ink into stone and raise up an impenetrable wall around it. Cyrene found her own fingers following the path his had taken along the edge where his lands met her woods.

Their worlds had touched for so long. They shared the same frozen winters, the same rains of spring, the same salty seas. Mayhap they could now find peace in a shared kingdom. Was that too much to wish for?

A solid stone settled in Cyrene's chest, and she curled her fisted hand over it, praying words that made no sense to anyone but the only One who could hear her heart and know the fear and worry it carried.

Truth-keeper. Named for a mighty huntress. There were so many things she was expected to be. Her mother had told fantastical stories of mighty women, her ancestors, who lived incredible lives.

Their blood flows in yer veins. Cyrene closed her eyes, hearing her mother's words as if she were beside her. *Yer heart pounds the same war-cry as the ancient warriors of old. If ye keep seeking An T-aon, keep yer heart surrendered to him, ye will find herself in these stories one day. Ye will walk the halls of legend in their company.*

Her mother had pressed a hand to her back, just over her right shoulder, then leaned over Cyrene's shoulder and whispered a promise. *Yer marked, Cyrene, lionheart. One day ye'll see as I see.*

Mayhap she did have a place in history. Mayhap her great contribution to the stories wouldn't be a loud, earth-shaking victory in battle. Mayhap it would be the simple, quiet sacrifice of her heart, a queen's duty.

Though if anyone knew of the fear that inched its way up her throat, the unbearable desire to tear off into the most hidden and secret places of the wood, there would be no stories worth telling. Ashamed, Cyrene sank into the fire-warmed chair by her hearth, practicing how she would deliver the news to her warriors.

"M'lady?" Revna's always-hoarse voice stirred Cyrene from her racing thoughts. "Are ye ready for me to take them away?"

She cleared her throat and stood to face her scout, so hard for her years of ten and five. "Revna, come . . . sit."

Revna's hands instinctively hovered over the blades attached to her belt, and her eyes scanned the hut for danger.

Cyrene smiled softly, beckoning the lass with a wave. Revna finally agreed and slipped soundlessly into a chair, though her posture was as rigid as the trunk of an ash.

"I have something to tell ye." Cyrene took a deep breath and shared her news.

"I'll carve his heart from his chest!" Revna shot out of the chair, knives drawn, and started for the hut's doorway.

"Revna!" Cyrene dove for the scout, catching her around the waist and nearly wrestling her to the ground to keep her from fulfilling her promise.

"He tricked ye, my queen." The scout's blue eyes blazed, reflecting flames from Cyrene's lanterns and making her almost dragon-like as she hissed. "He brings wicked tower-magic here. Release me! I'll kill him!"

"Nay," Cyrene soothed, her muscles straining against Revna's rage. "Calm, Revna. I need ye."

At those words, Revna found the ground with her knees, head bowed in service to her queen.

"I need ye to fetch the holy man of Tràigh from the church. Priest, he's called."

Revna jerked her head up, her eyes near silver with frustration. The hatred her scout had for the tower-dwelling king was unmatched, even by Cyrene, though she was only an infant when they'd first made for the woods.

"I ken we have our own holy man, but our union must be recognized by the people of his kingdom, or it will all be fer nothing."

Revna pounded her fisted hands against her leather-clad thighs, her frustration palpable. "I canna understand."

"I ken." Cyrene's answer was gentle, but she lifted her chin, straightening to a regal height. "But it must be done, and ye must accept my decision."

Cyrene pointed a look at the scout, ordering her to remain as she opened the trunk at the foot of her cot and withdrew a small satchel of coins.

"I need ye to gather some other things from the village as well." Cyrene offered Revna the coins and a bit of parchment marked with the list she and Duncan had made.

Revna took the money and parchment, rising as swiftly as she'd knelt, reading it over.

"Ye were but a bairn when Brígid took ye to the forest edge. I shouldna done it, but I followed."

Revna's expression remained impassive, revealing nothing.

"She whispered something to ye that day." Cyrene could still picture a small Revna tucked close beside Brígid, both staring in the direction of the tower.

She had never gotten the chance to ask Brígid what story she told, for that very night, Brígid was taken from them. Staring into Revna's darkening eyes, Cyrene changed her mind about asking the scout what Brígid had said, rubbing at the place across her ribs where a tender scar marred her pale skin. There were things about that day Revna needn't ever know.

"Her story made ye strong." Cyrene squeezed Revna's arm. "Made ye brave."

Cyrene didn't say it, but it had also made her hard. A darkness as black as her raven hair followed like a shadow. Revna became the night, slipping through the wood like a ghost, as quick and invisible a scout as a queen could hope for.

"That's why yer the only one I can ask to do this task fer me."

Revna's brows jumped together in question as if she knew Cyrene wasn't speaking of simply fetching the priest or the items from her list.

Revna neared at Cyrene's beckoning and listened as she whispered her final request. A piece of her own secret plan only shared with Revna.

Revna drew back and met Cyrene's steady gaze. Her eyes, nearly the same shade as Duncan's, filled with determination, and she dipped her head loyally. "I willna fail ye, m'lady."

Cyrene nodded, and Revna aimed for the doorway. She paused at the hut opening, speaking over her shoulder without meeting Cyrene's stare.

"His horse is loyal. As fine a stallion as I ever saw."

Cyrene breathed a laugh and wished Revna Godspeed with her nod. It was not an approval, but it was as best a well-wish as Revna had to offer.

Gertrud must have been waiting outside, because before the fabric of the hut opening had settled back in place, she shoved her way inside, eyes sparkling.

"You've heard?" Cyrene's brow neared her hairline.

"I saw the king when you left his hut. He whispered something to his friend, and I wondered what could be so profound it would end the battle of the ages between the captain and Astrid."

"That is all?"

Gertrud chewed her bottom lip as if trying to keep a grin from spreading.

"He may have asked how he might come upon a clean tunic. Nay, not for the return home, said he, when I asked. But fer a ceremony."

A burst of heat inside sent Cyrene's hands pressed flat against her stomach, unsure what to think of his request. Was this marriage more than a desperate attempt to survive for him? Was he trying to make their union seem less rushed, trying to include some semblance of propriety? Was he doing that for himself . . . or for her?

"He asked something else, m'lady."

Cyrene flicked her gaze back to Gertrud from where she'd been intently examining a knot on the hut's center beam.

"He asked fer it to be in yer favorite color."

That heat from her stomach spread through her veins until her entire body felt as if it were going to burst into flames. She rushed toward the door, cooling fresh air filling her lungs as she burst into the crisp morning.

Astrid rounded the corner, her sharp senses clearly assessing Cyrene's state of near panic. The captain's shoulders tensed, and she reached for her blade, only stopped by Cyrene's hand on her wrist.

"'Tis well." Cyrene made her voice low, an undercurrent of authority keeping Astrid's blade sheathed. "I only needed a breath. The fire was too warm."

Astrid's keen eyes still darted in all directions as she searched for danger before settling back on Cyrene, who assured her again.

"Truly. 'Tis well."

Though it was clear Astrid didn't fully believe her, she jerked her head toward the meeting place. "The warriors and scouts, save Revna, have gathered."

Cyrene drew in another lungful of morning air before following Astrid. Tension rolled across the gathering of warriors, but they remained silent as she delivered the news.

"I ken ye might have yer suspicions, but I ask ye . . . have I ever led ye down a path I wasna willing to walk myself?"

None spoke.

"Ye have trusted me since I was a child, and I ask ye to trust me now."

Her warriors answered in unison by the resounding thump of their longbows on the ground. Cyrene found Liam's scowl amongst their stone faces. He looked nearly as furious as Revna, and Cyrene bit back a grin. Especially after the defiant display he put on the day before outside her hut. She was tempted to thank Duncan for that engagement gift, though he wouldn't understand.

Backs straight, her warriors stood at attention, ready. Ready to follow their queen into the darkest pits of hell if she asked.

Cyrene lifted her chin, mustering every ounce of courage. She would be brave for them. Like Beli, she would give her last breath and the last beat of her heart for them. She would give her future, gladly.

"Ready yer weapons. For tonight, we make for the tower. As one wi' the kingdom of Tràigh."

Gertrud had not followed directly, but appeared before Cyrene's speech ended, remaining respectfully on the outskirts of the gathering place. As Cyrene approached, she offered a mug of some steaming liquid.

"Thought ye might need this today."

Cyrene drew the cup to her lips, overwhelmed by the scent of lavender. Without questioning Gertrud, she sipped the calming drink as they made their way back to her hut.

"Is there anything I can do for ye, m'lady?"

Cyrene resisted the urge to jokingly suggest Gertrud take her place as queen, and gave her question serious consideration. The request Duncan made of Gertrud still rolled around in her mind, unable to settle in a place of understanding.

"There is one thing."

Gertrud's face shone like the sun at Cyrene's request, and she dashed off, disappearing between huts before Cyrene could blink.

In the hours that passed before Gertrud appeared in Cyrene's hut with her arms full, Cyrene divided her time between praying, pacing, and gathering her few meager possessions into a trunk that would accompany her to the tower after the battle. If they survived.

She'd sent questions via Astrid to Eowin, who would receive the answer from his king. She'd never stepped foot inside a tower; she didn't know what to expect.

Astrid never verbally expressed her displeasure at the continued contact with the handsome captain, but Cyrene suspected it was more a denial of her unwanted respect rather than true disdain. Astrid had reluctantly admitted that if Duncan's whispered news hadn't caused Eowin to call the match, she might have actually lost to him.

Cyrene hummed a soft laugh at the thought of Astrid having to yield to anyone, and jumped when Gertrud burst through the curtain. She nearly dropped the quiver of arrows she was carrying to the trunk when Gertrud lowered one arm, holding up the other above her head to display her offering.

Dripping with delicate swirling vines of gold and detailed lace embellishments, Cyrene's dark emerald ceremony gown had been transformed into a breathtaking garment fit for any royal wedding.

She wiped her hands clean on her skirts, ran her palm over the soft fabric, and fingered each added golden trail.

"'Tis beautiful, Gertrud." Her words were breath. "How did you manage such artistry in so few hours?"

"Ye are well loved, m'lady. All the seamstresses were aching to be even a small part of this comfort for ye, after all ye . . ." Gertrud's voice broke, tears welling in her eyes. "All ye have given."

"'Tis perfect." Cyrene's own eyes burned with gratitude. If she were to face a stranger instead of a lover at her wedding ceremony, she would at least be wearing the gown of her dreams.

"Let's see how it looks on ye." Gertrud no longer hid her grin, and when she'd helped Cyrene into the dress, she could not contain her tears either. "He is a lucky man indeed. There is none as bonnie, m'lady."

Cyrene felt beautiful, but rising anxiousness quickly overtook any satisfaction. She sat in silence as Gertrud twisted her long red locks into swirls and braids, leaving a healthy section in waves down her back.

She was aware it was the fashion of the day—and even considered proper—for royal women, for all women, to pin all of their hair up under a veil, but Cyrene had never been one to bow to traditions, even those of her own people.

If it hadn't been from necessity, she would still have trained women as warriors like her mother. She didn't remain behind on hunts. She hadn't chosen a husband when she reached the age of marriage—although mayhap she should have—and she would not hide the brilliant auburn locks *An T-aon* had blessed her with.

It was a challenge, mayhap, to this man who wished to be her husband. Would he balk at her strong-headedness or encourage it? She tried not to hope for too much, but even what little hope she had turned to nausea as Astrid appeared between the folds of fabric at her hut entrance.

"M'lady." Her simple greeting was crisp with expectation and heavy with as much concern as Cyrene felt in her own limbs.

With a glance at Gertrud, who tucked a final pink blossom of herb robert into one of Cyrene's braids, she stood and followed Astrid along the path she'd traveled just hours before to meet with her warriors. Astrid gripped Cuddie's leather reins, the mare still strong and quick despite her age. She plodded silently beside her mistress.

The sound of pipes and softly singing voices met them long before they neared the clearing. As they passed rows of huts, villagers filed in behind them, bouquets of wildflowers and long stems of forest grass in their arms.

The procession broke away at the final row of homes, moving ahead to fill the clearing and greet their queen when she would meet the groom and walk alongside him into the clearing.

Before they rounded the final curve which would fully reveal the clearing and Duncan, Cyrene slowed, nearly brought to a halt by the twisting in her stomach. Astrid sensed her hesitation and turned, hands hovering and ready near her blades.

Cyrene didn't speak, but lifted wide, terrified eyes to her oldest friend. In a swift and unexpected move, Astrid drew her queen close. She pressed her forehead to Cyrene's as they used to do when they were children and the terrible unknown things that roamed in the darkness threatened to steal all hope.

Cyrene closed her eyes, focusing on Astrid's breathing, as she knew Astrid was also doing. When all other sounds were silenced, the certainty of their beating hearts, of each inhale and exhale, blanketed both of them with warmth, with peace, with hope.

No matter what the next moments brought, they were alive in

this one. It wasn't a promise that all would be well, but it was enough.

Her hands found the sides of Astrid's face, her friend with whom she had survived such sadness and despair that would have certainly crushed her alone.

"At least ye dunna have to marry Lanky Liam."

Laughter burst from Cyrene's lips. "Ye should have seen his face when I told them."

Astrid let her head fall back, a full throaty laugh filling the air. "I would give anything to have been there!"

Cyrene wrapped her arms around her friend, whispering into her sleek, silver hair, "Thank ye, my friend. I pray ye are always by my side."

"Only death could part me from ye, my queen."

"May death have a long wait and a long-fought battle."

Cyrene believed it would too. Even if her bones were crooked and eyes clouded from blindness. Images of a wrinkled, gray-haired Astrid still strong with fiery defiance and yielding a stone-sharpened blade brought a smile to Cyrene's lips as Astrid climbed atop Cuddie's back.

Together, they rounded the final bend and met their next challenge with chins high.

21

DUNCAN

821 AD - Late Afternoon

He barely heard the pipes and voices over the sound of his thundering heart, but when Astrid, high and astride her decorated mare, rounded the corner, even that fell silent. He waited at the outskirts, his back to a clearing full of villagers and warriors, only Eowin, atop Taranau, at his side.

For three eternal steps, Astrid blocked his view.

A collective gasp rolled through the crowd of spectators, their attention finally captured by something more interesting than the enemy king come to steal away their beloved queen.

Duncan's breath halted in his lungs at the first glimpse of her fire-red hair, unbound but for a thick braid that coiled around her head like a crown, jeweled with delicate pink flowers. Rebellion sparked in her eyes, stirring a longing in his spirit.

She was as wild and untamed as the woods in which she ruled, as the seas on stormy tides. A sudden desperate need to keep that fierce wildness, to protect it and cherish it, filled his heart with such force, it ached.

He greedily raked his gaze over her form, nearly knocked flat by the gown she wore. He wasn't expecting a gaudy monstrosity as was custom for royalty, but he also wasn't expecting . . . that.

It was a rich, dark green, with thin vines of gold that raced from the hem to the modest square neckline and down each arm, as if she'd stretched out her fingers while walking and the forest itself had become a perfectly fitted garment for its queen.

"Don't forget to breathe, sire." Eowin's murmured remark jerked Duncan back to his senses, and he released the air burning his lungs, clearing his throat.

"If yer cousin doesna want to kill ye for yer crown, he will certainly want to fer yer bride."

"That promised flogging will be waiting fer ye in the morn." Duncan's growl drew a chuckle from Eowin, although after his goading, some of the tension seizing Duncan's muscles had relaxed. He felt Eowin lean down again as if to make another remark, no doubt about what would transpire between then and the morning.

Duncan didn't take his eyes off the queen as she approached. He didn't think he could ever tear his eyes away from her again, but ticked his chin toward his captain. "Dunna ye dare."

Eowin laughed again, then spoke sincerely. "I wish ye happiness, sire."

Not many would care for something as silly as happiness for their king. "I am glad to have ye wi' me, Eowin. Yer a true friend."

Eowin stilled at the familiarity with which Duncan spoke. Not since they were children had the two escaped the scrutiny of the crown and propriety. The gravity of tomorrow still threatened to drown them all, but there, on that day, in that enchanted place, it almost felt as if they'd stepped out of time and the waiting world into a brief moment of freedom. For the first time since he could remember, peace settled over Duncan's spirit.

Astrid stalked toward them on her steed, a predatory warning in her eyes, her fingers twitching in a way that made Duncan suspect she would rather draw her blade and run him through than see this ceremony take place.

He felt Eowin and Taranau tense, protective and ready as always. "Seems ye have met yer match as well, Captain."

A rumble from Eowin's chest sounded at Duncan's side, and he couldn't help the teasing smile that curled at his lips. All humor evaporated into the warmth of the afternoon as Cyrene completed a final gliding step to face him. A blade of sun cut through the canopy above, bathing her in a warm, glowing light that made her hair even more like fire than before.

He couldn't be certain, but he thought he saw the tremble of her hands before she clasped them together at her waist.

Both Astrid and Eowin drew their horses side by side behind them, leaving Duncan and Cyrene to enter the clearing together, she at his left.

Duncan drew in a breath and lifted his hand, offering his arm to the queen. "M'lady."

He caught himself gaping when she lifted her chin, and slammed his mouth shut. The thick ray of golden afternoon sun poured over her face, nearly turning her emerald eyes to sea glass and giving her ivory skin an angelic glow. She captured his gaze, freezing him in place as she had done in the hut when he'd proposed. Once again, his heartbeat caught in his chest as if gripped by a hand that meant to squeeze out the truth.

She held him there until he was ready to beg for his life, then just as quickly as she had ensnared him, she released him with a blink and looped her hand through his offered arm. He placed his free hand over hers, his fingers curling around her slender wrist. At their touch, ladies playing pipes and flutes filed in front, forming a musical escort.

Without a word, they followed the ensemble toward the holy

man from her village and priest from his, who waited at the entrance to the inner circle.

It was custom for a bride and groom's parents to follow behind their best swordsman, but not much about this ceremony would be customary, and Duncan felt the corner of his mouth pull back at the thought. Custom had never sat well with him; not as much as authenticity.

Had they been in the tower, they'd have met the priest outside church doors and completed their ceremony before him, their parents, and the best man alone. Here, there were hundreds of witnesses to confirm their union.

Mayhap that was best, for her people, anyway. They were the ones about to march off to war with a strange king who was dumped on their doorstep.

Though she remained perfectly poised, with each step, he felt Cyrene's pulse slamming through her wrist against his fingers. He searched for the words to calm but not embarrass her.

"Ye are certainly bonnie, Huntress," he whispered between one step and another. "I must seem a pauper in rags next to ye."

He suppressed a grin at the slight squeeze of her hand on his arm. They were still ten steps away from the priests, but her pulse slowed, and she released a long breath.

"I already agreed to wed. Ye dunna need to try to woo me."

"Is it not proper for grooms to compliment their brides in yer kingdom?"

She hummed a soft reply that Duncan interpreted as amusement. "Is any of this proper?"

"Mayhap not, but I quite prefer it to pompous traditions." Duncan absently ran his thumb over the top of her hand, and as they completed the final steps, he leaned in to whisper against her ear, "'Tis true nonetheless."

He released her as they met the priest and holy man. She stayed to his left but turned to face him.

The priest began, issuing a rehearsed welcome and recognizing by name Duncan and Cyrene, Astrid and Eowin, then Cyrene's holy man, Alasdair, who was the only remaining elderly man residing in her village. The priest continued his portion.

"I must ask ye these questions as is law in the kingdom of Tràigh."

Cyrene nodded in agreement.

"Are ye both of age to wed?"

"Aye." Cyrene answered in unison with Duncan.

"Are ye related by blood?"

"Nay."

"Do ye both consent to this marriage freely?"

"Aye." Duncan heard only his answer and held his breath, keeping his eyes on the priest.

In the moment that he waited for her answer, he resolved that if she said no, he would kindly bid her farewell and face whatever lay in wait for him at the tower with no ill will in his heart.

"Aye." Cyrene's quiet response reached his ears on the tail end of a breeze that had slipped through the trees, cooling the sweat forming on his brow.

It seemed too warm for a day so near to winter, unless it was his nerves that kept him roasting in the tunic Gertrud had provided. A tunic that just happened to be the same shade of green as Cyrene's gown. He searched out Gertrud's round face in the crowd, finding her eyes wide and smile mischievous as if she alone knew a secret about the two of them. She clearly shared his request for the garment with Cyrene, and he wondered if she'd also told of his other favor.

"As ye are both monarchs of yer kingdoms, there is not a dowry agreement between ye, but instead an exchange of much greater value."

Alasdair stepped forward. A few wisps of silver hair that had escaped from where the rest were slicked back and tied with thin leather straps fluttered around his long, wrinkled face.

"Do ye, Duncan, agree to accept under your crown the entirety of this kingdom?"

"I do."

"Do ye swear to protect and keep them as yer own people, including the weakest among them?" Alasdair spoke slowly, gray eyes boring into Duncan's. His charge was no light matter.

"Aye, I do." Then to buck propriety once more, Duncan turned to face Cyrene, speaking to her directly. "Wi' my life and my crown, I do."

Something passed across her expression, a softening that gave him the smallest glimmer of hope for a future different from most arranged marriages.

Alasdair asked the same of Cyrene, and she answered with a quiet, "Aye, I do."

"Are ye prepared now to plight yer troth, Yer Majesty?" The priest drew his bound scripture from the folds of his robes, holding it open.

"Aye." Duncan nodded.

"Take the hand of yer bride."

Duncan lifted his hand, opening his palm and offering it to Cyrene. Again, he waited, giving her the choice. After a breath of consideration, she placed her hand in his, her fingers cool but sure.

The priest recited the scripture in Latin from the book of First Corinthians, chapter thirteen. From his studies, Duncan knew the text well.

"Yer Majesty, 'tis time fer the vows. Repeat my words to yer beloved."

Duncan nodded, centering his gaze on Cyrene's. He desperately desired to read the hidden thoughts written behind those green eyes.

"I, Duncan, in the name of the spirit of God that resides wi'in us all, by the life that courses wi'in my blood and the love that resides wi'in my heart, take thee, Cyrene to my hand, my heart, and my spirit, to be my chosen one."

Duncan echoed the words given by the priest, never taking his eyes from Cyrene's, hoping his steady voice would assure her that he meant to keep each one. But with each word, his heart beat faster, fear and longing fueling its pace.

"To desire thee and be desired by thee, to possess thee and be possessed by thee, without sin or shame, for naught can exist in the purity of my love for thee. I promise to love thee wholly and completely without restraint, in sickness and in health, in plenty and in poverty, in life and beyond, where we shall meet, remember, and love again."

Cyrene didn't move or hardly blink as he spoke. Duncan let his gaze drift to her chest to ensure she was still breathing. When he met her eyes again, they were as wide as he'd ever seen. A large rock of worry that she'd jerk free and disappear into the trees settled in his stomach, and he tightened his grip on her hands with the priest's final words.

"I shall not seek to change thee in any way. I shall respect thee, thy beliefs, thy people, and thy ways as I respect myself."

He expected the priest to next make mention of a ring, but Alasdair spoke instead.

"'Tis our tradition that a bride also take vows." Alasdair accepted the offered scriptures from the priest, holding them in the same manner but turning to a different passage. Instead of Latin, he spoke in their shared language, without reading but from memory.

"Set me as a seal upon thine heart,
As a seal upon thine arm:
For love is strong as death;
Jealousy is cruel as the grave:
The coals thereof are coals of fire,
Which hath a most vehement flame.
Many waters cannot quench love,
Neither can the floods drown it:
If a man would give all the substance of his house for love,
It would utterly be contemned."

He closed the scripture and faced Cyrene, prompting her to echo his words. Duncan wished to gauge her feelings, but Cyrene kept her eyes on Alasdair, as if he were the hand keeping her from drowning.

"Ye are blood of my blood, and bone of my bone. I give ye my body, that we two might be one. I give ye my spirit, 'til our life shall be done. You cannot possess me, for I belong to myself. But while we both wish it, I give you that which is mine to give."

At the slight nod of Alasdair's head, Cyrene finally slid her eyes to meet Duncan's, her strength meeting him with such force, he blinked in surprise. But there was something else hiding behind that wall of defiance. Something she tried desperately to hide. Something soft and vulnerable and pleading with him not to break it. She finished her vows, holding his gaze as he'd held hers.

"You canna command me, for I am a free person, but I shall serve you in those ways you require, and the honeycomb will taste sweeter coming from my hand."

The priest reached into the folds of his robes again, producing a thin silver band in the palm of his hand. Duncan allowed a half-smile at the widening of Cyrene's eyes and reminded himself to thank Gertrud for her discretion and the quick work of the only forge maiden in the village.

Cyrene's face paled, no doubt wondering how he'd produced such a ring. Then her eyes darted to his neck, noticing the absence of his necklace. He lifted one corner of his mouth as she combed those wide green eyes across his chest and up to his waiting gaze. Her lips parted slightly, a silent gasp slipping through before she smiled. A soft, genuine smile.

That simple silver necklace was precious to him, but at the sight of Cyrene's shy grin, he decided it was worth the sacrifice.

He took the ring from the priest and recited the proper words as he moved the band to her first, second, and finally her third finger.

"In the name of the Father, and of the Son, and of the Holy Spirit, I thee wed."

Cyrene stared at the ring. And stared and stared. The priest waited, as if she were supposed to speak.

"M'lady." Alasdair finally broke Cyrene's trance. When she looked up, Duncan was alarmed at the glisten of tears in her eyes.

She blinked hard several times and made a soft sound in her

throat before she nodded to Alasdair, who presented her with straps of leather similar to the ones she wore around her wrist.

She then offered her hand, and Duncan accepted without hesitation. She pushed back the sleeve of his tunic, her fingers cool on his burning skin. When she turned his hand over, he saw what she meant to do. His breath hitched when she turned her eyes to his.

"As I set these leathers as a seal upon thine arm and bind them to ye, so do I set thee as a seal upon my heart and bind it to yers." Cyrene finished tying the leathers and turned his arm again. "Until I breathe my last."

Duncan's heart thundered in his chest, his throat suddenly dry.

The priest drew strips of cord from his own robes and bound their hands together, reciting his blessing.

"Two entwined in love, bound by commitment and fear, sadness and joy, by hardship and victory, anger and reconciliation, all of which brings strength to this union."

Duncan could not break his gaze from Cyrene's as the priest continued. "Hold tight to love one another through both good times and bad, and watch as yer strength grows. Remember that it is not this physical cord, but what it represents, that keeps ye together."

The priest touched Duncan's shoulder. "I bestow upon thee a kiss of peace." He pulled Duncan down to his height and placed a kiss on his forehead.

Alasdair did the same for Cyrene before turning her to face Duncan again. She'd not released her grip on his wrist, and he could feel the strain in her fingers as she tensed.

The eyes of her entire village, nearly all of her warriors, Astrid, Eowin, even Thaedry were all centered on the two of them. But Duncan saw no one but Cyrene.

With his unbound hand, he gently drew her close, his fingers curling around her neck under her ear. Her pulse pounded against his palm.

He took a step, closing the space between them, and she tipped her head, wide emerald eyes never breaking from his.

"Dunna fear," he whispered as he lowered his head, his lips inches from hers. "'Tis only ye and me."

He felt her soften under his touch. "I'm going to kiss ye now."

He pressed a gentle kiss to her lips. It was simple and brief, but as he pulled away, he thought mayhap if she'd allow it, he'd like to do that again.

22

CYRENE

821 AD - Evening that Same Day

The hut was warm—maybe too warm. Cyrene felt beads of sweat trickle down her back under the thick fabric of her gown. She felt more heat rush across her cheeks when she found her fingers had traveled to her lips again, touching the place where Duncan had kissed her.

Astrid had been kissed once, when she was nigh ten and four. She said it felt like she'd kissed a slimy fish, and they'd giggled through the night.

Duncan was no slimy fish.

Her stomach nearly climbed her throat as she discovered her small cot had been removed, replaced with a large straw-stuffed mattress layered with thick furs. Big enough for two.

The rustle of fabric turned heat to ice, and gooseflesh rose along her arms. She wrapped those arms around herself, focusing on the embers that glowed in the hearth.

At the sound of his footsteps, she closed her eyes, her breaths growing shallow and throat dry. She expected his hands to turn her around, rushing and ready to get what was to come over with.

"I brought ye some food and wine." Duncan's voice was so husky, so reserved, that she turned, afraid that something terrible had happened.

He waited near the table, plates piled high with breads, dried venison and fish, and sweet cakes and tarts made by villagers for the event. Though it would be short, the elders who'd helped raise and guide Cyrene, the few who remained and loved her mother, would not allow her wedding to pass without a celebration.

Pipes still trilled in the distance, a melody to which the villagers would dance until Cyrene and Duncan emerged from the wedding hut.

The thought sent another wave of nausea-induced chills over her skin.

"I wish . . ." Duncan stopped and rubbed his hand over his bearded chin. "I wish we had more time."

"The world willna wait." Her words, laced with sadness and anger, barely made a sound past her lips. Her chest moved visibly with her breaths, and Duncan's eyes dipped as he noticed.

"Yer afraid." He didn't move, didn't approach.

"Are ye not?" she barked, irritated from nervousness more than his observation.

"Aye." His answer was short, and he seemed to ignore the bite in her tone. At least he was honest.

He finally moved, but only to the chair on his side of the table. "Are ye hungry?"

Her stomach was tied in so many knots, she doubted she'd ever be able to eat again. "Nay," she said, her tone softer. "Thank ye."

He nodded, reaching for one of the squares of cake. Cyrene watched as he took a bite, breathed a laugh, and lifted the remaining dessert as if giving a toast.

"S'good," he said, still chewing.

He didn't take another bite, but dropped the rest back on the plate, brushing his hands free of crumbs before lacing his fingers together. He kept his head bowed, and Cyrene felt like she should speak, but she had no words.

Duncan ran a hand through his curls, soft and shiny from being washed before the ceremony, then he grabbed the two cups of wine and rounded the table.

She remained rooted as he neared, but accepted the drink he offered. It was warm spiced wine and felt good as it slid down her raw throat.

He watched as she emptied her cup, then offered his, and she took it without hesitation. She knew time was short. She knew what was expected of a man and woman who were wed. She'd never once failed to do what needed to be done for her people. She'd nearly frozen to death at ten years old until she could return to the village with meat. She'd broken her back to build shelters, she'd gone without food when there wasn't enough. She'd wept over the ones they'd lost when sickness struck, and hunted down the necessary herbs to heal the rest herself.

She reminded herself of all these sacrifices, reminded herself how now she was warm and fed. Her people were thriving and healthy because of what she'd given.

She could give herself once more for the chance that they'd remain such. Still, her heart raced wildly, and she could barely contain the trembling of her limbs.

She added another hand to his cup, which she'd emptied, attempting to hide her shaking. When Duncan's hand covered hers, she did not meet his eyes, but closed hers instead. She felt him brush his thumb over the new ring on her finger.

"Was it verra special?" she whispered.

"What?"

"Yer necklace." She let the rhythm of his thumb across her finger calm her racing heart.

He hummed a response, and she finally looked up to see a soft smile on his lips.

"Aye. 'Twas verra precious to me." Duncan lifted her hand, twisting the ring around her finger. "'Twas a gift from Fiona. I loved her verra much."

Fiona. He loved Fiona too. He'd said it before, but Cyrene hadn't wanted to believe it. She pulled her hand away, closing her fingers in and pressing her fist to her chest. Hidden inside her closed hand was the bitterness and anger she could not release.

"Why would ye . . ." Cyrene felt the sting of tears and turned her back to him.

He was quiet for too long, but she couldn't bring herself to face him. She squeezed her eyes closed again when he cleared his throat.

"I dunna ken, truly." Duncan's voice sounded hoarse. "I just wanted to give ye . . . something that meant something."

Cyrene clenched her fist tighter to her chest as he continued. "'Twas all I had to give."

A hot tear slipped down her cheek, burning a path across her skin before she wiped it away with the back of her hand.

"Cyrene." There was something in his voice. Something that brought both relief and panic. "We dunna—"

"Nay." She spun to face him, hand fisted at her side, knowing what he would suggest. "It has to be real. And I willna lie. Not to them."

If there were any reason for their union to be doubted, her people wouldn't trust her, and it was crucial for their survival. If his people doubted, they could demand the marriage be annulled and drive them from the land again. Or worse.

Cyrene's skin burned. The fire was too hot. Everything was too hot. She stalked to the table, placing her empty cup next to the full plates of uneaten food. She had longed for a friendship with *An T-aon*. Now she found herself clinging to his presence with all her strength to simply continue allowing her lungs to bring in air and push it back out again.

She heard the rustle of movement as Duncan placed the other cup she'd drained beside hers. Then felt the warmth of his hands on her shoulders, gently turning her to face him.

"I wouldna ask ye to." Duncan's blue eyes held hers, his hands sliding down her arms to her hands. His breaths were as shallow as her own.

He gave her fingers a soft squeeze before dropping his hands to his sides.

"We ride for Tràigh in two hours." His statement was dry, a simple fact, but there was fear in his eyes.

"To battle." Cyrene finished what he couldn't.

"To battle." Agony pulled his head low. "I canna imagine what we will find."

He'd been kind to her. Even when he was hurt and held captive. Now he was her husband. She'd sworn for better or worse, knowing full well the worse was upon them.

Cyrene lifted her hand to his face, and when she touched his cheek, he covered it with his as if he'd been hoping, waiting for her to reach out. His hand was warm and strong; it fit perfectly atop hers. When she'd told him they were strangers, he'd reminded her of what he knew to be true. Finally, she knew what to say.

"I dunna ken what will happen before the dawn. Death may yet part us before then." Duncan kept his hand over hers but cut his eyes up to study her through his long lashes. "But I made a promise. I will go wi' ye. I will fight wi' ye, die wi' ye if *An T-aon* wills. Whatever comes for our people, for those we love, we will face it—together."

Duncan set his stare upon her, the depth of gratitude turning his blue eyes to the darkest shade of cobalt. She let her eyes drift from his and traced the strong lines of his jaw, the bow shape of his lips. She didn't dread the idea of looking at him for the rest of her life. He lifted his hand, reaching to brush her hair back from her face.

"A wife that is as brave as she is bonnie." His fingers grazed the skin of her neck, and she did not withdraw; she did not recoil. "I truly am but a pauper in rags compared to ye."

His fingers wove into her hair, and she placed her hand on his chest, finding herself leaning into him as his free arm slowly snaked around her waist.

"Please, dunna fear me, Cyrene." His breath was warm as he whispered into her hair.

"'Tisna ye I fear." She felt him swallow at her admission, and pressed her cheek against his chest, allowing the drum of his heart to match time with hers.

It was fear of what would come next that threatened to suffocate her. She'd seen the same in his eyes, heard it in his voice. They were the only two people in either kingdom who could lead, who could do anything to change what was coming.

They had begun the day as enemies, yet as Duncan blew a soft breath, extinguishing one of the lanterns, the remaining candle created deep shadows along the edges of her hut, its walls so thick, the remaining daylight couldn't penetrate. She didn't fear the darkness. Instead, she found comfort in his waiting arms. In those moments, he alone could truly understand the burden she'd borne all those years. She still faced impossible choices. But for once, she didn't face them alone.

"Two hours," she heard herself whisper as his fingers slipped into her hair. Such a short stretch of time to turn two strangers into a husband and a wife.

She almost laughed as she remembered the way Astrid had broken through her anxiety with a reminder that if it weren't for the impending battle, she might have found herself settling for Liam instead of this handsome stranger.

Though as his gentle fingers tugged loose the lacing of her gown, his breath warm on her skin, she melted into his strong chest and wasn't so sure she'd settled at all. Especially when his lips danced over hers, the shape of a smile lightening his words.

"Mayhap the world might wait just a little longer."

23

DUNCAN

821 AD - Later That Night

Taranau sailed through the forest, Duncan barely guiding him as his eyes were glued to Cyrene's slender shape expertly riding a chestnut gelding ahead of him. He hardly noticed any tenderness in his side, which was still dark purple with bruising and sensitive from Thaedry's quick-thinking branding. Distracted, he didn't hear the trotting hooves of Eowin's borrowed mare until he was beside him.

"Yer drooling, sire."

Duncan hissed a reproach at his captain, flicking his eyes back to Cyrene, hoping she hadn't heard. Though a husband should admire his wife, he wasn't sure it was normal for one to be unable to tear his thoughts away from memories of their short time together. He could still feel the softness of her skin, the eager kiss of her lips, and the pounding of her heart beneath his palm. He pushed his hand along the soft hair on Taranau's neck to dispel the sensation.

Mayhap it was simply the goodness of God, his mercy upon them, that they were granted a momentary escape from the weight of what was to come. Although Duncan still felt the tightness of worry in his chest, it was nothing like before.

"Together," she'd said. That simple word had snapped a cord inside of him that could never be rebound, opening a door in his heart to allow her in.

Astrid directed the gray-speckled mare she lovingly called Cuddie to the side, nearly touching Cyrene's horse, she was so close. The animals didn't seem to mind the nearness, and Astrid leaned over to whisper something to the queen.

Duncan noticed how Eowin stilled and straightened at Astrid's appearance, his keen eyes observing her every move.

"Ye have a bit of drool there yerself, Captain." At his teasing, Eowin glared and spurred his ride around to fall back behind Duncan.

The afternoon had faded into evening, and the last bits of light filtered in through the trees as Revna, atop her pure white stallion, led the group along a path only she knew.

When Cyrene's scout had appeared, reins in hand, at the edge of her village, Eowin had questioned Duncan's sudden stillness. He couldn't place the memory, but there had been something familiar about her.

"Her hair." Eowin had spoken quietly, nodding toward the young scout. "It reminds me of Fiona's."

While rare in their land, there were a few of his countrymen with the same olive skin and dark hair, which always sparked his memory of his stepmother and stole his breath.

Their similarities ended with her hair, skin, and straight line of her nose. Revna had no kindness to spare for him, and she'd not ceased to shoot daggers with every glance. He had no choice but to trust her lead, as the new moon was upon them and Cyrene promised Revna was the best hope for entering his kingdom secretly.

Duncan tugged on Taranau's reins, slowing him until he was even with Eowin.

"The scout . . ." Duncan lifted his chin, his voice nearly a whisper. "What do ye make of her?"

"She doesna trust ye, that is certain." Eowin eyed Duncan, seeming to read something deeper into his question. "She's about the age yer sisters would have been."

Duncan's thoughts slipped along a dark, forgotten cord as he rode, landing on the memory of two tiny faces. Eowin was right. Mayhap that's what kept his thoughts traveling back to Revna. He imagined her as one of them, taking the throne instead of him. She would make a fierce queen. Terrifyingly beautiful and severe in her rule. No one would dare cross her.

"Eowin, I think 'tis true . . . that my father was the one responsible for what happened to Fiona."

"Ye shouldna say such things." Eowin shifted on the bare back of his horse, scanning his surroundings as if to check for listening ears. "Though if it werna the Picts . . ."

"I dunna want to think it either, but too much of what she says rings true." Duncan's hand wandered to his chest, searching for the necklace he no longer possessed.

"What if it is? What can be done now? Ye've made her yer queen, united the kingdoms again."

Duncan remained quiet for a long moment, debating on sharing his thoughts even with Eowin.

"Yer pondering something." Eowin recognized Duncan's pensive silence.

"A terrible weight has been on my chest since the queen revealed what Eden said about my father." Duncan exhaled a slow, deep breath. "It feels as though a reckoning is coming. That . . . that atonement is required."

"Atonement for what crime?"

"My sisters." Some cold sliver of wind infiltrated Duncan's tunic, snaking around his torso until his bones ached from the chill. "I held such hate for the Picts for what I thought they'd done to them, but now . . . I just canna believe he killed them."

Duncan scanned the dim forest and suppressed a shiver as he found Revna staring directly at him as if she could hear his thoughts. As if he was the one who'd offered them to the sea.

"Do ye think 'tis possible he hid them away? Sent them to another kingdom?"

In a flash, he squelched the picture of Revna on a dark throne, a crown of obsidian and silver resting over her midnight hair. Instead, he forced his gaze to the light that was Cyrene.

"Nay. 'Tis impossible. No riders were allowed in or out of Tràigh from the moment Fiona was discovered. Even if he'd sent one that night before, he would have been seen and reported by the guards at the borders." Duncan kept his eyes on the queen. Even in the almost pitch black of a moonless night, she shone. A single star in a sea of onyx. "Our hope is for the future now, not the past."

A new vision filled his mind. Her people, watching her dance in worship at their ceremony. Her graceful movements, leading the way for them to follow and worship God themselves in joy and freedom.

As if she, too, could sense his thoughts, she tucked a look over her shoulder, her lips twitching at his waiting smile.

The weight remained, though, and his smile faded. Cyrene had been as broken over the loss of Fiona's children as he. They were of her people. Was he a fool to think there would be no punishment, no consequences for their loss, even if the one truly responsible was gone?

A high-pitched whistle drifted above the soft sound of hooves on the forest floor, and Duncan nudged Taranau to a trot, joining the others where they had gathered.

Cyrene had already slid from the back of her horse. She stood facing Astrid, each grasping the other's forearms as if someone would come to tear them apart forever. He kept quiet while dismounting and readying the weapons Cyrene's warriors had fitted him with.

Duncan turned his back to the women, feeling as though he were intruding. Over the back of his horse, he saw Eowin also moving unusually slowly, either from the discomfort of having traveled without a saddle or his deliberate intention of giving them privacy.

"Mayhap yer union can provide the woodland people with proper riding equipment." Eowin cut a jealous glance at Taranau's saddle when he caught Duncan watching him with amusement.

"Or mayhap the gentle captain can give lessons to our men to increase their skills if by chance they find themselves without."

Their teasing quieted when Cyrene started to sing a slow and haunting melody.

"May he be a light in the darkness. A path when the way is unknown. May he be the courage ye seek when yer heart is afraid and alone. May he guide ye, abide in ye, today, tonight and forevermore."

Even the animals were silent as her song for Astrid, for all her warriors, sailed on hopeful notes up to the obsidian sky.

"We will be ready, m'lady," Astrid whispered. "Our aim will be true."

Cyrene pulled Astrid close until their foreheads touched. "Only death shall part me from ye."

Astrid whispered something neither he nor Eowin could hear, but the men exchanged a curious glance when Cyrene smothered a laugh with her hand.

He glanced past the embracing women to see Revna also watching, her hand absently stroking the colorless mane of her stallion. She wore a look of resolved longing, as if their kind of friendship was something she didn't understand but secretly desired. When Revna sensed Duncan's attention, she pierced him with her narrowed glare and whispered something to her horse.

His ears flicked before he turned and trotted alone back in the direction they'd come.

"Ye ken the way now." Revna spoke to Astrid as the captain gathered the reins of all the horses. "I will lead the queen and the others to the tower. Gather the warriors, and I will meet ye here before dawn. We will have to travel a different route with the horses."

Astrid skillfully pulled herself onto Cuddie's back, clicking her tongue to coax the other animals to follow. Revna reached for Duncan's stallion, nuzzling her nose against his.

"Farewell, Taranau. Keep Astrid out of trouble now." With a pat to his flank, Revna watched Astrid guide the small herd back toward their hidden village.

Cyrene stepped to Duncan's side, keeping her eyes on Revna. "I believe ye'll have to fight her fer yer horse now."

"Better to just let her have him." Eowin shrugged past them, following Revna, who'd already started moving into the darkness.

Cyrene watched until Astrid completely disappeared into the black of the forest, the sadness in her expression threatening to tear his heart in two.

"Dunna worry." Duncan lifted his hand, then lowered it, unsure if she would allow his touch again just because she had a few hours before. "From what I've seen of yer captain, she will stop at nothing to be united with ye again."

A faint smile tugged at the corners of Cyrene's lips. She kept her eyes on the black void a few more seconds before turning to catch up with Revna.

"The path from here is treacherous. Watch yer step." Revna lowered herself into a crouch and silently picked her way through the thickest part of the wood.

Duncan followed Cyrene. He tried not to bear the entire burden for her situation, as he had not invited the attack from the Vikings nor his cousin. Mayhap if he hadn't wandered into her woods, her village would have been unprepared and destroyed without a chance. At least now they could fight.

They'd shared such tenderness in the hours after they'd wed, but he wasn't certain she could ever truly forgive him for what his family had done to hers. He wasn't sure he could forgive himself. If they survived, how long before she could no longer bear the memories and turned against him completely?

Loneliness settled on his shoulders, joining the weight in his chest until his legs strained to hold him upright. He searched for the sky hidden by the branches and vines through which they climbed. But even though he couldn't see it, he knew it was there. Waiting for him on the other side of his journey. It had always been there.

Mayhap this battle would claim the very kingdom his father had ventured to such dark places to secure. His search for purpose had taken him from war, to peace, to war again. Mayhap it was time to accept his place among the soldiers and do his best to defend those under his protection. But he needn't fear anything beyond this life. For that future was secure, and that punishment had already been taken for him.

Lost in his thoughts, he didn't notice Revna's signal, and only saw her near-invisible shape suddenly make some movement he couldn't discern and then disappear, as if she were swallowed whole by the earth.

Duncan charged forward, grabbing Cyrene's shoulders to save her from the same fate. Her yelp was silenced by his hand over her mouth, but before he could free his blade, she'd wrenched from his grasp, spun, drawn her bow, and had the tip of her arrow digging into his chest, a hiss on her lips.

Alarmed at the commotion, Eowin appeared at his side, his own blade at the ready. Cyrene was but a shadow, her shoulders rising and falling with heavy breaths. Eowin tapped his shoulder, silently telling him to stand down.

The captain seemed to ignore the fact that Cyrene was prepared to end his king right there, and crept past both of them to where Revna was waiting in the opening of an underground chamber.

"I thought there was danger." Duncan knew he'd startled her, but the quickness with which she'd turned her weapon on him sparked a hurt and anger he didn't understand or expect.

He snatched her arrow with such force its tip grazed his flesh, leaving a stinging trail. As he followed Eowin, he thrust the arrow into Cyrene's hand, leaving her blinking and stunned.

Once they were all below ground, Revna worked a rope that closed the hidden hatch, bathing them all in total darkness.

"We canna risk a torch. Animals have added their tunnels to ours, even the smallest bit of light could give us away. Put yer hands out, follow the walls. The path is smooth."

He'd already been uncomfortable to learn Revna had a secret path into his villages, but the sudden appearance of a well-constructed underground tunnel had him reeling. How long had it taken them to carve their way across the fields? What else was happening in his kingdom without his knowledge?

The thud of Cyrene's leather boots on the packed earth alerted him of her arrival. The others moved on, but Duncan was rooted in place. He felt the warmth of Cyrene's body as she moved blindly, stilling when she met the wall of his presence.

"Ye did this?" He spoke into the dark. His voice was ragged and hard. "Created this?"

He heard Cyrene's breath hitch, then the long inhale of a hesitation.

"Aye." Her answer was confident. Unapologetic.

Fire raced up his spine, and an infuriating burn of embarrassment at the vulnerability he'd allowed with Cyrene just hours before.

He heard a soft sound as if she were about to speak when Eowin's heavy hand dropped onto Duncan's shoulder.

"Yer Majesties. We canna tarry."

Duncan turned sharply, his hands stretched out until his fingers met the smooth, cool moisture of earth. Measuring the space by touch, he found the ceiling just inches above his head and secured with hewn logs at regular intervals. He followed the sounds of Revna's footsteps, her occasional whispered orders to hurry, and warnings to turn ahead.

He could hear Cyrene's breathing and knew she was close behind him, her hands occasionally brushing the fabric of his shirt.

Until a few days before, there had been clear lines between friend and foe. His kingdom had been the light, and the woods were the darkness.

But all that he thought to be true had been utterly shredded upon meeting Cyrene, who in a blink had somehow become his wife. He was lost in all the secrets, just as blindly moving through his understanding as he was through that buried passage.

Once again, he had no choice but to keep moving forward, hoping the next step would be solid and not another surprise that would swallow him whole.

"Climb." Revna's hiss reached him in the dark, and he listened to the rhythmic sounds of her feet on some kind of ladder before light flooded in a square of earth she'd pushed open.

When his head broke the surface, he was surprised to find himself inside a small village home. It could have been the dwelling of any simple farming family.

Instinctively, he reached for Cyrene's hand as she climbed the ladder, but she ignored his aid and brushed her skirts as she stood, not meeting his eye.

Whatever warmth and closeness they'd experienced had turned to ice. As his eyes grazed over her folded arms and hard stare, he felt no desire to be close to her. It was not only her heart that had chilled.

"Who lives here?" Even as he asked, Duncan noticed a set of blacksmith tools neatly laid out on a slip of deer hide. Next to it, precisely folded, a thick leather apron waited for its master.

No one answered. Duncan looked over his shoulder in time to catch Cyrene giving Revna an approving nod.

The scout narrowed her blue eyes and tilted her head as she said coolly, "A friend."

A few shared features were where her similarities to Fiona ended. Fiona was warmth and life and joy. Revna, though barely out of childhood, terrified him.

"A friend to whom?" It was Eowin who spoke the question brewing in Duncan's own mind.

"Today?" Revna leveled a look of hard stone at his captain. "A friend to all of us. Come." She didn't wait for him to agree before pulling a bit of parchment and charcoal from a satchel she wore across her body. "Ye can make yer way into the keep this way."

Revna scribbled a drawing on the parchment, not caring that Eowin hovered over her shoulder.

Duncan's fingers flew into his blond curls. "How do ye ken my own village better than even I?"

Revna didn't raise her head. She only flicked her eyes up, examining him through dark lashes, but it was Cyrene that answered.

"There isna time now for our full history, but the reason Revna ken of this way is because my people needed to survive." Cyrene's emerald eyes flashed with some memory that drove her gaze to the ground. Her hand touched a place on her side, rubbing some forgotten pain. When she saw him watching, she dropped her hand, eyes hard. "That is the only reason."

Duncan ground his teeth, but because of their union, he knew what lay beneath the fabric of her dress where her fingers had been. A wide swath of puckered skin. A scar that stretched the length of her ribs.

She'd carefully removed his hand when his fingers had discovered the scar, and he didn't dishonor her by demanding to know how she'd received such an injury. In truth, he hadn't wanted to hear for fear it had been at the hands of one of his father's men.

Her answer seemed to satisfy Eowin, who returned his attention to the parchment. He asked a few clarifying questions, which Revna answered with confidence as Cyrene hovered near the wall furthest from Duncan.

A woven basket was the home of several near-finished blades, which Cyrene browsed, testing each with practice thrusts.

Finally Eowin nodded and rolled the parchment as Revna approached Cyrene. The queen was turning a chosen blade in her hand and doing anything possible to ignore Duncan's presence.

He did the same, lingering near a window to scan the dark,

empty streets outside. Houses still stood unmolested, but all who were able had fled to the keep when William's army broke through his outer defenses and they'd heard rumors of the king's demise. He closed his eyes and listened. Only an occasional shout infiltrated the silence of the night. The battle must have died at nightfall. At least his cousin followed some proper rules of battle.

"'Tis time." Cyrene's voice was tight, and Duncan couldn't help but cast a concerned glance her way. "Ye ken what to do."

Revna bowed to Cyrene, then focused her stark, determined eyes on the queen. Every word Revna spoke sounded like a promise, or a threat. "I will gather the warriors. I will keep our people hidden. And I will find ye."

"Be swift, Revna." Cyrene placed a hand on Revna's shoulder, drawing the scout in close enough for their foreheads to touch.

Revna's shoulders stiffened under Cyrene's embrace. Although the response to their queen's affection was as different as the night was from the day, it was clear Revna loved Cyrene as passionately as Astrid did.

When the queen released her, Revna turned murderous eyes on Duncan. "The warriors will be in place. Our aim is true, and we will stand until the last enemy is felled."

Duncan opened his mouth to thank her, but she advanced on him, moving so quickly, he didn't see her blade until it was at his throat. A second blade he didn't even know she carried cut through the air, blocking Eowin's defensive draw, and the captain was stilled in his tracks, though she never took her eyes off the king.

"If any harm comes to my queen, I will end the battle myself, and my last arrow will find yer heart." She cocked her head to the side, the gesture more threatening and taunting than the blade at his neck. She spoke again, delivering her final comment slowly and deliberately. "I protect my family."

Duncan had seen his share of fighting. He'd witnessed the horrors of what the Vikings did to their captives, and he'd even survived a plague that left men begging for death before the end, but nothing terrified him as much as the promise in Revna's dark blue eyes. Just to drive her oath home, she flexed her wrist, the bite of her blade sending a trickle of blood racing down Duncan's neck.

"I will protect her." Duncan let his gaze drift over her shoulder to meet Cyrene's uncertain expression. "I swear it."

Revna's blade was sheathed, and she vanished through the tunnel's entrance before Duncan could exhale.

"Where was my captain?" Duncan rubbed his throat, wiping away the blood as Eowin moved toward the door.

"Yer on yer own wi' that one." Eowin flattened himself against the wall as he cracked open the door, scanning the streets. He cut a teasing glance back to Duncan. "She's terrifying."

The three of them moved through the empty village, following Revna's instructions that kept them hidden to anyone who might be spying from the surrounding wall, and soon found themselves at the church. Cyrene ushered them through the oak doors, which were always unlocked. Duncan was keenly aware of her eyes on him as he hesitated at the threshold.

It had taken near death, a rushed marriage, and an impending battle to coax him back into God's house. Each step he took across the cobblestone floor pounded conviction of his chosen distance further into his heart. But there was also the steadfast call of his Savior, pleading with him to return.

They passed rows of empty wooden benches, Eowin moving directly toward the massive stone fireplace embedded into the wall behind the altar. He knelt and pressed his fingers against the blackened back. After a few seconds of searching, a faint click preceded movement. A small door scraped open, and Duncan shook his head as an amused breath escaped his lips.

Another secret.

"It leads—"

"To the tower." Duncan finished Eowin's statement, raising his hand as an offering to let the others go first. "This, at least, makes sense."

If his father spent nearly every bit of hack silver fortifying his kingdom, he would certainly have had the foresight to create an escape route for himself. From the church, one could easily reach a waiting ship or the caves cut into the cliffs lining the shore if the tower was overrun.

"Keep a keen eye, Eowin." Duncan drew his blade, suddenly anxious to be trapped inside the passageway.

It was so narrow, they had to turn to the side to fit. It was steep and seemed to go on forever, but Duncan could feel the familiarity of the tower approaching.

Though he still felt immense turmoil regarding his father, he was thankful the man's distrust had led him to go through such lengths that provided Duncan a way back home. He did wonder, though, how many times Revna had stolen inside that home. He shuddered at the thought of her standing over him as he slept, talking herself out of beheading him with that blade she wielded with such deadly precision.

He'd never know the answer. The thought of confronting her churned his stomach in such a way that he had to swallow hard to keep his dinner in place.

"There it is." Eowin's hoarse whisper released a wave of relief as Duncan was beginning to feel the walls were closing in.

Slowly, Eowin eased through the opening of a final door before motioning Duncan and Cyrene to follow. Duncan recognized the small stair that would lead to the main hall, and turned to see that the door they'd exited was invisible, hidden by a tapestry. He'd explored every inch of this tower as a lad, then again as an adult, and never once noticed anything unusual about this small hallway.

By now, Revna would be stalking her way back to the woods to meet Astrid and lead Cyrene's warriors into position. They had to remain hidden, even from his own armies, until just the right moment. There was still a traitor in their midst, and any small slip of information could mean the end. Of them all.

They paused at the top of the stairs. The tower was silent. Whatever servants remained would have gathered in the keep with the villagers, praying for rescue.

Eowin flattened himself against the stone wall, glancing around the corner quickly before easing into the great hall.

"If ye see anyone about, ye have found yer traitor." Eowin drew his sword and nodded to Duncan before slipping off toward the southern bend of the tower. He would watch the waters. If they had correctly interpreted the cryptic last words of Cyrene's captured Viking, a fleet would arrive before dawn.

Duncan and Cyrene were left alone. He was meant to make his way to where the villagers were waiting, spreading hope amongst them at the return of their king and beseeching any able-bodied man to take up arms in defense of their people.

"This way." Duncan kept his voice low, inching toward the western wall and the stairs leading to the courtyard.

"Duncan." Cyrene's whisper halted him, but he didn't turn.

He felt her approach, and tensed at the warmth of her hand on his back.

"Duncan, I am sorry."

"Sorry fer what exactly?" Duncan didn't face her and was surprised when Cyrene didn't balk at his sharp reply.

Their union was supposed to unite their kingdoms. The whole point was to bring them together, but their suspicion and distrust had returned the second they'd stepped from the queen's hut.

He clenched his jaw, keeping his frustration in check. It wasn't just with her, but with himself for letting her reservations affect him so deeply. She'd warned him, after all. She'd been nothing but honest. He wanted to brush it off and continue with their mission, but there was no guarantee there would be a tomorrow. He remained frozen under her touch, sensing she had more to say.

"I'm sorry fer drawing on ye." Her hand remained on his shoulder, as if anchoring him in place until she'd said her piece. "I have lived my whole life at the ready."

A bit of a memory invaded his mind. The visage of a gaunt lass peeking out from behind a tree. An ashen face framed with wild licks of red hair. Trembling fingers wrapped around the hilt of a dagger and no more than a tattered semblance of a cloak to shield her from the bitter cold of winter. He'd always thought the lass he'd seen in the woods when he was a lad was only a vision created by his mind as some response to his desperate desire to find the legendary fairies of The Dorcha.

Her hand drifted down his arm as if she meant to let it fall away, but he caught it as she brushed his palm. She didn't pull away, not even when he threaded his fingers through hers.

"I survived by preparing for the worst. A sickness we couldna heal, a winter so harsh, we'd surely starve. I still wake up every day fearing it will be the day our sanctuary is discovered."

Duncan swallowed hard, barely able to make his tightening throat obey.

"I ken ye are angry about our secret ways into yer village, but I canna apologize fer that. 'Twas the only way we survived the years we were hunted by William's soldiers."

She stepped past him, her hand still captured by his, and turned to face him. She lifted his hand, and Duncan was forced closer as she flattened his palm against her ribs, just over her scar. He held his breath. Somehow this action felt more intimate than even the hours after their wedding.

"I was ten and six. Our healer, Brígid, was also our storyteller in my mother's stead. She took Revna to the forest edge, sharing some bit of lost history with her. I followed."

Duncan wanted to tell her to stop, that she didn't have to bare herself to him like this, but he couldn't. He could only swallow a dry lump forming in his throat.

"Whatever the story, it sent Revna racing across the open field toward the tower. Brígid gave chase and caught her. Revna tore back into the woods, but Brígid . . ."

Cyrene paused, pain reddening her cheeks and tears pooling in her eyes.

"Brígid was seen by a tower soldier. I went to help her."

Duncan wanted to lower his gaze, but he didn't feel he had the right to abandon her in her sorrow. Cyrene's throat moved as she battled to share the end of her story.

"Only I returned to the village, though."

Duncan moved his thumb, grazing it over the scar hidden by the coarse fabric of her dress. He knew how painful the wound must have been, how grave. He knew it was nothing compared to the loss of her friend. The thought ignited a rage more powerful than his reservations, forcing him to speak through clenched teeth. "He did this to ye?"

"Aye." Cyrene tilted her head to the side. "But I did worse to him. Brígid delivered the final blow, but . . . only to spare me the burden"

She watched his face, searching for his reaction.

"Does Revna ken what happened that day?"

"Nay." She released his hand, but he kept it at her side, picturing a young queen bleeding and grieving, stumbling through the woods alone and frightened. "I dunna intend for her to. I told a lie to protect her."

Cyrene cleared her throat and swallowed hard before continuing. "I still wonder if hiding Brigid's bravery to spare Revna was the right choice."

Duncan finally dropped his hand, but caught her cool fingers again, holding tightly.

"Brígid was the last true thread that tied me to my mother. I began plans for the tunnel the minute I recovered. We had no choice. Dunna punish the smithy. His mother was our kind, and when it all . . . well, she placed him in the arms of a village woman in order that he might live. And this . . ." Her voice dropped to a whisper.

Duncan tilted his head, watching her free hand as she pressed it against the bow strapped across her chest, then curled her fingers around its string. "Has kept me alive, kept all of us alive more times than I can count."

She ran her thumb across the twisted flax of the string. "I canna promise it willna happen again."

Duncan searched her face as she released the fullness of her green eyes on his.

"Be patient wi' me," she said.

Somehow, in just a few words and with the spell of her bright green eyes, she'd managed to tear through his doubts and suspicions. Her humble request sent a burst of heat across his skin, and had they not been about to sneak through the darkness to turn simple farmers into seasoned soldiers in a single night, he'd have wished to spend a proper wedding night with her. Instead, he hooked his hand along her jaw and pressed a kiss to her forehead.

He had to clear his throat before he could speak. "I must ask the same of ye."

24

CYRENE

821 AD - Minutes Later

The feel of Duncan's hand around hers kept her breathing as she trailed behind him through the cold corridors of his tower.

The long hall they traveled seemed to close in, and her breaths grew short from more than the running and tension of a coming battle. She couldn't see the sky; there was nothing green or alive. It was all stone and hardness and lifelessness. This was her new home. The place Fiona died. That thought bristled her skin, turning her stomach as if she were being led to a prison cell. Or a tomb.

The moment she aimed that arrow at his chest, she'd regretted it. It was only partially out of habit. If she was honest, she'd not stopped suspecting the worst of him, even after their tender moments together and a few shared smiles. Even though she'd told him about Brígid, a secret she'd never told anyone else, her mother's warning had never left her mind.

Dunna trust the tower king.

She stumbled several times, caught up by the sight of golden wall torches or elaborately woven tapestries. Duncan was gentle, promising a proper tour "when this is over."

He spoke as if they would emerge victorious, as if they stood a chance against the vast army she'd caught a glimpse of out of one of the arched windows. She desperately wished to share that hope, but all she could envision was that sea of bobbing torchlights which dotted the land surrounding Duncan's tower.

Theirs was a fool's hope. Even with her warriors' skill, they could not win. A twinge of guilt tugged at her when he launched a reassuring smile over his shoulder. Despite her own secret plans, she would still keep her promise to him and fight until the end. Duncan would never have the chance to test her mother's warning, so it didn't seem like a true betrayal to open her heart to him for a few hours. It was nothing but a bit of light before the dark.

Dread of that darkness tugged at Cyrene's nerves, creating an itch in her fingers to keep her bow loaded. She tensed at every corner, expecting to be set upon. Duncan's fingers jerked too; it seemed he felt the same.

When they finally crept down a long stone flight of stairs into the inner courtyard, they were greeted by cries of joy and surprise from the few villagers that were gathered near the entrance. Cyrene felt her lungs finally expand to their full capacity in the fresh air and open space.

Duncan gently shushed the chorus of "My lord"s and "Your Majesty"s. He let them embrace him, touched their heads, and patted shoulders. He knew them each by name.

"Spread the word that the king has returned." His voice was strong with confidence, and Cyrene watched in awe as the fear that drew their faces taut melted at the sight of their king. "Tell everyone he is alive and well. He has wed the powerful woodland queen of The Dorcha. Her armies are terrible and swift. Tell them help is coming.

Tell them to have hope and courage. And tell every able-bodied man to take up arms in defense of Tràigh."

They'd decided together not to reveal her Pictish lineage just yet, but instead to turn fear into courage as the things they'd always feared from The Dorcha were now fighting for them.

Duncan asked for several villagers by name, a group of women. Those listening greeted Cyrene out of respect to their king, but their eyes regarded her with wonder and uncertainty. She suspected there were few in the village who hadn't heard rumors of a fierce queen of the woods, and she prayed all those stories and legends would now give them hope, for she was on their side.

They bowed in agreement to his request, kissed his hands in gratitude, and whispered to each other as they began to spread out amongst the huddled groups.

The women he'd sent for rushed through the crowd, mouths covered with trembling hands when they saw he was indeed not a ghost. He hurriedly relayed instructions to them, making sure they felt confident to carry them out.

"Aye m'lord." One of the ladies reminded Cyrene of her mother—what she could remember of her, anyway. She looked to be about the age Derelei would have been had she lived. She stood tall and strong. A leader. Duncan had called her Sima.

"I willna fail ye." Sima bowed to the king, repeating the same words Revna had when Cyrene issued her own secret request.

Duncan turned to speak to a group of men that had gathered. Before she left to begin the task her king had set, Sima bowed to Cyrene, sharp eyes taking in the new queen.

"I ken who ye are."

Alarmed, Cyrene felt the color drain from her face as she scanned the crowd to see if any heard Sima's announcement.

"I ken yer mother." Sima's words froze Cyrene in place.

"How?"

"I was a maid in King William's household. I was released when he wed the Pictish lady, Fiona. But I ken of Derelei. I was there the eve she came to the tower and learned of yer father's death. Ye can be sure she loved him fiercely. I never saw such grief." Sima's sweet smile warmed Cyrene's chilled skin, easing her worry. "But even in her grief, the Battling Queen was lovely and wise. She kept to her principles despite the persistence of . . ." Sima's gaze flicked to Duncan, and her face reddened, as if she'd insulted him. "Well . . . she was lovely."

Sima bowed, moving to leave when Cyrene grabbed her wrist, tight breaths lifting her tone. "The persistence of whom?"

Sima sent another anxious glance toward Duncan, who was already instructing the men in the ways of warfare. By the time the woman returned her eyes to Cyrene, Sima had schooled her expression back to a sweet smile. "Just the persistence of those who would guide her down the wrong path. We are blessed to call Derelei's daughter our queen, m'lady. I ken what it would take for ye to return here. Yer courage this night willna be forgotten."

"Sima." Cyrene drew the woman close. "Please dunna tell anyone who I am . . . not yet. The time will come, but not yet."

Duncan had broken free from the mob, and Cyrene felt his warmth at her side. Sima nodded, gently pulled her arm free from Cyrene's grasp, bowed to Duncan, and disappeared into the dark sea of villagers, bound for her mission set by the king. Sima's cryptic message cinched Cyrene's insides into an uncomfortable knot. What other secrets and betrayals did this tower hold?

"Are ye well?" Duncan frowned, his fingers brushing loose strands of hair back from her face.

Cyrene took in a deep breath and forced a smile. "Aye. 'Tis overwhelming."

"Mmm." Duncan squeezed her arm gently. "Not the introduction ye would have desired, I ken."

Another villager approached, and again, Duncan greeted him by name. She found herself gaping at him. She had always imagined the people were oppressed under the crown, their lives sad and not much better than slaves. Mayhap that had been true with William. But they loved Duncan. Watching the lines of worry work their way across his drawn brow, she was certain he loved them too.

A shadow shifted, and movement from above caught her eye. She curled her fingers around his arm, drawing his attention.

"Behind ye," she said, fisting his tunic in both hands to keep him from turning. "There is someone watching from the upper wall."

Duncan kept his eyes centered on hers, his every muscle taut as if he was fighting an internal battle with himself not to turn toward the figure she was watching.

"Tell me."

"I canna see his face. He wears a cloak, but he is crouched, watching."

Duncan nodded and lifted his hand, fingers tucking a strand of her hair behind her ear without touching her skin.

"I'm going to kiss ye now and walk ye into the shadows so he canna see us." He tipped his brow, asking her permission.

"Aye." Her throat was tight, but she allowed him to lift her chin with his finger.

Heat flooded through her stomach when he pressed his lips to hers, then exploded through her chest when he wrapped his arms around her waist and started to move them backwards. Her eyes were closed, but she could sense when they'd reached the darkness of the hidden corner. Duncan didn't pull back right away. Instead, he slid his hand to the side of her neck, holding her in place as he deepened the kiss, encouraged by her willing response. He stole a bit of her breath when he finally pulled back.

"Ye make an excellent distraction, m'lady." He ran his rough knuckles across her cheek before turning to peek at their mystery observer. "He's still there."

Duncan watched for a silent second, hand hovering over the hilt of his blade. He spoke to her without breaking his focus on his target. "Keep him distracted."

Duncan crept deeper into the darkness toward an open stair. He took her hand, gently squeezing her fingers as an offering of confidence in her ability.

"Aye." Cyrene licked her lips, the feel of his kiss still lingering.

When he began his stealthy ascent, she stepped out of the shadows and moved through the crowd, making a show of introducing herself.

She felt a tug on her sleeve and looked down to see the round face of a wide-eyed little girl.

"Hello." Cyrene lowered herself to sit on her heels, face to face with the lass, whose golden ringlets bounced when she moved. "What's yer name?"

"Gwen." Her voice was a bell, a pure and innocent light in the dark worry and uncertainty that surrounded them.

"I am called Cyrene."

"Can I see yer ears?" Gwen blinked, unashamed of her bold question.

Cyrene smiled, tucked her hair behind her ears, and folded her hands into her lap. Gwen reached to trace the curve of Cyrene's ear, her little fingers cold on the queen's skin.

"They're not pointy." She sounded disappointed. "Are ye not a fairy?"

Cyrene couldn't help the grin that broke across her lips. She ran her finger over Gwen's round cheek and tapped her nose, making the little lass giggle.

"Nay. I am just like ye." As she talked, Cyrene kept a watchful eye on the crouching spy above.

"Have ye ever seen one?" Gwyn tilted her round face, curious eyes taking in everything about the queen.

Cyrene smiled again. "Only in my dreams."

A rumble of distant thunder shook the sky, and a baby cried, drawing the attention of several ladies, who tried to hush the infant. Cyrene made her way to the women and joined them in fussing over the little one, leaving Gwen to excitedly show her mother the thin leather bracelet Cyrene had taken from her own wrist and tied on hers.

She covertly flicked her gaze again to the spot where she'd seen the spying stranger. He was still there, crouched in the shadows. Duncan had not appeared yet.

"M'lady!" Sima rushed to her side. "Please, come, come and see!"

Her plea was hushed but urgent, and Cyrene handed the baby back to its mother before following the woman through a maze of people to the far wall that faced the back side of the tower. The lithe figure followed her movements, also turning to the outer wall.

Sima opened a small wooden shutter to reveal a perfect view of the sea. With no moon, it was near black.

"Where?" Cyrene squinted into the night.

"Watch. When the sky is alight, ye can see sharp lines just above the horizon. There are ships."

Sure enough, when Cyrene relaxed her gaze and waited for the coming storm to illuminate the clouds, sails of at least three ships appeared jutting up out of the ocean. They had not yet begun their journey through the jagged firths.

Another rumble of thunder shuddered the sky, shaking something loose in Cyrene's chest. She repeated the prayer she'd sung to Astrid and turned to Sima, who had wrapped her arms around herself in fear.

Cyrene grabbed Sima's shoulders, then placed her hands on the sides of the woman's face, capturing her wide eyes. "Have courage, Sima. The time is now."

Without waiting for Sima to respond, Cyrene ran back to the courtyard, her eyes immediately finding the dark space where the watcher had been. He'd disappeared.

Cyrene sprinted across the mass of bodies, searching the dark stone walls until she spotted his shadow again. Swiftly, he swept up his cloak in his hand and nimbly scurried along the wall toward a thin jutting tower looming above the top of Duncan's home.

"What's up there?" Cyrene grabbed the nearest villager and pointed to the silhouetted wooden turret where the stranger was headed.

"The signal tower," a man said in surprise. "To light the way for the ships at sea."

As realization set in, Duncan appeared on the wall where the stranger had been. At the same time, a low whistle drifted through the air.

Eowin's signal. He'd spotted the ships too. Cyrene chirped her own warning. Duncan found her in the crowd and she pointed to the tower.

The stranger's cloaked shape was flying up the thin stair, and Duncan raced after him. Cyrene searched for a way to get to a higher vantage point. She spied an unfinished bit of wall and pulled herself up, dancing along the jagged edge until she was one level higher.

At another flash of lightning, she could just see the tops of the sails from where she stood. They bobbed up and down on an angering sea. The wind had picked up, whipping strands of Cyrene's hair across her face.

Haste, Duncan. Make haste. Cyrene's unbreaking stare pushed her pleading thoughts toward Duncan, who scrambled up the stairs in pursuit.

Duncan was gaining on the man, and Cyrene held her breath as he overtook him. Duncan clasped the man's arms. They struggled, and the man's cloak hood fell back. Duncan froze, stunned for a split second, then Cyrene saw why. Long braids whipped free in the wind. Cyrene couldn't hear, but Duncan shook the woman and spoke to her like he knew her.

His shock gave her just enough time to rear back and kick out her foot, sending him careening down several steps. As he scrambled to his feet, she raced up the last few steps to the tower, slamming the door shut before he could catch her.

Cyrene's hands flexed as she watched, knowing she couldn't

reach the tower to help him before the woman got the signal fires lit. As if his shoulder was thunder, Duncan slammed against the door at the same time the sound exploded from the sky. It shuddered under the force but held firm. Cyrene scanned the courtyard. A few villagers had noticed her quick departure and were watching, grabbing anyone near enough to reach as they began to understand what was unfolding. They huddled together as the first drops of cool rain fell.

She narrowed her eyes, focusing on the dark window of the tower. There was a slip of a shadow, then a flash of light. Sparks! The woman was about to light the signal.

Her heart thundered in her chest. If the signal was lit, at least three ship loads of ruthless, bloodthirsty Vikings would be at their backs. From the north and the south. The captured Viking's warning finally made perfect sense.

Duncan was still working the door, but it held. A flash of flame soared across the sky from the far window of the signal tower. Was that a signal arrow?

Cyrene couldn't see where it landed from where she stood, and Duncan wouldn't have seen it at all. He slammed against the door again.

A hard ball of dread formed in her stomach. She had to do something.

The ringing of a child's laugh wafted up from the courtyard, and Cyrene caught the wave of Gwen's little hand as she danced between fat drops of rain. In the next instant, instead of her bright smile and flushed cheeks, she envisioned Gwen's dirty, tear-stained face, her tiny body bound by rough ropes and dragged onto the deck of a Viking ship.

The vision of that future settled deep in her heart, dread replaced by a stillness, a certainty that smoothed her movements and steadied her hands.

Drawing an arrow from her quiver, she loaded her bow and pulled back the string. She peered down the straight line of her arrow, focusing on the window, praying the woman would come into view before it was too late. The sky opened, and the heavens released a curtain of cold rain.

Breathe in. Breathe out. Release. The internal chant she'd taught herself as a child hummed in her mind. Raindrops stung her eyes as they slid down her face. It was too dark—the window remained invisible against the black shape of the signal tower. A sudden sharp line of lightning lit the sky, and Cyrene could see clearly. Just as the woman brought her hands together to strike a flint and light the signal, Cyrene let her arrow fly. Wind from its flight brushed her face like a gentle hand, but it found its target. The tower was once again cloaked in darkness, and Cyrene felt a hot tear mingle with the cold rain on her cheek, her insides as cold and tumbling as the sea.

Duncan finally broke through the door and disappeared inside for two breaths before he burst out again, first staring out across the sea before looking to the courtyard, immediately finding Cyrene's shape on the wall, her bow still raised.

He lifted his hand, motioning for her to meet him at the bottom of the stairs. Cyrene slung her bow across her chest and raced along the wall, winding her way up stairs and through doors until she found him.

"She fired an arrow . . . with flames. I dunna ken why." Breathless, her words stuck to the inside of her mouth as she wiped her face dry with her cloak. "And there are ships."

She wanted to ask about the woman in the signal tower. Who was she? Why had she done such a terrible thing? Had Cyrene missed her mark for once, and the woman lived? But those questions could wait.

"I ken." Duncan shook the water from his hair as he led her to a large window overlooking the sea, pointing to the faint jagged shapes dotting the shore. "Look."

In quick succession, bolts of lightning flashed, making the land as bright as day.

"There were three." Cyrene squinted into the night, clearly counting only two sails. "I ken there were three."

Another flash from the sky, and Cyrene grabbed Duncan's arm. Remains of a destroyed ship dotted rolling waters that crashed with foamy waves against the jagged rocks. Another ship was dangerously close to the same fate. Her heart leapt in her chest, both with dread of the remaining two but hope that God had indeed raised this storm to protect them.

"There is hope." Her hand slid down Duncan's arm and found his hand, her fingers weaving through his.

"Without the signal fire, if the storm doesna destroy them, the rocks will."

"At least they canna reach the shore until dawn." Cyrene felt Duncan's stare and looked up at him.

He released her hand and pulled her arrow from where it was tucked in the loop of his belt. She stared at it, unable to take it from him. The shaft was darker than before, marred by the blood of a traitor, but the tip was clean.

"Ye were nigh fifteen fell from that tower." He wiped the tear from her face with his thumb, and something passed over his expression, something that made Cyrene's insides warm again. "Ye have a gift, Cyrene. Ivna seen anything like that before."

She didn't touch the arrow. If she didn't take it back, it was almost as if it hadn't happened. As if she hadn't taken a life for the first time. Also, for the first time, she hated her gift.

"Are ye certain yer not a fairy?" When Cyrene didn't smile, Duncan's expression turned serious. "Cyrene, she—"

"Tell me after." She placed her hand on his chest to stop him from saying anything else. His heart thumped hard beneath her palm, and he covered her hand with his. She couldn't think about the woman who lay dead in the tower. The woman she had killed.

"Very well."

She gazed back out to the stormy sea. "Mayhap *An T-aon* is wi' us after all."

"Mayhap." Duncan's lips ticked up at one side before his expression grew serious once again. "Yer right, though. At first light, those ships *will* reach the shore. We must hurry."

They raced to the west side of the tower. He directed her to another large window, this one overlooking the outer section of the keep. With so few soldiers, they had no choice but to stage their defense there.

"If I dunna find ye before, I will meet ye at first light. Ye ken the way?" Duncan's blue eyes danced between hers, water still dripping onto his face from his soaked hair.

Her heart was climbing up her throat, so she only nodded. Duncan peered over the edge and placed his hand on the stones as if making sure they were sturdy. "This will give ye a clear shot."

Cyrene's chest was tight. Despite her childhood promise and mother's warning, she didn't want him to leave her. If he was felled, she would be a widow queen of a kingdom she didn't know. His cousin would enslave the people and destroy her warriors. Destroy her. Or worse, claim her as his own.

"Huntress." Duncan's hand was warm on her face. "Our plan is good. *Yer* plan is good. I *will* meet ye at dawn."

Their plans were foolish at best. All dependent on each small part unfolding exactly right. One deviation, and all would be lost. She clung to his strong arms, fisting the wet fabric of his tunic, and drew him close until her forehead rested on his chest. He wrapped his arms around her and buried his face in her drenched hair. She prayed for Beli's courage.

"I ken *An T-aon* is good. He hears us when we call. May he be wi' ye," she prayed. "Bring ye back to me, and may the wings of heaven shield ye from harm."

He drew back, and she lifted her chin to gaze up at him, surprised at the longing in his eyes. She wondered if he wished for the same thing as she. Time.

"May yer aim be true." His voice was low, his words heavy with meaning.

"I willna let ye fall."

His brows dipped, pain flashing across his face, evidence of a war within. As if deciding he must leave then or not at all, he lowered his head, kissed both her hands, and was gone before she could say another word.

25

DUNCAN

821 AD - The Same Night

Duncan crouched beside Eowin on the northeastern wall after he'd left Cyrene with three full baskets of arrows villagers had collected from the armory. As rain pelted his back, her prayer that God would bring him back echoed in his heart. Not just back to the throne, but to her. His skin still hummed where she'd touched him. His arms, his chest, his lips. A complicated thread weaved them together like a tapestry with two faces, one side trust, the other suspicion.

If there was not already reason enough to survive the night, the hope of the trust side emerging victorious pushed him to review the plan with Eowin once again just to be certain. Although he feared Cyrene was only warming to him because of their dire situation, and if they survived, her hate would bloom again.

The way she'd looked at him in the woods when she'd turned her weapon on him— He shook his head, reminding himself there was a battle he needed to think about, not his marital situation.

"The men are ready." Eowin's breaths were short, labored. He'd been scrambling along the tower walls gathering all the remaining soldiers and instructing them on the battle plan.

Duncan placed a heavy hand on his captain's shoulder and nodded in appreciation. They were about to stand when the sound of a horn rose over the sound of the rain.

A few blinking lights of William's camp still survived the sudden storm, but out of the darkness, lines of soldiers seemed to materialize from nothing. It was a trick. They weren't bedded down for the night at the camp. They were marching on the tower.

Duncan gripped the stone of the wall with such force, his nails threatened to break. This was not part of the plan—not yet. Why would they do such a thing?

The ships! William's troops had been waiting for the ships. That's why the spy had fired that flaming arrow Cyrene saw, but they wouldn't know the spy didn't succeed in lighting the signal fires. That tower was hidden from their position. They wouldn't know there were only two ships instead of three. This could work in their favor.

"They march, sire." Eowin's voice was cold, dread filling the air between them.

"Signal the men."

"The woodland warriors arna in place yet." Eowin's face was pale, and Duncan didn't know if it was rain or sweat that coated his forehead. He would be running through the impact this advance would make on their delicate plan as well. "Our men will be spread too thin."

"We canna wait. If they storm the keep before our people are secure, it willna matter. Pray her warriors are swift." Duncan placed both hands on Eowin's shoulders, allowing a moment of peace for two beats of his heart. "Fly, Captain."

Duncan tore off in the opposite direction, wiping rain from his eyes as he gathered his group of soldiers and armed villagers into position. Peering over the wall toward the sea, a determined grin broke across his lips with another flash of lightning. Only one ship. He sent a whistled song into the night, a signal to Cyrene.

He led his half of the warband through the halls until they stood in rows outside the barricaded doors of the keep. Eowin's soft whistle let him know he was waiting with his soldiers on the upper level as Duncan prepared his below. With the village men, they were sixty.

Sixty against three hundred, and Duncan stood before them. Outside the tower, they could hear the low drum of marching steps on earth.

All that had transpired to bring him to this place, this moment, rolled through his mind. The training, the study, the way he'd been chased directly into Cyrene's path. He still didn't understand every-thing, but he believed Cyrene was right. She was certain God was listening, that he was good, though they were facing insurmountable odds. He closed his eyes and drew in a long, deep breath, quieting his anxious spirit. A gentle breeze wafted through the keep, cooling his sweat-soaked brow.

I ken ye can hear me. I can finally hear ye, too, now that I've learned how to listen. Whatever the outcome of this night, of my life, I trust ye.

As if God was whispering the answers to all his questions, under-standing settled over his spirit. Eyes still closed, he saw the relief that had been on the faces of his people when he appeared in the courtyard. Mayhap there was one among them who'd been praying for a sign that God existed, praying that if he truly loved them, their king would return to fight for them.

If even for only that one heart, it was worth it. For he had been a stray sheep once, and God had sent someone for him. Fiona and Father Malcolm.

Then he remembered the way Cyrene clung to him moments before, hinting that some of her hard hatred toward the crown, toward him, had softened. Mayhap it was to heal the rift between their lands, to show their people they could exist together, fight together, die together. All those mayhaps, though they be just that, were enough. Enough that he would keep fighting.

Though he was surrounded by death, chaos, and war, he finally felt the peace Fiona had promised.

Duncan could hear the shallow breaths of his men and saw their exhales rising like smoke from their mouths. Fear was yet another enemy they would battle that night. They were tired, hungry, and defeated. The rain soaked through their armor, chilling their skin and weighing them down.

The thud of a ramming rod shook the walls and their resolve. Loose stones clacked down the walls and shattered as they landed.

One.

Two.

Three.

The wood splintered.

He felt his small army shift behind him, the urge to run almost unbearable. Duncan spun and faced them, speaking loud enough for the men on the upper levels to hear over the pounding rain.

"The night is upon us, and death is at our door. But inside those walls, our people still live! Our wives, our children, our future—they depend on us to defend the keep."

The men shifted, grips on their weapons tight, determination bolstered.

"Draw deep. Dunna let the darkness steal yer courage. The Lord is wi' us, I ken it to be true. Raise yer eyes and look to yer king, for I will fight wi' ye. I will die wi' ye. We willna give in to tyranny, to slavery, to death!"

The men pounded their spears on the stone floor, blades clapped together, shields as cymbals against their swords.

"Not one of our innocents will see death until the last one of us falls." Duncan raised his sword. "For Tràigh!"

The gates burst open, soldiers bearing William's crest flooding through.

"For Tràigh!" The shout of his men was the song of triumph, the cry of a people who would not give in.

Their voices were a shield as they rushed forward, swords and spears drawn, determined to hold the keep. As the courtyard filled with fighting men, Duncan's sword was a neverending blade of justice, meeting each foe with accuracy and swiftness. He prayed the instructions he'd given Sima and the other women were clear enough, that the ones he'd left in charge had understood the urgency and carried out his demands.

William's massive army pressed further in. Though his own soldiers were relentless, and Eowin's archers defended from above, if they didn't hold them long enough, every bit of this effort would be for nothing. The plan had to work in entirety or not at all.

There was hope still, though. They were pelted by stinging rain, but his men were unaffected. Storms were not uncommon along the sea, and his men were well-trained to battle in all conditions. Even the village men stood strong, having worked their fields in worse weather. William's men struggled to keep footing on the slippery stones and hold onto weapons with wet hands.

Duncan shouted encouragement over the battle, and his focus became singular—bring down any man bearing his cousin's crest. He was pressed in upon from all sides. He lifted his sword, swung wide, thrust, withdrew, blocked, attacked, thrust, spun, and swung again. Arms lifted in defense against a soldier's descending blade, Duncan felt another coming at his back. He raised his shield in defense while driving his sword through the target at his front, his chest exposed to yet another threat from the side. He bent, the man at his back tumbling over his shield, and rose to find the one who'd been racing toward him at his right, arms still raised, crumple at his feet, an arrow buried in his back.

Duncan sank his sword into yet another assailant just as an arrow sang past his cheek, feathers nearly brushing his skin, its target reached with preternatural accuracy.

He'd been here before. Faced with shadowy demons bringing

destruction and saved by an invisible angel with the aim of an eagle. She'd saved him then, before she even knew him.

He found her in the shadows of the turret. Bow raised and arrows sailing without stop. Even from that distance, her green eyes were alight with purpose, never once missing.

The rain slowed, then stopped as quickly as it had started, and Duncan shook water from his hair, surveying the courtyard. Some had fallen, but many still stood strong, leading William's troops deeper into the walled space, allowing them to fill the area and approach the keep.

"Eowin!" Duncan spotted his captain yelling orders from the upper level. "Hold!"

Duncan turned and raced back into the fray, the swish and stick of Cyrene's arrows clearing a path. Without fear or reservation of an attack from behind or beside, Duncan was a cloud of death over the enemy, emboldened by the fear rising in their eyes.

26

CYRENE

821 AD - The Same Time

Cyrene's eyes were like those of the hawk, searching out and felling her targets with otherworldly precision. *Draw, aim, fire. Draw, aim, fire.* Each arrow found its target without fail.

The sound of Duncan's shout to hold the line sent her scrambling to another window, where, if she leaned out far enough, she could see the inner courtyard.

All the women, children, and elderly had been herded through the secret, narrow escape tunnel by Sima and the other ladies Duncan had chosen. They would become a snake of bodies, slithering through that same hidden path that Cyrene and Duncan had arrived by, toward the village. The village now ignored by William's army because they'd seen the people escape to the tower.

From there, they'd find Revna waiting to take them through the underground tunnel and finally be introduced to their woodland neighbors.

They should have had more time. Much more time. The arrow the spy had let loose must have been a signal to the attacking army. Mayhap because she had seen the king return to his tower, or mayhap because she'd spotted the ships.

Grateful the rain had stopped so she could find sure footing, Cyrene pulled herself atop the ledge, gripping the lip of rock framing the window. She leaned as far as she could, her fingers stinging from the sharp surface of the stones. The courtyard was empty, save for the few village men who had been tasked with barricading any exits. Farmers, blacksmiths, stable hands. They stood in the shadows, ready, as brave and unflinching as any of Duncan's soldiers. It was time.

Cyrene leapt from her place, her palms once again scraping on the rough stone as she landed, but she ignored the sting and grabbed the special arrow Duncan had set aside.

She found him in the fray, relentless as his sword rose and fell, rose and fell. She loaded her bow, released, and watched as he stilled, his blade still embedded in the chest of an enemy soldier, when the arrow bearing a strip of scarlet fabric stuck true at his feet.

She didn't wait for his eyes to find her, but gathered the remaining basket of arrows and hurtled down dark steps to join the other half of Duncan's army, led by Eowin, that would fold in from behind, pushing William's army further into the courtyard.

Over the sound of her ragged breaths, she heard Duncan's voice calling to Eowin. A signal spurring on William's soldiers, but meaning something entirely different to Duncan's.

"Retreat!"

Following a tug on her heart, Cyrene broke from her path and raced along a corridor until she found a small window that looked out over the courtyard. Thinking Duncan's troops had abandoned their upper advantage, William's men gave a shout and rushed forward in victory.

Duncan's men worked their way around the sides of the courtyard, allowing William's army to reach the door of the keep undeterred. As the enemy rammed the massive wooden doors, Duncan's men continued their stealthy move toward the courtyard's entrance, urging more and more of William's army into the tower.

From inside the keep, the villagers were removing the massive planks that held the doors, allowing the enemy to break through. Duncan shouted to his men, and, as if they'd choreographed an elaborate dance, they channeled the invaders into an empty inner courtyard. The villagers and soldiers of Duncan's army closed off the doors behind a large group of William's men, cutting them off from the rest of their army. With all exits blocked, they were trapped, left for a handful of Eowin's archers to pick off one by one until they surrendered.

Cyrene tore herself away, racing to her next position. She flew down stair after stair, the basket of arrows beating against her back as she descended. She finally found the wide, open window Duncan had described.

Eowin was there, directing the remainder of Duncan's army to close in from both sides of the entrance to the tower, choking off William's army in the narrow space. But terror gripped her insides as she watched one after another of Duncan's soldiers fall. Despite their efforts, William's army surged forward. The small army of Tràigh was divided, Duncan's half pushed further back inside, and Eowin's half drawn out of the tower and onto the open fields.

Where were her warriors? *Hurry, Astrid! Oh, please hurry.* Just one level above the battle, Cyrene hurled her basket atop the window's ledge and toed jutting stones to pull herself up, straddling the opening.

Moving in a rhythm as smooth as the sea, she loaded and fired, loaded and fired until her supply was near gone. Despite their clever plan, William's army was too large. Duncan still hadn't emerged with his men, and Cyrene's heart threatened to burst through her chest as she scanned the field, watching soldier after soldier fall under the blades of the enemy.

Between shots, she withdrew a flint stone and scrap of oil-soaked fabric from her pocket. She glanced at her basket. So few arrows remained. She would wait. Until the last second, she would wait for another miracle.

Draw, aim, fire. Draw, aim, fire. William's army began to spread along the wall, some fighting their way further away from the tower and closer to the village. From the village, they might enter the forest.

She couldn't wait any longer. She wrapped the tip of an arrow with the fabric and struck the flint against the stone, creating a spark to ignite the fabric. The whispered instructions she'd given Revna circled in her mind. Another impossible choice. Flee or fight.

"Ye are the one, Revna. It has to be ye," she'd said. "Stay with our people and set a scout on the edge of the wood. Watch for my signal. If the tower is overrun, ye must flee. Take them all over the mountain. Even the people of Tràigh. Hide if ye must, but keep them alive. Yer the closest I have to a daughter. 'Tis ye who must act in my stead should we fail on the battlefield."

Another battle raged. The one in Revna's heart was visible in her blazing blue eyes as she buried her desire to fight with the warriors and nodded in obedience instead.

Keep them safe. A simple prayer was all Cyrene could offer as she loaded her bow with the fiery arrow and drew back the string. Tears as hot as the flame streamed down her cheeks. One last time, she scanned the black fields, her eyes straining for any sign of Astrid's pale braids.

Her heart ripped in two as she aimed for her target, a carefully placed wagon loaded with dry straw just beyond a curve in the wall not visible from fighting fields. The signal that would send Revna over the mountains. Cyrene would not abandon Duncan; she would keep her promise to fight to the end. But she would keep her promise to her people as well. They would not be slaughtered or enslaved. They would live.

Her fingers burned against the tug of the flax as she centered her aim, ready to let fly the signal arrow, when a streak of white blazed past her sight, accompanied by the buzz of dozens of soaring arrows.

Revna, atop her snow-white stallion, burst from the blackness, blades drawn, barreling over men from William's army. She left a wide path of fallen soldiers in her wake. Behind her, Astrid and her archers materialized from the night as ghosts. The captain was astride Taranau, her pale skin a stark contrast to his ebony fur. Cyrene scanned the squadron and found them all. Even Liam, on Cuddie's bare back, whose skilled hands wielded twin swords, charged through the mass of bodies.

A cry of relief escaped from her lips, and she sent her flaming arrow into the back of an enemy soldier who raised his blade against one of her warriors.

With a deafening shout, her warriors circled around and pressed in from both sides, cutting off William's army at the tower entrance. Tràigh soldiers who had been fighting inside the tower poured out to fight alongside her warriors and their countrymen.

Cyrene searched the walls, waiting for Duncan to appear. She couldn't find him. Revna's shout drew her attention, and she dropped to her knees to keep from diving headfirst off the wall as her scout exchanged her blades for a sling. Her leather-wrapped arm whipped the loaded leather strap around her head, releasing stone after stone with deadly accuracy. Then she pushed up and placed her feet on the bare back of her stallion, as swift and terrible as the storm that had dashed those Viking ships against the rocks.

Crouched for balance, she placed her hands on the lean muscled shoulders of her steed as he plowed through the mass of bodies. Cyrene followed the scout's seething gaze to her target. Cyrene held her breath, her hands clinging to the rough stone of the window.

Revna crouched deep, then propelled by his velocity, she leapt, soaring off the stallion's back as if she had wings. As she sailed,

Revna reached behind and withdrew her swords again, their blades glinting even in the moonless night.

Cyrene's cry cut through the sound of blades and clashing shields when Revna was devoured by a mob of enemy soldiers.

Snatching at a remaining arrow, Cyrene frantically searched the tumble of bodies for her scout. All she could see was flying blades and tangled limbs. Unable to distinguish friend from foe, she slammed her fist against the unforgiving stone.

With a breath trapped in her lungs, she determined to fire and trust whatever supernatural power guiding her aim to find the right target. She drew back, narrowed her gaze, and prepared to release, when a figure burst through the mob, uncurling like a phoenix from the ashes as men toppled backwards. Cyrene lowered her bow, her heart nearly stopping at the sight.

Revna. Blades gripped in her hands at her side, her face and clothes soaked through with blood, she stood alone in the middle of a circle of fallen enemies, her chest heaving with unsatiated rage. Even Duncan's soldiers crawled away in terror.

She was death itself, ravenous for a promised reckoning. Cyrene couldn't restrain the boiling tears that seared down her cheeks. Hate, bitterness, and vengeance at whatever life had stolen from her had so long resided in Revna's heart that she was truly the dark queen of war. And she was so young. So very young.

However valid and necessary, all of Cyrene's schemes to keep Revna away from the battle—from the chaotic swarm of swords and blood—had failed. She should have known Revna would come. To defend her home and queen, of course, she would have defied every order.

Revna moved like a shadow, stalking and slaying her prey as Cyrene's heart was torn into shreds. She was vengeance come to save them, but at what cost to Revna's soul?

Shouts from the east drew her attention, and the heat from her blood turned to ice. Duncan!

He'd made it to the outer wall but was cut off and surrounded by a half-circle of William's soldiers. Duncan's men surged forward, blending among the enemy and unaware of the danger pressing in on their king. Cyrene searched for a way to the ground. She was too high to jump, and if she wound down the stairs, she would be too late.

She scanned the field. There was no one close enough to call for help, and she didn't have enough arrows left to fell even half of the men closing in around him. Fist clenched, she slammed her hand onto the stone again, pain radiating from the thin band of silver around her finger. A reminder. A promise. A vow.

She'd promised not to let him die, and she meant to keep her word. A way. The last time she'd begged *An T-aon* for help, she'd been a child. Ever since, her worship and prayers had been faithful but heartless. Out of duty more than passion. Until a king, mistaken for a soldier, was dropped, dying and desperate, at her feet. It was for Duncan that she'd pleaded with *An T-aon* for help. And for Duncan she beseeched him again now.

An T-aon, help me, please, show me the way!

The whip of fabric in the wind caught her eye. A tattered azure flag bearing Duncan's crest jutted from the wall, attached to a thick wooden pole just below where she stood. She looked at her hand, at her mother's ring, the engraving nearly an exact match to the image Duncan had chosen to represent his kingdom. A reared form of a lion, ready to attack.

Then she saw Astrid, still astride Taranau, dodging enemy arrows and lobbed spears. Astrid hooked her leather-clad leg over the pommel of Taranau's saddle and slid to his side, arrows flying in smooth succession from her bow.

Cyrene climbed onto the window ledge, crouched and ready. She sent out a sharp whistle. Astrid jerked her head toward Cyrene's place on the wall. Her sharp eyes followed Cyrene's to the flag and then to Taranau, instantly understanding her queen's intent.

Astrid grabbed the pommel with both hands, unhooked her leg, and held the full weight of her body with her arms as she drew her legs up to her chest. With a click and hiss, she signaled for the horse to slow. Without breaking his stride, Taranau obeyed, and Astrid lowered her legs until she was running alongside the animal. With a flick of her wrist, she unlashed her quiver and released Taranau.

Cyrene glanced at Duncan again. He'd fought back half of his attackers. His sword was still drawn, but he was inching backwards toward the tower wall, one arm pressed close to his side, red seeping through his tunic at his shoulder. William's soldiers closed in.

Fierce determination gripped her nerves, turning them to iron. She placed her few remaining arrows between her teeth, slung her bow across her back, and dove from the window, her arms stretched so far in front of her, she felt her muscles might snap in two.

Eyes on her target, Cyrene caught the fabric of the waving flag and clung to it for her life despite the burn against her palms as it slowly tore and she sailed toward the ground. Knees bent, she braced for impact with the quickly-approaching wall, and kicked off as Taranau's pounding hoofbeats neared.

He galloped beneath her, and she released her hold on the flag, landing hard on his back. Cyrene shoved the three arrows from her mouth under the straps of the saddle and lowered herself until she was flush with Taranau's neck.

"To yer king, Taranau!" He seemed to understand her and kicked up his speed. Cyrene mimicked Astrid's trick and slid to the horse's side, snatching embedded arrows from felled enemy soldiers.

When she had a handful, she rose and began firing one after the other at the men surrounding Duncan. He continued his backwards walk until someone stepped from the shadow of the tower wall.

A man in nobleman's armor wrapped his arm around Duncan's shoulders, dagger to his throat.

White foam oozed from Taranau's mouth under the strain of his pursuit, his grunts telling her that he fully sensed the danger surrounding his master.

Two more soldiers joined Duncan's captor, one with a sword,

and the other, an ax, both pressed to Duncan's sides, freezing him in place.

Cyrene kept her chest low, moving in rhythm with Taranau's steps. There were three men still approaching Duncan and the three that had reached him. She pulled the remaining arrows from under Taranau's saddle and wove her fingers between them, holding all three at once. They were almost to Duncan when the horse of an enemy soldier reared and toppled in their path. Taranau didn't startle or turn, but in one smooth motion, hurdled over the obstacle.

As they sailed, Cyrene was lifted off the saddle. She drew her legs up, feet finding Taranau's back. When Taranau cleared the fallen animal, Cyrene pushed off the saddle as Revna had done and tucked herself into a ball, rolling across the wet grass and sliding to a stop on her knees between Duncan and the approaching soldiers. They froze at the sight of her three arrows readied in Cyrene's bow, each aimed directly at them.

Duncan hissed as his captors pressed their blades deeper into his flesh.

"Call off your queen, cousin," the man with his blade to Duncan's neck crooned.

The sound of his voice shuddered through Cyrene, boiling the blood in her veins, but she didn't turn, didn't flinch. She kept her bow drawn, still on her knees but back straight and tall, daring the soldiers to take another step.

The sounds of desperation and death filled the sky around them, but Cyrene only heard her heart, thundering beneath her bones, and Duncan's hitched breath as a metal blade threatened to pierce him through.

"Call her off, and I will let her live."

Duncan grunted, and Cyrene waited, her quick mind racing through every possible outcome. *I will let her live.* Not him. Her. Even if Eowin or Astrid had seen the attack, Duncan's throat would be slit before they could fight their way to his aid.

"Look around, Queen." The serpentine voice of Duncan's cousin sent Cyrene's teeth clenching in disgust. "Yer armies are falling. Surrender to me, and I will end this before they're all slaughtered."

She didn't bother to listen. She needn't look into his eyes to know he was lying. But it didn't matter if they won. If the king was killed, there could not be victory. He had to live. She could not rule alone.

"Huntress." Duncan's strained whisper was ice across her skin. She felt the sting of tears as she waited for what she knew he would say. "Ye must live."

"Ye promise to keep yer word?" Cyrene centered her narrowed eyes on the smirking soldiers.

"I swear it," William answered, but she heard Duncan suck in a breath as he realized her question was not meant for his cousin but for him.

They'd sworn allegiance to each other. To protect the other's kingdom no matter the outcome of this battle.

"Then I yield." She started to lower her bow as William ordered his men to force Duncan to his knees. The soldiers she'd drawn upon slowly advanced, and she bowed her head in defeat, her still-loaded bow resting on her knees. She secretly cast a look over her shoulder.

"Fools." William's dagger landed blade-first in the soft, wet ground and he turned to one of his soldiers, hand extended. "Give me yer ax."

In the split second he was distracted, Cyrene made her move.

She tilted her chin to the sky, an upside-down Duncan in view. Her eyes connected with his as she swung her drawn bow over her head and let her legs slide from under her until her back was flat on the ground. Arms outstretched above her head, the arrows were now aimed at William and his two soldiers.

Duncan's shout was too late. Cyrene released three arrows, and as the soldiers she'd turned away from fell upon her, she saw her aim was true.

27

DUNCAN

821 AD - Seconds Later

Duncan's heart stopped as his cousin and the two soldiers at his side dropped to the ground, leaving him kneeling alone. Unlike his men, who lay motionless and silent, William rolled on the ground, groaning and swearing in agony at the arrow that pierced his chest just inches from his heart. Duncan drew back his armored hand and silenced the wailing laird with a single blow.

Despite the fact that he still lived, terror as he'd never known gripped his heart at the three soldiers advancing on Cyrene. On his queen, his wife. The woman who had just sacrificed her life for his. The battle raged around them, but all he could see was her.

The pain in his shoulder was nothing compared to the resolve coursing through his blood. In one swift move, he retrieved the sword and ax from the lifeless hands of the soldiers at his feet and was charging forward.

Cyrene rolled to her stomach and tried to crawl away, but the closest soldier grabbed her foot and jerked her back down, her face hitting the wet ground with a slap. She flipped onto her back, kicking and clawing like a wild animal. He couldn't get hold of her, but she couldn't get up.

Duncan released a growl of rage when the soldier reared back and struck her with such force, her arms and legs went limp. Without slowing, Duncan flung the sword into the soft ground ahead of him, raised the ax above his head with both hands, and let it fly, ignoring the biting pain in his shoulder.

The soldier's chest absorbed the force of his weapon. It sent him soaring backwards, instantly still. Duncan dug his boots into the moist earth, aiming for the second sword he'd lodged in the ground. Blades before them, the remaining two soldiers were upon her.

A red curtain of rage coated his vision as his hand curled around the hilt of the waiting weapon. In the same second, he let his feet slide across the rain-slicked grass. Legs bent, he slid between the attacking soldiers and Cyrene, landing at her side. The bruising blow of a blade hammered against the leather vambrace coating his arm as he deflected an advancing thrust. He drew up his own sword, registering the bone-chilling slice as it met its mark. Faced with the open-mouthed expression of the enemy whose heart had met the sharp end of justice, he pushed the lifeless man aside and threw himself over Cyrene as the final soldier sailed toward them, bringing down his sword.

Breath pushed out of his lungs from the force of the soldier's body across his back. Duncan's arms buckled, and he felt Cyrene gasp beneath him. He expected the burn of the blade any second as his life would pulse out of his body from its wound. But the sting did not come.

Struggling under the weight, he pushed himself up on his elbows, finding Cyrene's wild eyes as she dragged in a jagged breath.

They shared the same air as their eyes met, each in shock that the other still lived. Cyrene followed Duncan's bewildered gaze to the felled soldier's sword buried in the ground so close to her head, a trickle of blood dripped from her ear.

Duncan drew his knees up until he was straddling her and groaned as he rolled the motionless man off his back to the ground.

He heard a soft, shuddered breath and dragged his eyes to the red-coated dagger gripped so tightly in Cyrene's trembling palm, her knuckles were white. Hands under her arms, he hauled her upright. She was alive. He didn't ask permission before he crushed her to his chest. His fingers tangled in her wet hair, lips pressed to the top of her head.

"Ye live." His lungs barely held breath. "Thank God, ye live."

Her arms clung to him as tightly as his to her. Their reprieve was short, though, as Eowin's panicked voice rose above the sounds of battle.

"Captain!"

Duncan jumped to his feet, dragging Cyrene with him, and they silently scanned the field, searching in the still dark morning for their friends. Eowin was pushing forward through a sea of soldiers, his eyes narrowed on a singular target.

With a shriek, Cyrene dove for the sword that had nearly ended her and raced toward a circle of William's soldiers, Astrid stranded dead center.

Duncan grabbed the armor of one of his men, jerking him away from the fight with barked orders to guard his injured cousin. He then retrieved his two blades and was at Cyrene's side in three steps. Cyrene fought her way toward her captain, but a rush of men blocked their way. Back to back, Duncan and Cyrene battled William's army.

"Astrid!" Cyrene's broken shout sailed above the battle.

Astrid had fallen to her knees, but the sound of Cyrene's voice reached her, and she rose again, strength renewed.

"Save her," Cyrene begged, her sword slicing through the air, meeting bone and dirt and flesh. "Duncan!"

As much as he fought, the wall of men seemed endless. All

around, his men and her warriors were fighting, falling, dying. William's men pressed in, threatening to separate him from Cyrene.

Duncan roared in frustration, his body automatically responding to the attacks around him as his vision was solely focused on Cyrene. They were still too far from Astrid, and Cyrene's calls were growing more desperate.

Duncan let out a long, low whistle and two short chirps. He heard Taranau's neighing response and saw the horse kicking and charging his way toward his master. He was closer to Eowin, and Duncan whistled another command, which Eowin heard.

Eowin let out a high-pitched song of his own, and Taranau changed course. Without slowing, the animal raced toward Eowin. He grabbed the pommel and pulled himself astride as Taranau passed.

A tumble of swords and limbs in their wake, Taranau and Eowin forged through the mob.

Cyrene screamed for Astrid, her blades slicing through the night, cutting a bloody path to her friend, who suddenly vanished under a swarm of soldiers.

"Astrid!" Cyrene was a whirl of fury, recklessly aiming for the place where Astrid had been.

Fighting off soldiers with one arm, Duncan gripped her wrist with his free hand, keeping her close until he'd dragged her to a hidden patch of dark shadow where they were safe. Cyrene screamed and cursed at him, but he yanked on her arm until she stumbled toward him, her back to his chest. He snaked his arm around her waist, jerking hard to get her attention.

"Look!"

Dawn broke the horizon, and the first rays of golden morning light caught the glint of Astrid's sword, still singing through the air as Taranau made two long strides and flew over a mass of fighters, his hooves clamoring against armor and shields. Eowin disappeared behind Taranau's muscular side.

For a moment, Cyrene stilled in Duncan's arms. He felt her draw in a breath and not release it until Eowin came up again, dragging Astrid with him.

The woodland captain slung her leg over Taranau's back and wrapped her arms around Eowin's waist, and they raced back into the battle together.

Cyrene was suddenly ripped from Duncan's arms, and a mob of William's men filed between them. As much as he fought, she was inched further and further away from him.

From the chaos, Cyrene's warrior, Liam, carved his way through the fray until he was at Duncan's side, even the slice across his thigh not slowing his advance. His pale eyes slid to Duncan's. Though he'd only ever had disdain for Duncan, Liam nodded and they turned back to back, pushing their way toward the queen. Duncan kept his blade moving as he plowed forward, trying and failing to gain ground.

Duncan and Liam continued their joint effort. Between swings of his sword, he counted fewer and fewer of his men. Panic pulsed through Duncan, his mind flying through every option to save his men, his people, his queen. He'd subdued William, but his cousin still lived. If Duncan's army was defeated, William would conquer Tràigh. The thought of what he might do to Cyrene sent a blaze of fire up his spine. Pushing one of William's soldiers away with a boot to his chest, Duncan turned and grabbed Liam by the vest.

"Get her away from here," he growled. When Liam's brows turned in confusion, Duncan shook him. There was no time to explain. "Take her! Make her go."

Liam didn't answer, but his expression settled into a determined glare, and he lowered his sword, becoming one with the softening shadows as he snaked his way toward the queen. Duncan continued fighting but kept his eye on Cyrene. Liam appeared behind her and wrapped his arms around her, one across her shoulders and one around her waist. In a breath, he'd hauled her away from the fighting.

"Release me!" She screamed and struggled, and a slice of guilt as painful as a blade cut through Duncan's chest when her furious green eyes found his, knowing what he'd done.

She would hate him for this decision, but he had to know that she would live. She alone could keep his people alive. She'd done it before with her own people. It was the only way.

Trusting Liam would honor his request, and resolved to fight until his last breath, Duncan threw himself back into the battle. The sting of a blade nearly reopened the barely healed wound on his side, and Duncan fell to his knees, his sword raised above his head. The shouts and cries of his men tore at his heart, but he kept fighting. A boot to his back sent him sprawling forward, his hands slipping on the blood-soaked grass.

He caught himself but came face to face with the lifeless body of one of Cyrene's warriors, her skin gray and wide, fixed eyes staring but not seeing into Duncan's.

Still, he wouldn't give up. Head spinning and muscles screaming, he pushed himself up again, sword plunging at his attacker. The dawn would see the Viking ship to shore, but there would not be much of a battle left for them to fight.

Some lonesome sound moved across the morning, and the soldiers surrounding him stilled. He expected them to pump their fists in victory, but instead, a long, low bellow from a battle horn filled the sky.

As the day overtook the night, bathing the horizon in a brilliant wash of pink and orange, a wave of Nàbaidh's soldiers coated the battlefield, joining what was left of Duncan's men and Cyrene's warriors. He would have collapsed with relief if it were not for the advance of three men with spears and swords aimed at his neck and chest.

Through the tang of swords and clash of shields, Duncan heard the familiar sound of Taranau's hooves pounding against the wet ground. Eowin, with Astrid behind him, guided the horse toward Duncan, stomping a protective circle around him.

Pushing himself to his feet, he forged onward, joining King

Laorn's army. They were still outnumbered, but hope resurfaced, and Duncan's men fought with renewed strength. Slowly, they worked their way across the field, gaining ground until he stumbled backwards under the weight of a slain soldier and rose to find himself free of the battle.

Eowin also reached the edge of the field, and Taranau slowed to a walk. Even though Eowin had rescued her, Astrid slapped at the hand he offered, jumping from Taranau's back on her own. Eowin turned Taranau back to the battle while Astrid stormed toward Duncan. He tensed, thinking she was going to attack him, but she blew past and into the arms of her queen, who appeared from a cloud of morning mist.

Duncan sucked in a sharp breath, scanning the hazy dawn for Liam. The warrior was at her heels, one knee on the ground, wheezing and bent at his middle from whatever violence she'd unleashed on him.

Cyrene's hands flew to the sides of Astrid's face, touching her hair, her shoulders, as if to ensure she wasn't a ghost. Then she drew their foreheads together, and after an exchange of words he couldn't hear, Astrid turned and flew back into the waning battle. Cyrene approached, turning her gaze upon Duncan, her green eyes as hard as emeralds.

"I have faced enough impossible choices to understand why ye did what ye did." Her words kept him in place, as if he were anchored by chains to the ground. "But that doesna mean I forgive ye for it."

He wasn't offended by her scolding, but he wasn't ashamed of his decision either. "I willna ask ye to. But I would do it again. One of us had to live."

They stared, their own battle raging between them. He broke his gaze first, unable to ignore the swelling that spread across her cheek. Without thinking, he lifted his hand to touch her, but she jerked away. He dropped his hand to his side, accepting her distance. She was hurt. He'd taken her choice and made a decision without her permission. He understood, even if he still stood by it.

The first waves of relief at what they'd survived filled him with emotion.

"Ye did the same." His throat was raw, words raspy and broken. "Ye saved me too."

She didn't answer, but he could see the pounding of her pulse at her neck. She dragged her eyes back to the field where their countrymen were cheering at their victory.

"Ye dinna save me. There's a difference between what ye did and what I did. I keep my promises."

Her words felt like a slap across his face, and Duncan didn't try to stop her as she turned to help Liam to his feet, a murmured reproach for him, too, on her lips.

"Duncan!" A stout man adorned with royal armor approached, riding a mare with a shining copper coat, Eowin on Taranau at his side.

His captain dismounted, handing the reins to Duncan. Eowin flicked his gaze between Duncan and Cyrene, his chin jumping in curiosity. Duncan gave him a slight nod that told him not to ask. Cyrene didn't meet his eyes again before she left to gather what warriors survived for the second part of their plan. Duncan drew in a deep breath to regain his composure.

Leaving Liam to trail behind the queen, Duncan climbed onto Taranau's back and joined the king of Nàbaidh on the battlefield. With the help of Laorn's troops, they drove the remaining soldiers into the tower, herding them into the keep with the ones Duncan and his men had trapped earlier.

Laorn and Duncan's soldiers worked their way through the captured soldiers, collecting weapons and securing bonds to keep them subdued.

"There is yet another danger." Duncan faced the king of Nàbaidh from their place on the corridor overlooking the courtyard-turned-prison. "Will ye stay and help us end this for good?"

"Aye." Laorn nodded, shoving a thick hand toward Duncan, who took it in his own. "Yer grin tells me ye have a plan in place?"

"I do." Duncan tipped his head to something over Laorn's shoulder, and the king turned, balking at who approached.

Flanked by her maidens, Cyrene glided toward Duncan and Laorn, a cloak of rich blue flowing behind her like a dark wave. Her maidens followed, dressed in the same deep blue fabric, a secret purchase Cyrene had bid Revna make on the day of their wedding.

The king of Nàbaidh tipped a brow in intrigue and rubbed his hands together. "I canna wait to see what ye have in store."

Cyrene joined Duncan but noticeably kept her distance. Duncan forced a smile and turned to Laorn. "My queen is as skilled in theatrics as she is in battle."

Once Duncan had explained their plans, Laorn nodded in approval. "I pray yer plans go unhindered. I shall take my men to their place. We will be ready." He bowed to Cyrene, who tipped her head in a gracious acknowledgment.

Duncan clasped his hand on Laorn's shoulder, thanking him once again before he disappeared into the darkness of a corridor. Duncan remained standing next to Cyrene in the shadowed hall leading to an open walkway overlooking the keep.

"Are ye ready?" Hoping she would somehow understand him enough to make peace, Duncan lifted the royal blue hood of her cloak over her head. She didn't pull away, and he took the chance to explain. "I ken ye understand what it means to be faced with only terrible choices and have to choose between them. But can ye not see that I made that decision because I trust ye?"

He raised her chin with his finger and examined her face. It was always a guess as to which woman would gaze back at him. The tragically beautiful ice queen that only had daggers for him, or the softened woodland ruler whose emerald eyes were as warm as a summer evening? The woman looking back at him then was a mix of both. He tilted his head, begging her to understand.

"Because I trust only ye with my people, Cyrene. I ken ye dinna need me to save ye. I just needed ye to save them."

She held his gaze for a long minute, that familiar tugging sensation gripping his heart. Finally, she lowered her eyes and handed him a small jar filled with some thick, oily paste the same color as her cloak. It was a gift, a silent treaty struck between them—at least for the moment.

"Another of yer secret purchases from the village?"

When his mouth quirked in question, she nodded and dipped her fingers into the color, spreading it across her cheeks. "As the legends say."

"The legends say something else about how the Picts enter battle." Duncan tested the waters with a rise of his brows.

"If we appeared in such a state, I doubt our words would find listening ears." She didn't smile, but her dry humor still filled his heart with hope that they could recover from this breach of trust.

"Aye." The abnormal fluttering beat of Duncan's heart forced him to cough.

He attempted to bring his own memories under submission as he dipped his fingers into the berry-scented paint and traced a Pictish symbol on her arm.

When she was adequately decorated, she passed the color to the rest of her maidens. He tucked a loose strand of her wild red hair behind her ear. "Even battle-bruised and blue, ye are bonnie."

Heat filled his chest at the blush that crept up her slender neck, and she tipped her head in a slight acknowledgment before leading her maidens around the upper level corridors around the keep.

Inside, steep walls kept the morning light at bay, the sky growing from black to a light blue that cast long shadows behind every archway and overhang. Soft torches held below their hooded figures, Cyrene's maidens sang a haunting melody. Duncan knew it was a song of worship, but to the men in the keep, it sounded like a ghostly curse, and they cried out in terror.

The song, starting soft, rose to a beautifully dreadful crescendo as it echoed off the cold stone of the tower, filling each empty hall. When every captured soldier had fallen to his knees, the women's voices went silent.

Cyrene stepped forward. Men cried out as she tossed back her hood, revealing her painted face. The torch she held illuminated her pale skin and created deep shadows over her eyes. To the men below, it would appear as if her face was nearly skeletal. Her maidens followed, mimicking her movements.

"Yer leader is captured." Cyrene held out her hand, William's bloodied armor in her grasp.

"These lands dunna belong to ye." Her powerful voice rang clear in the dawning day. "They are protected by ancient magic, and any who come against them will find death."

Duncan felt the lift of a half-smile at the corner of his mouth. The ancient magic was nothing more than rumors. But there was a force, invisible and swift, that had fought for them that night. A force strong enough to change calm waters to raging seas and direct soaring arrows to a true target.

"Go. Tell of what ye saw here this day, and dunna ever return."

In unison, Cyrene and her maidens stepped back into the dark shadows of the corridors, vanishing from sight.

"Do ye have the strength for one more display?" Duncan caught up to Cyrene as her maidens silently filed through the empty halls of the tower toward the now-quiet battlefield.

"Aye." Cyrene's shoulders sagged, though. He knew she was as weary as he.

Leaving William's terrified troops trapped in the keep, they gathered on the battlefield with Nàbaidh's soldiers, forming silent ranks. Dew on the blood-soaked grass turned to red diamonds in the morning light, and steam hovered above the ground as if the final breaths of the slain lingered, waiting for permission from the dawn to escape.

An eerie calm settled over Duncan's kingdom. Even the horses' prancing stilled. The earth held its breath as a soft call floated across the morning from the watchtower. A signal that the remaining Norse ship had reached the shores.

Duncan closed his eyes, imagining their confusion as they tore through the village, finding it empty and abandoned instead of teeming with promised slaves.

"Sire." Eowin breathed the word.

Duncan followed his captain's squinting gaze to the highest window in the tower. A reflected flash of light, created by a bit of mirror and the sun, signaled the arrival of the Vikings at the tower.

"They'll be reaching the keep now." Duncan could feel his heart racing, waiting for the outcome of their enemies' meeting.

Their hope was retreat at the sight of William's defeated and imprisoned men, but instead, a terrible roar rose from the keep. Duncan winced at the clashing sound of swords, the screams of men, then a deafening silence. The soldiers at his sides shifted, a murmur of disbelief and horror rippling through the crowd.

He glanced over his shoulder at the queen. Her face was as pale as the dawn, and she closed her eyes for one long moment, a single tear racing down her cheek.

Duncan couldn't bear the sight, and whipped his head around to face what was coming.

The sound of swords and spears beating against shields filled the air, echoing off the stone walls of the tower. The heavy thud of booted feet grew louder until a seething horde of angry, blood-splattered Vikings poured through the tower entrance onto the battlefield.

They made ranks, weapons at the ready. Growls and threatening stamps of spears on earth hid any surprise or fear at the army that waited for them.

With Laorn's borrowed troops, the armies of Tràigh outnumbered the Vikings, but these were a people known for their viciousness, for sacking armies much larger than his.

Duncan and his troops remained perfectly still, as if in a trance. When a delicate touch brushed his shoulder, Duncan stepped aside, creating an opening in the middle of the front row.

Cyrene advanced, her head hooded once more. A trail of maidens followed, each with the same blue-painted stripes across her face and arms. They were equally beautiful and terrifying.

She stopped midway between the two armies, too far for an enemy arrow to reach her, and the maidens that followed delivered the same performance as before.

The superstitious nature of the Vikings was known in all the land. Duncan silently pleaded with God that Cyrene's warning would be so laden with supernatural power, these Norsemen would find themselves frozen with fear.

Duncan marched from his place, dragging a wounded and whimpering William by his shoulder like an unwanted dog. He released the fallen leader to the sound of growls and curses from the Vikings.

Duncan shoved William with his foot, a final degrading show. "Yer alliance is broken. Whatever he promised is neither his to give nor yers to have."

A mocking laugh erupted from the brawny leader, spurring the rest of his crew to do the same. Cyrene drew a single arrow from beneath her cloak and loaded her bow. The Norseman continued to laugh, thinking her much too far for her shot to inflict damage. When the arrow with brilliant blue feathers landed dead center in the chest of their leader, their laughter was silenced.

As he dropped motionless to the ground at their feet, a single heartbeat passed before the Vikings turned and ran for the shore, Nàbaidh's army at their heels.

28

CYRENE

821 AD - Two Hours Later

When Duncan met her on the seaside wall after a pass through the keep and a short visit to the healer to wrap his wounded shoulder, his pallor was near green and eyes ringed red. Cyrene didn't have to ask why. She was still angry with him for sending Liam to pull her away from the battle, but she recognized the look he wore. She'd worn it herself many times. He was on the edge of breaking, and it would only take a nudge to send him over.

She hadn't seen a single one of William's captured soldiers exit the tower. It had been Duncan's decision to stage them in the keep for the Vikings to find, though he couldn't have imagined the outcome of that meeting.

A wife would comfort her husband. But she was more than just a wife. She was a ruler of a people, and she, too, had been forced to make decisions that meant life and death. Pity and even compassion sometimes made it worse instead of better. Nothing could bring back the dead. Words to heal that kind of pain didn't exist.

Despite their forced proximity the last few days, he was a little more than a stranger, and after what he'd done earlier, what little trust she'd built was close to toppling. But in some ways, she knew him as well as she knew herself.

Now was not the time for arguing. She put aside her frustrations and simply stood at his side as he watched the last remaining Viking ship set sail, stone-faced and silent. At Duncan's merciful request, Nàbaidh's army allowed those that laid down their weapons to board.

A strange longing tugged at her insides, as if this moment was their only time of truce, and it would sail away with the Norsemen.

"What has become of yer cousin?" She kept her eyes on the shore.

"He was taken to the gaol cell." Duncan's voice was raw, his exhaustion evident. "Eowin is leading those of our men not being treated for injuries in a search of the battlefield for any surviving from his army and . . . taking care of those who didn't."

Cyrene had kept her back to those fields. A peaceful sea stretched before her. She could almost forget the thick black clouds of smoke that marred a brilliant sunrise. Were it not for the ache of her bone-deep bruises, the bloody night might seem like nothing more than a bad dream. Light chased away shadows and bathed the world in glorious color, life from death.

Cyrene's thumb brushed against the smooth band encircling her finger. It still felt foreign on her skin. She supposed she would get used to it, even if she couldn't get used to him. Duncan's own hands were clasped in front of him, but she noticed he rubbed the pads of his fingers across the marked surface of the thin leather bracelet she'd fastened on his wrist. Back and forth his finger moved, soft, like waves kissing the shore.

A bit of metal and a strap of leather, symbols of a lifelong bargain made in haste in exchange for a slim chance at survival. And it worked. They'd prayed for a miracle, and *An T-aon* had answered with one after the other. Enemy ships dashed against rocks, the arrival of the troops from Nàbaidh, and most importantly, none of the innocent villagers they'd sent through the tunnel were injured.

It was over. She'd kept her promises. All oaths fulfilled.

Except those that would only end with death. The thought sent a chill racing across her skin. Cyrene stared out over the shore, the hush of waves against rocks whispering a reminder of another promise and a warning given on dying lips. A new conflict brewed in her spirit.

She'd been a child—a broken, lonely child—when she'd sworn the oath to never allow her heart to be subject to the crown. Still, snaking tendrils of the past wrapped around her promise, cradling it, holding it close. Was there any way for either of them to cross the bridge of pain and grief and distrust?

An T-aon had answered when she called. Mayhap he had one more miracle left for her, if she only dared ask it of him.

"What of the spy?" Cyrene asked Duncan instead.

He rubbed his hand across his forehead, as if coaxing the memories forward. "Her body was retrieved and has joined the others of William's army."

"Do ye ken why she would do such a thing?" She could feel the pressure of his stare as she tried to control the anxious bouncing of her knees. Though she'd taken many more lives during the battle, she'd never escape the memory of that first arrow sinking into the spy's heart.

"Nay." He sighed and turned his back to the sea, leaning against the waist-high edge of the wall. "Mayhap my cousin can answer for that."

"Did ye ken who she was?" She didn't want to discuss his vile kinsman just yet.

"Aye. Well—I dunna ken for sure until I speak with my kitchen maid, but she had appeared recently as a maid on my household staff."

Cyrene turned from the sea at his answer. "In yer household?"

"Aye." Duncan's jaw was tight, the muscles feathering in frustration.

"She wasna from the North?" Cyrene's stomach cramped at the thought.

"She dinna have the look of a Viking, but her speech was much the same as Astrid's." He crossed his arms over his broad chest, brows furrowed. "There was something about her, though."

"What do ye mean?"

Duncan shoved a hand through his hair, his matted curls catching his fingers. "I ken 'tis but an impossible coincidence, and I'm certain it was just because it was dark, but when her hood fell back, I thought her to be Revna."

"Revna?" Cyrene drew in a breath to ask him to explain when a flash of white at the edge of the woods near the shore sent Cyrene to the cold stone edge of the wall, her nails scraping against its rough surface.

"What is it?" Duncan's hitched breath brushed her neck as he leaned in to investigate.

A pale stallion nervously pranced back and forth just inside the line of trees. Alone.

"No," Cyrene breathed, the word caught in her desert-dry throat.

"What's wrong?" Instantly tense, Duncan's hands went to the blade strapped at his side.

Cyrene's fingers fluttered to her lips, pressing back a wail of denial as her heart ached within her chest.

I'll bring them all back. Another sworn oath, a dark promise, wound its way through Cyrene's memory. Agony permeated her voice as she croaked a single heartbreaking word.

"Revna."

Duncan's anxious eyes darted from Cyrene to the stallion, to the ship already adrift on gray, foamy waters. He stilled, seeming to understand what Cyrene immediately knew. Revna was aboard.

Cyrene couldn't fetter the thoughts that set sail in her mind, imagining what Revna's purpose aboard that ship could be. The scout would wait, bide her time, as the crew steered the ship homeward, but when it docked . . .

If Revna allowed a survivor, he would have such a terrible tale to spread, they needn't ever fear the Vikings' return.

If Duncan bore the responsibility for the fate of the captured enemy soldiers in the keep, the souls aboard that ship of death belonged to Cyrene. Shame, guilt, and regret stretched icy fingers from her chest, constricting her limbs until they wrapped around her body.

"I should have done more." For once, Cyrene couldn't hold back the tears that burned her eyes.

"What could ye have done?" Duncan's question was gentle. He didn't attempt to touch her, and she was grateful. Despite her hesitations, she would have used him and let him comfort her in that moment.

"I ken of her rage, and I . . . fed it when I should have starved it. I shouldna have allowed her to fight. She's but ten and five, barely more than a lass." Cyrene's lungs felt as though they were shrinking inside her chest. "I should have loved her more."

"A starving man will find food wherever he can. Ye couldna have kept Revna from battle any more than ye could have held back the tide." He touched her then, gently taking her shoulders to turn her to face him. "I havna ken ye for long, but I say this with assurance: no one could have loved Revna more than ye." Duncan tipped his head, demanding her gaze. "No one."

He was right. Revna was loved. From the moment she was placed in the arms of a Pictish woman, she was as loved as if she'd been their own.

"Vengeance is a choice, Huntress, as is anger and wrath and unforgiveness."

As terrible as the Vikings were, darkness could never defeat darkness. Only light could drive it out. He'd been speaking of Revna, but she couldn't help but wonder if his message was meant for her too. Cyrene turned back to the sea. They didn't speak again until the sails neared the horizon.

"How will she get home?" Duncan's quiet question was heavy with compassion, drawing Cyrene back from the edge of allowing her heart to sail off with that ship.

"I dunna think she plans to." Cyrene closed her eyes, refusing to believe that would be the last time she'd see her young scout. "Not until she finds what she seeks."

"What does she search for?"

Cyrene turned her back on the sea. Her throat burned, eyes still stinging with salty tears that she'd wiped away.

"I dunna think she ken herself. Mayhap she seeks escape from her own heart, from the hate that has burrowed deep. It traps her."

"I pray she finds peace."

Something in his tone sent Cyrene's gaze gliding his way. She found his blue eyes waiting, laden with sadness. That prayer was not only for Revna.

His arms hung loose at his sides, open. Willing. She wanted to lean into him, to forgive and trust and live the kind of love her parents had. Something was holding her back.

Revna left all who loved her to keep her promise. Was Cyrene doing the same? Was keeping her word worth a life of loneliness for the both of them?

"Sire." Eowin's haggard voice rasped from behind. "What of yer cousin?"

William. The name alone conjured such painful, wretched memories, she wanted to spit it out of her mind. Duncan scanned her face, eyes darkening at whatever he saw there. If he'd asked for her opinion, she'd have hissed any number of disgraceful means of dealing with him.

Throw him into the sea, tie him to a post and leave him for the animals, tear him to shreds and send the pieces out as a warning to any kingdoms close enough to be a threat.

"Send the healer." Duncan's gaze still centered on Cyrene, his tenor calm, resolved. "He lives for now."

The last hint of sails snagged her gaze again. Revna's darkness directed her toward compassion. Yet when it came to William, Cyrene so easily turned to the vengeance Duncan had said was a choice. How was her heart so two-faced? She dropped her eyes to the stones beneath her feet, afraid that if she met either man's eyes, they'd see that hypocrisy as if it were a band across her head.

Eowin tipped his head in acceptance of Duncan's order. "King Laorn waits for ye in the meeting hall."

Duncan drew in a deep breath and swept his eyes over his disheveled appearance, making a half-hearted attempt to straighten himself. "I'm expected to make good on my promises now."

Cyrene blinked back at him, still unable to rationalize his civility toward his cousin after what he'd done.

"Will ye join me?" Duncan's tired eyes drifted past her to the field below, still crawling with soldiers as they carried away the dead and injured. "Even though he came to our aid, we should make a strong showing of unity."

In other words, he was asking her to pretend not to hate him. She could do that. But not for him. For the sake of their kingdoms.

29

CYRENE

821 AD - An Hour Later

Asimple wooden table, surface polished and shining, and six large chairs were the only pieces of furniture occupying the large space of Duncan's meeting room. The only other thing in the room was a wooden trunk tucked in the corner as if it were meant to be forgotten.

The servants of his household had escaped with the villagers from the keep, and he didn't seem concerned at the absence of his advisors. He didn't seem fully present himself, and when Cyrene paused at the foot of the table, uncertain of where to sit, Eowin drew close behind her, leaning to whisper in her ear.

"Take your place by the king, m'lady. Ye are the queen."

Duncan stood behind a high-backed chair at the head of the table, elaborate scrolling artwork carved into its arms. Aside from a fresh tunic, he still wore his battle clothes, as did she. They didn't look anything like royals ready to hold talks of peace with a neighboring kingdom.

Cyrene moved to the space beside him, but he pulled back the chair and motioned for her to be seated in the place of honor.

Cyrene clicked her chin a fraction, challenging his decision; he answered with the teasing arch of his brow. Just as she did by having unbound hair, Duncan was showing his own disdain for propriety and tradition. Mayhap he was perpetuating the threat of the mysterious woodland queen a little longer. Cyrene offered a regal smile, her face freshly cleaned by a quick scrubbing of cold water before entering.

The king of Nàbaidh and his military leaders watched Duncan and Cyrene's show of power unfold, eyes capturing every movement.

Duncan took Cyrene's hand, a courteous gesture, as she lowered herself gracefully into the royal chair. He placed a soft kiss on the top of her hand before seating himself beside her.

The room was silent until to everyone's surprise, King Laorn let out a deep, boisterous laugh and pounded the table with his fist.

A round-faced man of nearly fifty with a short whitish-yellow beard which had probably once been bright orange, the king nearly wept from whatever amused him. Cyrene exchanged a concerned look with Duncan before Laorn wiped his eyes with the back of his chubby hand.

"I ken I would like ye, Duncan." He pounded the table a few more times before his laughter subsided. "They called ye bold, and bold ye are!"

"I guess I have Eowin to thank for bringing that dead nickname back to life." Duncan seemed to relax at Laorn's explanation, and Cyrene released her talon-like grip on the chair's arms.

"I have no time fer politics. Let's talk trade agreements." Laorn folded his hands together on the table, a wide grin revealing a mouthful of large white teeth. He looked hungry, but not in a predatory manner that would have made Cyrene uncomfortable. It was more of a joyful expectation. "Tell me about the sea."

Duncan's lips pulled back in a matching smile, and the men opened the discussion. Cyrene knew the way of things outside the woods. Leadership was a man's job. To Cyrene's surprise, Duncan frequently asked her opinion, carefully considered her thoughts, and conceded to most of her suggestions.

She held back her emotions, keeping her expression cool, but caught him offering grateful nods and soft smiles when she participated in the discussions. She wanted to believe it was because he saw her as an equal, but the seed of distrust planted long ago and watered on the battlefield when he'd broken their agreement had developed a healthy stem and stood strong in her heart. Could he have known that was what she truly desired more than anything, even more than love and passion?

A partner. A friend.

Never trust the tower king. Her mother's warning visited her again. It was always there. Always lingering around the edges of her mind.

What would happen when they came to a matter they didn't agree on? Would he make the decision without her again? The thought released a bitter taste in her mouth, and she grew quiet. Duncan frowned when he moved to touch her hand and she discreetly slipped it into her lap, pretending not to have noticed his reach.

Morning broadened into day, and word of the villagers' return to their homes reached the meeting. Lines were drawn, agreements made, and Laorn yanked Duncan to his broad chest for an aggressive embrace, vigorously slapping his back. When he moved toward Cyrene, she tensed, and he laughed again, offering his hand instead.

"Ye are as bonnie as ye are wise, m'lady." She felt the burn of a blush on her cheeks as he followed Duncan's lead and placed a kiss on the back of her hand, his whiskers rough against her skin.

Trays of food were brought by the returning servants, a celebration of victory over the enemy and new alliances formed. The humble feast and lingering rush of energy from the battle almost kept the overwhelming exhaustion at bay. Laorn and his entourage were shown to guest chambers, his army having already set up camp around the tower to rest and tend to their wounded. Duncan kindly offered whatever supplies were left in his storehouses. He asked after the villagers, ordering special gifts of gratitude for Sima and the ladies who'd so boldly led the people to safety.

Cyrene watched as he worked. He spoke gently to his servants, treated them as equals—if not in position, in humanity. He was good. So unlike what she'd expected. She wanted to believe what her mind told her, that all she witnessed was true. But the wispy vines that grew from her little garden of doubt kept tugging her back, wrapping their sticky tendrils around her heart and filling her head with warning memories of death and betrayal from long ago.

The surviving advisors of his council were among the last to return, and once Duncan satisfied their questions, Cyrene alone remained in the meeting room with the king. He stood at the table, braced on his arms, poring over stacks of parchments inked with the agreements he'd signed with Laorn.

Uncertain of what to do or say, she found herself hovering over the lonely trunk stashed in the corner.

"My father's things."

Cyrene jumped at the sound of his voice and felt heat creep up her neck when she turned to see him watching her. He still stood at the table, but he'd straightened, wincing in pain when his hand explored the injured place on his shoulder. "Open it if you like. I meant to go through it months ago, but . . ."

His voice trailed off as something on one of the parchments caught his attention, and he sank into his chair to study it.

Cyrene examined the trunk. It didn't seem like something that would belong to a king. It was simple and ordinary. She lifted the lid, wincing as it released a long, whining creak.

There was not much inside. There were a few pieces of jewelry— one an ornate wedding ring, which she assumed had belonged to Fiona or his first wife. Stacked on one side were some crumbling parchments filled with curling script, a set of quill pens and dried-up ink flaking on the sides of glass bottles, and a small box. It was made of wood, intricately carved and inlaid with silver.

She opened the lid and tilted her head curiously at the stack of small ink-drawn portraits. The one on top was of a woman, her belly round with a bairn, embraced by a lad, his arms draped around her shoulders. Cyrene drew the portrait closer to her face, squinting at a small detail sketched on the woman's ring finger. It was the wedding ring from the trunk. Mayhap this woman was Duncan's mother and his brother. Had the king been an artist in secret?

It was strange and unnerving to be touching the personal belongings of the man whose blade had killed her mother. She'd only ever imagined him as a monster. Her hand shook as she looked at the next drawing. It was Fiona, that same ring decorating her finger. Her dark, piercing eyes seemed to speak secrets that were never meant to be shared. Things too painful to know.

She lifted Fiona's portrait, ready to view the next, when the stiff hinges of the meeting hall doors screamed as they were shoved open. Cyrene spun, her heart racing. She absentmindedly tucked the rest of the drawings into her vest but remained rooted in place as Eowin appeared, dragging a young sentry by the neck.

He tossed the lad onto the stone floor at Duncan's feet, the captain's expression twisted with rage. He aimed a finger at the trembling soldier and shouted one command.

"Speak!"

Cyrene remained unmoving near the trunk, watching as the lad groveled before Eowin shoved him again and ordered him to reveal whatever information was so dire that he'd barged unannounced into the king's private meeting hall.

"This fool is the reason we were betrayed!" Eowin's roar filled the room, its force sending Cyrene back a few steps until her shoulders met the cold hardness of the wall.

"Explain yerself." Duncan seemed calm, but the veins in his forearms bulged at the tight fist he kept at his side.

"She came to me . . . I thought she be a village lass. I dinna ken, Yer Majesty, I swear to ye."

Eowin shoved him again.

"She was so bonnie, so soft, I dinna ken she was using me."

The captain, tired of waiting for the lad to get on with his confession, threw his hands in the air. "He told her everything. She wanted to ken where on the outer walls they could meet where none would see, so he pointed out the weakest spots in our defenses. She wanted to visit the caves by the sea, so he led her right to the perfect place for the Vikings to hide. She wanted him to sneak her into the signal tower to view the sea at dawn, so she ken the way to go unnoticed. She wanted a job in the tower so she could go in search of her long-lost sister. So he brought her to Hilde. She wanted a token of his undying love—a dagger with the castle crest."

Eowin spun and leaned over to shout in the lad's face. "How could ye be so stupid?"

"What was her name?" Cyrene's soft question seemed to startle the men, as if they'd forgotten she was there.

The lad turned to face her, his face drawn from fear. "She called herself Vidarra."

Duncan sat back against the table as if pushed over by this revelation. He stared at the floor, his face draining of color. "Take him to the gaol cell."

"I should run him through, sire." Eowin trembled with rage, his blade already drawn.

"Nay." Duncan's objection was barely audible over the lad's pleas for mercy. "I'll question him more later. Just . . . take him away."

"Ye'll na execute me?" The young soldier's question turned Duncan's placid expression stern. "It's just . . . I ken about what happened to the guards when King William . . ."

"I am not my father." Duncan stood, his fists clenched and face crimson.

Eowin snatched the lad to his feet and hurled him toward the still-open doors. His apologetic cries reached them long after they'd disappeared around the corner. Duncan turned back to the table, slamming his fist on its surface. Then he raked his hands across the table, sending the parchments flying and fluttering to the floor.

Cyrene didn't understand this reaction. These actions the sentry described were those of a spy; he already knew that. There had to be something else, something more than the weariness that ringed his blue eyes with red.

"Who was she?" Cyrene stepped away from the trunk, her arms wrapped around herself.

Duncan didn't answer. He only stared at the empty table in front of him.

"Who was she?" Her pulse raced, blood pounding in her ears.

He'd said he'd mistaken the young woman for Revna. He'd said her accent was like Astrid's. In her story to the sentry, she claimed to have a sister—a lost sister. Cyrene's mind swirled in a violent storm of dark possibility. She saw the truth, but in jumbled pieces.

Lovely Fiona, with the same dark skin and hair as Revna. A sickly child, the age Fiona's daughters would have been. Brígid sharing a secret, and Revna racing in a rage toward the tower.

Something else. Another bit of a memory blended so seamlessly with grief, it was nearly forgotten. Eden. Kneeling at her mother's bed as the queen was dying. Answering a cryptic question.

Where were ye, Eden?

I had to . . . there's something I need to tell ye, but I dunna ken who to trust, m'lady. The queen cried at her whispered secret, but there was relief in her sigh as if there was hope amidst the anguish.

"Ye said that yer people were slaughtered by the king." Duncan didn't turn, but something in his voice sent Cyrene's hands to her lips, quieting her breaths. "He was a hard man, capable of such things . . . but he was also greedy."

His voice was trembling, laced with such pain, he gripped the edge of the table until his knuckles turned white.

"He dinna waste the treasure he'd collected." Duncan sank into the chair at the head of the table, his head falling into his open palm.

"I saw them marched to the shore and loaded onto ships. I saw them. Men and women and children . . . and bairns."

She shook her head. What was he saying? Her people lived? All the ones taken still lived?

He stood suddenly, the chair loudly scraping against the stones as it was pushed back. He looked up at her, his blue eyes glazed with tears, and he aimed a shaking finger at the stone wall visible through the open window behind her. "That wall was built with the money he was paid for their lives."

"He sold them." Her words were but a breath. A secret too horrifying to be spoken, and Cyrene backed against the wall, sliding down the rough stones to the floor, her legs unable to support her.

"If yer people dinna sacrifice my sisters to the sea . . ." He was begging her, his grief on full display, his heart flayed and placed as an offering before her. His voice broke at his next question. "What happened to them?"

As if a secret lock had found its key, a door was opened.

"Eden." The name of her mother's captain sparked one last memory, one she didn't even know she had.

Eden's whispered words had been so quiet, Cyrene hadn't heard but one, one that was so painful for Eden to speak, her voice had broken, making it loud enough for Cyrene to hear. *Separated.*

Another lock, another key.

Cyrene blinked at Duncan, not believing the words that tumbled out of her mouth, nor the calm with which she spoke them. "The story Brígid told us about Eden was a dark fairytale. There were bits of truth, but not complete. I was but a child, but I have memories, and I . . . I think I ken now the true story. She did fall ill. She did see yer father leaving Fiona's chambers, and she did find Fiona dead. But if what ye said about the ladies is true, and they'd have taken the bairns to yer father . . ."

Duncan rocked back on his heels, slipping back into the seat of his chair before he ended up on the floor like Cyrene. Any remains of that rush of energy were gone. She lifted weary eyes to Duncan; she saw the same was true for him.

"She dinna find the lady murdered." His hand covered his mouth, and his words slipped out through his fingers as if he was trying to catch them.

"Nay." This story was true; she knew it even as it formed in her mind. "Eden ken the king had slain Fiona. She must have feared he would do the same to her children. *She* wielded the blade against Fiona's lady. *She* took the bairns, and *she* hid them amongst the Picts. Separately, so no one would suspect they were the lost children of the murdered queen. She couldn't have known just how far the king would go to exact his revenge."

Duncan looked as if he were going to be sick. "He sold his own children."

"Child." Cyrene pushed herself up off the floor, using the wall at her back for support. When Duncan looked at her with questions in his eyes, she turned toward the window, gulping down deep breaths of fresh air. "One daughter was sold. The other came to us."

"Revna." He nearly choked on her name. She couldn't imagine the emotions tearing through his heart. He'd been so close to his sister all this time, never knowing she lived.

Her thoughts slipped to Beli, just for the length of a blink. As much as she wished she could hope he lived, he couldn't have been among the ones sent away. She'd seen him fall in the woods. She never even got to bury him. Her eyes burned at the thought. At the unfairness and mercilessness of it all.

Cyrene walked to the door, the heat of Duncan's eyes warming her back. Beli was gone, but she could do for Duncan what had not been done for her. A servant was waiting outside, and she forced herself not to look back at Duncan as she gave her orders.

"Find the king's captain. Tell him to retrieve the spy's body and have it brought to the tower. Tell him to take great care; all will be explained later." After an acknowledging nod, the servant hurried away, and Cyrene closed the door to the meeting hall but didn't turn around, her hand remaining on its solid oak surface.

She heard the sob that leaked through Duncan's shaken resolve, and her tired eyes released the tears she'd kept back. Revna was the lost daughter of the murdered Fiona. And Vidarra was her sister. Vidarra, who had been sold as a slave and returned a spy against her own people. Vidarra, who was now lying amidst a heap of enemy soldiers, dead. Cyrene had killed her. She'd killed the tower princess. The first arrow she'd ever let fly at a human target with the intent to end a life had slain Revna's sister. The gaping chasm in her chest that had slowly sealed shut over the years wrenched painfully open, nearly sending Cyrene to her knees again.

At that realization, she wished she'd left Duncan in the wood at the mercy of the Vikings. Even if war had indeed come to them, she'd have been spared this agony. In that moment, she hated him more than she'd ever hated him before. Mayhap even more than she hated his father. William had done wretched, horrible things, but it was Duncan that had turned her into a killer. She finally turned, taking two forceful steps, prepared to unleash her feelings upon him.

But Duncan's head fell onto his arms. His shoulders shook with silent sobs as he, too, unlocked the devastating secret, and she stopped, her breaths shallow. What would he do with this knowledge? Would he hate her as she hated him?

He said he wasn't like his father, but Eden had taken his sisters, even though she'd done it to save their lives. His entire life, he'd believed them to be dead, and now Vidarra was. At Cyrene's hand. And Revna . . .

Cyrene's heart ached so much, she bent, forced nearly to her knees by the sting. Revna was gone.

Duncan raised his head, his eyes red with sorrow and anger. He despised her. He must.

Dunna trust the tower king.

Cyrene backed toward the doors again. Duncan flew from his chair and crossed the room in three long strides. She retreated until her back made a hollow thump against the doors. He stopped just inches from her, his jaw tight and eyes blazing.

She tried to step around him, but he slammed his palms against the door on either side of her, caging her between his arms.

"Did ye ken?" Though quiet, his voice was hard, demanding. Like a king.

But she, too, was a queen, and she would not shrink under his burning gaze, under the condemning look of fury that turned his eyes dark. He slammed his hand against the door again, making her flinch. "Did ye?"

"Nay. Of course not." Cyrene's own anger sparked inside, the desire to flee near unstoppable.

"Did Revna ken?" he demanded.

Cyrene ground her teeth, infuriated by his interrogation. Revna's secrets were not hers to share. "She was but a bairn when she came to us."

"Ye mean when she was stolen."

She ducked under his arm and stopped a safe distance from him, her tone set in defiance. "They'd have met the same fate as Fiona if she hadn't."

"Ye dunna ken that!" His forehead met the wood of the door with a thump, and he rolled to the side, his hand moving to hold his injured shoulder. A fresh stain of red blossomed, soaking through the fabric of his tunic.

It had to be done. They canna be used now. She did know. She knew then what must have transpired in that meeting between the king and her mother. What threats must have been made. Whatever the king wanted from Derelei, he was willing to use his infant daughters to get it. Ever the Battling Queen, she refused.

"I do ken." Cyrene aimed a shaking finger at his face. "And Eden tried to save Revna. To save them both."

Duncan straightened and let his head fall back, a sarcastic, cruel laugh rumbling in his chest. "Fine thing too. One is dead and the other might as well be."

Cyrene stepped back, his words a harsh hand against her cheek. Was this cruelty a side effect of their exhaustion, or he revealing his true nature?

"What will ye do, then?" It was one thing when his father had been the only villain. Now Eden was guilty, too, and her mother was complicit, however noble their intentions.

"What?" he snapped.

"What is yer plan? Now that ye've won yer kingdom back. Made yer alliances with Nàbaidh. Ye dunna need us anymore."

He didn't answer. He only stared, his eyes darting between hers.

"Where will the woodland people live? In the forest . . . the village? In caves on the shore?"

"I dunna ke—"

"Or will ye finish what yer father started?"

It was Duncan's turn to back away from her. The sting of her accusation sliced a wound that drew his expression into shock. His eyes darkened again, and he marched forward, nearly nose to nose with her. Jaw clenched, he spoke through his teeth.

"I am not my father." Each word was pregnant with sincerity.

As much as she resisted, her gift could not let her miss the suspicion in his heart. But there was also undeniable truth behind his words. She couldn't trust that gift. Not anymore. She'd trusted Brígid and believed the lie, even if it was told to protect the innocent. She'd trusted her aim, and Vidarra had died. What if her people suffered from her naive belief in some fairytale of supernatural abilities?

"I would have died for ye today, and still ye dunna trust me." His tone softened, though anger still burned in his eyes. "What happened in the past . . . as horrible as it is . . . it doesna belong to us."

Dunna trust the tower king. In her mind, Cyrene caressed that warning, curled it in her arms, and cradled it close to her heart.

"We were fools to think this could ever work." She stared at the silver band encircling her finger.

"Cyrene." He reached for her, but she jerked away.

303

"Dunna touch me."

He froze at her hiss, dropping his arms to his sides. Her head swam with confusion. Promises and oaths, agreements and exhaustion, all swirling in incomprehensible vapors. The pain of his accusations. The agony at what she'd become because of this union.

She rubbed her palms along the dirt-caked fabric of her fighting leathers. Though they appeared clean, her hands were so caked with blood, they'd never truly be free of its sticky remains. The enormity of what she'd done punched a hole in her heart, destroying the small amount of trust she'd begun to store there. Then there was the empty, burning hatred that settled in the bottom of her heart, weighing it down until it felt as though it might fall right out of her chest.

And what of *An T-aon*? How could she ever hope to find closeness with him now?

"This canna work. It was never going to work."

Duncan's frustration matched her own. "How can ye say this, Cyrene?"

"Ye got what ye wanted." Even as she spoke them, Cyrene wished she could take the words back, yet they just kept coming. "Let me go."

He dropped his hands to his hips, eyes searching the floor. He shook his head and looked up at her again. "We are both tired. We just need to sleep and . . ."

"'Tis more than that."

"Cyrene, please."

"Stop saying my name!" Her hands flew to her ears, blocking out his voice, the frozen silence of the prison that was his tower taking her to a state of near panic. "Let me go."

"Go where?"

"Home."

"This is yer home." He pressed his fist to his chest. His voice was hoarse, eyes red, and hair a wild tangle of blonde curls. Like hers, his clothes were still filthy from the battle; splashes of blood now dried in dark brown spots on the fabric and leather.

She was used to dirt beneath her nails, but this—it was a different kind of grime. As she narrowed her eyes, voice turning to ice, that filthiness seeped deep into her heart, coating all of it with a repulsive blackness. Fists clenched, she stood tall, an awesome and terrible queen. Untouchable. Invincible. "This will never be my home."

30

DUNCAN

821 AD - The Same Time

Every word he'd spoken, every move he'd made in the hours since the battle, flashed through his mind. What had he done? What had happened? Anger and confusion and grief, magnified by the pain in his shoulder and the weight of exhaustion, swirled inside of him until he couldn't discern one emotion from another.

Flames burned in her eyes, and Duncan fought the urge to drop to his knees and beg her for mercy. He'd done it before, for Eowin's sake. Now he wanted to again for his own.

Every sprout of hope that had bloomed since the ceremony, culti-vated by tender moments, soft smiles, and touches, withered and died at the pure disgust etched across her beautiful features.

As he looked at the queen, her face became Fiona's face. He saw his stepmother walking the empty halls as if searching for the affection his father had promised but never delivered. Her loneliness had matched his own.

Duncan tore his gaze away, catching his own reflection in the glass of the window. His features were so much like his father's. Would he, too, become a cold, uncaring husband? A ruthless and vengeful king? It was clearly what Cyrene expected of him.

And why wouldn't she? He'd forced her into this position, this marriage. She chose to say yes, but truly, what other choice had he given her? And now she was the killer of Revna's sister. Of his sister. No wonder she hated him.

"Why dinna ye just let me die?" He didn't mean to say it aloud and certainly didn't mean it to be another accusation, but if his future were to mirror his father's and Fiona's, he would have rather perished in defense of his kingdom. At least there was honor in that.

"I keep my promises." The chill in Cyrene's tone gutted him.

"How? Ye are asking to leave me."

"I amna ending the arrangement."

Nay. She was simply taking her residence elsewhere. It wasn't unheard of in the lives of monarchs. But it felt like she was giving up hope.

"What other promises have ye made?" What deals were struck in the darkness as she was forced to lead a scared and hunted people when she was just a child herself?

She didn't answer him. Mayhap that's what gripped her so tightly. Fear. Fear that he would be just as cruel as his father. She wouldn't accept his promise that he would never become such a man.

Why? The question plagued him. He needed answers, and not just from her. Why had his life taken him down so many paths, only to end up back where he started? Why had he lost two mothers? Why had God allowed the plague to yank him from the abbey where he was doing the Lord's work? Why had his father done such unthinkable things?

That answer was the only clear one. *The sea, brother. 'Tis all about the sea.* He'd said it himself: his father was greedy.

"What do ye want from me, Cyrene?"

She turned her back to him, head lowered. "Nothing."

He stepped beside her but didn't touch her. "Did I not meet my end of the bargain? I kept yer people safe; they dinna have to face battle. What did ye expect from me?"

"Nothing." Her answers grew quieter. He was losing her. Not that he had any part of her to begin with.

"Ye had to have thought about it. About what our future would look like."

She whipped her head around to face him, tears pooled at the corners of her green eyes. "Nay. Just like ye, I dinna have any thoughts about what would come next."

"Why?" Her accusation wasn't unfounded. They'd never discussed what life would look like moving forward.

She brushed the back of her hand across her cheek, tears vanishing in its wake.

"Because there was no reason to. We were not supposed to survive this. There was not supposed to be a tomorrow."

"Then why did ye agree?" He stared at her, but she didn't turn around. Frustrated, he took her shoulders and made her face him. "Why?"

"To give them a chance." Tears poured down her face. "Revna was supposed to take them over the mountain. All of them . . . yers and mine. If the tower fell . . . she was supposed to keep them alive."

Dunna let it happen again.

He didn't know where that memory had been hiding, but a ghostly Fiona's plea from a long-forgotten nightmare rose to the surface of his mind. He'd always assumed she'd meant the betrayal of the crown, of Tràigh.

But as he looked upon Cyrene, watching the wheels of her mind whirling out of control, he knew Fiona meant something entirely different. She meant for him to protect the Picts, to keep them from suffering such pain again.

Like Fiona, Cyrene's commitment to her people was unwavering, unbreakable, and when he looked at her, he saw a woman who had only ever belonged to the hearts of those people. She had never once belonged to herself. She'd known her purpose since the minute she was crowned queen at eight years old.

She'd measured every step since then, knowing one wrong move could cost lives. Even he couldn't fully understand the weight of that burden, and he was asking her to lead her people into some great unknown where she couldn't see the ground in front of her. He was asking her to trust him, a stranger. Her enemy.

There was no assurance he could offer that would calm the storm he could see raging inside of her. The only gift he could give was time.

He released her, and his gaze traced the edges of the gray stone floor before rising to endless bare walls. This was no place for the queen of the wood. She needed life to survive, music and trees and nights spent under stars, not endless days buried in his stone tomb. He could give her that.

"I'll take ye home."

Her eyes widened, then narrowed again, suspicion flattening her full lips into a hard line. It was a dream to think they could be one, that they could find peace between the fields and forest.

The favor they'd been shown in battle had faded with the dawn, and now they stood before each other, empty and depleted. Their true selves were exposed in the raw exhaustion of the day. Mayhap this was the first truly honest moment they'd shared.

"I promised not to ask ye to love me. I promised to give all I had to ye." Duncan turned and swept out his arm as if to present the kingdom and all it represented to her. "Ye may go wherever ye wish."

Cyrene didn't move. She looked as if she were waiting for his condition. She was right. He did have one. One last hope flung between them.

"I'll take ye, but ye must rest first."

She opened her mouth to protest, but he leveled a hard gaze that snapped her lips shut.

"I'll find a maid to tend to yer needs, and will escort ye myself when ye've rested."

With a formal bow, he moved to the wide wooden doors of the meeting room, looking over his shoulder as he paused in the grand opening.

"I keep my promises, too, Huntress."

31

DUNCAN

821 AD - Later That Afternoon

Steam rose around his face, warming his skin until it was almost unbearable. He hissed as he sank into the tub and again when the long though shallow wound in his shoulder met the surface. His bathwater turned a murky brown from the blood and filth. He scrubbed until he could finally see his own skin again and run his fingers through his hair without them getting tangled in matted curls.

Once the bath was drawn, he'd sent his servants away, insisting on bathing alone for once, a simple privilege he'd always desired but never demanded. Since he was throwing all manner of propriety out the window anyway, he might as well indulge himself a little. He'd never take for granted the endless comforts awarded his position: the food, clothes, protection . . . but privacy—he would always envy the villagers for that luxury.

As he dried and dressed the wound at his side with a length of clean cloth, he tried to ignore the silent call of his bed. If he lay down on its soft surface, he might not wake for days, and he had a promise to keep to the queen. The bath had done wonders for his muscles, but his heart still beat a steady rhythm of defeat.

Instead, he snatched a pillow and a woven blanket from the foot of his bed and stretched out on the floor. A soldier's training allowed him to force himself to sleep, but the hard surface of the stone floor kept him from resting more than a few hours. He awoke to the sun beginning its descent and the same question that had chased him into a dreamless slumber.

What is yer plan?

She'd asked a fair question. The truth was, when he'd decided to follow through with Eowin's suggestion to propose, he didn't have a plan. Not beyond the battle. He'd not given one minute of consideration to what this union would realistically look like once the fighting ceased. He'd only been concerned with survival.

Once again, overwhelming turmoil plagued his mind, spawned from that one question he constantly asked: *Why?*

He had never desired this position, and yet against all odds, here he was—still king. He'd not been seeking to marry, and yet here he stood—a husband. None of these things had been in his plans. He didn't want any of this.

Without his advisors, had it not been for Cyrene, negotiations with Laorn would have been a disaster. It was her thoughtful suggestions and decisiveness that won the king of Nàbaidh over and peacefully brought talks to an agreeable end. Laorn even returned the silver Duncan had offered to tempt him into the meeting with Eowin.

Ashamed to voice his doubt aloud, Duncan closed his eyes, fists balled at the sides of his head.

Why? I am not the man for this place, for her.

Silence was the only answer, and, resigned to the frustration, Duncan heaved a long breath before opening his eyes again. The late afternoon sun poured through his windows in golden rays; iron bars across mottled glass created the long silhouette of a cross on the floor.

He stood at the foot of that shape, hands limp at his sides.

"Ye gave us all we asked for." Duncan ran his hand through his still-wet hair, letting it land on the back of his neck. "Gave us victory when there was no way."

His weary eyes stung from exhaustion, but he refused to tear his gaze away from the shadow cross.

"Why does it still feel like we lost?"

In the five years he'd spent studying the scriptures, how many times had he read about patience? About waiting on the Lord? About trusting the heart of God?

"Is that what ye ask of me? To wait? To trust?"

With Fiona's guidance, he'd decided as a child that God was true. He was real, and if he was real, he had to be good. And if he was good, he was all good. Worthy to be trusted. Worthy of Duncan's full allegiance, of his whole heart. It was Duncan's choice to give it over or not.

Duncan's throat grew tight with emotion as he faced his doubt and weaknesses. With broken, barely whispered words, he confessed to the shadow of the cross.

"I dunna have enough faith on my own. I need yer help."

A knock interrupted his prayer. Given permission, Eowin entered as Duncan wrapped his brat around a clean tunic, wincing not only at the ache in his shoulder, but also at his reflection in the polished mirror above his table. The captain wore a clean uniform and looked as if he had found as little sleep as Duncan.

Eowin's mouth turned down as he surveyed Duncan's expression. Seeming to think better of it, he didn't mention the redness of his king's eyes. "William wishes to speak to ye."

"I'm certain he does." Duncan huffed an annoyed laugh and pinned his brat in place. "He can wait. I must escort the queen back to her kingdom."

"Sire? She . . ." Eowin's brows met over his gray eyes, and he lowered his voice to a whisper, even though they were alone. "She willna remain wi' ye?"

Duncan let his gaze wander back to the shadowed cross spread across his floor. He remembered well the day they laid Fiona to rest. His father didn't even remain until the priest finished his prayer, and after that day, he couldn't remember sharing more than a few words with his father. The king's mission to rid the kingdom of Fiona's people had filled his heart, suffocating any life that once warmed his chest.

Mayhap Duncan had buried his heart with Fiona's that day. But if there was one thing he'd learned from his time with Father Malcolm at the abbey, it was that Jesus had come to bring life to dead hearts like his. Hope to hopeless situations.

He believed in God, and he knew the truth, but he'd never let it seep into his soul—to change him so deeply that he became something new.

Duncan stared at the cross. If he didn't give all, why bother giving any?

His hand traveled to his chest, remembering that strange sensation when Cyrene had seemed to peer into the very depths of who he was. Mayhap that's what she saw—the empty, passionless husk he inhabited. Mayhap that's why she wanted to run.

He couldn't force her to forgive him for who he was, couldn't change her heart or heal whatever pain dug so deep inside of her. But he could wait, and he could fight for her, for them.

He could give his own heart completely to Christ and become something new. Mayhap she couldn't love who he'd been, but maybe she could learn to live with who he would become.

"Sire?" Eowin's voice seemed far away.

When Duncan blinked him into focus, Eowin's mouth ticked up at one side, as if he sensed the blooming of life inside his once-dead king.

As he shoved his feet into his boots, Duncan flashed a glance at his reflection again. Sparks of hope lit the dull gray of his eyes to a blazing cobalt. Rising to his full height, he answered Eowin's curious half-smile with a grin of his own.

"In time, Eowin." His heavy hand gave Eowin's shoulder a reassuring squeeze. "In time."

32

CYRENE

821 AD - That Evening

Taranau's smooth gait carried Cyrene across the open fields of Tràigh. Duncan galloped beside her on a stone gray mare. They'd not spoken since he'd asked if she had everything she needed for the ride. She'd answered with a nod.

The discomfort in her gut was not just from the foreignness of the leather saddle but from the feeling that she was making the wrong decision. It worked its way through her nerves, but she only straightened her back and held tight to Taranau's reins in defiance of her own insecurity.

When they reached the edge of the wood, it was nearly nightfall, and Cyrene pulled back, bringing Taranau to a halt. She made to dismount when Duncan drew close beside her, still astride his horse.

"Do ye mean to walk?"

"Aye." She moved again, and he stilled her with a large hand over hers where it rested on her leg. Cutting a slicing glare his way, she expected him to unhand her. When he didn't, she curled her lip and explained, "Ye can take Taranau back wi' ye."

"I will go all the way."

"I ken the way home, Duncan." Her comment was terse, the bite making him flinch.

The muscles of his jaw bulged as he clenched his teeth, and his hand remained in place, firm and authoritative.

"I will go all the way."

When she opened her mouth to argue, he squeezed his fingers around hers. "Our people need to ken their king. They need to see my face and ken that I will protect them and care for them as ye do. No matter where they live."

The fervor in his words sent a chill up her spine, as if she were a child being scolded for some misdoing. *Our people*, he'd called them.

He lowered his head, centering his gaze on hers, telling her even if she continued her dismount, he would only follow on foot if necessary.

Jerking her hand free, Cyrene nudged Taranau onward with her heels and tried to swallow the smoking, angry words burning at her lips. His demand wasn't absurd. Even if she didn't stay with him in the tower, he was still their king. The irritating metal band around her finger kept reminding her of that.

At the click of Duncan's tongue, Taranau stopped, and Cyrene sent a daggered look over her shoulder. He'd dismounted, and with a rub of his hand between his own horse's ears, whispered a command that sent the mare trotting back toward the stables at the tower. She scowled.

Curse him and his well-behaved horses.

"Since yer staying, I dunna need two animals for the trip back." He marched to Taranau's side, the animal annoyingly obedient to his master. "Front or back?"

"Pardon?"

"Do ye want to ride in front or back?"

"I'd rather walk." Cyrene shifted, preparing to slide to the ground, when Duncan reached around her and threw himself onto Taranau's back, keeping her in place in front of him. "Front it is."

He didn't give her the chance to complain before whistling a chirp that spurred Taranau forward. She had a mind to drive her skull back into his wounded shoulder, sending him hurtling to the ground while she took off, but Taranau was too loyal. He'd never leave Duncan. Not like she was doing.

She wanted to hate him, but the warmth of his strong arms around her, his broad chest at her back, made her head swim with confusion. She smothered memories of the night they'd shared with a huff and clenched her teeth at the sound of his chuckle, as if he could read her mind.

"I told ye I used to explore these woods as a child. But when I was ten and two, I convinced Eowin to come wi' me." Duncan's breath was warm on her neck. She tried to lean away but lost her balance and nearly tumbled over Taranau's shoulders.

Duncan caught her waist, steadying her, but kept talking without mention of her embarrassing falter. "He was much more timid then. Scared of his own shadow."

He kept his hands on her waist, but relaxed his grip once he was assured she wouldn't try to dive off Taranau's back.

"We went searching for the fairies from the legends. Maybe we went looking for courage too."

"Why are you telling me this?" Cyrene spoke through her teeth, seething at his nearness, at the way she wanted to cringe but couldn't.

Duncan leaned close again, his lips at her ear. "Because I think I saw one. Wi' locks of fire like yers." When he tugged at a strand of her hair, she slapped at his hand, fuming that he didn't seem to care and dropped his hand to her waist again.

He didn't seem bothered when she stiffened under his touch either, but he moved his hands so he was no longer touching her.

"I had the feeling she gave me a gift that day."

"What gift?" Cyrene couldn't help herself. The memory of two lads laughing as she battled the desire to release frozen fingers that held back the string of her longbow was too strong.

"She let me live."

Mercifully, he kept quiet for the next hour, and he kept his hands to himself. Their only contact was when Taranau bounced over a log and she was forced to lean into him.

She'd taken his offer at the tower. She'd bathed and accepted clean clothes brought by one of the maids. She even attempted to obey his order to rest, as difficult as it was in the strange place. The few hours' sleep she'd found were plagued with dreams of swirling gray ghosts that whispered warnings and showed her bits of forgotten things. She knew he'd hoped that a little sleep was all she needed to change her mind, but it was all she could do to not race across the courtyard to the stables when he appeared at her door and gave his permission for her to leave. Mayhap she was a coward, but the woods beckoned, the rustle of leaves offering promises of safety —of answers to questions she didn't know how to ask. So many questions.

"It seemed ye ken who she was. When the sentry said her name?" she asked without warning, but she didn't have to identify the "her." Duncan would know she spoke of Vidarra.

He hummed at her question, and she waited, letting him formulate his response. She had no right to ask such intrusive questions, especially after her harsh accusations. The back of her head thumped against his injured shoulder as Taranau climbed another steep, rocky incline.

"Vidarra is a Norse name." He shuttered a pained groan and placed a firm hand on her waist to hold her still.

Cyrene straightened at his answer, and Duncan reached with his free arm, taking the reins from her. It made sense that she'd been given a Viking name, but it didn't explain his reaction. Just as Brígid took great care to keep Revna's true identity secret, Eden would have done the same. So much so that when the captured Picts were taken aboard the ship, an infant princess was among them, and no one from Tràigh knew to rescue her.

More locks and keys found each other. Clicking into place and opening the way to dark, unfathomable truths.

I will bring them all back.

Cyrene shivered at the memory of Revna's chilling promise, and Duncan curved his arm around her middle, tucking her tighter against him. She couldn't imagine what that must feel like—knowing your father sold infants as slaves. Even had none of them been his own, it was still too terrible to fathom. Her father, though taken too soon, had been kind and loving. She knew nothing of Duncan's pain, and though she didn't trust him—didn't even like him much at the moment—her heart ached for him all the same.

"Ye spoke to her . . . on the steps. What did she say?" she asked, hoping against hope there was some comfort in Vidarra's last words. Mayhap something she could tell Revna if she ever returned.

"After I realized she wasna Revna, I recognized her from my household and thought she was from Tràigh. I asked her why she would betray her own people."

Cyrene's throat felt dry; she wasn't sure she wanted to know the answer and wished she hadn't asked.

"All she said was if I had ken her name, I would understand."

"What does that mean?"

His voice was gravelly, and he cleared his throat. "Vidarra means vengeance."

"If she was but a bairn when she was taken from Tràigh, do ye think she ken of her life before?"

Duncan sighed, rubbing his hand on her side before releasing her and holding the reins with both hands.

"I dunna ken, but if she hated Tràigh enough to wish such destruction, she must have at least learned what the king had done, even if she dinna ken he was her father."

Taranau plodded along; Duncan needn't guide him. He knew the way. She had no more questions, none that she wished to voice out loud, anyway.

"I'm sorry." Duncan's voice was soft, penitent. Cyrene waited, letting him take the lead. "That ye had to . . . that I didn't catch her before she went through that door."

A costly delay. Cyrene was sorry, too, and rubbed her fingers across the fabric of her dress. She hadn't been able to shed the dirty feeling of blood on her hands since she fired that arrow. More lives would have been lost if she hadn't. And mayhap Duncan would have had to deal the final blow against his sister. It was too horrid to imagine. It had been war, and war was messy, but she would grieve what it had taken from all of them nonetheless.

"Before that, I dinna . . ." The words stuck in her throat, and she coughed, forcing their release. "I hadna ever taken a life before."

He didn't respond, but she felt him tense. He wouldn't understand how it was possible; she didn't really understand herself.

"'Tis true," she said. "I trained with my warriors. We faced many enemies, but . . . somehow it was always another who took the final blow."

He stayed quiet, his breaths hitching with emotion. The sounds of the woods at night drifted up around them, wrapping them in a private cocoon. There was no one else to hear, and Cyrene felt the urge to share some deep, hidden part of herself that no one else would ever know.

"There is a legend amongst the women in my family. That some are chosen to be blessed with gifts from *An T-aon*. They're never to be used to her glory, only for his. My mother said I would receive such a gift, and I'd be marked. When I realized my arrows always reached their targets, I thought it to be the gift she spoke of. I thought *An T-aon* gave it to me to save our people, that he was sparing me from having to end a life. So I made sure that the Picts kept worshiping. We honored him. Or . . . they did. I spoke the words and led the dance. I thought it was enough. But my worship was empty."

Cyrene found herself breathless, her chest tight. Duncan still remained quiet, as if he were letting her reveal as much as she was willing.

"I dunna ken why I thought I deserved to escape the pain of death when all those around me had to bear its burden. As though I'd earned his grace somehow when I ken I can earn nothing. 'Tis all given from his goodness. And I am learning to accept that, even if I never receive my mark."

"Yer mark?" He finally spoke, his voice soft.

"My mother's was here." She placed her hand on her chest near her shoulder. "'Twas there from birth, she said. Distinct and the color of browned honey."

He leaned back then, and Cyrene craned her neck to see why. "What is it?"

"Ye have a mark, too, Huntress." He pressed his palm to her back, in the spot opposite her mother's.

Cyrene reached back and touched the place. "Ye've seen it?"

"Aye."

It could have only been in the hours after their wedding. If that was true, then it had been there before the battle. Before that arrow pierced Vidarra's chest. Cyrene's heart pounded, her thoughts racing. "Is it still there?"

She tore at the strings lacing her tunic together in the front. When it was loose enough, Duncan gently brushed her hair aside and pulled the fabric off her shoulder. She drew her arms to her chest, keeping herself covered.

She felt the warmth of his hand as he brushed his fingers across her skin. "Aye. 'Tis here. Why wouldna it be?"

She squeezed her eyes closed, heavy breaths pouring from her lungs. She didn't have an answer to his question, only one of her own. "What does it look like?"

"I see a lioness." His fingers traced the shape, and a tear raced down her cheek. "She's standing on hind legs. A warrior. Like ye."

Cyrene's shoulders curled inward, and Duncan lifted her tunic back in place as she tightened the laces with trembling fingers. She was marked. Even though her faith had been as dry as sand, even though her hands had been buried in blood. He kept her. *An T-aon* kept her as his own.

Even though she'd had a few hours' sleep, the physical exhaustion of battle and the emotional toil of all the revealed secrets still drained her. Cyrene's eyes begged for rest, true, peaceful rest, and she was grateful when Duncan finally spoke again.

"Question for a question?" Duncan leaned to the side, catching Cyrene's glance.

She shrugged an agreement. If she was talking, she wasn't sleeping.

"Why did ye let my cousin live?"

"What makes ye think I did it on purpose?"

His chest brushed her back as he shifted on Taranau's back again, and she felt his hand move to rub his shoulder. "Ye never miss, Huntress."

She pursed her lips to hide the smile that threatened to break across her mouth. Cyrene stretched her neck and cleared her throat before answering.

"Despite his misery, he was still yer kin." Chills raised the hair on her arms when Duncan's rough beard grazed her neck, and she lifted her chin, becoming queen instead of wife. "Besides, a leader killed in battle becomes a fallen hero. He becomes someone who needs avenging."

"A coward that's captured, though—"

"No one remembers him."

"Yer a wise queen, Cyrene."

"I told ye already . . ." She didn't bother to hide her grin, knowing he couldn't see. "No need to woo, I already said the vows."

"Canna a husband compliment his wife?"

Husband. Wife. The words didn't seem fitting for them, for what they were. They weren't friends, nor lovers. But they weren't exactly strangers either.

The complexity of it all made her head ache, and Cyrene pushed her fingers against her temples. A breath of winter wind snaked through the trees, chilling her skin, and Duncan reached into the satchel attached to Taranau's saddle, retrieving a blanket that he draped around her. Once settled, she felt herself relax into him, the feel of his heartbeat thrumming against her shoulder.

She could live with that. When it was just the two of them. She just Cyrene, and he just Duncan. Not king and queen. Not ruler of wood and ruler of stone. It was when she returned to the reality of who she was and where she'd come from that it all fell apart.

The vibrant sounds of her people infiltrated the silent, private world they'd traveled through, and she grew tense again. Before she could shuck off his loose embrace, Duncan slid off Taranau's back, taking the reins and leading the horse the rest of the way into the village.

Cyrene allowed herself to watch as he walked. During the meeting with Laorn, he was uncertain, almost relying on her decisiveness instead of his own. Now he seemed different. Confident and assertive.

She didn't know what had changed, but she approved, if not for her sake, then for his.

When word of their arrival spread, her people rushed from their homes, greeting them with baskets of wild forest flowers, hugs, offerings of sweet cakes and warm ale. They were showered with tears of joy and thanks.

At Gertrud's insistence, they visited the hut she used for healing, not entirely surprised to find Thaedry still present. He inspected the wound he'd tended when Duncan had first arrived and redressed his new injury before clapping the king on the back in a grateful display.

Throughout Thaedry's examination, Cyrene tried to settle on the right words to offer Duncan a place to rest for the night. Her hut was the obvious choice, but given her decision to return to the village, mayhap it was best if they kept their own quarters for the night.

She didn't get the chance to offer. As soon as they stepped through the hut's opening, ladies grabbed their hands and dragged them into a skipping line of dancers snaking their way through the cluster of homes to the music of pipes and flutes. When she lifted her eyes to the sky and whispered a prayer of thanks, for the first time, her words were not empty but laden with every bit of passion she possessed.

Cyrene found herself searching for Duncan in the crowd, unable to hold her laughter at his stumbling through the unfamiliar dance.

Night was in full bloom by the time they broke from the celebration and collapsed next to each other beside a healthy fire. When most of the ladies had exhausted their reverie, they, too, settled in small groups around their own fires, music giving way to the sound of easy conversation.

Duncan pushed himself to his feet, offering his hand to her. Aware of watching eyes, Cyrene accepted and allowed him to fold her hand around his bent arm.

"I want to meet them." He leaned toward her but scanned the scattered groups of villagers.

"All of them?" She laughed, her eyes bouncing over the dozens of thatched roof homes that dotted the woods.

He didn't answer, and when she looked back at him, he was watching her intently, a look of appreciation etched across his features.

"Not tonight." He tilted his head, his eyes taking in every detail of her face. "Ye need to sleep. But eventually I want to meet them all."

When a young woman called Aberdeen placed her bairn in Duncan's arms, something took flight in Cyrene's stomach and fluttered around until he returned the infant to his glowing mother. On their way to the stables, Cyrene introduced him to the eager villagers they passed.

"Thank ye, m'lady." Duncan released her arm and folded his hands behind his back with a slight bow before stepping toward Taranau, who had been enjoying his own bucket of hay and grain.

"Ye dunna have to go." The words were out before she could stop herself.

Duncan stood by his horse's side, rubbing lazy circles on the animal's thick neck. He didn't ask what she meant, only watched her stumble over her words with a confident half-smile.

"I just mean, 'tis late. Ye need sleep as well. Ye could wait until the morn to leave."

His lips twitched as if he were reining in a grin that would change her mind and send him on his way with a curse and a swift kick. He turned back to Taranau, who nuzzled his nose against Duncan's side, enjoying a vigorous scratch between his ears.

Duncan seemed to be carefully considering her suggestion. She felt small, exposed, and fought the urge to take it back.

"I must go, but will ye do something fer me?" He kept his eyes locked on Taranau. "Will ye meet me at the tower three days hence?"

"I . . . what is in three days?"

"A gathering." Duncan turned his gaze loose on her, blue eyes pleading. "Ye dunna have to stay, but the people of that village need to ken their queen too."

She caught herself taking a step away from him, lifelong suspicions taking over reason. Had he only come to play nice and lower her defenses, let her people see them happy and smiling—then convince her to return to the tower to trap her there when everyone would think she went on her own?

"I ken that look." He surprised her with a smirk. "I ken ye dunna trust me yet."

"I . . ." She almost apologized, but despite their marital situation, she'd known him less than a full week. Surely more time was needed to form trust. "Do ye trust me?"

His half-smile broadened a bit, but he only said, "Bring Astrid, bring whomever ye'd like, all of them, if that's what ye desire, but these people . . ." Duncan lifted his chin in the direction of the huts, then toward the tower. "All our people deserve a crown that cares about them. Who will ken their names and their troubles. Who *they* can trust."

Duncan slid the leather reins of Taranau's bridle through his hands, clenching his fingers around the ends.

"I mean to give them what they deserve. But they need ye, Huntress. Not just the woodland people, but the villagers of Tràigh too." He pulled himself onto Taranau's back, turning the animal toward the blackness of the wood.

Taranau pranced a few steps closer to the queen, and she reached out, holding his halter to keep him still, looking up at Duncan.

"I willna force ye," he said, his tone soft. "But I'm asking ye. Please, come."

Cyrene examined Duncan's face, finding no hint of a teasing smile, of untruth. When her eyes met his, she locked onto his gaze and searched deep. She heard him draw in a sharp breath. *True. True. True.* The word pulsed in her mind as if connected to his heart. Warmth flooded through her down to her bones, like she had been immersed in a hot spring. He felt . . . right.

In a blink, she broke their trance and released Taranau with a kiss to his warm nose. Duncan didn't ask for an answer, and she didn't offer one. She only watched as the stallion carried her husband off into the night, wishing she'd done more to make him stay.

33

CYRENE

821 AD – Midday the Next Day

"**W**hat will ye do?" Astrid's quiet question drifted over Cyrene's shoulder as she filled mugs with the elderberry and rosehips tea that Gertrud finished brewing.

Cyrene examined the many cuts her healer had doctored, fingers finally coming to rest on her bruised cheek. After a cup of Thaedry's tea finally helped her slip into a truly restful sleep, she'd woken alert but on edge. She'd shared the king's request with her friends, partially for advice and partially because she had to hear his words again, even if in her own voice.

But first, she'd shared the shocking discovery of Revna's tragic lineage, which had stunned the room into silence for a long, grieving moment.

"I dunna ken." Cyrene met their eyes, uncertainty widening her own. "What should I do?"

Taking the offered cup, Cyrene let her eyes follow curls of steam rising from the liquid. Astrid leaned against the hut's center beam, nursing her own drink.

"Ye ken my mother was a great storyteller." Gertrud slid silently into a neighboring chair.

"Aye," Cyrene answered after a slow sip, flashing a lazy smile at Astrid. "We fell asleep to many of Brígid's tales as children, dinna we?"

Astrid lifted her mug in agreement.

"My favorite was the love story of Derelei and Bercilak." Gertrud moved to the hearth, her stick stirring up sparks as she poked the fire.

"The Pictish queen and the brave son of a laird-turned-soldier." Astrid's smile beckoned the same from Cyrene.

As Gertrud continued the story, Cyrene allowed her mind to explore long-forgotten memories and fill in missing pieces with imagined ones.

"Derelei, daughter of Rhona and Darron, was bonnie and wild, her temper as untamed as her spirit. They say as a lass, she would disappear for days into the caves along the shore of the sea, her parents having to send trackers to return her."

Cyrene could almost smell the salty air of the sea. How many times had she and Beli walked the shores, their small hands wrapped safely in her mother's?

"War came to their land, and the Picts were spread thin, foreign men wi' foreign weapons overpowering their spears and bows. Darron was slain, Derelei forever wounded by the wails of her mother over his loss. She made a promise to herself then, even though she was but a child."

Cyrene knew of her grandparents, but had never heard this story. A quietness settled over her hut, as if she, Astrid, and Gertrud had escaped to some other realm where they were the only ones who dwelt.

"She swore to never give her heart to another, for she couldna bear the pain. And thus Derelei became as the stones she collected from the sea. Hard, cold, strong."

Cyrene flicked her eyes toward Astrid, wondering if she knew this story. But her captain remained motionless, as if a single flinch would break the spell and the story would be lost.

"When Derelei became of age, the most handsome and greatest of Pictish men couldna capture her heart, for it belonged to the sea. Even kings sought her hand, but she dinna give mind to any."

A flicker of a memory, a much more recent memory, sent a flare of fire across Cyrene's brow. Sima, the woman from Duncan's kingdom, hinted at something Cyrene didn't understand. Sima had stopped herself before saying more and looked at Duncan as if he would be offended at this information. Gertrud's soft voice drew Cyrene back to the past, locking her into the mystery of her parents' story.

"Strengthened by her heartache, Rhona became a great warrior, rising to lead an army against the foreign invaders. Years and years, she ruled. A neverending battle hardened her until Derelei no longer recognized her mother. She was ruthless, a black wave of death across any battlefield. But even she was not enough. The men from the south were too many, and Rhona ken their only chance was to ally wi' the neighboring kingdom of Tràigh."

Heart pounding against her ribs, Cyrene dared not even swallow. A dread settled in her bones, its ache threatening to pull her through the floor, deep under the soil of the earth to a dark and lonely grave.

"Rhona looked to Derelei. Bonnie, fierce Derelei."

The image of her mother's sparkling eyes danced through Cyrene's memory, longing taking the place of dread.

"A union wi' the son of a wealthy laird and the king's most esteemed soldier, Bercilak, would bring the Pictish lands under the protection of Tràigh's army. In exchange, the king of Tràigh gained the coveted access to the firth. So Derelei became a wife, and Bercilak, a husband."

Cyrene couldn't move, couldn't breathe, couldn't speak. Surely this was some fairytale Brígid had created to entertain a toddling Gertrud. Surely this was not the truth. In the version Brígid had told, her parents were something of a fairytale. They fell in love, married for joy. Theirs was not a forced alliance.

Astrid had dropped her feet to the floor, now sitting rigid in her chair. She, too, was captivated by the tale. Cyrene turned her eyes on the healer, who met her stare with equal determination. Cyrene sucked in a sharp breath. It was true. Every word.

"Together, they drove back the invaders, gaining glory and land for his king and safety and peace for her people. But what was left when it was over was a broken, divided nation. A kingdom in need of healing."

Her mother's story so much mirrored her own, Cyrene could almost feel Derelei's presence at her side, and she longed to turn and see her standing there. She dared not, lest she break the spell cast by Gertrud's fairytale, losing even the vapor of that presence.

"As they worked to mend a divided land, Derelei began to see goodness in Bercilak. She began to admire his strength and compassion. The heart of sea stone in her chest began to soften into a heart of flesh, but she could not give that heart to him. She was reminded of the teachings spread by the Irishmen who had come many years before. *An T-aon*, the one true God, who through his own sacrifice, took blackened, dead hearts and made them live. Something captured Derelei's own stone heart. She believed their words. She prayed that he would do the same for her."

Gertrud didn't have to finish the story. Even though she'd been but a lass, Cyrene had vivid memories of her mother and father. Their love was as impassioned and trustworthy as the waves against the shore, as certain as the sun rising.

"'Twas nay a quick transformation." Gertrud lowered her chin, looking up through her lashes. "Both learning to die each day to themselves, to live for *An T-aon*, and through their love for him, they found a love for each other to rival the ages."

Cyrene didn't bother to fight the tears that slid down her cheeks

—she was too centered on the stirring in her chest. Her own heart of stone trembled against the truth of her mother's story.

"I wish ye'd shared this before I wed." Cyrene finally wiped the salty drops from her chin with the back of her hand.

"Nay." Gertrud turned to the table, pouring unused herbs back into the pots and carved wooden boxes from her supply satchel. "Ye werna ready to hear it until now."

Cyrene shot Gertrud a glare but knew the young healer was right.

"Do ye have a story for Astrid in that satchel?" Cyrene laughed when Gertrud scrunched her sweet round face in confusion. Astrid shot her a warning glare. "I fear the force of her bursting heart will level the entire kingdom if she doesna release it soon."

"My heart?" Astrid snorted, tossing an annoyed look at Cyrene. "What about yer—"

"So 'tis true then." Gertrud stilled her cleaning, a bright smile aimed at the seething warrior. Cyrene stifled a laugh. "I heard rumors of a certain braw captain."

Astrid's face flamed red as she snatched her quiver and longbow from where they rested against the table before flying through the doorway into the night.

"Careful, Gertrud. Astrid isna as civil as I when given instruction by young healers."

Gertrud's pink lips popped open, feigning surprise. "I only shared a favorite childhood fairytale, m'lady."

For the first time in days, the weight of the world lifted from Cyrene's shoulders. It happened so quickly, she thought she might float off the ground as she and Gertrud walked to her own hut.

"Did Brígid share any other stories wi' ye, Gertrud?"

Gertrud's brows met, curious as to Cyrene's meaning.

"I just wish I ken what truly happened to make the king who had been her friend turn against her." Cyrene's peace remained despite her unanswered questions.

"I canna remember any that would explain." Gertrud's tone was soft, apologetic.

"Mayhap we will never ken the full truth." They'd reached Cyrene's tent, and she held back the curtain for Gertrud to follow her inside.

"Shall I help ye gather yer things, or will ye put them back in place?" Gertrud lifted a wrap and the cleaned fighting leathers Cyrene had worn in battle from the table and held them to her chest, waiting for Cyrene to make a decision.

"I dunna ken yet."

The trunk she'd packed on her wedding day still sat in its place. She'd only made a half-attempt to load the box with her few belongings, certain she wouldn't return from battle.

She lifted the leather straps fastened to its carved wooden lid, surveying her meager possessions. She retrieved a small wooden box containing a single item. Pulling open the top, Cyrene turned it aside until the contents spilled into her palm.

Her mother's ring was cool against her skin. A gift from the handsome Bercilak, pride of Tràigh and friend to the Picts. It struck her then that he'd come from the tower. Even under the cruel reign of the elder William, something good had come.

Gertrud went to place the clothes in the trunk when something fell from its folds. A small stack of square parchments scattered on the floor.

"What are these?" Gertrud bent to pick them up.

Cyrene joined her, explaining when she saw the inked portraits. "They were in a trunk belonging to Duncan's father. I tucked them in my vest and forgot to put them back."

Gertrud handed the parchments she'd collected to Cyrene but kept one, examining it. "He drew these?"

"I think so," Cyrene said, gathering the rest and rising to her feet.

Gertrud remained crouched, staring at the portrait in her hand. "This one . . ."

"What is it?" Cyrene asked, placing the stack on the table.

Gertrud stood, wide eyes lifting from the drawing to Cyrene's face. "I barely remember her, but—"

Cyrene took the portrait from Gertrud's outstretched hand, nearly stumbling backwards into the table when she recognized the likeness.

"My mother." Fire spread across Cyrene's cheeks, and she shook the portrait at Gertrud. "Why would he have this?"

"I dunna ken." Gertrud wasn't fazed by Cyrene's outburst. "It looks as if it were crumpled and then smoothed again. And look. There's writing on the back."

Gertrud was right; it wasn't smooth like the other drawings; it was marred with lines. When Cyrene turned it over, she read aloud the scripted words angrily scrawled in jagged indigo ink.

Only ye between the sea and me.

"Look at her hand." Gertrud tilted her head to see Derelei's likeness again. "That doesna look like a Pictish ring."

Cyrene turned the parchment again, examining the ring drawn on Derelei's hand. That same one that he'd drawn on his first wife and Fiona. "'Tis a wedding ring."

It was more than a ring. It was a key unlocking another secret.

"What does it mean?"

Tell me about the sea. King Laorn had been most interested in Tràigh's access to the firth. The land that under her mother's rule had belonged to the Picts. Cyrene's gaze centered on that sketched ring.

"I . . . I think I ken why he turned on her."

Gertrud waited with wide eyes for Cyrene to explain.

"The sea. He wanted that land . . . not just permission from the Pictish queen to access the firth. He wanted control of it."

Gertrud pulled a chair away from the table, motioning for Cyrene to sit before sitting herself in another chair.

"A union with Derelei would have meant their lands would become one, but she was married to my father. I remember when he was sent to the west. There was no danger to Tràigh, but the king sent him to the front lines anyway. I remember my father saying the king had chosen him because he was the only one who could keep the fighting from reaching Tràigh."

Cyrene rubbed her hand across her brow, already slick with sweat at the story the drawing had unlocked.

"When Mother was called to the tower, she learned of my father's death and the next day of the king's wedding to Fiona. She came home and prepared her warriors. She was so angry, and I over-heard her telling Eden she wouldn't be threatened."

Gertrud didn't speak. She didn't seem to even be breathing.

"I thought she was talking about the kingdom in the west, but Gertrud . . . I think the king sent my father to die. I think to gain control of the firth, he tried to wed my mother, and when she refused, he took Fiona instead."

"If he gained the land he wanted, why would he have killed Fiona?"

"He didn't. Fiona's father had the power to allow him in, but the queen was still in control. King William ken she would come when the bairns were born because of the gifting custom. I think he took the opportunity of my mother's visit to arrange a scheme." Cyrene leaned forward, tapping her finger on the table with each point she made. "We ken he killed Fiona. We ken he called my mother into a private meeting, and we ken when she emerged, they learned the bairns were gone. That news sent him into a rage. I think he tried to persuade her again in that meeting to form a union, and I think he used the princesses as leverage."

She kept to her principles despite the persistence of . . . Sima's words joined with another memory to form a theory in Cyrene's mind. As she lay dying, her mother had said, *They canna be used now.*

"I believe she refused to wed him again. She'd never have given him power over the Picts. When he discovered Eden had taken the princesses, his plans were ruined, and the king decided to take the land by force, using Fiona's death to blame the Picts as his excuse. That's when he drove his sword into her side and his soldiers turned on her guard."

Gertrud collapsed against the back of her chair, pushing wisps of her blond hair away from her face.

"I dunna ken if 'tis all true, but . . ." Cyrene arranged the three women's portraits in a row. "Why else would he have drawn her wearing that ring? 'Twas certainly not because he loved her."

They sat in silence for a long while before Gertrud finally straightened. "So what will ye do?"

Cyrene, who had been staring at her mother's portrait, raised her eyes to the healer.

"If all ye say is true. If 'tis indeed how it happened, ye are still wed to Duncan. He was a lad and ye a lass when it happened. What will ye do now, wi' *yer* future?"

She thought for a long moment before answering. "Duncan's sister died at my hand. How can I be forgiven for such an act?"

The young healer examined Cyrene, wisdom beyond her years narrowing her eyes. "If Revna walked through the door right now and asked the same question, what would ye tell her?"

Cyrene was taken aback by the question. "I would say there is nothing *An T-aon* canna forgive. Ye have but to ask."

"Wouldna ye also tell her *An T-aon* not only came to give life eternal, but also abundant life while ye yet live? Would ye not tell her of hope and grace? That it can be found not only from *An T-aon*, but also between his followers?"

Cyrene only stared at Gertrud, who smiled softly and began placing Cyrene's belongings in her trunk. All that Gertrud said was true—but the fear that, even though he never said as much, Duncan would forever hate her for killing his sister still pulsed a warning beat in her heart.

She opened her mouth to say such when Astrid, red-faced and panting, burst through the curtain, scrolls of parchment clenched in her fists.

"A gift from the king." Her jaw barely moved as she dumped them onto Cyrene's table.

"Who delivered these?" Cyrene abandoned the trunk for the pile Astrid had brought.

"His captain."

Cyrene and Gertrud both threw fascinated glances at Astrid. Gertrud placed the fur she'd been folding into the trunk and hedged the outer wall of the hut, inching her way toward the exit with Astrid eying her warily.

Before she darted out, Gertrud said with a wink, "I'm certain he is weary from his travels. I'm sure he needs rest and a good meal."

Astrid bounded after the healer with shouts of "Dunna ye dare, Gertrud," leaving Cyrene alone with Duncan's gift.

Cyrene unrolled the parchments, suddenly serious when she realized what they detailed. She sucked in a sharp breath as she examined each page. Searching through the rest of the delivery for explanation, she finally found a letter with words inked in perfectly formed letters.

Gertrud stumbled back inside, breathless and giggling.

"I see she hasn't killed ye yet." Cyrene offered the healer little more than a glance before examining the letter again.

"She's deadly, but I'm quick." Gertrud pushed away from the doorway and joined Cyrene at the table, her eyes immediately finding the map Duncan had drawn. "Is this . . ."

"Aye." Cyrene pushed her fingers against her lips, managing the smile that forced its way across her mouth. "He's suggested a verra organized solution to unite our people."

At a nod of permission from the queen, Gertrud thumbed through the rest of the parchments. "Impressive."

Cyrene didn't respond as she finished reading. Under the discreet, watchful eye of her healer, Cyrene skirted the furniture, making her way across her hut to where their ceremonial staff lay in its place of honor.

She ran her fingers across its smooth, carved surface, remembering the last time she stood in that spot, Duncan at her side. When he'd learned of her faith, a visible tension left his shoulders, and she could almost hear his thoughts. They were the same. She pictured him standing in his meeting room, a look of deep sincerity cut across his features, telling her his tower was her home.

No. Not his tower. When she squeezed her eyes closed, she saw him clearly. When he'd said it was her home, he hadn't gestured to the stone walls; his hand had been fisted over his heart.

Cyrene considered Gertrud's story. Her grandmother, Rhona, had come to the end of her life trapped in the sharp claws of bitterness. Derelei could have chosen that same path, as her life was not what she'd chosen for herself. The difference was that Derelei sought *An T-aon* and surrendered to his sovereignty. Now two roads emerged before Cyrene as well.

"Have ye now made up yer mind?" Gertrud's prompting question sent Cyrene's fingers tapping across the stack of parchments.

"Aye." Cyrene whispered her answer to Gertrud. "I have."

34

DUNCAN

821 AD - Three Days Later

Three long days and three longer nights passed. Nervous angst sent Duncan pacing stone halls well into the night. His instinct was to ride back to the village, sweep her away, and throw every bit of his charm and wealth at her until her walls crumbled and she could learn, if not to care for him, to at least tolerate his presence.

But the cross had called him to wait. The Lord beseeched him to have patience. In the length of those days, God's Word had also called him to return. To read and fully commit his heart to not only believe but to follow. The words didn't promise happiness or a life without struggle. They suggested the opposite, in fact. But they did promise hope. Assurance of an eternity of peace when he was done with this world.

That would be enough. He wasn't enough, and because of Christ, thankfully, he didn't have to try to be.

He could finally stand in front of the mirror in his chambers and not despise the reflection of the man he met there. He finally saw a creature made in God's own image, someone he could love. Someone God could use. Someone with the purpose of leading a kingdom toward the true High King.

The sound of a hundred voices wafted through his window, a pleasant buzz of conversation and excitement as the entirety of the kingdom gathered for a celebration. Almost the entire kingdom.

No word had come of her arrival; none had even spotted her approaching. Neither had he received a response to the package he'd sent by Eowin. They'd been careful plans, though drawn in haste, detailing changes to his kingdom, including the expansion of his walls to make room for new homes available to any of her people that wished to live within. He'd also scribbled a proposal requesting her warriors train his soldiers in their arts of stealth and archery.

Duncan surveyed that man in the mirror once more, straightening his tunic and brat with a deep inhale.

He was confident in his decision to leave her the choice to return and decide what should become of her village. It would always be her choice.

"Sire?" Eowin appeared in Duncan's open doorway, his own clothes bright and freshly laundered. When he noticed the hopeful expectation of Duncan's lifted brows, he bowed his head in apology. "No word yet."

Duncan forced a smile and slapped his friend on the back. "I have faith, my friend. There is still time."

"While ye bide yer time, kindly find another messenger fer yer love notes." Eowin's lifted brow spoke of teasing, but there was also some sincerity to his request.

"Ye weren't met wi' open arms then?"

"If the fair captain thought she could get away wi' it, I'd have been met wi' the entirety of her quiver." The less than sincere way Eowin said "fair" was not lost on Duncan.

"I thought ye enjoyed a challenge."

"I do, but I dunna have a death wish."

Duncan couldn't help but laugh at Eowin's predicament. Never had he seen his friend show fear, but when faced with the storm that was Astrid, he nearly trembled.

"What of my cousin?" Duncan asked when he'd reined in his laughter.

"He has accepted yer offer. A ship is ready. He'll be on his way to Ireland wi'in the hour."

"He understands the terms?"

"Aye. If he's seen on these shores again, there'll not be a warning, only the slice of a blade through his heart."

"I still canna believe it was mere chance that he encountered Vidarra when he visited the Viking lands seeking an alliance." Duncan shook his head, unable to fathom what that meeting must have been like.

"I canna believe he escaped alive from their shores."

The men remained quiet for their next few steps.

"Ye think me foolish fer letting him live?" Duncan watched his steps, asking himself the same question. His father would have ended William's life on the battlefield in front of what was left of his army, family or not, but Duncan had come to realize his father was not a man to model himself after.

Eowin didn't answer right away but clasped his hands behind his back as he walked.

"Nay," he said finally. "I believe ye are a good man. A good friend. A good king."

"Good kings rarely meet a sweet end." His tone was light, but doubt drew his brows together.

"Sometimes they do." Eowin's shoulders lifted, a friendly nudge bringing a smile to Duncan's mouth.

"Aye," he agreed. "Sometimes they do."

A crowd of advisors, household staff, and soldiers were waiting outside the doors to the throne room. Duncan searched their faces, finding Hilda's. He offered her a smile and nod to further assure her that her compassion, though it had brought Vidarra's wrath into the tower, was not to be punished but encouraged. There was always a risk of pain when loving broken people, but the risk should always be taken.

He stepped onto a sun-drenched balcony overlooking the court-yard to the joyous eruption of shouts and cheers from the crowd.

Duncan raised his hand, and the noise grew louder. After several minutes, it finally died to a level he could speak over.

"Welcome, my people, my friends. Today we celebrate a great victory and the union of two kingdoms." He scanned the crowd, still hoping against hope to spot a fiery shock of auburn hair amongst them. "Long have our armies held the borders of our lands, and long have our shores been safe. But this is no longer so. The enemy came, they tried to take what was precious to us, but the enemy did not gain victory. For wi' the union with the woodland warriors, the skill of their archers and fierceness of their blades joined wi' ours, we were not defeated!"

Another round of applause and cheers filled the sky, echoing off the surrounding stone walls. Duncan lifted his hand, this time bringing the crowd to silence. He'd planned his speech carefully, knew exactly what he wanted to say, but as he gazed across the faces of those who depended on him, who loved him, his prepared words seemed empty.

"I . . . I want to give ye, all of ye, more. More than just a safe place to run to when danger comes. More than land on which to build and farm. I want to give ye a home."

The courtyard was silent, almost as if no one was there. "I want to give ye a king who loves ye wi' his whole heart, holding nothing back. A king who will give himself and his life fer all of ye. I want to be that man."

Duncan's chest was heaving with passion, his hands clenched around the stone railing.

"I will be that man."

The crowd remained frozen and silent long enough for a pair of figures to move in their midst, hooded shapes that wove through tightly packed bodies until they stopped beneath the balcony. Slender, pale arms emerged from beneath the fabric, rising to fold back the hood.

Duncan wanted to cheer when thick braids of fire red tumbled free from under the cloak and Cyrene's beautiful face peered up at him. Astrid revealed herself next to the queen, making no attempt to hide her longbow.

Cyrene turned to face the waiting crowd. Ladies raised their clasped hands to their mouths, and men lowered their heads in respect to this strange new queen.

"Because of one man's hatred, long have I feared the king of this land. Long have we hidden away in the wood because of that fear." She didn't raise her voice, but it carried across the crowd as if she were shouting. "I swore an oath to never be subject to this crown, and I meant to keep that oath."

Duncan held his breath, his heart thundering so hard in his chest, he feared it would burst through his bones.

"But the king I hated . . ." Cyrene lifted her eyes, emerald green irises locking onto Duncan's. "He doesna exist. The danger that kept us imprisoned died wi' the past."

Burning lungs reminded Duncan to exhale, but he never broke his hold on her stare until she looked away, dusting the crowd with her confident gaze.

"We come to join ye, to ask ye to join us. As one kingdom. One people." Cyrene slid her eyes to Duncan's again. "One family."

From the edges of the courtyard, more bodies stepped forward, having been hidden in the shadows. Duncan's eyes grew wide as he recognized faces from Cyrene's village, faces he'd met the night he brought her home. He felt a tug at his lips and didn't resist the wide grin that spread across his face. Her people worked their way through his villagers, a welcoming murmur floating through the courtyard. When he looked back to where she'd been standing, she was gone. His smile disappeared as he searched the crowd, unable to find her.

He was turning to Eowin, prepared to call down the guard, when Cyrene's warm hand slipped into his. He laced his fingers through hers and brought their hands to his chest.

When he faced her, her eyes danced back and forth between his, searching, asking, pleading with him to be true.

"Thank ye," he whispered, allowing her to see all of him, every bit of his weary heart. She didn't have to reach inside, for it was all laid bare before her.

Duncan felt his household retreat behind him, including Astrid, who still had nothing but daggers for the captain standing stone-faced beside her.

"I canna promise ye much, Duncan. I only have myself to give, but I am willing to give it."

Despite the hundreds of eyes watching them, Duncan took Cyrene in his arms.

"Any amount of ye is more than I could ever deserve." He wrapped his arms around her. Hidden under her cloak, he recognized the hard form of her bow against his arm.

"Yer armed." One side of his mouth pulled up.

She lifted a shoulder. "I heard the king was a rogue."

He couldn't help the breath of laughter that escaped his lips. He was aware of her every move, the rise and fall of her chest as she breathed, the bump of her pulse beneath his palm.

"A rogue who canna believe such a bonnie huntress agreed to be his bride."

She pressed her full lips together, repressing a smile at some secret joke. He cocked his head to the side, narrowing his gaze in curiosity. "What?"

"I guess ye dunna remember, but in yer fever, ye swore ye'd make me yer bride."

He let his head fall back, body shaking with laughter. Her

accusing reaction when he'd proposed finally made sense. "I prayed that was a hallucination."

"Would ye tease me if I said I am glad ye made good on yer promise?"

"Aye?" Suddenly sober, Duncan could feel his racing heart thunder against his ribs.

"Aye." Cyrene attempted to lower her eyes, but he lifted her chin with his finger. Tentatively at first, and then when she didn't resist or pull away, he slid one hand along the side of her face, the other around her back. She trembled beneath his touch.

"'Tis only me and ye."

She relaxed into his hold, and he'd never felt anything so wonderful in all his life. Lifting her face to his, he lowered his head until his lips hovered over hers.

"I'm going to kiss ye now."

She breathed a laugh, and he closed the distance between them. When their lips met, she melted into him, her hands finding his waist, drawing him closer.

A cheer from the crowd below encouraged them, and his lips drew back in a wide grin against hers. He kissed her again and moved to turn back to the crowd when Eowin's broad hand fell on his shoulder.

"Sire!" The panic in his captain's voice sent Duncan's arms tight around the queen, drawing her protectively to his chest. "William's surviving troops attacked our men. He escaped!"

Duncan's gaze skipped over Eowin to the breathless and bloodied soldier in the doorway who had delivered the news. A shout rose from the crowd, and Duncan whipped his head around to see a villager in the courtyard, his arm raised, finger aimed at the opposite wall, where the shape of a man had appeared.

It was William, bow in hand, arrow loaded and ready to fire, lip curled into a seething sneer. Duncan narrowed on his cousin's eyes, near black from the hate. But William's ire wasn't centered on Duncan. His fury was focused solely on Cyrene.

Duncan was in motion. As he turned his back to William to shield Cyrene, she ducked under his arm, throwing the cloak off her shoulders and the king off balance. He stumbled into a charging Eowin.

William shifted to release his arrow. Duncan pushed away from the captain, lunging for Cyrene, but she had already reached the edge of the balcony. A flash of bright purple lashed to the end of the arrow Cyrene held between her fingers sent a fire of panic through his nerves.

"NO!" Duncan launched himself at his wife, William's arrow in flight, aimed straight at her chest. Even if her arrow brought William down, there was no stopping the one he'd fired.

He became a wall between Cyrene and the danger flying over the courtyard, bracing himself for the pierce of its tip as he pushed her away.

Cries soared from the courtyard as the villagers realized what was happening. Duncan's muscles were so tight he couldn't breathe, but the sting of death never arrived, and Duncan opened his eyes, finding Cyrene with wide eyes and labored breaths. And an empty bow.

She only blinked at him.

Behind her, Astrid lowered her own bow from where she stood, Duncan noticed, protectively in front of Eowin, who had somehow ended up on the ground.

"She pushed me." Eowin's explanation seemed a surprise to the captain's own ears.

Duncan slid his eyes to Astrid's, the blue of her irises so pale, they seemed white in the rays of the morning sun. He dipped his head in gratitude, and she returned the gesture even more subtly before turning her glare toward Eowin again. "My debt to ye is paid."

Shouts of alarm from the courtyard finally broke the trance that froze Duncan in place and he turned. William was no longer on the wall. A group of villagers crowded around something in the court-yard just below where his cousin had stood. When they parted,

Duncan winced at the sight of William's lifeless body, his unmoving limbs bent at unnatural angles, and Astrid's arrow with brown fletchings protruding from his chest.

Duncan searched William's still form for Cyrene's arrow. It seemed trivial, given that they'd almost just died. Again. But he couldn't believe it. She'd actually missed a shot. And so had William, thank goodness.

"Yer Majesty!" a man called from the center of the courtyard, waving at Duncan.

He lifted his hand, waving William's arrow, which was split in two at the middle by another, its pale ash shaft bearing Cyrene's violet feather fletchings. An impossible shot. He looked over his shoulder at her.

"I would have taken him, but I ken ye would shield me." She shrugged.

Duncan spun, stalking toward Cyrene with a gaze so fierce, she retreated. He caught her wrist, jerking her to his chest. Both hands on her face, he gave her no warning before kissing her deeply. She was breathless when he finally pulled back, pressing his forehead to hers.

"Ye saved me. Again."

Cyrene covered his hands with hers, a smile playing at her lips.

"I keep my promises." This time, her declaration sent a wave of fire through him instead of ice.

Duncan dragged Cyrene to the edge of the balcony. Her hand tight in his, he raised it high as the people shouted.

"Yer queen!" He stepped back, allowing Cyrene to take her place in front of him. "Cyrene. The mighty huntress!"

Before the ceremony ended, the priest and Eowin came forward to give testimony to Cyrene and Duncan's vows, solidifying the validity of their marriage for those in his kingdom. The priest led a liturgy of prayer and thanksgiving for God's protection during the battle.

Throughout the event, Duncan did not release his grip on

Cyrene's hand and thought mayhap he might never find himself able to do so. She smiled, laughed, and blessed him with sidelong glances as they made their way to the courtyard, but she'd done so before only to suddenly give in to the doubt and fear.

Mayhap it was different this time. He was different. Dragging her hand to his lips for the hundredth time, he resolved to be patient. No matter if her affection ebbed and flowed like the tide, he would not surrender in the battle for her heart as God had not surrendered in the battle for his.

"Question for a question?"

Cyrene's soft request caught him off guard as they worked their way through the crowd of their combined people, Eowin, Astrid, and two other soldiers flanking irritatingly close.

He peered down at her. She stopped to embrace an older woman he recognized from her village with her free arm, as he'd still not given up possession of her hand. Cyrene placed her hand on the side of the woman's face, pure adoration gazing back at his queen.

"I ken yer mother would be so proud of ye, m'lady. Ye have her heart."

Cyrene whispered a few words before stepping back to Duncan's side, her eyes frosted with emotion. He curled his arm, tucking her hand tightly to his chest.

"Ye had a question for me, m'lady?" His blood heated at the curve of her lip into a soft smile.

"What was it yer priest read at our wedding? 'Twas from the scriptures, but I dinna understand."

As they continued their journey through the crowd, stopping occasionally to greet a villager, Duncan thought back to that day, still finding it hard to believe it was real.

"It was from the first book of Corinthians. He spoke of love."

"What kind of love?"

"All kinds, I believe. The kind a parent has fer a child, one friend fer another, a king fer his people, a neighbor fer a neighbor. God fer his people." Duncan slid a curious gaze her way. "A husband fer a wife."

"What does it say?"

Duncan lifted her hand to his lips, pressing a kiss to her smooth skin before he recited the verses.

"Though I speak wi' the tongues of men and of angels, and have not love, I am become as sounding brass or a tinkling cymbal." Duncan's voice deepened as he leaned close, whispering memorized words into Cyrene's ear. "Though I have the gift of prophecy, and understand all mysteries, and all knowledge; and though I have all faith, so that I could remove mountains, and have not love, I am nothing. And though I bestow all my goods to feed the poor, and though I give my body to be burned, and have not love, it profits me nothing."

The tug of Cyrene's hand as she stopped prompted Duncan to do the same. She stared, a question floating just beneath the surface of her gaze. He took the step to bring himself before her, hooked his finger under her chin, lifting her face until he could fully capture her gaze.

"Love is patient and is kind. Love doesna envy or boast, nor is it arrogant. 'Tis not rude or self-seeking, 'tis not irritable, and doesna keep a record of wrongs. Love finds no joy in unrighteousness but rejoices in the truth. It bears all things. Believes all things. Hopes all things. Endures all things."

He watched the rise and fall of her chest as he spoke, saw the tightening of her throat as she fought to keep back some strong emotion. His fingers sought the feel of her skin, the smooth texture of her hair, and his lips longed to kiss her again. And again and again.

He tucked a wisp of her hair behind her ear and brought her face to his, speaking the final words of the verse in a soft breath over her mouth. "Love never fails."

Her eyes fluttered closed, lips parted, and he felt the heat of a blush across her skin against his palm. Duncan kissed her, and kissed her, and kissed her until the sound of Eowin clearing his throat reminded him they weren't alone.

When Eowin opened his mouth to comment, Duncan's warning glare sealed his lips shut. Astrid smothered a laugh before she remembered she was supposed to be sneering at Eowin.

"Did ye learn that in yer years of study?" Cyrene's cheeks were still flushed, as if she, too, realized they had an audience.

"The kissing or the scripture?"

Cyrene flushed again at his teasing and nudged him softly with her shoulder. "The Word of *An T-aon*."

"Aye." Duncan felt his brows meeting, familiar doubt and unanswered questions rising from where he'd managed to keep them subdued the last few days.

Cyrene didn't answer until after she'd greeted another villager with a friendly embrace.

"Ye said once ye dinna ken why ye had studied. Mayhap . . ." She drew in a deep breath before continuing. "Mayhap it was because ye'd need to be able to share those words wi' yer wife one day."

She kept walking, but Duncan spied a sweet smile creeping across her lips. If he could only make these moments last, if he could somehow capture this time and store it forever, he would be the happiest man on earth.

"Fer many years, I wished to have my questions answered. I wished to ken why our lives had been so troubled. It consumed me and stole what joy I could have shared with *An T-aon*. Mayhap we dunna have to have all the answers to ken that *An T-aon* is good." Cyrene's suggestion settled in his spirit. "Mayhap we can just trust that he is. We can allow him to be our friend and give us life, both here and fer eternity."

During his time at the abbey, he'd mastered Latin, memorized scripture, and learned the entire history of the modern church, yet in the span of a single sentence, Cyrene managed to convey more understanding and wisdom than he'd acquired in all his education.

She was a delightful mystery. An enigma he had a lifetime to figure out. Starting now. Duncan thought for a long moment, threading his fingers through hers again.

"'Tis yer turn to answer."

"I just shared my thoughts."

"Ah, but I dinna ask, 'twas a gift ye gave freely." Duncan breathed a laugh at her groan. "This was yer idea, dunna ye remember?"

"I ken, I ken. Just dunna make it too embarrassing."

"The day I asked ye to marry me, ye'd come to see me off, and ye had something in yer hand. What was it?"

"Ye have the memory of a fox!" Cyrene laughed, a sound that could power Duncan's heart even if he'd been long dead in the grave.

Her laughter faded, and she grew quiet. Pulling her hand from his, she reached into the pocket sewn into her skirts.

Cyrene lifted Duncan's hand, folding open his fingers to place something in his palm.

"I had wanted to give ye this that day. Since ye had admired mine so." It was a tiny replica of her ceremonial staff.

He stopped walking again, eyes glued to the small wooden trinket. He took both sides in his hands, pulled it apart as she had done, revealing the hidden length of leather in its hollow middle. He ran his thumb over the carved surface, each symbol meaningful to her faith. Their faith.

"I dunna ken what to say." He couldn't stop staring at it.

"Ye dunna have to say anything." Cyrene shrugged, as if she'd not just given him the most precious gift he'd ever received, and continued her stroll.

He stared after her until she nearly disappeared into the crowd, Astrid at her side. The Pictish captain linked arms with Cyrene, leaning in to whisper something that caused Cyrene to tip her head back in laughter. Sparked by Eowin's own movement, Duncan pursued his bride, resolved to chase after her all the days of his life.

35

CYRENE

822 AD - A Year Later

Sweat coated her brow, pains coming in crashing waves such as she'd never experienced before.

Astrid paced at her bedside, hand fidgeting about the hilt of her blade, as if she could battle whatever invisible force was attacking her queen. There was more than the uncertainty of birth fueling Astrid's nervous pacing, but Cyrene was unable to split her thoughts from the bairn she was about to bring into the world. Gertrud issued a gentle rebuke, stilling Astrid before whispering instructions to the other maids, who assured Cyrene her time was near.

Though it was expected, her pains had come on strong and quick, not even giving her enough time to notify the king.

When she cried out at the next wave tearing across her abdomen, Duncan's voice boomed beyond the closed wooden door of their chambers, demanding to enter.

It was not proper for a husband to be in his wife's chamber during labor. For an instant, Cyrene forgot her discomfort and felt the icy sting of panic race through her bones. Had something happened? Were they under attack? He burst through the door and raced to her side, the salty smell of the sea still clinging to his skin.

"Sire!" One of the maids clasped a hand over her mouth, appalled enough at his behavior to speak but afraid enough of the king to make her voice not more than a whisper. "'Tisn't allowed."

"Dunna tell me what I am allowed to do in my own home!" Duncan's roar sent the maid cowering.

His calloused hands found Cyrene's face, brushing her sweat-soaked hair away from her face. "I'm sorry."

When Cyrene's brows tipped in question, he lowered his head to rest on her shoulder.

"What news?" Her heart picked up its already hurried pace.

"Later." He was nearly breathless, stroking his hands up and down her arms in a soothing rhythm.

She lifted his chin with her finger, needing to look into his eyes, and was met with only sincerity.

"I dunna mean to dishonor ye," he said, keeping her gaze. "I ken ye are strong, I just . . . I need to be wi' ye. The world can wait."

The midwives bristled at his presence, frowning and chattering about impropriety until Cyrene spoke with such authority that any objections were silenced.

"He stays."

He'd shared the pain he'd felt at losing his mother before he could know her. She knew his worry stemmed from fear of her suffering the same fate as well as the seemingly endless threats against their people—his own thoughts always torn between protecting his kingdom and protecting his family. She melted into his touch, the comfort of his presence enough to carry her through the pain. She needed him as much as he needed her.

"'Tis time, m'lady." Gertrud's soothing encouragement ignited a mixture of excitement and terror inside Cyrene.

She grasped Duncan's hand and found his wide eyes mirroring her own emotions as he whispered, "I promise I willna leave ye."

With a hand behind her shoulders, he helped her to sit, sliding behind her on the bed. He let her grip his hands. She bore down so hard, she feared she might break his bones, but he held firm until she released him to take their bairn in her arms.

Duncan's chest shuddered at her back as he took in the sight of their son's round, red face. His tiny wails were the most enchanting melody, and Cyrene allowed tears to flow unhindered down her cheeks. She felt the same from Duncan as his strong arms encircled their little family, his heavy breaths saturated with joy, every other worry forgotten in that precious moment. *The world can wait.*

At Cyrene's assurance she was safe with Gertrud, Duncan presented their son to the waiting crowd of his household, their cheers and shouts slipping through the cracks under the door. He was a blossom of color in the stark gray of winter.

"Where is Astrid?" Cyrene scanned the room as Gertrud worked with gentle hands.

"She must have slipped out when His Majesty arrived."

Of course she would have taken his place where he'd been nearly day and night for the last three days—watching the seas. She gave up her place at Cyrene's side for the king.

"Did I hurt ye, Majesty?" Gertrud stopped at the sight of Cyrene's tears.

"Nay." She wiped her cheeks with the back of her hand. "Nay, Gertrud."

When Getrud and her maidens had finished their ministrations, seeing that Cyrene and the bairn were well, Duncan was allowed back into her chambers, returning to his position as a supporting pillow at her back.

"He's perfect." Cyrene's voice gave way to emotion.

Duncan's beard tickled her neck, his lips finding the soft skin below her ear. "How couldna he be? Look at his mother."

"He has his father's eyes." Cyrene couldn't hide her smile as she leaned forward, lowering her gown off one shoulder to allow the babe to nurse.

The deep blue of her son's eyes was the same as Duncan's. The same as Revna's. Despite his villainy, their father had given them both that beautiful gift. She felt Duncan's thumb graze over her shoulder, caressing the place where she was marked, his deep voice rumbling a hum through his chest.

"What is it?"

"I was just thinking that our son would be a lion, just like his mother."

Duncan drew her back, close to his chest, chills raced along her arms as warmth from his sigh bathed her skin.

A full year had they lived as husband and wife. A year they'd battled their way through differences, through generations of bitterness, through their own selfishness to reach this perfect moment.

A sudden sadness crashed through her heart, and she choked back a sob, not understanding where such sorrow came from.

"What is it?" Duncan shifted as if he were going to leap from the bed and call for the midwives.

Cyrene grabbed his tunic, pulling his arms back around her. "Nay, dunna go."

He didn't leave, but he didn't settle either.

"'Tis just . . . I wonder if Fiona ever got to feel such happiness." The words slipped out without fetter. "I look at him and think of how much she must have loved them, how she must have wished the king would . . ."

Duncan didn't hold her; he clung to her. "'Tis not me." She felt his lips on her shoulder, then his forehead on her back as he lowered his head. "I'm not him."

"I ken." Her answer was so soft, he lifted his head as if he wasn't sure he'd heard correctly.

"'Tis not us." He was pleading with her, begging her not to turn to stone as she had done so many times in the past year.

"I ken, Duncan." She craned her neck to see his face, letting him know she was not going to draw away. "Ye are nothing like him."

"Ye've forgiven me?"

His question stung, along with the shame she felt for allowing him to live under a cloud of suspicion and angst for all that time.

"Ye were never like him. There's never been anything to forgive." She pressed her forehead to his. "'Tis I that should ask ye to forgive me. I made ye feel that way fer so long."

Cyrene reached for a small wooden box resting on the table next to their bed. It was just beyond the stretch of her fingers, and Duncan placed it in her hand.

She removed the carved lid with her thumb, setting the box in her lap before removing its contents.

"This was my father's gift to my mother." She held the ring between her thumb and forefinger, lifting it for Duncan to examine.

"Those markings . . ."

"I ken. They match your flag."

"And yer mark."

Her eyes traced the unending circle of the ring, then drifted up to find Duncan's blue eyes. She felt . . . complete.

"I'm still sorry fer what he did to ye, to yer family." It wasn't the first time he'd apologized for his father's evil actions, and probably wouldn't be the last, but she was finally to a place where she didn't need to hear it anymore.

It was so much, and she was so tired, it made her head swim. As Cyrene drew the bairn to her breast, she tucked the ring into her palm. Duncan raked the back of his fingers along her jaw and tenderly brushed strands of her damp hair away from her face. Their infant's tiny hand worked its way loose from his swaddling, and when he wrapped his little fingers around one of Duncan's, she thought she felt the king's heart nearly beat through the bones in his chest.

"Are ye well?" Cyrene's teasing question prompted an amused exhale from Duncan.

He took a long moment to collect his emotions, clearing his throat before answering.

"I imagined what this would feel like, but all my dreams were lacking. The best of them was but a fog-covered moor in the dead of winter compared to this." His words settled over her skin, a warm blanket woven from everything she'd ever hoped for. He shifted so as to look directly in her eyes. "Ye are the sun, my bonnie Huntress. Ye are every summer day, every blossom of spring flowers, every warm breath of wind across the seas."

He cupped her cheek so tenderly, she wanted to weep, for she felt the depth of his heart in that single touch. She needn't search for truth; he offered it freely.

"What my father did, though he claimed to love this kingdom —'twas not love. Yer right, I am nothing like him, and I have been slowly accepting that for many years."

Cyrene's breath stilled in her lungs, her own heart ready to escape through her lips. In the year since their union, they had grown in friendship, even in sparks of passion, but still they'd both held something back.

"I promised not to ask ye to love me, and I will keep my promise, but I never promised not to love ye." Duncan dragged in a long breath, as if gathering his courage. "I do love ye. And not just because ye gave me a bairn, though I will be eternally grateful." His gaze drifted to their son before centering back on her face. "I love ye because of who ye are, because of yer heart, yer compassion, yer wisdom. All yer faults and all yer strengths—I love every bit of ye. And even if ye never can love me back, I will be grateful just to spend my life under the blessing of loving ye."

The rough surface of his thumb stroked her cheek, nearly her undoing. His burning blue eyes grazed over her face, brows turning inward at the expression he saw there.

"Yer trembling," he said, lifting his hand. "Are ye hurt?"

Cyrene placed her free hand atop his, pressing it back against her face.

"Nay." She closed her eyes, hot tears flowing freely. Emotion tightened her throat so that she needed to swallow twice before she was able to speak.

"I made a promise to myself when I was a lass. A broken and grieving child. I promised my heart to my people and only my people. That promise served me well, and so many nights, it kept me alive—kept us all alive."

Muffled grunts from their bairn drew her gaze to his delicate form. As she examined every curve of his face, the fullness of his pink lips, their shape nearly identical to Duncan's, she couldn't imagine him making those same promises. The thought of him living with such bitterness that it snuffed out all hope of love—it was enough to tear her heart to shreds.

If she would never desire that for her child, surely her own mother didn't desire it for her. Her warning had been against another king. One she'd have been wise not to trust. But Duncan was not that king. She lifted their child to her face, breathed deeply his sweet scent, and peppered his soft head with kisses.

"The promise was made to protect my heart, but to keep it now . . ." She turned back to Duncan, hope etched in every feature. "It would mean hurting my heart. To keep my promise, I must break it."

Water pooled at the edges of his blue eyes.

"I do love ye, Duncan." She slipped her mother's ring on his smallest finger.

He released the breath he'd kept back, touching his forehead to hers, his shoulders tight with emotion. A single tear slid across the palm of her hand as she touched his face, and he sniffed before lifting his head. Breathing a soft laugh, he kissed her unashamedly.

"Thank ye," he said against her lips before kissing her again. When he finally drew back, they were both breathless.

"What shall we call him?" Duncan stroked his finger along the side of the sleeping bairn's cheek.

"Ye dunna want to wait until the naming ceremony?"

"Nay." He didn't elaborate, and she didn't need to ask why. His sisters never received their names, and with the latest threat edging closer to their borders, they might very well be in the middle of war with the dawn.

"Ye ken, I havna even thought about it. I thought the entire time he were to be a lass."

"Did ye hope fer a lass?"

"I dinna prefer either, I just felt . . . I felt I'd have a daughter." Cyrene traced the line of her son's button nose with her finger. "Maybe he'll have a sister."

She grinned at the hopeful squeeze of Duncan's arms.

"He does need a name," he said. "Tradition demands he take my father's name, but I dunna think I care to hold to that."

"What about yer grandfather?" Cyrene asked. "What was he called?"

"Erick."

Cyrene gazed up at Duncan, who was still staring at the child. "Is that what ye desire?"

"He was a good man. I loved him verra much." He lifted a shoulder, and the corner of his mouth ticked up, some sweet memory lightening his mood. "What is yer people's tradition?"

"'Tis the same."

"Bercilak is a strong name."

They sat in silence for several long minutes, exhaustion from the delivery nearly stealing Cyrene's consciousness.

"I had a brother." She wasn't sure she'd even said it out loud until Duncan's chest vibrated with a hummed question.

"A brother?"

"Aye." Cyrene's lips moved, but she felt like she was already asleep, lingering in that foggy place between consciousness and dreams. A place where it was not so painful to remember him, where the secret door she kept his memory drifted open. "He was a lion too. The bravest and boldest Pict ever to live."

Duncan's lips warmed the top of her head. He didn't speak as she sleepily told him all about her brother. Of his quickness. His unending hunger. His wisdom beyond his young years, and she thought she felt a shudder in Duncan's chest when she shared how he'd saved her with his own life.

"His name was Beli." She tasted the salt of her tears as her lips pulled back in a smile.

"Beli," Duncan repeated. "I like it."

Cyrene enjoyed the deep, peaceful slumber of a woman who was truly loved and protected while the world indeed waited. She dreamed of a tower, but instead of cold, lifeless walls, they were covered with climbing green ivy and flowers of every shade. She strolled through the halls, windows flooded with golden sunlight. There was color, so much color everywhere. Carpets of deep blue and rich green lay thick beneath her bare feet, and curtains drifted in the wind like angels' wings blazing with the same brilliant hues. The stones of her dream home were alive with laughter, breathing life into those who dwelt within and all those who were loved by them.

Adorning the walls were endless tapestries bearing the likenesses of generations to follow. Sons and daughters, a legacy of love that was hard fought, treasured, and selfless. Faces of families, most of whom Cyrene and Duncan would never meet in their lifetime, but who would gather together in eternity because of the example of their faith.

Cyrene wandered through a sparkling arched doorway, basking in the glory of a sunrise over the sea. Warmth flooded through her as Duncan's fingers slipped between hers. They stood together, always together, facing whatever future might unfold, the laughter of their children and children's children echoing across the shores of their kingdom.

EPILOGUE
CYRENE

825 AD - Three Years Later

"More have arrived, Yer Majesty."

Cyrene placed her infant daughter in Gertrud's arms, the healer's own belly so round, they'd just spoken of how it must be near her time. Thaedry came behind his wife and gazed at the little princess over her shoulder as Cyrene pulled on her cloak.

"Go." Gertrud nudged her arm when Cyrene asked a silent question. "Aislinn will be well wi' me."

After a hurried kiss on her friend's cheek, Cyrene raced through the halls and down the stairs of the tower until she reached the outer stone wall facing the sea. Mixed with merchants and soldiers, frail, cloaked figures disembarked a large wooden vessel, loading onto smaller boats aimed for the shore.

"Is she among them?" Cyrene turned desperate eyes to Duncan, who had followed at her heels, golden-haired Beli giggling from his place on his father's strong shoulders. The child was ever in his shadow. Even at his young age, there was none he admired more.

"I dunna ken." The king's large hands rested on their son's bouncing legs, keeping him safely in place.

Cyrene couldn't ignore the doubt in Duncan's tone and struggled to hold onto her own hope.

Beli wiggled, whining to be released, and Duncan swung him from his shoulders to the ground as the lad filled the sky with his laughter. Beli pressed himself to Cyrene's side. His little hand worked its way into hers as she lifted a prayer, pleading that this arrival would be the one she'd been waiting for.

"Would ye like me to take ye to greet them?"

She narrowed her eyes at the distant figures on the shore, wishing for some magic device that would allow her to see them with clarity.

"Cyrene?"

"Aye." Cyrene straightened, realizing their need to make haste. "Aye, of course."

She always greeted them.

It had been four years. Four long years since Cyrene and Duncan's armies had battled against his cousin and invaders from the North. Four years since her midnight-haired scout secretly boarded the remaining Viking ship, leaving Cyrene to guess at her grizzly intentions.

The first ones had arrived less than a year after. Women, men, and children stolen by ruthless Vikings in the months and years before, now returned. Each one with the same story.

A dark angel had found them. Whether they'd been sold, traded for goods, thrown in prison, forced to work in fields, or bound to serve on Viking ships. She'd come. And they were home.

Where Vidarra had chosen to use her vengeance to enslave and destroy, Revna used hers to free those held captive. She was death to those who enslaved. Merciless and swift. Those she sent home spoke of her with fear and admiration.

Duncan led Cyrene, with Beli by her side, to the beach as the shore boats slid to a halt among the rocks and sand.

"Welcome home." They embraced weeping travelers, then released them to find their waiting families among those who gathered expectantly at the arrival of each ship.

"She's not here." Cyrene's tears had stopped stinging her eyes after the first year. She kept telling herself not to expect to ever see Revna again, though her heart couldn't help but race at the sight of sails on the horizon.

Duncan's hands wound around her waist, his arms strong enough to hold her together when she wanted to fall apart. She covered his arms with her own. He waited with just as much anticipation for a sister once lost to be found.

"Have hope, Huntress." His lips found her shoulder, her neck, her jaw. He rubbed his thumb in a circle over the spot on her back where the lion had appeared. The place where her hand reached to retrieve her arrows from her quiver. "If God can direct your aim with every shot, he can direct Revna back home."

She let herself be folded into his embrace, tilting her chin until she felt his breath on her face, and let her eyes drift closed.

"I'm going to kiss ye now." She felt the brush of a wide grin peel back his lips as she repeated the phrase he'd said so many times to her.

She kissed him, and kissed him, and kissed him until Beli giggled and tugged at their hands.

Duncan swept the lad up between them, his blond curls soft on her cheek. She prayed with all her heart that *An T-aon* would do just what Duncan said he could. Until then, she would do what Revna could not. She would lean on the strength of *An T-aon* and fight with everything inside of her against unforgiveness, against darkness. She would seek out the light and chase after the God who, no matter how small or dim, could breathe life over colorless embers until they blazed into an undying flame.

More from this Author

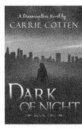

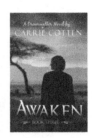

The Dreamwalker series is a speculative fiction trilogy following Andromeda Stone, an ordinary girl with the extraordinary ability to walk in dreams.

The Huntress is a Medieval Christian Fiction series featuring a vibrant cast of strong female warriors, swoon-worthy heroes, and epic faith-filled adventures.

ABOUT THE AUTHOR

Carrie Cotten is a writer of Christian fiction, an accidental farm-girl, homeschool mom, and ministry wife. She lives with her husband and four precious cherubs in a small town in North Carolina.

Carrie is a life-long writer, but it wasn't until 2019 she published her first novel, Dreamwalker. The idea for the story was conceived almost a decade before it's completion. It was not originally a novel that included faith elements. During the years, Carrie came to the important realization, that she simply could not separate who she was as a writer from who she was as a follower of Christ. Once she submitted her whole talent, ideas and creativity, allowing the story to become what it was meant to be, words flowed authentically and the manuscript was completed within a few months.

She hopes that her books inspire readers to share their own faith through everything they do. Above all, she strives, through her words, to share the wonderful news of the saving grace of Jesus Christ.

From Carrie,

I've always had a lot of words. As a child, I would talk my mom's ear off about anything and everything. It's a privilege to get to use my words to share the love of Jesus with readers now.

If anything in this trilogy sparked a flame in your heart to know more about the saving grace of Jesus, or if you're at all unsure where you will spend eternity, please don't let another day pass without finding answers.

You can start here. www.carriecotten.com/gospel

Made in United States
Orlando, FL
26 November 2024

54504324R00232